# Beyond the Dark Gate

Book Two Of

The Flow Of Power

# R.V. Johnson

Publisher's Cataloging-in-Publication data

Names: Johnson, R.V., author.
Title: Beyond the dark gate : book two of the flow of power / R.V. Johnson
Description: South Jordan, UT: Lost In New World Publishing, 2016.
Series: The Flow of Power.
Identifiers: ISBN 978-0-9861655-2-8
Subjects: LCSH Magic--Fiction. | Fantasy fiction. | Swordplay--Fiction. | Science fiction. | BISAC FICTION / Action & Adventure | FICTION / Fantasy / Epic | FICTION / Fantasy / General.
Classification: LCC PS3610.O37265 B49 2016 | DDC 813.6--dc23



This book is a work of fiction. Names, characters, businesses, organizations, places, events and incidents either are the product of the author's imagination or are used fictitiously. Any resemblance to actual persons, living or dead, events, or locales is entirely coincidental.

For information contact; http://www.authorrvjohnson.com

Cover design by DHMDesign

ISBN: 978-0-9861655-2-8
EBook ISBN: 0986165535
First Edition: December 2016

*For all those who enjoy losing themselves in a new world, if only for a few bells. I am of like mind.*

# ACKNOWLEDGMENTS

I would like to thank my editor, Kelly Hartigan of
XterraWeb. To everyone in my writing group, every little bit
noticed helped. To my beta readers, and ARC reviewers, thank you.

Most of all, I would like to thank readers and reviewers like
you.

# CURTAIN OF DARKNESS

*Not another week of stinking drudgery,* Cord moaned in silence. *I don't know how much of this I can stomach.* He wondered what he had done to anger Onan at some point in his miserable life to cause him to draw such duty again. This time around, the seventy-first had patrolled deeper underground than any of them had ever gone, even Durm.

As he marched along the old carved ramp of black limestone leading ever down, that one fact surprised and worried Cord as he mulled it over in his mind. Durm had *not* wandered this deep into the slime pit under the Dark Citadel before now. The scarred patrol leader often bragged of his intimate knowledge of the dim, green glowing tunnels, putrid channels, or cold, dank catacombs in the underbelly of the citadel. Yet, the past half day, Durm seemed subdued. As though he anticipated something and dared not reveal it, or no one would follow him. What was so important they go this far? What *were* his orders?

"How much farther are we going to tramp through these forsaken tunnels, Durm?" Gorem called ahead, echoing Cord's thoughts. "There isn't a thing down here but us and this blasted pooling water."

Durm halted at an intersection of three tunnels. Waving his torch between the three, he hesitated. "Funny, I seem to recall you saying nearly those exact words right before we ran into those ingrots. While killing them was the only time you have not complained."

Gorem's snarled reply came quick. "That's different and you know it. Those fiends would have taken any one of us for their bloody cook pots."

Cord agreed with Gorem: ingrots were nasty unpredictable things. From the murmurs and the added creaking of armor going to rust that drifted around the watercourse, so did many of the others. The slimy creatures had slunk from the darkness coming at them from two side tunnels at the *same* time. It did not make sense. Always before, the frog-faced creatures had fought among themselves as they floundered around humid areas in twos or threes. When had such primitive creatures learned to cooperate?

"Why not find someplace dry to hole up for a while and then head back?" Gorem asked. As the only User in the patrol, he stood alone gripping a glimmer shard, smug in the knowledge of its frail light, for a time. The light would fail in a few bells, but at least he had not had to taste the acrid stink of burning torches dipped in crude oil, like the rest of them. Most of the patrol envied Gorem the shard even as they despised the small display of his wealth and power.

Not one of the soldiers much cared for Users, anyway. They were an arrogant lot, prancing about in silk robes lined inside with kell leather while they slung aggressive magic around. A fighting man should wear proper armor joined with steel and wield a sturdy weapon. Still, Cord supposed they did help in a bind. No one would refute a User's ranged capability at destruction. Yet, more than once, Cord had voiced his notion of banning Dark Users from the great lord's service and replacing them with archers for the distance kills. Unfortunately, half the lords at the citadel were Users, as so many were throughout the citadel's turbulent history.

Durm waved his torch at the left and center passages. "We

continue on until I decide we have ranged enough. Any that does not want to finish his duty can stand guard beside these tunnels. The rest of us are following the right branch for two bells, or until it ends, whichever happens first, then back here in four."

"We are ankle-deep in putrid water," Gorem protested. "What am I supposed to do, stand here and shiver for two bells?"

Durm stomped to the gaping tunnel of the right-hand branch, splashing through murky water that glistened darkly in the torchlight. "Standing is advisable. Your pristine robe could not sop up this much water; it would weigh as much as the Dark Oracle. Besides, you never know what parasite is floating around, waiting for a tight skinny orifice like yours to crawl inside."

A chorus of guffaws ensued from most of the men.

Cord did not laugh with the others. His lean stature almost matched the User's, and the laughter seemed hollow and out of place. The dark holes of the tunnels grew blacker, as if having taken great offense for such a sound in the deep.

As Durm waved the torch back and forth, bright curved lines flashed redly in the air from cobwebs caught in the flame. With a final barked chortle, he plunged into the tunnel. The torchlight did not swing behind him to see who followed.

Cord waited for the rest of the soldiers—fifty strong—to slosh single file into the tunnel until he and the Dark User were the last two at the junction before he took up his customary place at the back. The rest of the patrol believed his training made him an expert in guarding against a rear attack, a belief he had carefully promoted for seasons.

Early on, he found there was less risk at the back of every guard patrol he had accompanied beneath the citadel under orders. He figured it unlikely that an enemy would flank them in such narrow confines; trouble would lie in wait ahead. He hoped. As miserable as his life may be, he wanted to be around to watch his children grow, though they seemed to respect his wishes less and less every season. Something he did not understand. Was he not a good father?

After a quarter bell spent staring into the tunnel, Gorem splashed past, cursing under his breath. Cord smiled, his respect for Durm growing. It took an intelligent and confident person to make one's followers believe your leadership would keep them from harm as you led them into danger. Durm had pulled it off with some skill. Cord knew Gorem would not want to wait at the junction alone. There were far worse things skulking in these caverns than the web-limbed ingrots with their green-glowing skin.

The tunnel dragged on endlessly, or so it seemed. Cord's leaden legs tripped over snags unseen in the water with greater frequency. Finally, the torch flickered; the meager light it gave off drowned in the immensity of a great cavern.

He was about to request a rest halt to the man in front to relay forward when a commotion broke out beyond his light. Indiscernible shouting echoed about. A lightning bolt sizzled, revealing a downward slope leading into an underground ravine. A flash of red flame bloomed in the dark. As most of the light faded, he got a glimpse of ingrots swarming eerily silent out of the darkness below. Some of them burned with red and yellow flames providing a growing luminescence as they caught their neighbors on fire, yet they made no sound.

"Blast you all! Fight! Now, before we're surrounded!" Durm's bellows rang through the cavern.

The sharp *thrannng* of released cross bolts mixed with the grunts of hand weapons thudding into ingrot flesh ceased in a short time.

"What are you doing? Keep fighting!" Gorem's shrill voice floated back to Cord from a weak flicker of torchlight not far below, near where he assumed the cavern floor leveled out. Silence settled in, made starkly eerie by the torchlight winking out nearly at once, as if a single hand carried them.

Lightning bolts again crackled through the blackness, three in rapid succession.

Cord blinked as they faded. Durm and many of the others were out there, but they were not fighting. They stood with the ingrots! Shuffling forward, they led the beasts toward the few still holding weapons, and the sole person carrying light…they came for *him*!

Cord ran, moving so fast back the way they had come he splashed fetid water into his eyes. Wiping desperately with his free hand, he slowed a little, fearing he may have extinguished his torch. He was heartened to see it flickering. The loss of its sputtering feeble flame meant death.

Keeping to a disciplined pace through shin-deep water was maddening—barely above a fast walk—but he stuck with it. The terror of what was coming behind spurred him on. He had to escape the tunnels.

After a long grueling tromp, walking as fast as he dared, he halted at the three-tunnel intersection, holding his torch high and gulping air as he looked back. The tunnel mouth brooded dark and ominous. No light flickered from it. *Perhaps those things hadn't followed.* Still, he would take no chances. Ingrots would not leave their dark and dank dwellings.

Setting off, he slogged through the center of the intersection, the upward ramp to safety and freedom beckoning in the torch's meager but stable light. He smiled despite the immediacy of the situation. The hooded man would not now dispute his story of survival if he were the only one left to tell it. And perhaps, this frightening ordeal would work to his favor, providing he reported it in such a way as to show how Durm had ordered the men to stroll into ambush. Yes, it was a good plan. Did he not have to inform the citadel what waited below? *It would work nicely.* If he worded it right, showed a proper amount of horror lurking in his eyes, it might even get him a higher rank commendation and added scrip.

Dropping from above, a curtain of darkness draped over him.

An alien intelligence, old when his world was young, permeated his mind. The scream bubbling in his throat vanished, erased from him by an overwhelming sense of dark and utter supremacy.

# BROKEN MIND ON A VIOLENT WORLD

Stretching to the end of her reach, Crystalyn Creek grasped the top of the ledge's jagged edge and pulled herself higher, scraping with the under toe of her boots for a foothold. After much scuffing about at the limestone rock face, she met success with something large enough to support her. Pushing and stretching upward, she got her forearms upon the ledge's rocky surface, allowing her long legs to dangle in empty air space as she crawled forward then rolled onto her back when she deemed it far enough for safety's sake.

Gasping for breath, she lay gazing up at her smallest companion, Atoi. The little girl had scrambled up the mountainside as quick as a goat, which was no surprise. Though she looked and sounded not a day over ten seasons, in reality she'd had more than four hundred of them to develop that agility. When she'd first arrived on Astura, Atoi had used that same quick speed on her when the little vagabond had sunk the poisoned dagger into her stomach. Crystalyn no longer held it against her. After all, it had been an accident, sort of.

Standing, Crystalyn looked around wondering at Hastel's choice for their route. Her link mate, Broth—her *Do'brieni*, in the warden's language—may have a rough time with the final hurdle of their strenuous morning, not to mention she worried if her younger sister Jade could make it.

Her fears proved groundless. Broth cleared the ledge in one smooth leap, landing on the cushioned pads of his big paws; Jade swung herself up with ease, the big hammer at her side behaving by following the contour of her thigh without a single hitch.

Perusing the path they'd taken up the mountainside, she noted the owner of the Muddy Wagon Inn, Hastel, had chosen the route with an exceptional eye. As far as she could see, there was no other way. Deadfall timber and a rockslide blocked the south. A sheer cliff rising to the north deterred anything without wings. They could have gone around either side toward the west or east, but it would cost days. From the reports Hastel had received regarding the Vibrant Vale, they did not have days, hours perhaps.

Crystalyn looked toward the one-eyed warrior. "How much farther is it?"

Hastel wiped the sweat from his brow with the same rag he used for the weeping scar glaring from his forehead to nose and centered across the missing eye. Crystalyn wished he would let her attempt her healing symbol on it, but he'd flatly refused without offering a good explanation why. "It will take us one full bell to scout along the ridge, then another for the jaunt down into the Vale," he replied.

Jade's quick smile flashed white in the shade of the pine trees lining the ridge. "You make it sound like we're going for a stroll instead of a battle."

Hastel's one blue eye glinted in the early afternoon sun. "I suppose *some* battles are a leisure stroll around well-built fortifications, like the present day Dark User siege of Surbo I've heard tell is. Most are pure chaos. Yet, chaos has its own kind of excitement." His one eye grew brighter as he spoke.

Crystalyn stepped closer to the Vale's rim, gazing upon its wide green canopy. In spots, smoke hung in a thick pall above it, and an occasional boom sounded now and then, the only indications something was not right in the peaceful forest. That, and the fact no birds soared throughout the treetops. "Somehow, I don't think we're going to find a glimmer of fun down there," she said softly.

Hastel sighed in agreement. "You're right as usual, we'll find only conflict. Come, we should continue. The hike along the Vibrant Rim is easier, but I would prefer we gradually work our way to the southern end. Our best chance of meeting up with the Lore Mother and Lore Rayna is at the main outpost there." The grizzled warrior set out along the ridge going slightly down into the inner rim of the valley and into a patch of evergreen pines, avoiding the openness of the aspens.

Crystalyn walked beside Atoi as Jade followed close behind and Broth guarded the rear. They easily fell into their customary patrolling order they'd taken upon themselves since leaving the Muddy Wagon Inn weeks ago. Often, Atoi ranged ahead, sometimes even ahead of Hastel. For now, the enigmatic little girl seemed to seek companionship. "Have you ever been to the Vale before?" Crystalyn asked as they walked.

Atoi regarded her, her emerald eyes unreadable though starkly vivid against the background of her too-pale skin. "I have memory of the place of great trees."

Crystalyn was mildly surprised. Such a reply didn't sound like the usual Atoi. She never knew if she was speaking with her or the Dark Child the little girl hosted inside her tiny, four-hundred-season old body. "What are your memories of it? Tell me what to expect."

With a decidedly little girl gesture, Atoi shrugged. "Large flowers, bigger trees, meandering water, and plant people."

"What do you mean? What are 'plant people'?"

"The ones who nurture the flora, you know them as naturists."

Now Crystalyn was surprised. "You think of the Lore Mother, Lore Rayna, and Cudgel as plant people? Why?"

Atoi's green eyes shone with added brightness before fading as they entered the trees. They were so vivid on her white skin. "All floras listen to them and thrive."

Crystalyn stopped, staring after Atoi as she continued down the path without slowing. Soon she was gone from sight. Jade took her place.

"Are you okay?" Jade asked.

"Yes and no. After all that time spent traveling with my companions, now I find some of them are plant shepherds. But I'm glad we're back, impending battle or not."

"Huh? You're not slipping again, are you, sister?"

Crystalyn laughed with little mirth. "There's a term from our world I haven't heard for a while. No, I'm not slipping, not yet. I'm as stable as someone with a broken mind can expect to stay on a world prone to violence. Plant shepherds are my words for the naturists, like the Lore Mother, Lore Rayna, and Cudgel. You haven't met them yet, but you will. They're part of the Green Writhe, and apparently, they tell plants what to do with themselves."

"Camoe said he was with the Green Writhe. Do you think it is the same one?"

"I would imagine."

*"Have you heard of the Green Writhe?"* Crystalyn sent through the link, adding a slight feeling of annoyance into the psychic flow. The Green Writhe sounded important enough her link mate and protector should have spoken of it by now.

Broth's response was hesitant. *"I have, my Do'brieni. Wardens have pledged service with them in exchange for training with much frequency for many seasons. They are a bonded group of druids, naturists, and monks of the strongest ability with the Flow in some form."*

*"Why haven't we discussed this before?"*

*"They do not speak of it often; they are a solitary group with vows of secrecy."*

*"Should you ever believe I should know additional hierocracies or anything else pertinent, feel free to confide in me, my Do'brieni."* Crystalyn sent a bit of love and affection into the link to soften her feeling of annoyance. Broth would not intentionally withhold such important knowledge from her.

Unconditional love flowed back through the link. *"I shall, my Do'brieni, I shall."*

Crystalyn smiled.

"Do you think the naturists or those of this Green Writhe will have heard of Dad's whereabouts?" Jade was asking.

"Hastel and Atoi seem to think so, but they hadn't expected the Vibrant Vale would come under another attack when we set out from the inn vanquishing battle lords either. I hope it isn't going too badly for their side when we get down there."

The path narrowed. Crystalyn motioned Jade ahead.

They moved in silence for another hour, and then Broth left the rear to scout ahead. He did not have to mention his intent; she felt his presence wherever he went and received snapshots of the type of terrain he traversed sometimes, usually when it was a difficult environment.

Having a link mate gave her warmth and support. She found it hard to recall how it was before without him. Nor did she want to dwell on it long; it was too frightening to consider. They were a family now, even Atoi and Hastel. Once they found Dad, they could all settle down somewhere, perhaps at the Four Bridges helping with the upkeep of Hastel's inn.

The ridge they followed downhill sloped toward a small hilltop showing a tantalizing bit of meadow and a possible view of the Vale beyond sparser copses of pines and oak brush. The smell of smoke grew palpable as it thickened, stinging the eyes. Her tear ducts and moving farther down the path supplied the relief she hoped would come.

*The scarred human, the Ancient One, and I await your arrival at an overlook. It is an acceptable view.*"

Broth's designation for Atoi made Crystalyn wonder if he considered four hundred seasons as old or if he somehow knew the Dark Child she hosted was far older, but current urgent matters took precedence in her thoughts for now. "*Good, stay hidden. I am almost there.*"

The path dropped under a large ponderosa pine and then curved back onto the ridge at the north roots of the tree. Beyond the tree, a wide, though shallow, pit created an opening in the greenery where flakes of sandstone rock lay strewn below a ledge of the same but thicker material. Scarring from chisels glared stark testament of human intervention upon a natural landscape. Stepping gingerly on the broken pieces, Crystalyn made her way farther inside the old rock quarry.

At the bottom of a shallow pit, she dropped to her hands and knees and crawled up a short incline between Jade and Hastel. The view of the Vibrant Vale was better than she expected, for the ledge jutted out from a small cliff ten or so stories from the Vale's eastern edge.

The Vale had a rounded pit-like shape. Perhaps an enormous, ancient meteorite had smashed the great hole out of the soft earth. A winding, slow-flowing stream cut through the bottom, originating from a misty waterfall, which dropped from a small plateau at the east. An army was camped below the fall, spread toward the south below them.

Sprouting upward at the north and west, the great falun trees—dwarfing everything, even the ponderosa pines—rose through the smoke above.

Crystalyn grew alarmed. A few of the bushy, fern-like boughs glowed orange-red from flames, but then ice formed on a nearby falun tree, smothering the flames. For now, the Light Users were combating the attack. How long could they hold out?

"Someone's in those huge trees," Jade suddenly said, her voice soft though urgent. "We have to do something."

"Oh, we will."

Jade turned to look at her sharply. Crystalyn brushed a stray auburn lock of her flowing hair from her little sister's eye with her fingers. Crystalyn smiled with affection, though it quickly faded. Serious matters needed spoken about. "I have my symbols, little sis. With the power they contain, I intend to do something—many somethings. That force attacking the Vale won't appreciate it; a lot of them are going to die."

Letting her callous words hang in the air between them, Crystalyn hesitated. Jade had to understand what was at stake. When Jade's vivid emerald eyes rounded, she continued. "But I need your help. Are you able to do what it takes?" Crystalyn hated herself for asking. Jade was an innocent. Though her somewhat new ability to read images rotating in the auras around someone had helped her escape the Dark Citadel, she'd never had to end a life to save her own. The friends she'd made on her harrowing journey had done the killing.

Now she was asking her little sister to lose her twenty seasons of innocence and help her with life-threatening destruction on a wide scale.

Jade hesitated, her emerald eyes darker and rounder. Terror and resolve warred within. Finally, there remained but one. Jade held out a steady hand. "Together we are at our strongest," she whispered.

Clasping her sister's hand, Crystalyn formed one of her most aggressive symbols in her mind. Octagonal in shape, thin, crooked lines formed a myriad of pinwheels tipped with round spikes at the octagon's points.

Picturing the symbol hovering before her, she brought it out from within. Glowing with the black radiance of a dark flame in the morning sun, the symbol flickered with impatience, ready and waiting. Crystalyn formed another of the same type, bringing it out beside the first, and then one more. With Jade boosting her power with the Flow, the two of them would send chaos thundering rampant through the enemy forces, she hoped.

A thought struck her. There was so much going on with the battle she knew nothing about. Perhaps it was time for a change in tactics. Instead of tearing about the land wreaking havoc on whatever assaulted them with the power of her symbols, why not implement a concise attack?

There might be alternatives for helping her friends with the war and uncalled for assaults besides blowing things up. Perhaps she may even save a falun tree or two. After all, she couldn't continue going around ripping Astura apart in the name of good intentions forever. Eventually, luck would abandon her little band of warriors.

# SCREAMS OF FURY

Garnet Creek kept well back from the battle. The flashes of white light tinted with yellow did significant damage to everything close to the detonation area, including *anyone*. The white-haired man with the young features wearing the black robe of a Dark User seemed to have them in endless supply. Amidst the chaos of battle centered on the Dark Oracle where the hooded man had his contactings performed by Dark Users, it had taken him time to track the flashes back to the source. Most of his confusion had stemmed from the fact the man and every User in the invading force wore black or red robes though they cast light magic.

Bunched together in a circle in order to protect those inside, the intruders moved away from the Oracle, one hard won step at a time. He hadn't yet found a way to get within sword range; they fought well, employing elite tactics he'd yet to encounter on Astura. What they wanted with the Dark Oracle was unknown.

To a person, they were better than any fighter, man or woman, the Alchemist had pitted against him throughout his enslavement. When a man fell from an errant bolt or was impaled by the sheer number of pikes jabbing at gaps in the shield wall, they closed rank in an instant or slipped an armored soldier in to fill the gap from inside.

The white-haired man was one of those protected by the moving human fortress. Most bore a resemblance to the overall form of a human, but there were two who had…discrepancies.

Forced backward by Garn's soldiers outside the writhing fortification, a giant woman flailed about alone battering his men with tree-branch textured arms and legs that flowed along the floor. It was a remarkable sight and a first for him since his arrival on world many months past.

An old woman towered behind the white-haired man. Garn hadn't yet discovered her function, yet the group protected her as well as the man detonating the white-yellow flashes. A memory struck him then, one he'd learned not long into his captivity, when he'd nearly made the fatal mistake of believing the Dark User he sparred with had drained of power. They guarded her for good reason.

Unseen by most, including him, the old woman interrupted the river of power flowing under the land and then funneled it to one who could use it, a User, the white-haired man whose shoulder her large hand rested on. The woman was an Interrupter though different from those who halted the Flow for Dark Users. Dark Users would put themselves behind an Interrupter.

With the body acting as a conduit, eventually the interruption would fail. Handling such a volatile substance would cause a leak; her energy would drain with the Flow back into the river.

Garn could almost applaud the white-haired man for his attempts to provide aid to those around him; he had to know it wouldn't be long now. The woman hunched lower with his every cast, and they were outnumbered five to one; his black robes were pouring in from the side corridor. Many of the soldiers who had protected the group as they moved from the Oracle lay smoldering, cut down along their back trail. Others fell by the moment.

Abruptly, a golden dome encased much of the human bastion.

Facing the great hall, a brown-haired woman inside—a User, yet heavily armored with black plate mail—had raised a staff topped with a clear crystal above the crowd. Four red-robed men and two women held firm to her shoulders. They shuffled backward as one unit.

Garn studied the dome. The dark, light-consuming cones hurled by his dark robes slid from it, exploding on the ground below. Illuminating the hallway with a brilliant ruby radiance, missiles streaked toward the dome. Striking en masse, they too bounced harmlessly away.

Underneath the dome's golden radiance, most soldiers lowered their swords as the tree-branch limbs without the leaves of the large female retracted, reforming as a big woman wearing a short, leafy, green dress, beautiful in a tall formidable way, if not for her glowing eyes.

"After destroying a third of our forces, Sureen has raised a sphere," Kara Laurel stated matter-of-factly from close behind Garn. "I cannot believe the strength she possesses."

Garn's breaths stilled at the mention of the woman's name. He had a strong feeling he should know her, yet no memory came to mind.

"Are you certain it's her?" the hooded man asked.

Garn didn't have to turn around to know his captor and his captor's magic User stood close behind. He had kept them close in order to protect them from the battle as the intruders had moved away from the Dark Oracle for the simple fact he had use of them. Kara Laurel, Garn needed for her magic, and the hooded man— the Alchemist, his detested master—he would protect until the opportunity arose to kill him and escape.

"I was *informed* she'd been destroyed," the Alchemist continued with a hiss. His tone left no doubt he would be speaking to whoever gave him that information at the earliest opportunity. Garn would not want to be that person.

Kara Laurel's voice rose with excitement. "As did I, yet there she is, and she has cast a sphere of magical protection over many. Such a feat requires a huge amount of the Flow. I am astonished she has the strength left after covering the retreat from the Oracle, though I imagine having that great artifact adds tremendously to her ability. Do you see how the white crystal mounted on Sureen's staff blazes to form the golden dome, Garn?" Kara Laurel pointed over his shoulder, pressing her firm body against his backside.

"You sound as if you admire her," the Alchemist sneered. His soft black cowl brushed against Garn's other shoulder. His quiet but steely voice irritated Garn to no end, even as the mention of the woman's name sent a thrill through him.

The Alchemist's foot tapped the stone floor with impatience. "Signal for the attacks to increase, but if it appears the sphere will fall, desist. Take as many Users alive as you can and the Vale woman. Destroy the rest."

Slipping a dagger from his left hip sheath, Garn held it outstretched high in his right hand, the blade pointing to the dome. He followed through with the order though the command seemed to contradict the Alchemist's intended result. He did not question the hooded man. Since the violent takeover of the citadel the past winter, the Alchemist had executed a third of the Obsidian Table, the citadel's political and militant leaders. Some of the executed members had offered only the slightest hesitations to his commands.

Garn had performed the executions as commanded, which gained him a small amount of trust in the Alchemist's eyes but had also had the adverse effect of offering fewer opportunities to kill the man and escape. Now, the hooded man usually took him with him wherever he went but rarely alone, anymore.

The User Kara Laurel had garnered some trust too—as much as the hooded man was capable of offering—during the time of strife at the citadel. Either Garn, or Kara, or both had stood guard beside the Alchemist every second of those months. Likely, the hooded man wanted to keep an eye on them both, him and either he or his retinue of elite guards he did not go anywhere without were always watching Garn. A contingent of ten men and women kept fresh by eight-hour-duty rotations trailed behind the hooded man. They stayed out of earshot but were close enough to keep Garn and Kara in sight, even as they slept. The man trusted no one fully.

Guarding the arduous man had become crucial now that the hooded man had set in motion two sieges at the same time: one at the White Lands' capital city of Surbo and one aimed at the Valen tree city, the Vibrant Vale. Likely, the intruders hailed from the latter with the Valen woman part of the force. Garn hoped his two daughters weren't at either place since he couldn't yet see a way out of his predicament to continue his search for them.

True, the Alchemist had saved his life, but then he had forced him into servitude as payment. The takeover of the Dark Citadel after the disappearances of Lord Charn and General Darkwind had been a major detriment to Garn killing the hooded man and his continuing after his daughters. All he needed was a small hint of their whereabouts and a map of the land, two things that had eluded him for months. Once he had them, he would run the hooded man through and fight his way from the Dark Citadel, though doing so wouldn't be easy. The Alchemist had a fortress of soldiers and magic Users, most notably Kara Laurel, a powerful Light User in her own right. Kara Laurel's motives for keeping the man alive were no doubt different from his own; she had yet to divulge them.

The drawn dagger was the agreed-upon signal for his general. The general's black helm, constructed to resemble an alien spider and bee like creature with its myriad of eyes, faced his direction as it had throughout the fighting. Protected by a small company of shield-bearing soldiers, the general saluted in acknowledgment and then relayed the signal.

At the general's relayed signal, orange fireballs, trailing their long comet tails, joined the missiles and cones peppering the golden dome. Immediately following them, a cloud of burning dark rain struck. From his military training as head of security on his home world, Garn noted how he would defend against such attacks should he end up on the receiving end after he escaped.

Unable to withstand the onslaught, the dozen or so Users and soldiers caught outside the dome's protection dropped within the first couple of rounds, their personal protection domes winking out and the armor bursting into flames, some pierced with holes. The golden dome wavered but held. Another volley struck, and two of the five red robes gripping the soldier woman's shoulder collapsed. Each volley of crackling energy hammering the dome thinned it, the golden color of the dome fading almost to transparency.

Raising two daggers, Garn signaled the cease-fire. Then he sheathed them.

The lull of the attack surprised the staff-bearing woman. She glanced around, her eyes coming to a rest not on the Dark Users who had cast the assault but on *him*. As her lovely green eyes widened, the dome rippled.

"Now, signal the steel!" the Alchemist hissed loudly in his ear.

With great reluctance, Garn wrenched his eyes from the woman. Drawing and raising his great sword at a forty-five-degree slant, he pointed toward a darkened hall entry. Shields at the forefront, his pike-wielding soldiers marched out, shoulder to shoulder.

As soon as the last of his men stepped into the great hall, a hail of arrows from the intruders assailed them. A wall of blazing white flame engulfed the front three rows, cast presumably by the white-haired man. Garn's men screamed as they died. White flashes of light behind the flames indicated the white-haired man's explosions had begun again in earnest.

Garn readied the signal to bring in the reserves. Raising his sword high, he waited for the command.

The Alchemist's voice was loud in Garn's ears, though he spoke to Kara Laurel. "Without having an attunement to the gate, they cannot activate it, they are trapped. We can finish them."

Kara Laurel's voice pitched high with excitement so close to his ear made him wince. "The gate *is* activated, how?"

Garn looked to the green-eyed woman soldier holding the white-crystal-topped staff. The golden dome's protective covering had vanished. Tall and defiant, the woman stood exposed. Dark-robed Users and their soldiers, some with silver hair, ran headlong toward the topaz gateway.

The Alchemist screamed, "Stop them! Signal my Users! Destroy them all!"

Garn hesitated, ostensibly assessing the situation, waiting as long as he dared. "I cannot," he said after two of his pumping heartbeats. "They are behind our soldiers and the wall of flame." He halfheartedly poked his sword toward the great hall's ceiling, again at a forty-five-degree angle. "My signal is too distorted for them to see."

Already, the fastest intruders were slipping through the gate, including the old woman. The tree-branch woman casually knocked aside one of the gate guard's pikes, then pulled an arrow from the quiver on her back, and rammed it into his throat. The way clear, she stepped between the obelisks.

"Is that so? Why aren't you attacking, Kara?" the Alchemist asked, his tone casual but menacing at the same time.

Stepping beside Garn, Kara Laurel began picking off the

soldiers who paused to slay the few men and women left guarding the gate. A half dozen dropped as her white spears of light struck.

Their numbers small from the start, the remaining gate guards did not last long. Most had left their posts to assist with the assault at the Oracle, something he'd discuss with the general who'd given the command, soon.

A few tense seconds passed as the desperate group, their path clear, ran through the gate. Soon only the white-haired man and the staff woman remained. Facing the great hall, they walked slowly backward.

Firing golden spears of her own, the woman easily deflected Kara Laurel's white ones, her eyes focused on the hallway where they stood, fixed…on *him*.

The white-haired, long-bearded man sent a final flash of light exploding into Garn's soldiers. Then they both vanished, the woman last. Garn fought an almost overpowering urge to follow her.

With the last explosions dying in the hall, the Alchemist ran to the Oracle and gazed inside.

His screams of fury echoed throughout the great hall.

# THE SKY ABOVE

The symbol Crystalyn Creek sent floating across the battlefield, an octagon as wide as a building wall, displayed giants swinging weapons as sapling-tree-sized arrows struck in clouds all around. Enthralled, she watched as the image reflected upon it magnified the struggle below hundreds of times.

Cyclone-sized black cones swallowed patches of sky as they flew toward silver-armored soldiers, sent from a row of Dark Users at the back of the line. Jagged, upside-down lightning trees flashed in the midst of a large group of white- and yellow-robed Light Users striking many at random and hurtling into the air, not always in one piece. A deadly array of red missiles and white ones as long as spears fell in clusters like shards of heat rays expelled in bursts from a dying sun. Waterfalls of black and golden flame appeared in midair and flowed upon troops and robes caught between the two opposing armies melting the carnage of the gory battlefield along with the greenery. White flashes of light preceded explosions in areas thick with men, and walls of black flames sprang up blocking retreat and engulfing those nearby.

Crystalyn let the symbol fade from the battlefield; if she and her companions could see it, so could anyone from the ground.

Jade slumped beside the rock ledge they used for shelter. "Well, that did us a lot of good, the imagery was too large to really see what we're up against. We had to give it a try, I suppose."

Crystalyn thought about the latest attempt of combining each of their abilities together in order to gauge the enemy's strength. Perhaps they'd been going about it the wrong way. Quickly, she redrew and recombined the familiar magical absorption symbol she'd just used, visualizing it in her mind and then willing it to hover before her. Floating as it did cost her little. The big drain happened when the symbol detonated. "Let's try this: let your aura images absorb into my symbol instead of mirroring the battle below. They should stay contained inside until I retrieve it, I hope. Each attempt this way drains me a little, but I have to know where to land my symbols for the most damage. The Dark Users will return fire, and possibly their archers, once I start."

A small grin lit Jade's tired face. "That might work. I'll give it a go. Don't take too long, though. There are a lot of auras down there. I can't feed them all to you, though I should pull enough to view you circle."

Crystalyn gazed at her sister with a silence that stretched.

"It will be a serious drain, likely we'll only have one shot," Jade continued. Then she froze. A brief, lopsided smile tugged one corner of her mouth upward a moment later. "Am I stating the obvious again?"

Crystalyn flashed a quick smile of her own. "We've been at this long enough. I have a second wind and the pacing down, I think. I gave you a little time to rest. It's too bad *grounding* won't work with your ability as it does with mine, it really helps slow the symbols' drain on my life."

Jade shrugged a lock of her auburn hair from an eye. "It works for you and every User of the Flow, but I've tried it countless times. Either I'm not getting how it works or it will never happen for me. I have visualized a path from my feet to my mind and back again to the ground as you've taught, but it hasn't lessened the energy required each time."

"Do you regret coming back here?" Crystalyn asked, changing the subject. In a way, if they hadn't come back, Jade wouldn't need her ability so much, nor would she. "I know we have to find Dad, but once we have, do you want to go back? We have the extra set of sapphire obelisks Lord Charn—I mean, Ruena—stashed in the mausoleum. They're probably the same ones the Dragon Lady somehow got Dad to go through; we could go back to the Muddy Wagon Inn anytime you want to activate them."

Jade's fine, red-brown eyebrows rose as she thought it through. "They could be the same ones, but who's to say there aren't others? We only took the time to go through perhaps a quarter of the warehouse. As for regretting our return, I'm not certain yet. I do want to let Camoe know about Burl, though." Her voice broke at mention of the dark creation who'd been a dear companion.

Crystalyn felt a pang of guilt, but she'd done what needed doing.

"Besides," Jade went on, "we're going to help those people down there. We can make a difference."

Crystalyn was heartened her sister had arrived at the same conclusion she had. "From the little we've seen so far, it looks like the Vibrant Vale is losing. Our friends will have nowhere to run. We cannot fail at finding a way to get to them. Let's give this symbol another go, if you're up to it."

Hastel slid into the ancient quarry site from underneath the ponderosa pine growing in the middle of the old wagon road leading to the pit made from harvested stone. "I heard that. You're right. From what we've managed to scout, the Valens *are* losing," he said.

Crystalyn glanced beyond the tree, but nothing moved. "Is Atoi with you?"

Hastel studied her as he responded. "No, she's watching the hillside below. She'll let us know if anyone gets past your Broth. His warden eyes are good, but it's a big area."

Like Jade, he'd stated the obvious, though he looked at her as if she had. "Which is precisely the problem; things are going to escalate soon. I'm about to disturb that anthill down there, so I'll call my link mate back. Broth can bring Atoi with him. The three of you need to scout our seeming escape path. Make it look like we are running for our lives, then find and mark where we leave the path to begin circling back. Once Jade and I discover the best targets to scatter for the diversion, I'll pummel the area with symbols. We won't have long before they converge on this little hillside, but it should give us the time we'll need."

A little too late, Hastel masked the look of relief that flitted on his wounded face, his one eye glossy.

Did he think they would just give up and go home in the face of such a sizable force? Perhaps he had.

"Aye, I will find the way," Hastel said. He slipped under the tree and made use of the quarry road. "Don't take too long." The soft admonishment hung in the air after him.

Crystalyn looked at Jade. "If we can't get through, we go to Brown Recluse. Perhaps we can persuade the monks to aid us with helping the Valens with their plight."

Jade's brow furrowed. "You're putting a lot of faith in the belief Camoe's brother Caven is still prominence at the monastery. He helped me get to you at the Dark Citadel. Doing so cost the lives of four tavern workers. That couldn't have gone well for him."

Crystalyn wanted to assure her sister everything would have a happy conclusion, but such words would sound as artificial as they were to both of them. Those types of endings were for normal people going about mundane, nondescript lives. Their family and new friends were as far from normal as a world full of warring magic Users, both Dark and Light, had forced them to get. Though they both longed for it, they would never have ordinary lives. Jade knew it as well as she did. "Then hopefully, what we do today will be enough to make it through, though attacking an entire army by our lonesome is a tad bit reckless or unstable. You get to decide which it is."

Jade glanced at her sharply.

Crystalyn smiled as she spoke, adding a bit of self-recrimination to lighten the gravity of the situation. "I daresay, you know which one goes better with my broken mind. It's always been a tad unstable. Well, perhaps more than that, two tads."

Even with Jade feeding her tiny increments of the Flow—the river of power running beneath Astura—to augment some of the huge energy requirements to cast her symbols and the black candle artifact enhancing them by touch, they wouldn't stand a chance against even one-fourth of the Dark Citadel's forces besieging the Vale.

Jade kept silent.

*"Broth?"* Crystalyn inquired. The telepathic link resided like a fond, unforgettable memory in her mind. It was always there, ready for her to access. *"Are you here?"*

*"I am your link mate, Do'brieni"* came the reply, along with a faint sense of amusement.

She always seemed to amuse him a lot for some unfathomable reason. *"Do you have anything different to report?"*

An image of dark-armored soldiers, afoot and on horseback, crowding the open areas below a grove of falun trees flowed through the link.

*"As I suspected,"* Crystalyn added into the link. *"We're going to attempt something new. If it works, they'll be on us like a swarm of spiderbees. Gather Atoi and make your way here, quickly."*

*"I come,"* flowed the voiceless reply.

Crystalyn looked at her sister. "Everyone is ready. Are you?"

Jade's nod was small, resigned.

Crystalyn combined her familiar absorption symbol with another she'd read about in the *Tiered Tome of Symbols,* tier three, tucked under the heading seek. The curvy leaves with diagonal lines symbol had provided limited-range audio, but combining it with the absorption one had been a stroke of genius mixed with sheer luck.

Jade's ability to glimpse disjointed images in auras, fragments of their lives and their possible futures swirling around them like maelstroms, could prove useful for surveillance, now and in the future, if they got it right. "Here we go. Feed me all the power you can, but don't overdo it. You have to be able to run when I hit them. They will retaliate." Contact made the effect much stronger, so she held out her hand.

Jade took it without hesitation.

Crystalyn smiled grimly. Her sister trusted her implicitly, but would she after the death toll climbed? Jade would use herself as a conduit to the Flow, interrupting the raging river of power underlying the land and feeding it into Crystalyn through their touch. As Dad had always said, together they were stronger.

Crystalyn prepared herself by mentally attaching a path of least resistance through the quarry rock beneath her feet. *Grounding* herself ensured she would pull energy from around her, instead of from her. It still cost her traces of her life energy though at a fraction of what it had the first months of discovering her ability with symbols.

Standing, she peeked over the ledge at the carnage happening below. Her symbol formed in the air before her, an intricate hexagon with squiggly lines and long spirals making up the center. "There," she said after a time, pointing. "In the center and the farthest right appear to be the most concentrated areas. We'll aim for them."

Jade squeezed her hand.

Attaching her awareness to the white-gold pattern, Crystalyn sent it moving about the valley. They made it to the outskirts of the fighting before the symbol gained notice. A volley of black cones and red missiles converged upon it, only to be absorbed. The added power would boost Jade, though not long.

The enemy's next attack was a hail of gleaming, onyx arrows sent from a regiment of archers that passed harmlessly through the symbol. The attack stalled after that for some reason, likely the enemy Users waited for someone with authority to tell them what to try next.

Crystalyn made the most of it. Stepping up the pace, she swept the symbol past the center of the raging battle feeling as if she stood in the midst of it. She was afraid of leaving the symbol out too long or sending it too far afield; it might leave her too drained to pull her consciousness back. Today was not a good time to become a mindless shell.

Moving on to the right side of the meadow as far as she dared, she swung the symbol into the Vale itself. Some few brave or foolish souls rode after the symbol on horseback, only to fall to a hail of green-hafted arrows. Partway under the battered, green canopy of the great falun trees of the Vibrant Vale, Crystalyn decided to make do with whatever she had for now. The strain of holding on to it was too great.

Pulling back quickly—too fast—her perspective snapped from the symbol to where she stood in the quarry. Her awareness of her present surroundings mixed with her body's demand for equilibrium assaulted her at once.

She collapsed.

Crystalyn found herself looking up at the bright, though

brisk, afternoon sky. Growing on the rim of the quarry pit, fragrant mountain flowers exulted in new spring.

A rock scraped against another.

Jade sat beside her, concern furrowing her fine eyebrows. "Looks like you're back—your eyes aren't blank now. I never know if you're going to return from one of those jaunts. Flinging your mind around the countryside like that can't be good for your health. One of these times, I won't catch you in time, and you're going to get hurt." Jade paused, regarding her closely. "Well, did it work?"

Blinking rapidly, her mind still adjusting, Crystalyn stood and brushed the moist soil from the back of her legs. "We'll see in a moment," she said and then paused, allowing her racing heart to still before going on. The trips 'around the countryside' as her sister so eloquently put it, were starting to take a lot out of her. Finally, her heartbeat slowed. Crystalyn brought out the symbol, setting it to hover in the air before them. Restoring the link to the symbol, she took Jade's hand, signaling her to bring up the aura images it had captured.

It worked better than expected. Replacing the symbol's intricate pattern on its white side, frozen images of men and women in various battle poses popped into being. Crystalyn motioned the images across the symbol with a wave of her hand from the will of her mind.

Frame after frame of images flickered by as if it were a three-dimensional holo projection, though not how she remembered it. Something was off. The scenes seemed more brutal. Granted, the perspective was closer then when she'd guided the symbol, but the damage was so much greater. Large areas erupted with the earth exploding under the feet of many soldiers and Users.

Then she had it. They watched a future projection of the battle below, the brutal carnage of a war that *would* happen when men and women died. Jade's ability had drawn the moment of death images into the symbol with a show of staggering power.

The soundless screams of the dying showed on anguished faces as those caught in the violence clutched weakly at their horrid injuries. Arrows and magical bolts flew sizzling through the air; blood splashed a vibrant red as weapons connected.

Armored men and women charged forward, pikes held at the ready, only to drop with an arrow to the throat or wiped apart by a huge boulder flung from a catapult. Worse, vines lying dormant on the ground would suddenly reach up and tighten around limbs, squeezing until they sliced through.

Crystalyn concentrated on the densest areas of the dying, looking for the highest concentrations of the enemy. The view swung to the right side, where the Dark army fared better. Cavalry prepared to sweep toward the right center where a group of tall, muscular Valens, some with eyes glowing radiant white, made their stand. Most had visible injuries, some with black arrow shafts impaled through arms or legs, while others had blackened, still bubbling wounds.

A contingent of robed Users waited behind the relative safety of infantry, presumably until the cavalry rode back to the rear after a foray into the front lines.

The image froze, ending halfway along the writhing mass of dark-armored, robed, and green-clad bodies of forest warriors, the Valens, and some dark creations, the magical beings manifested by Dark Users. Crystalyn played it through again before dissolving it. Now she knew what symbols to use and where to place them. The future scenes had made the decision easy by showing her. "Okay, I'm going to use my acidic drop symbol on the right side, then send the explosive rings through the center, working on their Users as much as possible. I'll get three to four symbols off before they pinpoint our location."

Jade's brilliant green eyes were wide with horror. "Oh, Great Father! That was hard to watch. How do you do it? You're so…so clinical sometimes."

"I have to be hard with some of this. Think of it as a festering wound to cleanse before it will heal, as I do. Otherwise, we wouldn't be able help anyone, not even ourselves," Crystalyn said. She hesitated. "Once I begin, we won't have long. Are you up to it?"

"I know we need to help them, I just hate it is all. Those attacking our friends are bad, but they're still human. Well, some of them are."

"They would not hesitate to destroy us."

"I suppose. So, I'll do my best to keep up."

Crystalyn let the matter drop. Jade had her own convictions, something she admired about her, but she would do what she had to, to keep her sister safe and save a few of their friends.

*"How close are you, Do'brieni?"* Crystalyn asked, and Broth's reply came as an image of a grove of evergreen trees below the quarry a short meadow away. Atoi ran some distance ahead. *Close enough,* she thought.

Crawling to the slab's edge, she formed the symbol she'd once sworn she wouldn't use again. The symbol was black on one side, white on the other, and octagonal in shape; the pattern inside was thin, and stick-like lines formed a myriad of pinwheels tipped with round spikes at the points. Though she dreaded using it, it had proved effective against large forces. Releasing it, she formed her second symbol, a black and brown eruption symbol she'd only recently mastered. The first was halfway toward the large group of Users on the right side as she launched a second and a third, releasing them toward the middle group of Dark Users, and then prepared a fourth one to target the left.

The black symbol slowed to a stop above the enemy where

she'd envisioned. There, it rotated, spinning with greater and greater speed until it spun itself apart and threw out countless black teardrops. Judging by the chaos rippling in a widening circle below, the acid droplets fell, taking a horrible price on anything coming into contact.

Her second and third symbols expanded as they struck the ground brown side up; blazing with a rich black radiance briefly, they erupted with a series of explosions the size of a small meadow as they faded. Bodies, and parts of them, heaved high into the air.

The other side retaliated swiftly. Three differing clouds of dark cones, red splinters, and something dark resembling a storm cloud launched from several directions bearing down on their position with uncanny precision.

Dissolving her last symbol, Crystalyn pushed away from the quarry rim with her free hand. "Time to go, Jade, they're not going to let me send another one!"

The drone of the incoming retaliation filled the air, getting louder the closer they came. Though it slowed her down a little from the necessity of keeping it grounded, Crystalyn draped her absorption symbol over the two of them. Then she scrambled uphill past the ponderosa, pulling Jade along with her.

Several cones slammed into the evergreen. With a loud *pop* and great *cracking,* the ponderosa toppled slowly toward them, gaining speed. Crystalyn angled away from it as fast as she could, but a quick glance behind and up showed they would not run clear of the falling behemoth. The top of the tree was too branchy.

Stopping and turning, Crystalyn dissolved the absorption symbol and released the one that came to mind, her black netting symbol. Unfolding to triple its size, black pole-length spikes, as sharp as a double-edged sword, sprang from every knot on its octagon shape and snowflake interior.

The symbol sliced through the tree branches, clearing away

many of them as the dark cloud launched from the Dark Users dropped into it, visible now with what it contained. Black bits of broken sword tips and chunks of other black metal common to Virun mixed with the bright steel of the White Lands tore through her netting, *clanging* and *dinging* against wood. The larger chunks of steel shattered branches, drenching them with wood chips, and a wave of red spikes *thudded* into the tree adding to the chaos. The tree fell faster, falling with the weight of long life and great height.

Jade screamed something, tugging on her hand, but there was no time. The canopy of wood and foliage met the ground with a deafening *crash*. A huge, main branch landed with its thick fork on either side of them, the force of the impact whipping their hair back.

The once mighty tree shuddered with a final *creak* and then lay still. Crystalyn gazed wide-eyed at a red spike protruding an inch from her eye, buried in the crook of the branch. Fragments of metals lined a good portion of it.

Oddly, the face of the First Light of the Circle of Light, Durandas, popped into her mind at that moment. Crystalyn swept the image and the fear of the narrow escape to the back of her broken mind. Now was not the time to slip again, to spiral into the madness lurking within waiting to claim her. For the first time in months, she once again wished she hadn't run out of meds.

Jade tugged on her hand. "We have to keep moving, we have to keep moving," she babbled.

Turning away, Crystalyn raced uphill hand in hand with Jade. They ran toward a concealing patch of trees, glancing often behind and at the sky above.

# ALLIES AND FRIENDS

The great topaz gateway of the Dark Citadel deposited Lore Rayna and the rest of the survivors in the Old Town Coliseum in Gray Dust where the mirrored obelisks resided. In all probability, using the gateway for the escape was the boldest part of the planned conversion of the Dark Oracle led by Durandas. The topaz gateway on the Gray Dust side also had sentries, though less than a third of those guarding the Dark Citadel, and most had arms.

A pair of the black-armored sentries stood on each side of the topaz obelisks. Four others were spread along the east and west walls. Three unarmed soldiers, two women and a man staffed a like number of podiums placed away from the topaz gate. The podiums' purpose made for allowing or denying use from travelers who stood single file along a lengthy great room with a high-vaulted ceiling.

The four guards at the gate had drawn scimitars, presumably when the Lore Mother had come through. They moved toward the two of them even though Captain Wron—one of Sureen's great commanders—and his surviving fighters disguised with the black kell livery of the citadel's warrior apparel had come through first. They stood in a group not far away. There was little point in claiming she had an affiliation with them, or anyone of the Dark Citadel, not as a Valen. Neither Lore Rayna nor the Lore Mother, or any of their kind, had ever interacted with those of Virun ancestry.

The podium keepers had already halted the people lined in three rows from using the gateway. The east and west guards strode toward her, their long strides purposeful.

Halting near the fighters, a woman with deep golden hair cropped above her black plate-armored shoulders regarded her with hard blue eyes. Then she turned to the group of fighters. "Traveling from the citadel is restricted during earlier bells to avoid unpleasant merges. Worse, you have violated this protocol two-fold by allowing two members of a large mass race through at such times. Your marker must reflect the great lord's command of this, give it to me."

Though no one drew sword, many a hand hovered near the waist or rose to a shoulder where a large sword haft peeked over a shoulder within the band of fighters.

"I shall handle this," Durandas said, tramping from the topaz gate.

Behind him, Sureen appeared. Turning around, she faced the great gateway for a brief time and then moved to follow Durandas.

The male soldier beside the golden-haired woman cursed. "Blast it! You two," he said, jabbing his scimitar at the other male guards who had accompanied him from the opposite side of the gateway, "go back to your post!"

Giving a brief nod, they strode away, marching past Durandas and then Sureen.

Durandas worked a medallion from his neck, pulling it over his head. Gripping it by the rugged chain, fine silver flashed with its slow rotation. "This should clear the air," he said, raising his arm higher and putting the medallion level with the woman's eyesight. Centered within silver, an onyx heron rotated into view.

The woman snatched the medallion by the chain, ripping it

from his hand. "I've only seen a single other pendant such as this. That one graced the neck of a great lord. Where did you get it?" she asked, her voice filled with awe or impending violence; Lore Rayna could not determine which.

"The details of my coming into possession of the black heron are of no concern to you. Suffice it to say, this proves beyond doubt the importance of our mission," Durandas said quickly. He reached for the medallion.

The woman drew back. "So you say, User," she sneered. "Yet, you travel with those who believe themselves chosen of the land."

"Have no concern over the Valens!" Sureen said, moving beside Durandas, the tone of her voice imperious. "The naturists have some use for this mission, for the moment."

The woman regarded Sureen, the light tone of her complexion darkening. "Though you wear the garb of Virun, I do not recognize the house of your insignia," she said, slipping easily into a fighting stance.

Raising his curved bladed weapon, the male guard moved away from the woman a few paces, giving them both room to swing.

The *clinks* of plate armor sounding softly nearby informed her that Sureen's warriors had drawn weapons, matching the guards who were nearly there, coming in from both sides of the room. Gently pushing the Lore Mother behind her, Lore Rayna prepared her first attack. Though she could not slip her branches through stone, she could send them snaking along the floor.

Ignoring those nearby, Sureen took a step toward the woman, banging her staff on the granite beneath her feet. "Nor will you, House of Black Corral."

Sureen's words had a profound effect, and the woman straightened, dropping her fighting stance. "You recognize me?"

Sureen allowed a tiny smile to thin her lips. "I know your sigil. Though your house has garnered some respect, the great one has sent his most elite on this mission, a *house* he deems effective only if left in the shadows."

The woman lowered her scimitar, gripped in a steady hand, letting the sharp tip hang an arm's length above the floor. "But how shall I truly know then?"

"Present the medallion to the great lord," Sureen said.

"No!' Durandas cried. "The great one entrusted me with it, it is not yours to give!"

"Though the great lord may kill you for simply possessing it, there is a small possibility you shall be deemed worthy for elite service," Sureen continued as if she had not heard the outburst. "Make your choice quickly, woman, the time for our delay has passed."

The woman cast a wide-eyed glance at the medallion in her hand as if seeing it in a new way. "Mira, I am Mira, and I shall go straightaway to the lord of our citadel."

"Very well," Sureen said. Turning, she strode away from the great topaz gate. "Bring the Valen women, Captain."

"What!" Durandas exclaimed.

"Wait! Who do I tell our great lord who gave this to me?"

"The great one shall know," Durandas said. "It is doubtful he shall be pleased." Slipping his black hood over his head, he strode away.

Six warriors fell into place, surrounding Lore Rayna and the Lore Mother.

"Move out," Captain Wron ordered.

The woman, Mira, stared after them, even as they marched through the high-arched doorway exiting the Old Town Coliseum. Once outside, Lore Rayna strode beside the Lore Mother. Durandas and Sureen sprinted ahead. Without the need to speak of it, they picked up the pace, causing the warriors to jog. They ran without protest. Dashing under the stern eyes of the old statues carved by humans who had passed into dust long ago, they caught up and slowed, matching Durandas and Sureen's fast walk.

Durandas was speaking as they strode down the small incline of the ancient roadway leading to Gray Dust.

"What have you done, Sureen? That medallion was far more valuable than you are aware," Durandas said.

Even while wearing the hot black robes of a Dark User in the midday heat of Gray Dust at his seasons, Durandas traveled at a considerable pace for a human. Though older, the Light User continued to surprise Lore Rayna with his prowess.

"I am aware of the black heron's worth. Shall I remind you of a lifetime spent interrogating those of Virun? I know my enemies well. One might ask you how is it you were able to obtain such a rare artifact without my knowledge or the awareness of anyone else on the Circle of Light?"

"One is curious to know how you acquired a black heron without the rest of our order knowing," the Lore Mother said, the tone of her voice soft.

"I suppose it did save us from fighting our way out of Old Town Coliseum," Durandas admitted, ignoring the words of his Interrupter, the Lore Mother.

Lore Rayna had clamped her mouth closed. Not even the First Light on the Circle of Light should have the audacity to speak to the Lore Mother in such a way, yet the Lore Mother must have a reason for not responding to such an affront.

"Precisely," Sureen continued. "I am not certain about you, but I need a bit of a rest before engaging with the Flow again so soon after the Oracle. That took much from me."

"Aye, from me as well, your quick thinking likely saved lives, perhaps my own," Durandas said, though grudgingly.

As they turned onto Dust Stir, the main thoroughfare going in and out of Gray Dust, Lore Rayna stopped listening. A busy street demanded some attention for pocket lifters, bag thieves, and flesh catchers who preferred crowds for the added marks it gave them. The experienced lifter and bag thief rabble would avoid a large observant group, yet there were still a few bold or foolish enough to try, though she herself was safe from any such attempts. Her living dress would deter all; it only revealed pockets to her.

Mostly, she had to maintain vigilance for the flesh catchers paid by slavers for new product. Her kind was rare in the southern cities, the heat too unbearable for most to remain long, fetching a high price at the flesh market for her race alone. She and the Lore Mother's luminous eyes would set them above that.

A middling march through several back alleyways put them in the wine cellar of a private dwelling in the heart of silver quarter at the close of midday. A pair of gray obelisks hidden behind a hinged set of wine casks in the cellar took them to the outskirts of Grit Eye City.

From there, the remainder of the small conversion assault group on the Dark Oracle had raced through the back streets and dark alleys of the city's seedier side until reaching the Lovely Stupor Pub's back entrance. A surly human woman wearing scanty silks opened the door for them and then demanded a few words in private with Durandas. Sureen uncovered and activated an emerald gate disguised well as a wardrobe.

The emerald gateway deposited Lore Rayna in the Vibrant Vale's command room. Nothing had changed much from when they had left, just the passing of a few bells. The live, interwoven leaf rugs still crawled on parts of the Great Tree's floor, and the living oak coaxed from the tree to form the grand desk that stood off to one side had the unrolled maps of the Vale—weighted on the four corners with small river rocks—right where they had left them.

Captain Wron spoke with the Valen commanders who had gathered at the viewing window overlooking the battlefront of Silver Meadow, though it was only a small area from this height. The rest of the men had raised the trapdoor and were climbing down one at a time.

Across the room, the Lore Mother gave the grave news to two Valen warriors their only son would not return. Lore Rayna would not want such a duty and respected her mentor for doing it.

The cost of the undertaking was high, but the result was better than they all had hoped for, due in a large part from Sureen's powerful assistance. Without her using, it was unlikely no one would have returned.

Lore Rayna looked to the area kept clear by the north wall for the gateway. Sureen materialized walking backward, followed by Durandas a mere step apart. He also put a foot behind him, keeping a watch right up until touching the spiral curtain on the other side. Though the emerald gateway stood hidden inside the living quarters of the pub's owners, it had resided inside a lawless area of Dark User supporters.

Lore Rayna relaxed a little with the arrival of the final two to cross through, though she should not have worried. Durandas and Sureen were adept enough to step through one at a time, stemming from the tangible danger of reforming as one mass of deformity that loomed each time one used a gateway. Her kind going through alone was always binding; added mass meant a higher the risk.

"Report, daughter," the Lore Mother said abruptly.

Lore Rayna jumped, vibrating the boughs of the Great Tree. The room shuddered. Standing beside her, her old mentor's wizened face held no mirth for startling her student. Her duty had seen to that. "Though neither Durandas nor Sureen has confirmed it, I am certain it worked, Mother. The Oracle was converted."

The Lore Mother nodded, pleased. "Stuck with providing the Flow to Durandas, I had no opportunity to look into the water. Did it clear?"

Lore Rayna nodded. "Yes, the Dark Oracle cleared, becoming as pristine as the pools below Plunging Falls."

The Lore Mother gazed off into the distance, though the wall kept barren for gated arrivals stood in the way. "With surprise as our ally, I had expected less resistance. Yet they gathered a formidable force quickly. Someone powerful with the Flow struck Sureen's barrier once we gained the topaz gateway, and overall, an expert military mind led the soldiers. Our escape was nearly thwarted."

"All of you should be proud," Durandas said, coming over. "We have struck a historical blow this day. A major instrument of Dark User intelligence gathering is now lost to anyone not wielding the Flow of Light."

Lore Rayna wondered where the First Light found his energy to move, let alone calmly stroll about the room. After nearly a bell of nonstop using, followed by a risky sprint through Gray Dust and Grit Eye City, she expected him to express a need for rest. His smooth face showed little trace of fatigue despite his words spoken to Sureen. Lore Rayna felt the drain after calling upon the Flow Mother to bless her with the living form for so long. Contact with one of the great falun trees had boosted her energy slightly as soon as she had arrived.

Sureen's soft voice grew softer with sadness. "They hurt us as well, Durandas. I lost fully two-thirds of my warriors. Was their sacrifice worthwhile? Did you find her after we converted the Oracle?"

Though high already, Lore Rayna's respect for Sureen rose. The warrior User had expended an amazing amount of the Flow protecting them and covering their retreat *after* performing the cleansing rite on the Oracle with a double handful of her Interrupters with Durandas and the Lore Mother's aid. It had come at great cost, as she said, though not only to the humans. Only two of her Interrupters had escaped and seven Valen warriors had fallen, a great loss for the Vale. Their numbers were too few as it was.

Durandas flashed a brief smile. "I did find her. As luck would have it, Crystalyn's here. By here, I mean in the outskirts of the Vibrant Vale. At least, I believe so, judging from the quick view of her surroundings. Running from Dark Users, I suspect, she brushed off the Oracle contacting almost immediately, but it is enough to know she lives."

"Thank the One Mother!" the Lore Mother exclaimed.

Sureen smiled.

"That explains something," the Lore Mother said. "One commander reported a disruption occurred within the Dark Users' ranks, we've managed to scatter their left flank. I must act upon this," she said, striding away.

Lore Rayna was ecstatic. "Then I shall go to her!" She dashed ahead of the Lore Mother flinging open the trap door the warriors had closed, exposing it to the windy heights below.

Speaking quickly, Durandas halted her with one foot poised above the top of the living ladder the Great Tree provided. "I am not certain you can reach her, Rayna. I need to look at a map, perhaps I can figure out where Crystalyn attacked the Dark Users." He strode toward the map table with the raised terrain painstakingly made over several seasons by the monks of Brown Recluse.

Lore Rayna put her foot down on the smooth flooring of the landing, the sanded Four Bridges boards held snugly in place by the tree.

"Make room for the First Light," Captain Wron said to those

grouped at the table. Two men moved to one side leaving a wide opening.

Durandas froze as he neared the table, his right eye vanishing behind a brilliant white radiance, the left illuminated with a vivid black that flickered as a dark campfire would without sound. "What do you want?" he demanded of the empty air in front of him. "You know Dark Users have intercepted transmissions."

"Someone contacts Durandas," Sureen said, the tone of her voice urgent. "Lore Rayna, can you listen in on the conversation? Don't press too hard, he's weak after so much using this day."

Lore Rayna slipped her contact stone from her dress pocket. Tying the kell leather band to the back of her head, she centered the clear stone on her forehead.

Durandas drew a sharp breath. "So, he's lost to us then," he said.

Lore Rayna interrupted the Flow and dribbled a minute amount into her body infusing the white crystal on her headband. Energy filled her, giving her a vibrancy she accepted gratefully. A drain would come later, once the Flow's pure energy had released into her system.

"Bring him to Surbo. I will see he gets the training needed to keep him from becoming a mindless shell," Durandas commanded.

Lore Rayna focused on Durandas' white eye, shying away from his black one. The Flow of Light was the only one she'd have a chance of joining. Whoever contacted Durandas had trained with Dark Users in some form, which made that link beyond her. Gathering her will, she added her stream of the Flow to Durandas with as much delicacy as she could muster.

An image bloomed in her mind. Five men and a woman sat at a table; extensive handcrafted raised maps depicting much of the western White Lands covered a wall. Lore Rayna was familiar with only one at the table, though the two men dressed in the same livery beside Duke Durniss denoted the men as his own.

"Now I must go," Durandas was saying. "The Vibrant Vale is under siege. Arelya, if your apprentice has sufficient training for short communications, leave her with the duke, I need you here. Your long-range talents will keep me in touch with Surbo. Durniss, prepare for the worst; the Black Wolf Valley shall not remain unscathed for long now that the darkness awoken has found it. It will not rest until—"

"Didn't you say it was time to break off this transmission?" a handsome human man seated beside the woman Contactor, Arelya, interjected.

Lore Rayna knew she was a Contactor since her eyes glowed white and black and the white stone wrapped tight to her forehead.

"Right you are, Laran, sometimes I get to barking orders and forget to keep track of the time, besides, we are draining Arel and—"

Suddenly the image wavered, the top and bottom corners began swiftly turning black. Lore Rayna glimpsed Arelya's right eye bleeding bright red. Then, the Flow wrenched from her at a staggering rate. A supreme will, containing staggering power, brushed the edge of her awareness from deep beneath the Dark Citadel. Her mind shied from it, severing the contacting.

Lore Rayna fell to her knees. She fought the urge to heave the contents of her stomach; she was so very close to closing her eyes and succumbing to blackness. Giving in may prove fatal. "Are you badly hurt?" someone asked, but she dared not reply.

Once her stomach calmed, she pushed her way to her feet.

Putting her shoulder under Durandas, Sureen helped him stand.

Lore Rayna crossed the room and stood before the First Light. Durandas looked up at her, gray shades of weariness evident in his blue eyes, though there was no fright from such a narrow escape.

"You have my gratitude," he said. "Without your strength to draw upon, I would have been overcome."

"What was it?" Lore Rayna asked. "That was no Dark User attack. I sensed something else."

Durandas looked around the room, urging the commanders back to their discussion with a long stare. Once they had their back to them, he met the Lore Mother's and Sureen's eyes, raising an eyebrow. Both nodded. "The Green Writhe believes as the Circle only recently suspects, something grows with power in the southeast," Durandas confided, the tone of his voice low.

The Lore Mother laid an arm on her shoulder, gently drawing her close. "Something stealthy has awoken, daughter."

Lore Rayna was puzzled. "Where did you say?"

Sureen spoke. "The Stair of Despair, southeast of here." The tone of her voice was lower than the previous ones.

Lore Rayna shook her head. "No. This came from below the Dark Plateau, under the citadel." Though she whispered, the trio glanced quickly around.

Satisfied of their privacy, Durandas' words were no louder than a breath of wind. "You are mistaken. The Green Writhe has had secret vigilance, passed on to each generation for ages. We suspect this is the very thing we have watched for, perhaps even akin to the mind worm that afflicted you in Surbo, though stronger. Its existence is not something all here should know about, or a great panic would ensue, nor is it speculation. I now confirm it. This evil is the greatest threat our world has ever known."

Though frightened by the grim words, she was puzzled too. Their geographic description was off; she knew what she sensed. The arrogance and evilness came from *under* the Dark Citadel, not to the south. It was the same great plateau though wrong location.

Something resided under the citadel, something big and bad,

and not something she ever wanted contact with again. The mind worm was a child compared to it. "This did not originate from the southeast of the great plateau, Durandas. It came from the bowels of the Dark Citadel, somewhere so deep, I do not believe even the Dark Users know it's there. Whatever it was, it knows how we contact now. It shall be *waiting*."

Silence filled the room broken only by the soft wail of living wood holding back a small errant gust of wind.

"I do not know if these two incidents are related," Sureen said softly, breaking the silence at last. "But there is a looming…presence…in the southeast as Durandas has mentioned. I sensed its malice in the Dark Oracle during the conversion. Something best left slumbering has awoken. It moves under the plateau there as well."

"Did we awaken it by transforming the Dark Oracle to the Light?" Durandas asked, his light blue eyes intent.

"No," Sureen replied. "It was already there when we began. It searches for the one who woke it, consuming all within its grasp."

The Lore Mother leaned one hand on the trap door. "Who woke this power or powers as the case may be?"

"I wish I knew," Sureen admitted. "The key to its defeat may well lie within that knowledge. It searches ardently for the awakener, for it knows unease. Of what, I do not know. I do know it desires this one being above any other, though I could not discern the motive. I fear we now have to discover whom it seeks, get there before it does, and destroy that power before allowing the darkness to consume it. I do not believe our combined might shall have a chance at destroying it otherwise."

Sounding too loud in the silence that followed Sureen's statement, a gasp escaped Lore Rayna's throat as a frightening thought occurred to her.

The Lore Mother glanced at her sharply. "We both have the same thought, do we not?"

Lore Rayna nodded. "Crystalyn is the strongest person I know of with her symbol magic, though she may not be a match against the collective strength of the Light. If she is the one you think you have to destroy, then you shall find a Valen blocking the way. The only part in this for me is to protect *her*."

The Lore Mother's luminous eyes flared brighter. "Hold your tongue, daughter! No one has said that may happen, but you shall do everything necessary to protect Astura. That has always been our mission on this world."

"I shall not do anything of the sort! She saved my life *and* my mind, have you forgotten so quickly, Mother?"

"If the choice ever comes upon us, you shall do as the Lore Mother commands," Durandas said, the tone of his voice low but strong.

Sureen raised a hand. "Please, everyone! There is time yet to make those hard decisions should it come to that. Our first priority is to send a scout to discover more about this threat so we can better combat it. Is there someone you trust to lead a small group on such a mission? That someone would have to have high skills of stealth and observation. Does anyone come to mind?"

Lore Rayna looked toward the Lore Mother. The wise one gave an almost imperceptible nod. "Yes, there is such a one here overseeing the defenses. It was his suggestion we convert the Oracle into something only those of the Light could control while much of the Dark Citadel was busy attacking the Vale."

Sureen smiled. She looked as vibrant as when they had left for the Dark Citadel, giving credence to Lore Rayna's belief that the warrior User thrived during adversity. "Then by all means, bring him here. We have to set goals and stratagem to attain them. Durandas, do you have a candidate?" Sureen asked next.

"Yes, I do. She will be a valuable asset to the group in many ways. There is a problem, however. To get her gated here from Surbo, I will need to attempt another contacting."

Sureen rested her gold staff on the ground and straightened. For a human woman, she was tall. At least, Lore Rayna thought so. "I think we have to risk it. We need to know how to combat this great evil.

Leaving the trap door, the Lore Mother strode toward him. "I suppose you shall need an Interrupter, keep it short, Durandas. Give the command to gate here, but nothing else."

Durandas's jaw tightened. "As you advise," he said. Tying his focus orb at the back, he made direct contact with the skin of his forehead where the neural Flow was strongest. "Blocked from communicating this way has us at a huge disadvantage for this war. I hope the other side is hampered with it also," he said, clasping the Lore Mother's hand, the white stone already illuminating.

While they were involved, Lore Rayna dropped through the open hatch and slid down the wooded rungs two at a time before anyone could command her otherwise.

Descending quickly, she almost missed the first landing. Pausing to regain her composure, she looked upon the writhing shapes dotting the landscape below. In tune with the tree, she swayed with the rail-less landing, studying the darkest spots, the highest concentration of fighting.

The far sight inherent to her people—when she called upon it—enabled her to view the scene below without too much trouble. The enemy's right flank had collapsed back to the left to strengthen its failing line.

She was saddened to see two of the great falun trees burning closer to the front. The naturists' fire protection shield was strong and repelled most of the fireballs thrown at it, but there was not enough of them to keep it maintained upon the huge trees.

Swinging over the side, Lore Rayna caught the guide rope to the next landing with one hand, bypassing the ladders. Once on the ground, she ran to the hillock where Camoe shouted orders to the generals directing the battle. He was not going be happy with the new turn of events, but he was the best druid for the task, or human for that matter, now that he appeared to have turned the tide of the battle in their favor.

Nor was he going to be happy she was not going with him on the mission. With Cudgel sent away by Durandas on Circle of Light affairs, she would find the friend she was proud to be indebted to, one who needed to know she was in danger from several sources. Even some Crystalyn may have thought of as allies and friends.

# ONE MIND

Cord was the designation the remnant of the humanoid mind considered itself. It was a weak title, one not befitting an entity of sublime intelligence. Nevertheless, it would do as long as it was predominant in this mass.

Having a host pleased the entity, the One Mind, for it would sow fear throughout the land thereby making the species easier to consume. Humans, as they thought of themselves, exuded emotion, which raised neural activity. Higher activity increased its power. Fear was one of the strongest for producing the highest frequencies when such creatures were near.

In the distance, human minds with the greatest active frequency caught at the One Mind's, Cord's sensors, beckoning at its innate sense for such things, coming in as bright spots of motion moving about the land. Two areas in particular drew interest.

Of the two, one pulled at it as much as the molten core of the planet had drawn it in after making the only error ever made in its long existence. For, from the darkness of cold space, the great energy source underlying this planet with its connection to a massive store of neural activity of synaptic pulses had singled out this solar system from countless others.

The mistake came only days after landing with the first attempt to absorb the neural connectivity entwined with the river of power flowing through the land. Instead of absorbing it, the river had almost erased Cord's existence by siphoning much of its stored neural supremacy into its raging mass. The One Mind had fled to the planet's depths, only there could it sever the connection.

Weakened beyond the ability to travel, the One-Mind was nurtured by the coldness underground and relative heat compared to space as it fought to retain a presence through an eon, while gaining the unexpected benefit of raising its frigid inner core. Now, direct dominion of life without the use of offspring was possible. Attempting dominions in the past had resulted with the fragile vessel's life on the planet crystalizing instantly, forcing an abandonment of the host as soon as it had entered.

Now, Cord knew wariness, something it had never known throughout the billions of ages of its creation, and uncertainty. Travel through the galaxies after harvesting the neural pulses of the planet with its core temperature raised may not now be possible.

With the Cord human, and many others powering it, it would then determine the truth of it. For its supreme intellect, gathered from a collective pool over the ages, had a theory. A notion it would test soon with little risk; the power of the river would affect it but little if the process failed.

The offspring it had created while still cocooned underground stored centuries of the planet's neural waves. Once it consumed those and boosted the considerable power it already contained, the minds within them would be absorbed into the One Mind. Nonhuman or human, it made only a small difference.

Cord issued a command into the One Mind and the Over Mind passed it through neural pathways, transferring it from mind to mind of its subjugations, the speed of the transmission near instantaneous. The Over Mind sent a query outward from all controlled, and the One Mind, Cord, searched until finding two compellable intelligences roaming near the bright spots of energy.

The One Mind, Cord, clamped the coercion upon the first immediately, an instinctive creature led by baser hungers, and one of its own. Even so, compelling some of the offspring took large amounts of its limited power and only sustained partial success with a quick frontal assault. Satisfied with having the flicker controlled in the background, the Over Mind moved on.

The second target, a beast, resisted the compulsion for two discordant beats of its cold-blooded heart. Interestingly, as the One Mind blew away all self-aware thoughts, there was a touch of darkness compelling it from underground. The hold the darkness had on it was tenuous; the Over Mind severed it with ease.

Viewing the planet through lime-colored vision took several seconds of adjustment as it sought a place of height. From there it settled in to wait. The radiance its alien intellect knew as the galaxy focus—most of the planet's denizens thought of as the sun and the baser intellects considered it simply as heat in the sky—was moving at a steady rate toward it. The beast exulted in the feeling of it, and the Over Mind gained a tiny boost from the primitive, though strong, neural activity.

Benefitting from the simple act of basking in the heat, Cord drank hungrily on the brain waves though it halted from ever coming close to fully sated. Drawing too much would make the host a useless husk. As it waited, one of the many facets of the Over Mind—the human formerly known as Cord—alerted it to a beacon the stone fortress above the main host.

Though dimmer, another bright spot gathered there with the tool—the one human it had left intact for implementing the notion of using humans as feelers for neural power—sent confusion through the Over Mind. Compelled from the initial meeting when the human had sought it out in the cocoon, the tool had no alternative but to report exceptional neural waves to the community intellect, yet no record existed.

It was but a small concern. Once finished with the beast and the instinctual life form, it would gather its superior intellect back to the present host and then consume the brightness. The tool too, as it had little use left for it.

The One Mind, Cord, was pleased. Soon it would absorb two-and-a-half complex intelligences in a single day, a rare occurrence.

Shifting its awareness back to the swarm of its vessels moving about the planet, it tracked the progress of the two bright spots, one of which had awoken it. That one was the brightest, nearly a hundred times superior to the others, and strong. As great a mind as it had ever discovered on any world. Absorbing it would ensure this world's total domination.

At present, the other spot generated increased emotional neural activity, and it was moving close.

At the same time, halfway across the land, the great mind neared an encounter with the dark offspring. After the flicker went for it, Cord, the One Mind, would then overtake the Dark One and the mind it held.

Each strike would occur close to the same moment, though at different places on the planet, not a difficult endeavor for the power of the One Mind.

The Over Mind shifted back to the wait. As it waited, it changed its awareness to the main host.

Cord recognized the ramp the main host had used with the rest of the patrol to access the caverns below the Dark Citadel. That patrol now marched toward the Black Gate with the ingrots—a slightly lower level of life form than humans—though the underground dwellers would not believe so.

Once at the gate, control of the underground fortress would swell as it absorbed the humans guarding the main entrance, a holdover left behind by the Ancients. The Over Mind's vast, timeworn memories recalled the Ancients as a large group of powerful Users who had inhabited the world at the time of arrival.

No great neural bounty awaited the Over Mind back then; most Users had encountered the great darkness dwelling under the Dark Citadel and had succumbed to *its* control. Though the flickering darkness was a colossal energy source, the One Mind avoided it by staying hidden in the shadows while the redundant mind in the southern hemisphere stored and developed contingency intellect. There it waited, gathering strength in its best offspring before taking on such power, if ever. The darkness had a strong, though corrupted, connection to the river of energy.

For now, Cord was careful not to permit the controlled User minds access to the great river or to go near the great darkness.

Though it had absorbed many of the two-legged denizens into the Over Mind—the bulk not long ago, additions from its offspring while it slumbered—the One Mind's supreme intelligence knew surprise at the lobe adaptation of the species. Humans' thought processes and memory storages had infinitesimal variations.

A shudder of excitement rippled throughout the One Mind. This one, which had thought of itself as Cord, had a strong ability the host had not known existed. The One Mind could see the great potential controlling it had provided. The discovery of the ability had come from an extraneous, but fortuitous, event.

A contacting—as the host mind thought of it—had occurred between two Light Users. The host's ability had intercepted the contacting on instinct, perhaps triggered when the brain lost the ability to function on its own. Had the One Mind been aware of its host's ability, it may have attempted to absorb the minds of those performing the contact.

As it was, the Over Mind knew satisfaction. The human with white hair had made contact only for a short time, but it was enough and attracted the One Mind the same way as the dark creature—a flicker, the hominids referred to it—was attracted to the light ray essence inside and around humans, the soul.

The mind the Light User contacted was far different from any other the Over Mind had experienced in its long past. It was a strong mind, but it was a mind in turmoil. A power resided there like no other on this alien, power-infused world.

The mind that had awakened it was there also, the bright beacon. This one mind it now desired above all others. It too, had a latent ability. Combined with the Cord host ability, the new host would know no end to the dissension it would reap from this primitive planet. No longer would the restriction of not allowing the minds it controlled access to the river of power have relevance, for it did not need to control them all, not at first. It only had to govern the leaders; the rest would follow those the One Mind placed in command.

With the bright mind's ability, Cord would know if the species were a User *before* absorption. Consuming the humans holding authority without the ability to access the river would allow use of the Users with their abilities intact.

After absorption of the bright mind, whenever another contacting occurred between two of the world's denizens, the One Mind and its new host's innate alarm would trigger. Cord would then choose to listen in or destroy the minds contacting. The desire for the bright mind rose.

Excitement rippled through all the minds in the One Mind. The long conditional search for the exact neurological and environmental makeup central to the long-range stratagem was now a possible outcome.

The Over Mind had done well consuming Cord as a start to fulfilling the great desire, but the host had a mate and offspring. As a precaution, the One Mind would assimilate them all to add to the cloak of normalcy.

The One Mind continued up the ramp the host had originally ran toward, working out the stiffness of its motor control as it went, smoothing the arduousness of controlled muscles. Moving without complete fluidity would draw unwanted attention. Soon it would shift back to its lime-colored vision, where it basked in the sun, and spring the trap.

# DARK SHAPE

To Jade, the forest seemed like a protective friend. The cloudless sky above and the open spaces between the trees permitted anyone or *anything* to see them. Someone or something spotting them now would mean another attack. How long could they go on before a dark-armored soldier crept close enough to hurl a spear through the magic-resistant dome?

As they fled from the Vale, they'd kept a constant vigil on the dome; hand in hand, she'd supplied Crystalyn with energy, dribbling the Flow through her palm. Filtered through Jade first was the only way they'd found her sister could use the Flow in small bits, like the perfect spice on the meat of her symbols.

A shudder racked Jade. From the fatigue of funneling the Flow for several bells or scrambling with all the stealth they could muster while attempting to circle through a dense forest, she knew not which. Nor did she care; she was too tired think about it.

Atoi came into view racing down the steep incline they'd only recently made their way down. "Incoming!" the little girl shouted, bursting into the absorption symbol Crystalyn kept tented around them as they walked. The beautiful interlocked white crosses on the black background kept them sheltered from User magic attacks, but it had the downside of standing out, the black-and-white translucence unnatural in a forest.

Hastel dived inside the dome's protection as fireballs

exploded ahead and to the right of them. Pushing to his feet, he matched their slow pace, staring at the barrage for a time. "They're fishing!" he declared, daubing the wicked scar running from his forehead to his cheek.

Jade noted that in times of stress, it tended to break open again. When they got out of this, she was going to pry it out of him or his aura how he got a scar. Perhaps then, he would let Crystalyn heal it. So far, she hadn't read the images twisting around him as she had those spinning around Atoi. Dark and cloudy, Atoi's aura hadn't slowed for a viewing, even using all her willpower. Jade hadn't tried the arrowhead amulet and the white crystal candle artifacts on the little girl yet. Perhaps they would give her the boost required.

Hastel was so touchy about healing every time her sister had offered. Why wouldn't he want it mended?

Crystalyn's dark blue eyes regarded the one-eyed man with her customary sharpness. "What do you mean?"

Hastel's smile was grim. "They're throwing out a blanket net of explosions hoping we'll break cover or get caught in the fallout. Look, they're already moving away, bombarding as they go."

Jade concentrated on the explosions. "He's right, if we stay away from that area, we should be able to swing around the ridge ahead while staying out of sight under those ferns and…whatever those are," she said, giving a quick gesture toward a hedge of branches. Thick and twisting, the tree-like limbs entwined a foot or two above Crystalyn's six-foot height.

"Rubble brush," Hastel offered. "I suppose you mean those root-like branches wrapped around rocks below and to the right of us?"

"I do," Jade said.

"Try and angle that way; they will make good cover," Hastel said. "As I was saying, the Dark Users don't know our exact location in this thicket. We could follow the fireballs back to the Vale as long as a fire doesn't force us to put it out again with your rainstorm symbol. Those take serious energy, don't they? If you throw anything larger than that last one out there, we run the risk of catching ourselves in a flash flood."

Though she kept her eyes on the brush- and boulder-strewn route ahead, Crystalyn had heard Hastel. "Is it safe to drop the absorption symbol?" she asked.

Hastel nodded. "For now, but stay close to each other, it's possible they want us to think we've lost them."

Jade gratefully released the link she kept with the Flow. Weakness flowed through her limbs, and she stumbled, gripping Crystalyn for support.

Crystalyn stumbled with her, though Broth supported her under one arm. The warden's powerful front haunches held their combined weight easily.

Atoi's wide, emerald eyes gazed up the mountain. "Methinks little sister is correct, we should go around the ridge by going through the brush. As thick as it is, we would discourage any stragglers."

The closer they came, the more overgrown the hedge wall looked, and Jade was already regretting mentioning it.

Crystalyn strode up to it and stopped, considering. "Okay," she finally said. "Everyone down on their knees, let's lead our pursuit into the thickets if they're still tracking us. I'm almost beginning to believe the whole battle at the Vale was bait to bring us running to the rescue. They've been relentless with hounding us. If that is the case, it has worked for them."

Hastel dropped to his hands and feet. "You might be onto something there, but I'm not going to go ask them right now. Follow me as quiet as you can." He crawled into the twisted gnarls of the rubble brush before him and was soon out of sight.

Atoi's small frame disappeared behind him without a backward glance.

Jade curbed a sigh. Crawling was physically demanding to their overtaxed bodies, but it was their best chance at escape. She would find the energy somewhere. Dropping to all fours, she crept into the brambles.

At first, it was as tough as she feared, and the thorn-like dry sticks caught at her clothes. Breaking free meant flinging the sharp sticks snapping through the countryside with loud *cracking* noises—sound traveled so far in the forest. Jade cringed each time it happened.

After a while, she learned to bend them out of the way or crawl around thicker clumps when possible, though it lengthened the route. The wrist-thick brush entwined anything in its path, gripping small and large boulders in its wooden grasp, even digging some from loose dirt.

Her white flame hammer kept catching on forked branches, and she'd have to stop and pry it free. Several times, she had the wild urge to use it to smash through a thicket wall instead of going around, but it would make a world-deafening sound, louder than a round rolled boulder crashing through dry timber.

Broth pushed past Hastel, taking the lead. Following him, their pace picked up notably. Already moving on all fours, the warden's cat body was suited to the terrain. Even so, it was grueling work.

Exhausted, Jade laughed with quiet glee when they broke into a gloomy branch-covered clearing hours later. Broth had led them to a small, sunken dell inside the thicket jungle.

Atoi and Hastel sat together at the opening. Even they were not immune to the horrid trek, and both looked ragged. Dried leaves and twigs had tangled in their hair and neither one made any move to rake them clear. Broth sat on his haunches in the center, as placid as usual, though his great jaws were open, expelling heat.

Jade prostrated onto her stomach beside them, ecstatic to stretch to her full height without moving. It felt *glorious!* Crystalyn plopped beside her, sitting and extending her legs, a grateful smile lining her tired dust-streaked face.

Jade glanced around their oasis inside the cruel rubble brush forest, their little grotto. The clearing funneled toward a dark overgrown tunnel of jumbled deadfall that nearly roofed the farthest side. Beyond it, the forest thinned. Patches of grassland glinted with golden sunrays. *Good,* she thought. *I'm getting tired of scrambling around like a kind of forest crab.*

For some reason, she disliked the looks of the tunnel, finding it odd simply by the fact of what it was; no drainage had ever flowed through the snarls to create it. So how had it gotten there?

Why did it matter? Forests had a way of piling deadfall in reason-defying stacks. She must be tired. At least there was an easy way out to an easier hike.

Crystalyn shifted next to her, rustling dried leaves and grass. "As long as we're taking a break, I would like some water."

Her sister's gentle admonishment reminded Jade of her own dry throat. Lifting the flask of water off her shoulders and over her head by the strap, Jade pulled the stopper from the leatherneck, handing it to Crystalyn first.

Leaning back, Crystalyn squirted a half cup down her throat. Broth padded in front of her, and she squirted a stream into his wolf-like jaws and then passed the flask to Atoi. After the little girl drank, Jade watched Hastel gulp several swallows before he handed it back to her.

Though she was tired and low on energy, Jade drew upon her ability and slowed the rotation of his aura spinning around him in a cyclone. Like Crystalyn, his aura was dark. Unlike hers, Hastel's took a great deal of her willpower to halt it enough to view the images rotating inside.

After a few moments, she made out definite images though the rotation tugged at her mind as a horse would with an unwanted tether. Jade gathered her will and forced it slower. The images sprang into clarity.

In one, a stooped white-haired woman with glowing eyes held a leaf outstretched. The second started to the forefront. A bloodstained axe, facing another dripping with blood, spun into view. The third held several shapes, but she couldn't hold it. With a sharp wrench, his aura spun away, whipping around him faster and faster, blurring to cyclone speed.

Jade let it go, dropping the sight; she had no strength for a second attempt. Hastel stared at her, his blue eye narrow. She considered him, wondering about the old woman. He looked away.

Jade understood the axes. He carried a pair, one on each hip, but the woman's offering meant something. However, she had no notion what secret he carried without asking him. Someday she'd broach the subject, even though the taciturn warrior had not confided in anyone of his past.

Raising the leather bottle to her mouth, Jade found it nearly empty. Suppressing a sigh, she finished the last of it with two mouthfuls, just enough to wash the grit down. They'd have to find water soon. Standing, she stretched and worked the kinks from her back. The tunnel called to her with a small sound, nearly enough to make her drool. Somewhere beyond, water trickled.

Leaving the others where they sat or lay, Jade went to the tunnel, pausing to verify what she first thought. Besides the way they crawled in, the tunnel was the only exit. The rubble brush thickets were native to Astura. At the heart, its root-like branches entwined with everything nearby, living or not if one stayed too long around it, creating a barrier dense enough a rodent would struggle to get through in some spots, yet the brush had left the odd escape route. She wasn't going to complain. They couldn't stay, and already she'd felt the tiny vibrations of the brush moving.

Jade only had to bend at the waist, making it faster and easier than a crawl, though the shadows inside the tunnel darkened deeply. Something sticky and stretched taut touched her face, causing her to cringe. Thrusting her arms in front of her at a defensive angle, she kept the cobwebs at bay as best she could, hating when her mind conjured the image of something black and writhing dropping on her hands and racing toward her each time a filament stuck.

The light of mid-afternoon blazed as she stepped free at last and straightened.

In the shadows, off to one side, a dark shape writhed with tendrils outstretched…flicker.

Warmth, security, and divine happiness flowed through her. *No! She knew this for what it was!* Flicker.

*Glee, there was no escape from its touch, it was going to feed…finally, it would feast! It had been so long, glee…*flicker.

*No, please! This can't be happening again!* To survive, she had to *run,* just as she had in the Dark Citadel. Flicker.

*Why was she afraid? Why would she run? Was she frightened of something as gentle as her own mother was?* Flicker.

It was near…she needed to scream…but she couldn't…her voice had failed. Flicker.

It had only one base desire, to feed on a soul. It was coming…Flicker. Flicker.

# COHERENT THOUGHT

Crystalyn watched Jade as she doubled over and vanished inside the tunnel at the end of the clearing. She envied her sister's energy. How did she do it? They'd been fighting and circling around the Vale, trying to break through to their besieged friends for most of the day. Jade must be as tired as she was, though she had the added benefit of two seasons of youth less than she did.

*"Something comes, Do'brieni!"*

Crystalyn scrambled to her feet. "Which direction, show me."

Broth leapt to her side, gazing into the trees behind her.

"Everyone, someone is coming," Crystalyn said. Atoi and Hastel needed little urging; they'd heard her side of the conversation with Broth.

Drawing her dagger, Atoi stalked beside her as Hastel wound a crossbow bolt. When it locked in place, he indicated his readiness with a nod.

Crystalyn visualized the pattern for her black gale symbol she'd read in the *Tiered Tome of Symbols,* tier three, in the last chapter titled much and greater. So far, she hadn't used it or any of those under the heading during battle. In effect, this test would decide if she ever used it again.

Bringing the symbol out to hover before her, Crystalyn sent a silent query to her link mate. *"Have you caught a scent yet?"*

*"Aye, though it is not strong. Whoever it is mixes the scent of many*

*trees to mask the true scent."*

Crystalyn motioned Atoi and Hastel to move to the center of the clearing to wait.

The wait was not long. The rubble brush at the back parted. The branches sidled out of the way, scraping and screeching loudly, as they drew to the side. A large form stepped through.

Breathing hard, Lore Rayna paused at the new entrance, her green, leafy dress slithering back and forth with constant agitation, revealing too much of her bosom and thighs. The big woman appeared not to notice, her eyes sweeping past Crystalyn to the end of the clearing. "One…of your companions…is in grave danger. There is foulness…in the foliage," she said between gasping breaths.

Dread raced through her. She looked to her companions, and then toward the rounded opening. Crystalyn dashed through the passageway of deadfall.

Jade stood straight and rigid to the left of the tunnel's exit. Black tendrils had wrapped around her waist and upper torso, dragging her toward a flickering shape writhing with multi-wisps of dark radiance.

The shape exuded a petrifying fear.

Earlier in Crystalyn's life, on another world, the sight of such evil might have frozen her in place, hammered her with dread. Not now, not after the betrayals, or going through the impalement of a spiderbee, and the many other brushes with death. Now it made her angry. The bloody thing thought to take her sister from almost right beside her. Did such foulness believe she'd ever let that happen?

Thinking to sever the tendrils gripping Jade, Crystalyn brought out her absorption symbol and sent it chopping through them. The symbol dispersed on contact. Jade's motion never ended. If anything, the darkness seemed to sense the attempt, pulling harder. Soon, Jade would encounter its flickering embrace.

Hastel shouted from somewhere near. "Do something, Lore Rayna! My bolts do not affect it!"

The tunnel dispersed, reforming as a giant wooden fist, which wrapped around the flicker and squeezed. Then, exploding, it threw wooden shrapnel and rubble ringing outward.

Crystalyn somehow escaped harm.

Blood welled and then streamed from a gash on Jade's head.

Tinged with anxiety for her sister, Crystalyn's anger mounted. Reaching under a tendril, Crystalyn gripped Jade's hand and brought her silver and gold healing symbol out. Part of its oval edge brushed the flicker.

The creature shrank back from it.

Crystalyn had little time to marvel. Attaching her awareness to the symbol, she let it sink into her sister.

"It's too late! It has—"

Hastel's shout cut off abruptly. Silence descended as she floated the symbol to where she'd viewed the crack in Jade's skull.

It was easy to find. Floating inside a vein growing ever smaller, her symbol rushed toward it, swept along as if it were silk webbing caught in a storm pipe, causing a moment of panic. The flow nearly carried her outside before she thought to paste part of the symbol into the opening. Then she plugged the vein from the inside.

Most of the symbol remained, so she passed through the capillary, attached it to the gray matter of Jade's brain, and nearly recoiled, receiving a brutal shock. Jade cognizance wasn't Jade's. Something dominating, alien with its base desires of hunger and subversion, shifted its awareness to her.

Only from instinct, Crystalyn clung to her symbol after severing the connection to the gray matter, her mind in turmoil.

The creature was aware of her, but she cared not. What

mattered was how to help Jade without killing her. She'd have to fight the thing, but how to start? If she somehow managed to destroy the creature, would it leave her sister a mindless shell? Or was she already? *No!* Crystalyn squashed the panic rising within. It would do Jade no good with her mind slipping, looped inside another anxiety attack.

Crystalyn attached the symbol to the gray matter, at the left side of the frontal lobe this time.

Concentrated at the front, pure instinctual thoughts bombarded her, an all-consuming yearning for self-awareness, any self-awareness, as long as it *was* an awareness of one's self, something it had never had. *It wants her soul,* Crystalyn knew with a certainty that repulsed her.

The creature lusted for something it could never truly know. Even if it consumed all the countless little filaments of Jade's central nervous system, swallowed all the minuscule dots of her sense of self, and overrode all her synaptic compilations moving around in her brain, it could never discern truth. The creature's own sense of inner vitality and purpose had not been included in its makeup by the evil that had created it—an old, and chillingly strong, power. What such power wanted with a soul, Crystalyn wished she knew.

She had no time to think about it. The rush toward the frontal lobe slowed as the creature gained in strength.

Without a second thought, Crystalyn pushed into the rush of alien thoughts careening forward, flowing to the front lobe before her perception changed. Now she was at Jade's prefrontal cortex, the part of her mind that held her consciousness, precisely where she'd expected the alien thought pulses were streaming.

Crystalyn had no doubt they were aware of her now. Many of the pulses racing toward a ball of throbbing blackness stopped. Uncontested, Crystalyn kept going, though not long. Swarming her symbol, the dark pulses stacked about her in a sphere, keeping back from her symbol. The ball surrounding her crashed into something and halted. Dented, the sphere compressed inward on one side.

Floating onward, her symbol plowed through the pulses and burst them on contact, obliterating a partial line of her pattern but opening a tiny window through to a transparent bubble. Her symbol and awareness contacted the dome. Coherent thought flowed into her mind.

She'd found Jade.

# FORETOLD

The swarm of black pulses clinging to her bubble covered it completely, but Jade felt it was holding. The flicker was as powerful as the mesmerizing ability of the dominion wraith in the Dark Citadel. Her attempt to expand her dome outward by sheer force of will had failed. She'd only fought off the stupor the creature exuded just as the psychic swarm of its essence reached her, installing her tiny bubble of protection at the last moment.

Now she wondered about the rest of her. Trapped inside her own mind, it was an odd feeling losing the sense of her body. Disjointed and disconnected, she was at a loss what to do. Black and oblong, the pulses swarmed along her barrier. They seemed unable to penetrate the shell, for now.

Eventually her body would grow weak. When that happened, her strength at maintaining the shield would weaken also. She'd give it a moment of rest, and then she'd work on pushing the swarm outward, bubble and all, throwing her fright into it. She didn't want to die like this, but at the back of her dwindling cerebral hemisphere, Jade feared there was no escape.

Then her bubble bulged inward on one side. Crystalyn's strong but chaotic presence flowed inside her awareness, filling her with the warmth and familiarity of her big sister. If she'd had access to her tear ducts, she would've cried with joy.

*"Is that you, Jade?"*

Crystalyn's thoughts flowed through hers.

*"Oh, Crystalyn, how did you get to me?"* Jade asked with a thought.

*"Not now, those black pulses are attacking my symbol. They die upon contact, but it wipes out a small portion of it, and every strand counts. I had to use a part of it to heal you, though I still have the golden side of the symbol left. If it holds true, like when the mind worm had taken control of Lore Rayna, we should make it. Wait! They've stopped."*

Crystalyn was right. The swarm had ceased pulsing. As one, the entire ball shuddered, and the oblong shapes dropped away. *"Come on, Crystalyn, I can expand my barrier and sweep them out,"* Jade thought, expanding her barrier a little.

*"Something is coming."* Crystalyn sent. Anxiety came with it.

Ancient and vast, a great malice slammed into Jade's barrier, shrinking it by half. Then, a gale of malevolence, as strong as a radiation hurricane blowing about Low Realm, gusted into her bubble with a crushing, indomitable will of monumental power.

Frightened, Jade pushed back with all she had, denying it access but barely. Intensifying, coming at her with a sense of unlimited power, an immense force of malice thundered into her dome, crushing her with the strength of an exploding nebula. Her bubble shrank, compressing smaller at an alarming rate. Soon there would be nothing left of her resistance.

She couldn't stop it.

All at once, the gale of malevolence stopped.

Jade sensed why immediately. Crystalyn had shifted her symbol between the alien intelligence of black malice and her bubble.

With the pressure off her, Jade expanded her barrier, rising above and to the side of where Crystalyn had previously been with her symbol. The malice attacked as soon as she did, slamming into her bubble around Crystalyn. Hard-pressed, Jade recoiled, sending a query to her sister. *"Can you push it back? I'm not getting anywhere."*

*"It's too strong; my symbol won't hold it long even though I have the black crystal candle artifact. Can you access the Flow?"*

Without control of her body, Jade felt certain she could not, but she made the attempt. Surprisingly, the Flow was there but not the endless supply of the great, frothing river. There was only a remnant, a single brilliant strand floating within her mind. Having no time to analyze, she transferred it to the comforting awareness that was her sister. *"It's all I have. There is no more."*

*"Then it will have to…what's it doing?"*

Shying away from her sister's symbol, the darkness split and stretched around both sides, reaching for *her.*

*"Crystalyn, can you move forward?"*

*"Good idea"* was the reply as the symbol began to move.

Jade kept in contact, moving with it. The darkness receded noticeably. *"It's working! Push the bloody thing to the edge of my mind!"* With the darkness receding, as fast as Crystalyn swept her symbol forth, Jade expanded her bubble, reclaiming lost neural synaptic imbalances. Vague connections to some of her internal functions became available as the front of her mind came into view, apparent by the two cornucopia-shaped tubes leading to the back of her eyes.

*"See you on the outside,"* reverberated through Jade's thoughts along with a black snarl of unbelievable rage from Crystalyn. Then nerve endings, muscles, and body weight crashed upon her making her reel. Sight returned all at once with skull-searing brightness. Jade nearly swooned, only saving herself from a fall by snapping her eyelids closed.

When she opened them, Crystalyn was close, her blue eyes round and moist. Her wonderful sister, the best sibling ever on two worlds, no *any*, leaned forward putting her forehead against hers.

"It is good to have you back, my sister," Crystalyn said.

Tears blurred Jade's vision. "I couldn't have done it without you. How did you do it?" she asked, sobbing with relief between each question.

Crystalyn wrapped her in a fierce hug. "It is an aspect of the healing symbol, I suspect. It requires guidance in order to perform the right mend. I've adapted it to include mind afflictions," she replied, speaking softly, scientifically, into her ear. Crystalyn's scent was uniquely her sister's—all strength and determination with an underlying vulnerability. Jade had smelled it all her life and loved the warmth and security it gave her, though she only now recognized it for what it was. "It's too bad I cannot use it to cure my own," Crystalyn added, though much softer than before as she moved away.

Jade heard it. "No! Don't think that way, my sister. I love you the way you are, don't change."

"What just happened?" Hastel asked.

"Why did the flicker withdraw to the shadows?" Lore Rayna asked.

"Not leaving, fleeing," Jade corrected.

"Methinks we should go after it and destroy it then," Atoi said.

Broth moved beside the little girl, his great form throwing her into shadows.

Crystalyn looked to the east; she seemed to know the way the vile thing fled.

As Jade had known, the thing's malice left behind a fading sense of arrogant evilness. Even though it fled at a colossal rate of speed, it still believed itself far superior than they.

Crystalyn looked at Atoi and Broth, shaking her head. "It is moving faster than we can travel, even for you, Broth. Besides, I don't want you confronting it, that creature nearly overcame both my sister and I."

Jade sniffed and wiped away a final tear. "It's more than a flicker. I don't know what it is exactly, but it isn't just that."

Crystalyn glanced at her sharply and then back to the rest of the little group circled protectively around them. "Well, there you have it. We let it go, for now."

Hastel's broad, grizzled face swiveled between the two of them. "There's something you're not telling us, but it can wait. We should keep moving. Stick with the original plan?"

Crystalyn looked up at Lore Rayna and smiled. "I take it you're here for a reason. I mean, besides giving a warning to dangers when sorely needed. I owe you a lot for that. A minute later may have been too late…"

The big woman's eerie, glowing eyes brightened, but her beautiful, round face stayed placid. "It is nothing. You would have done the same. Do not think of it as counting toward my life debt to you; it does not. Nonetheless, you are correct. I have sought for you. The Vale is in grave danger. Bad things attack. Dark creations stalk the land. Dire portents and momentous events have occurred and have yet to occur. With some of these, you are mentioned."

"Yes, yes, we know about the codices, how Jade is an anomaly, and I'm the ruination or savior of everything," Crystalyn said. The impatient tone of her voice matched her words. "Can we get through to the Vale?"

"I believe I can get us there," Lore Rayna replied, though she didn't sound confident.

Feeling weak after the encounter, Jade shivered. At least the tunnel was gone, replaced by a wide swath of bare earth; with the characteristics of the rubble brush, it wouldn't last long. "Please, let's move away from this foul place," she said.

"What codices?" Hastel asked.

Crystalyn kept her eyes on Lore Rayna. "Not now, Hastel. Jade's right, we should leave this place, it's not safe. Lead the way,

Lore Rayna. Broth will help, alerting me if you two run across Dark Users or something."

Hastel scowled. "You'll probably never tell me then, you rarely do," he grumbled as he moved behind Atoi, taking rear position.

Crystalyn clasped Jade's hand and led her into the forest using the path Lore Rayna and Broth had taken.

Jade glanced back. Hastel still frowned. She found it hard to feel sorry for him. Knowing what the codices foretold would not lighten his mood.

# HOST MIND

The One Mind, Cord, was not pleased. Having the host terminated while still ingrained deep inside its motor functions and neural processes created discordant ripples throughout the Over Mind as a whole. Such an action temporarily weakened the compulsion tendril, blocking instantaneous travel to the Cord host, the Over Mind, forcing it to jump to a rodent. Losing a tendril seriously weakened it. Too many lost would quash its ability to reproduce replacements.

Both of the bright beacons it had targeted for absorption into the Over Mind had failed. Something it struggled to comprehend as it grappled with a second, odd sensation, unknown to it. Sifting through the dulled limbic system—a side effect of the compulsion—in the forebrain of the one named Cord, the One Mind found two emotions matching the sensation—worry and fear. Apprehension was a form of fright, and Cord had much familiarity with both according to the human's memory processes.

Cord dwelled upon this new revelation moving slowly upward through the caverns below the Dark Citadel. Either the main host it now resided in was weaker than most or its compulsion ability had lessened from the forced eon of sleep. The One Mind did not fear. It thrived on it.

Only one mind had ever resisted it, before this day. Overcoming that threat had required making it an offspring by infusing it with some of its essence as it had the dominion wraiths. It was a precarious move absorbing the flicker as it had, considering its former master was too strong for the One Mind to absorb. That darkness, the ancient evil that resided under this citadel, was as old as this world, or older. The One Mind would not attack such power until most other minds on the planet had joined with the Over Mind.

Movements of the human Cord had deteriorated. The question of why this loss of leg muscular movement had occurred so early Cord streamed through the Over Mind. Then the One Mind selected the suggestion with the highest success logistics, and a quick scan of the host body gathered the information. The host's core temperature had dropped.

The human's brain was dying from the intrusion; the weaker minds had an unfortunate tendency toward such an occurrence according to the knowledge stored in fragments of the Over Mind as a whole. When the brain failed, motor control inevitably went first.

It was a small matter for a time. The frail human's limp added proof to the lie prepared of how the ingrots had destroyed the rest of the patrol. This may have the benefit of helping the One Mind gain the necessary proximity of moving to another host when the time came. It intended to use the host's ability at intercepting a contacting until the host was but a husk and no longer mobile.

Cord continued along the rough stone hallway slowed only slightly by the unnatural gait of the cell-decaying limb. The One Mind found the two guards stationed at the entrance to the great hall, precisely where the host recalled them.

Larka, the short, broad one, coaxed his bulk from the stone bench he sat upon using his spear for support. "You have returned early. Lord Braddert informed us to watch for it. We are to escort you to him, immediately," he said, wheezing. He wiped at the sweat on his brow with a shaky hand.

Cord smiled. "Why yes, take me to him."

Salman, the tall one of the two, folded his lanky arms across his chest, a morose expression ingrained within his grizzled face. "I do not see why you are so happy, Cord. Lord Braddert has looked for an excuse to lock you away. This will likely do it. None of the rest of the men skulked back here before the patrol had finished."

Cord widened his smile. "Nor will any of them. The patrol is now of one mind."

Larka's heavy-lidded eyes bulged, and Cord knew a moment of satisfaction. "What do you mean? My sister's husband is down there with Durm. He would not follow the likes of you."

The One Mind allowed the smile to fade. "If you know him well, you may recognize his thoughts."

Reaching out, Cord touched them both on their bared skin, a cheek and an arm, adding two minds to the Over Mind. The One Mind had the power to penetrate clothing, but it took more energy and added a risk of resistance.

As the Over Mind shuffled the two minds to the back, Cord reflected the One Mind was getting crowded with all the fresh additions, not a particular problem for it, but it slowed the communication chain. With so many thoughts and experiences to pick through, some information had delays. For the next while, it would have to use stringent selection—selecting those with authority—from now until most of the minds' memories and consciousness were absorbed into the whole permanently, still some months away.

Sending the command to the two newest horrified minds to continue to their leader—Lord Braddert—Cord squashed the incessant gibbering from each.

Dragging the right leg, Cord shuffled along behind, the limp becoming more pronounced as they climbed higher into the Dark

Citadel. Another command slowed his escorts. Strolling in unison, they presented an armed wall in front of the host, and the decaying body was able to stay with them.

Cord was pleased.

A long hallway brought them to a short flight of steps leading to a dual guarded door. The sentries nodded at Cord's controlled soldiers as they topped the last step. The nods went unacknowledged. One of Cord's controlled turned the latch, and the other pushed the door open. They strode through into daylight, the first the host had seen in a long while.

A glance behind revealed one of the door guard's looks of suspicion, or offense, as the door closed. Cord sent instructions to the controlled to use ordinary interactions, whatever their collective minds recalled as normal, around free minds.

The One Mind again contemplated the sensations of worry and fear as the host moved along the bottom of the massive structure known as the Dark Gate, his two guards leading the way as if an escort. How had it come by such base emotions? The One Mind requested a reading of the memory bubbles that drifted through the Over Mind—with so many from the patrol, it would take time. The One Mind waited with the patience of eons of existence as the Cord body shuffled along behind the guards, the dark gate dwarfing the human's frail body.

Cord was pleased.

The Dark Citadel would provide a secure base of operations.

The request granted, the One Mind interrupted a stream of memories and read them, finding an answer with some of the freshest immediately. There was no power like the one in the northwest that had blocked it from the great mind the One Mind had nearly absorbed. That power was unlike the darkness residing below the citadel.

Though not at first, two minds had worked together to push

it from the most compatible mind it had ever known. A mind with the ability for discerning the spark of life and reading a possible future; such a thing had the power to fold the future with training. It had to have the mind, and whatever else it absorbed on this world, or any other, was now secondary.

Yet a symbol, a symbol of power, had defeated it. A great concern, yes, but it was not the cause for the sensations; the origin of the sensations stemmed from the awareness those minds possessed of each failed attempt. It was imperative to destroy the angry mind and gain control of the great mind. Or terminate them both. The One Mind savored the thoughts of destruction.

Even so, the sensation the host mind knew as fear grew.

Cord, the One Mind, was not pleased.

They left the brightness of the Dark Gate for the darkened interior of the citadel and began the short climb down to the guard post. A diminutive hallway brought them to a wide common room. Soldiers sat at tables drinking or watching two men setting stone figurines upon a marked table depicting structures of some sort—a game of cities, Cord's memory informed it. Such activity would end in the near future.

No one spoke to them as they crossed the common area to a door at the back. The One Mind's controlled soldiers entered without knocking, holding the door until the Cord host shambled through.

From a high-backed chair placed behind a small desk, Lord Braddert rose tall and imposing in his plate armor, his hazel eyes shiny with irritation. "Larka, Salman, if you ever barge in here like that again, I shall have you flogged at the Dark Gate for everyone to appreciate." Without waiting to see if his threat had the desired effect, he strode across the room, halting before the Cord host. "So, the coward returns early without the patrol as I suspected. How far into the caverns were my men when you skulked away like the little rat you are?"

The One Mind was pleased.

This human specimen should last longer with its size, *and* it had a position of authority. It would fit within the One Mind's overall scheme well.

Reaching out, Cord froze partway there. The host had intercepted a contacting between Users of the Light. A human woman initiated the contacting with a white-haired human who thought of himself as Durandas. The human male had knowledge of a symbol power and the great mind the One Mind sought. Taking the opportunity, the One Mind installed a tendril into the human male and closed the contacting.

The One Mind was greatly pleased. The Over Mind knew where next to travel.

"Too frightened to speak, rat? I imagine so, you are as pale as a filthy ingrot, and you stink of rotting fish, like them. Speak, coward. I may spare your miserable skin and lock you in the dungeon to rot, depending on your story."

Cord smiled. "Soon you will know all there is to know."

Lord Braddert's large, black eyebrows drew together. "Not soon, you impudent little rat. You will—"

Grabbing the back of Lord Braddert's hand, Cord made the transfer.

The One Mind was pleased.

The new host's physical condition was sound of mind and body, and had a title worthy of the One Mind. Distributing Lord Braddert's thoughts and memories as it read them into the crowded mix of the Over Mind; the One Mind regarded the body of the host it had left behind. Without the Over Mind controlling it, the human's body slumped, standing from muscle memory alone.

What little was left of the mind—perhaps enough to

intercept a final contacting—resided within the Over Mind. The dying body had no further use.

Directing the Cord body to sit at the desk, the One Mind sent a request for Lord Braddert's newest memories. The wait was not long. The human had recently received a requisition for exemplary soldiers. A *great lord,* a person of high authority, had ordered the guards doubled outside the Onyx Room, not far from here.

The One Mind, Lord Braddert, was pleased.

The great lord designation of the new host mind was worthy of the One Mind.

# REVERED ONE

Though his pudgy head and braided black goatee bobbed from side to side when Guail, the rotund spice merchant, clapped his thick hands together, Darwin Darkwind did not once believe the man was slow of thought. The merchant promoted the image by dressing in mismatched rainbow silks too big for him, yet his sunken black eyes were predatory as he watched the flurry of activity his audible command brought upon the wide pavilion. Carrying tables and chairs, sultry dressed maidens and bare-chested men dashed inside the structure from the end wall tied open to the heat of the Searing Sands Desert.

Hinged for folding, a long table was set below and to the left of the spice merchant's oversized high-backed chair. A smaller table settled in front of the merchant. The two young maidens who'd carried it bustled about placing food and drinks from trays held by scantily dressed others.

Chafing at the delay, Darwin sat at the long table, motioning for Malkor to do likewise.

Malkor leaned close. "I am sorry, Master, but it is a custom of the nomad merchants to entertain honored guests. As a lord of the citadel, you are beyond honored, bordering on exalted, in Guail's simple thinking."

Darwin kept his voice low with difficulty. "No one is to know my identity! I had not thought you such a fool!"

Malkor's narrow face darkened. "Your features are known far and wide, Master. He did not ask, so he is already aware. I merely went with the opportunity for you to regain the strength lost with our travels through this fearsome desert."

Though still wary and annoyed, Darwin calmed a little. Malkor had left something out. His servant missed having all the countless preferential treatments he considered his due when serving a Dark lord. Perhaps his loyal servant did deserve better than trudging over endless sand dunes for months after healing him from the wound Lord Charn had inflicted, which would have meant certain death if left untouched. He would never straighten his left arm again, but he was alive.

Nevertheless, he would punish Malkor severely when they returned to their bland room in Shimmer. Too many powerful lords, both Light and Dark, sought to destroy him, particularly at the Dark Citadel. Confirming the merchant's assumption by failing to dispute it was foolish. Eventually the wrong person would garner the truth of his past.

He would not have that happen, not until he was ready to storm the citadel and take it back under his own terms, exacting his revenge with power no one could deny. First, he would find whom he sought—Lord Charn or the hooded man. He had heard the hooded man controlled the dark throne now, but it made little difference. Whoever controlled the Dark Citadel would grovel on his bare stomach before him begging for mercy. Neither one would receive it.

When both tables bowed under the weight of various meats, fruits, pies, and drink—Rallan red wine from the look of it—Guail tapped his spoon against a tankard. The servants scurried to one side and stood in a row waiting to fulfill a need. Two maidens remained near, holding dewy glass pitchers.

Guail tapped a silver spoon against a glass pitcher, three

times. "For the pleasure of my new friends, let us drink to shade and prosperity," he announced loudly.

Malkor lifted his mug with gusto, sloshing a few drops on the back of his hand. "May shade and prosperity nurture the clan!"

Their host's squeaky voice had grated, much like Malkor's raspy one, but Darwin shunted it aside. Guail claimed to have knowledge of the Servants of Eons. He raised his glass, toward his host briefly. "Your hospitality is commendable, Merchant Guail. However, there is a small matter I wish to discuss with you concerning the Ser—"

Guail's palms slammed upon the table, sloshing the red liquid over the side of his tankard. Then he flashed a quick, humble smile. Or was it placating? "The opportunity for a private discussion will be arranged after the meal. Please partake of my humble offerings," he said.

Darwin fumed at the interruption, masking it by lifting the mug to his mouth. How long would he have to endure the merchant's blatant show of affluence? Darwin cared not. He only wished information from the man.

Darwin took a sip of the wine. Surprisingly, it was good. Guail had stout connections for real Rallan Red somewhere in his dealings, not the watered-down stuff sold at taverns. Savoring the smoothness of a rich full-bodied flavor, he drank deep. When it he set his glass on the table, it was empty.

A willowy woman, one of the serving maidens, wearing a silk-stringed halter-top dashed to his side and refilled his mug before he could decline. Not that he would, yet he had a tinge of irritation that she had not inquired if he wished another. Draining it, he set it down, leaving his palm covering the rim, stopping her from refilling it a third time. He gazed into her round blue eyes when she made to pour again, her arms outstretched, the glass pitcher held in both slender-fingered hands

"Do you find her appealing?" Guail asked loudly in his squeaky voice. "I will order her sent to your sleeping arrangement tonight. Where in Shimmer are you staying?"

Darwin considered. She was beautiful. Her hairstyle and color reminded him of the woman he lost; she was slender and lovely, like her, though not nearly as tall. He motioned the woman back to her station with a wave of his hand. If she was disappointed, she did not show it. "I shall speak of my accommodations, Master Merchant, during our discussion after this fine meal."

Guail inclined his head, his black-braided goatee slapping against his chest. Tied loosely at his sternum with a wide black ribbon of silky material matching the turban wrapped around his head, Guail's multi-colored silk robe lay bare to the waist. "As you wish, My Lord, simply indicate to me if one of my household, of either gender, pleases your eye; eunuchs are also available. Now, partake of what you will of the meal undisturbed. Both of you enjoy."

Resting a hand on the small of the back of the maiden pouring his drink, Malkor smiled. Older and heavier than Darwin's slender serving maiden, the woman lowered the pitcher with only a slight shake of her hand. "Your generosity is renowned, Master Merchant Guail. I shall accept," Malkor said, his brown eyes leering.

The woman failed to hide the fright that shone briefly in her eyes.

Darwin did not address his servant's comment or Guail's nod of approval. If things happened the way he wanted, the lawlessness of Shimmer would be long behind them by tonight with no opportunity for dalliances; his servant's urges could wait.

Stabbing an olive from a serving plateful, he popped it into his mouth and chewed. The slightly sour taste was pleasant. He ate another and then heaped his plate with all foodstuffs within reach, eating with vigor.

The merchant's supply line was diverse, more so than expected. The fish, though salty, retained moisture. Darwin suspected it shipped packed with ice bound from the Flow, which made it expensive. The Users' cost on both ends of the supply line was additional to the fishery. Meaning Guail had to retain a User to dissolve the packing. His estimation and wariness for the spice merchant grew. Why expend such extravagance on the two of them? Guail had to know how far he had fallen since fleeing the citadel barely alive.

As Darwin pushed his plate aside, Guail's second set of three taps startled him.

Seven voluptuous women, two with skin darker than the rest, dashed inside the tent, coming to a breathy rest in a row at the table's edge. Sultry music coaxed from fluted, drummed, corded, and shaker instruments started up from the back. The women danced, undulating from shoulders to hips, their sheer silk tops and skirts adding only a sense of color to bare skin.

Slurping wine, Darwin leaned back in his chair to watch. The women were in fine shape and pleased him. He gave an appreciative nod to the host, who flashed a brief smile.

At his elbow, the slender woman refilled the wine. He brought the mug to his lips, glancing at Malkor. His lanky servant was slumped over the table, his bony arms tucked under his narrow head.

Darwin was surprised to find him asleep. True, they had braved the desert's heat through the morning interviewing the merchant caravans camped at the outskirts of Shimmer, but it had not been that far. So why did he too share Malkor's exhaustion?

*****

Strong arms pulled Darwin across a hard surface, then blazing light reddened the inside of his eyelids, and unrelenting heat baked his lungs each time he took a breath. A pressure under his shoulders indicated someone carried him. He opened his eyes when the left side of his cheek and head burned. He lay on his side in the red desert sand.

"They awaken," a pleasant female voice said.

Darwin blew sand from his nose and fought to sit up, no small feat with one hand tied behind his back and the other as good as useless, yet he eventually succeeded. Nearby, with both hands tied behind him, Malkor squirmed as if a larval snake fed on him from the inside out. He, too, finally made it to a sitting position.

Squinting from the midmorning sun, Darwin looked around, shifting the pain of his throbbing head to the background, likely a side effect of the sleeping draught.

A group of five men and women wearing light armor over kell leather clustered together in a tight circle. The pudgy merchant, Guail, sat atop a high-sided caravan wagon pulled by a team of six horses close by. Several men and women with curved scimitars—the servants from the tents of last night—sat on camels that ringed a small circle of wagons. Beyond them, the desert city of Shimmer flickered tiny with great distance.

"As you are now aware, the delivery arrived intact," Guail said. The self-assurance in the merchant's smooth voice bespoke command; gone was the squeaky placating tone of one who only desired to please.

*How did I not see the traitorous scum for what he was?* Darwin asked himself.

Of those grouped in the circle, the tallest man replied to Guail, though he kept his icy blue eyes on Darwin. "You have earned the bounty, which you shall receive as soon as they are shunted back to the Dark Citadel through the nearest gateway."

Guail's face darkened. "We did not agree to anything of the kind. I had it from the highest assurance the Red Rock Clan was trustworthy, yet you speak of delaying payment. In keeping with the bargain, I have delivered the Spear. Now make it right or I leave with the property; there are other buyers. Five silver daggers as we agreed, for each man."

Guail's tone had slipped back into his familiar whine at the end of the tirade.

The tall man's hand rested on a long sword at his side. "The red robe is not required. You may do with him as you will."

The soft *shurrup* sounds of swords drawn quickly from wooden scabbards lined with animal hide and wrapped in leather made Darwin glance sharply around the circle of wagons. All of Guail's servant-mercenaries held the bared steel of their scimitars.

A woman strode from within the circle of six Red Rock clan people and pulled Guail roughly from the wagon, her sword at his throat as soon as his silk shoes touched sand. "Tell your people to sheathe their weapons and you shall have your ten daggers. Is this not so, Bronz?"

The woman's voice was the same pleasant one Darwin had heard upon awakening. He spoke to her, striving to keep the tone of his voice amicable. "Where do you expect to locate a gate in the desert?"

Her blue eyes shifted toward him briefly and then continued her perusal of those around the camp as she talked. "That is not your concern, Dark User. You would do well to ask if we need you alive for delivery. We do not. As for the rest of you," she said, raising her voice, "put away your swords *before* the rest of the clan draw. Once they do, your lives are forfeit."

"Do as she commands!" Guail shouted.

The dark-skinned women who had danced at the pudgy merchant's tent stabbed their blades into their scabbards last, glaring fiercely at the desert clan woman.

As soon as they had, Darwin drew upon the Flow, trickling it from his mangled arm to the rope binding his right hand behind him. It heated, searing his hand. Though he could smell his flesh, he kept going.

The clan woman's gray eyes widened. In one swift movement, she kicked the back of the merchant's legs, forcing him to his knees. "I told you to bind *both* their hands behind them with their palms facing upward," she said, her voice a hiss.

"We tried, but his mangled arm will not bend behind him," Guail whined. "Please!"

"Then why did you not break it!" Roughly, she kicked the merchant between his shoulders, sending him sprawling face first in the sand, and then strode past him, marching toward Darwin with her sword raised.

Darwin snapped the charred rope and brought his right arm forward in a scooping motion as if he had dug into the sand at his feet. His mangled left hand drew the Flow as his right raised a physical barrier from the brown desert sand as the woman lunged at his chest, jabbing with the point of her long sword. The translucent sparks repelling the steel an inch from his heart flashed a warning how close it was, but he didn't dwell upon it. He moved to Malkor and worked at the knot binding his hands, keeping his body between him and the woman.

The woman chopped at the shield at his head. "Help me, you imbeciles!" she screamed.

Darwin steadied the robe with his mangled arm and picked at the knot with his right hand. Finally, Malkor's hands pulled free, installing his own barrier.

The clan warriors came to the woman's aid. Revealing strong discipline, all of them took turns chopping at Darwin's shield, leaving Malkor's unblemished. Long jagged cracks opened above his head running beyond his neck; he hadn't much time. He leaned toward Malkor until repelled by his servant's shield. "I need room to end this. Replace my physical shield with your own."

Malkor's eyes widened with the knowledge the command would leave him unprotected, but he drew upon the Flow, the translucent conduit of glowing red-tinged energy running from his left palm to the raging river below the sand visible to all who used.

"The red robe uses!" Bronz shouted, swinging his sword at Malkor.

The moment Malkor's barrier enclosed his, Darwin dissolved his own and then raised it around Malkor.

Malkor cringed, but the clansman's sword chopped at his neck and bounced harmlessly away with a flash of light, as if it were a steel rod striking a stone of flint. "Bah! The red User is protected too," the Red Rock warrior snarled. Turning, he rejoined the clan with trading blows on Darwin's barrier.

Darwin counted on the precise discipline of the Red Rock clan's training. As soon as Bronz's blow landed on his barrier, he dissolved the protection around his servant and then released an explosion of air that swept outward ripping those surrounding him from their feet and hurling them into the cloud of sand it created.

Darwin dissolved his barrier and then reinstalled it as the sand cloud cleared. The clan warriors wearing the supple but flexible kell leather armor struggled little to regain footing, coming to their feet almost as soon as they stopped moving. In rapid succession, four of his dark cones streaked to the warriors. Exploding on impact, the cones blew the warriors high into the air, rending them apart and ceasing their struggles. Bronz died with one of his black javelins impaling his heart. His body thumped to the hot sand.

Darwin finished with black netting, pinning the gray-eyed woman's arms and legs to her body. Tugging on the part of the net tied to her feet, he pulled her legs out from under her and let her fall hard on her back to the hot sand. Satisfied she was out of the way for a time, he looked around. Though no one made to flee, the merchant's people looked at him with glazed eyes and pale faces.

He had no patience for them. "I should destroy you all. Who speaks for the caravan?"

Sliding his pudgy arms under him, Guail pushed away from the sand with a whimper. "Thank you for your—"

"Put your treacherous face back to the sand, Merchant. I have not yet decided if you shall live."

Guail dropped to his stomach, lowering his head to the ground without protest.

A woman climbed out of a high-walled and unadorned wagon. The willowy auburn-haired female who had served him wine in Guail's tent took a step forward. "Permit me to act as the voice of my clan," she said.

Hearing her speak for the first time, Darwin was pleasantly surprised. He liked the sound of her, and she was even more beautiful than he had seen the night before. "How can I trust the wine-bearer, the one who brought the stupor of unconsciousness?"

The woman's green eyes widened, but she kept her face smooth. "My lord, Guail has purchased the clan from an old debt; I served only the drink given unto me without being privy to the pitcher's contents."

Darwin believed her though it had little bearing with the present situation. He had little inclination to exact revenge, only to make a point. "Very well, then tell me. Will your clan follow you?"

For an answer, she waved a delicate hand at the wagons.

"Tell him what he asks. Does the Searing Sun clan listen to me?"

A chorus of masculine ayes and feminine yeses sounded all around.

"I do believe you," Darwin said when the voices grew silent. "The Clan of the Searing Sun follows you, which is unfortunate," he added.

The woman frowned with confusion, which detracted none from her beauty.

Darwin drew upon the Flow. His black cone struck the slender woman full in the chest, flinging her into the wagon she had climbed from with a sickening *thud*. "I need them to follow me," he said softly as her broken body slid to the ground. The bright stain of her blood trailed down the wagon's wall, darkening quickly in the heat of the sun.

"No! Blast you, you filthy User!" a male clan member sitting upon a horse yelled. He spurred his mount and charged, pulling on the scabbard of his scimitar.

Drawing deeply from the Flow, Darwin's thrice-sized cone carried horse and rider beyond the clan's ring of wagons. Then he drew a minuscule amount of the Flow into the bottom of his lungs and abdomen, enhancing his voice. "How many of you shall I destroy before you accept me as your new leader?" His words, though soft-spoken, boomed to the farthest wagon with ease.

No one spoke; none moved. All looked sullen. Two men and a woman glared at him boldly, stark hatred shining in their blue-gray eyes. He'd have to watch those. "How many strong is the Clan of the Searing Sun? Is this all of you?" His questions rang loud all around but not to anyone in particular. Gauging the cooperation level of the camp with accuracy would determine his next move.

The silence lengthened. Then, a woman, one of the dark-skinned dancers, spoke. "Someone give him the answer he seeks or your clan's blood will drench the Searing Sands. He is prepared to destroy you."

Scowls darkened many a face.

Darwin waited. He allowed ten full heartbeats for a reply to the woman's plea. As he had expected, none came. He drew from the Flow, creating his dark net again, wrapping it around Guail. Tying the net to his hand, he lifted the merchant from the sand.

Guail squealed. "Please! It's too tight!"

Ticking against his barrier, crossbow bolts created small sparks that flashed brilliantly before vanishing, even in midday. He ignored them. Swinging the merchant toward the bloodstained wagon, he tightened the nets ropes slowly.

Guail screamed. "Too tight! Release me!"

Darwin cinched the net again.

Guail's second scream was weaker, though prolonged. The constriction to his lungs left his cries a croaking gasp, as the excess skin of his rotund body bulged through the squares in the net.

Darwin prepared a final squeeze. He drew upon the Flow, pulling the drawstring he'd created. He would pull the net through the flesh and bone of every member here if he had to.

Too weak to scream, Guail moaned.

"Stop!" a man sitting on a roan horse to his right shouted. The yellow robe he wore was open at the front, revealing the suppleness of brown kell leather beneath. He slid to the ground and walked over to Darwin. "Merchant Guail has the answer you seek, no one else. Kill him and you shall hear only lies given in desperation after you have destroyed many of the clan."

Malkor laughed. "You have the volunteer for the next example, My Lord."

Darwin considered. The clansman had the haughtiness of confidence, and no fear shone in his brown eyes. He would die bravely protecting his beliefs, a good man to have on one's side. "What is your role and designation in the clan?"

"I am Long Sand, sand reader for the Clan of the Searing Sun. I know you for who you are, Great Lord."

Darwin swung his burden to the right side. "Then you admit to freely aiding this one with our abduction from his tent of hospitality."

Long Sand wore no cloth wrapped about his head, yet his face and skin remained light, showing no sign of burning despite his bright red hair and clean-shaven face. "Nay, Great One, I advised against it. The clan has enough enemies without adding a lord to those wishing to darken the sand with our lifeblood."

"Kill him, Master. Kill them all," Malkor hissed.

Darwin regarded his longtime companion. Malkor lowered his eyes. Then he continued as if there had been no interruption. "You would vouch for this one?" he asked, giving the bundle a shake.

Guail moaned weakly.

Long Sand's muscular shoulders rippled with his shrug. "Nay, Great One, there is no affection in the clan for him. Yet he has far-reaching connections. He can show you the way to the knowledge you seek."

Wary, Darwin glanced around while drawing in more of the Flow's sweet radiance. He filled every nook inside the vessel of his body, drinking until he thrummed with power, an inferno raging for release. "How would you know what I look for, Sand Reader? What have you read?" he asked, the tone of his voice mild though he was ready to burst.

Long Sand gave a slight bow. "Forgive me for not speaking of it sooner. Clan leader Sia, the woman whose blood streaks the wagon and darkens the Searing Sands, informed many of the clan of your inquiry about the Servants of Eons."

Darwin glanced at Guail floating above him. The robust man deserved death for his devious actions, but he had asked the merchant of what he sought at the meal the former caravan leader hosted.

Reluctantly, Darwin severed the link to the Flow. With a puff of black radiance at every knot, the net dissolved. Guail thudded to the sand. Curling into a fetal position, he lay moaning softly.

Again, Darwin enhanced his voice. "Your sand reader is now clan leader, do not forget this."

No one spoke.

"What is your wish, Great Lord?" Long Sand asked, breaking the silence.

Darwin dropped into his normal way of speaking for Long Sand's ears alone. "Do not address me as great lord outside my personal chambers again. Inform the clan. Should anyone inquire, I am but an advisor to you. Have someone bring my servant and I clan attire."

Long Sand bowed low. "As you command, oh, Gre— Revered One," he said.

Still bound by the Flow, Darwin bent over the gray-eyed woman, blocking the sun with his body. Her tanned face looked up at his, failing to mask the fright her brief quivers revealed. "Do you know where the Servants of Eons may be found?"

The woman shuddered, longer this time. Her eyes dulled as she nodded.

He expected so; it was likely she was a Servant of Eons or one of their mercenaries. With every revelation, Guail's use descended. For now, he would keep him around for eyes on the clan, if nothing else. The merchant would desire to ingratiate himself at every opportunity. He turned to the sand reader. "Instruct your men to erect a tent to shade us as we wait."

Malkor came close. "What do we wait for?"

Though he replied to Malkor, Darwin kept his eyes on his new clan leader. "Long Sand is going to send his most trusted into

Shimmer to sell the wagons. Where we travel, the wagons cannot."

The sand reader blinked with surprise, but his deeply tanned face remained impassive. "What of Guail, Revered One?" he asked.

"Malkor shall heal him. After that, put him to work tending the horses."

Long Sand bowed and then turned to make the preparations.

"There is one other thing, Clan Leader," Darwin said.

Long Sand froze.

"After the wagons are sold, instruct them to purchase sixteen camels. Load them and the extra horses freed from harness with provisions for one month. Make certain to locate a shade tent for the horses."

Long Sand's back stiffened, though he did not turn around. "I shall ensure it completed, Revered One," he said, striding away.

"Are you certain you can trust them in the city?" Malkor asked, bending over Guail.

"I cannot, that is why you are going with them."

Malkor froze. Looking up, a frown creased his forehead. "Is that wise to separate us?"

"I can handle this rabble; it is you who has to stay alert. Watch for signs of anyone passing a message. Kill all involved and then report to me as soon as you return. Do you understand?"

"Aye, Master."

Darwin contemplated the beautiful woman lying in the sand at his feet. His entire plan hinged on her knowing the way to the elusive Servants of Eons. For her sake, he hoped she had spoken the truth.

# HELPLESSNESS

Garnet Creek thought little of the red-robed Dark User, but the black robe didn't seem bad; at least he'd flashed a wide smile when he entered the room. Though Garn didn't return the gesture, he assumed better of the man for it. He'd seen both men attend the Obsidian Table meeting before, but he'd never been privy to their names.

Closing the door to the Obsidian Table's meeting room behind the two, Garn leaned his weapon on the wall at his customary position beside the door, which kept it within easy reach and put his back to a wall.

His chosen weapon for the day was a two-handed onyx broadsword he'd taken from Lord Charn's armory—now his armory—provided by the generosity of the Alchemist. The armory's previous owner apparently didn't need it. He'd never come back from wherever he went after his confrontation with the hooded one.

Garn studied the man wearing the dark robe. His smooth, tanned face showed confidence in the set of his jaw, though his blue eyes contained a world-weary blankness he was too young to have. He was not smiling now.

"I requested a private meeting, Dark One," the black robe said. He frowned at the red-robed woman sitting at the Alchemist's right. Garn noted the man's eyes did not include him in the request for privacy. He must have recognized his role as the hooded man's personal guard.

The Alchemist's golden hourglass eyes sparkled with irritation. Garn was likely the only one to notice.

The hooded man's soft words carried throughout the room. "Kara Laurel is much involved, Pasquin. She is the only one here who can now make use of the Oracle. Speak what you will or leave my sight."

The man in the red robe spoke. Though his hood shadowed his features, his voice had a nasal quality one would not soon forget. "Is this wise, Great Lord? Kara Laurel is high on the Circle of Light and now the only one who can use the Oracle. What is to deter her from simply contacting the Circle when no one can hear?"

The dark hood of Garn's master swung toward the red robe. "Do not think to question me, Drayne. Though your Flow saturation is great and you sit high at the Obsidian Table, you are not irreplaceable."

Drayne's jaw set. He glared at everyone in the room—except the Alchemist.

Clasping her hands together, Kara Laurel leaned forward, covering a smile tugging at the corners of her full lips.

Pasquin appeared not to notice. "I shall accept your wisdom on this as I have from days gone past, hooded one, though I wonder if her beauty has clouded your judgment. Such a thing has happened to great lords, some not long ago, and should merit eradication from the start."

The hooded man's soft voice came as a deadly hiss. "I am not such a fool as you choose to believe. Your subtle threat, hidden within your words, shall now have the immediacy you have bestowed upon it. Is it your wish to meet me at the Dark Dais for a challenge this day? I sense greater power in you as well. Is it sufficient to destroy me? Consider your next words with some care."

Garn had gripped his great sword's pommel as soon as the first words left his captor's mouth. By the end of the Alchemist's statement, he'd slid his fingers around the grip.

Kara Laurel slowly unclasped her hands, slipping them onto her lap.

Pasquin and Drayne considered the offer, gazing at each other and then at the Alchemist with interest. The silence lengthened. Garn eased from the wall. Finally, the black robe spoke, his tone mild and almost clinical. "The two of us have offered to protect you as you travel to the forefront of the battle, yet you forsake us. One is simply curious as to why you would pass on our considerable power."

The hooded man's unblinking hourglass eyes regarded both men for many heartbeats longer than necessary, revealing nothing. "I shall mention this only once," he finally said, softly. "My motives are my own. Do not voice an inquiry about them in my presence again."

Garn moved into a battle form, *Water Flowing from the Mountain*, one of his best for magical defense. Seeming at ease, Garn had his sword and stance set at the ready. If anything were to happen, it would come soon and fast.

Pasquin glanced his direction and then back to the Alchemist. The younger man's reaction was so fast most would not have seen it. Nonetheless, it heightened Garn's alertness. The black robe had taken him and his weapon into account. The man was more dangerous than he'd first believed.

The smile that flashed upon Drayne's broad face held no mirth. "We simply wished to allay a curiosity we have carried. Is it safe to ask how you disposed of Lord Charn? A historical battle on the Dark Dais with the end result of the great lord lying broken and destroyed. Such a great challenge would merit a stamped official ledger recorded by a historian and stored in the Death Watch Hall. We found nothing. Tell me, was his a slow death?"

There was no hesitation to the hooded man's answer. Garn relaxed slightly. "I have not destroyed your *great lord*, though I may if he should ever feel foolish enough to come back here."

Pasquin's composure dropped a little as he leaned forward. "He is alive then?"

"I have no knowledge. Your Lord Charn went inside your General Darwin Darkwind's chambers with the prophecy vessel and the anomaly. The Dark Child, the warden, and a creation entered with them. No one came out. The sapphire obelisks were recovered," the Alchemist said. "His failure to destroy your Lord Charn has cost us, dearly."

Leaning forward, Drayne had perked up at the mention of the obelisks, almost as much as Garn had, but then he seemed confused. "You have the entire Dark Citadel at your disposal and the gateway you sought. Why are you still here? Surly someone could activate them?"

Kara Laurel interrupted, adding to Garn's annoyance. The red robe had dared ask about the sapphire obelisks. The hooded man had a way for him and his girls to return home right under his bloody nose all along. "You are a blasted fool, Drayne, if you cannot see the implications our great lord has mentioned. No one came out!"

Drayne's look at Kara Laurel was scathing, but then his face cleared. "Perhaps you have just cause. Losing the vessel and the anomaly is a loss, though perhaps for the best. I have spoken of this before. Relying too much on prophecy is oftentimes fatal."

Garn felt a bloody mute fool. *What in the Great Father's name were they talking about? What prophecy?*

Garn regarded his captor. The hooded man's hourglass eyes

stared unblinking at Drayne, his expression unreadable.

The room fell silent. Drayne's glare was gone, replaced by a confident air of superiority. Garn returned his grip to the great swords hilt.

The hooded man broke the silence. "My greatest weapon could kill you both where you sit in seconds; your adeptness with the Flow is of no concern to him. A wise man would use these next seconds to convince me to hold my weapon at bay."

To Garn, the Alchemist's soft-spoken words were a direct order. He moved to the other side of the table, their side, his sword positioned at the ready in front of him.

Pasquin glanced at him and his eyes grew wide.

Too arrogant to acknowledge the danger coming for him, Drayne sneered at the hooded man..

Garn shuffled closer. Briefly, he wondered about the political implications of killing the pair, they both sat at the Obsidian Table, but he put it from his mind. It would soon not matter; neither one seemed inclined to speak for their lives.

The sound of folded steel meeting beaten steel rang out from the hallway.

Garn leapt upon the table, sliding beside the hooded man in time to deflect a bolt of red flung at the Alchemist from Drayne. Then a transparent barrier encompassed them. Aimed for Garn's head, Drayne's next bolt rocketed from the obstruction, slamming into the wall beside him and chipping the stone.

Pasquin was on his feet bellowing. "We are not the enemy!" His words came too late. The Alchemist's vial broke apart on his chest. Encasing the Dark User's head, black smoke billowed from it to the ceiling. The black robe crumpled to the floor.

"No!" Drayne shouted. Encasing Pasquin's torso in ice, he went to his knees beside the fallen black robe. The ice melted away taking the oily black smoke with it.

The door to the room crashed open. One of Garn's soldiers he'd ordered to stand watch fell inside. Landing facedown, blood spread in an expanding circle from underneath him. Grant and Lynn, the other two soldiers he'd stationed there, stepped over Davram, and shuffled into the room. "Explain your actions quickly," Garn commanded. He glanced about the room, searching for the one preparing the next move.

Silent, the two men halted partway to the table's edge with weapons raised, their eyes blank.

A rotund soldier he hadn't met entered, followed by the pompous Lord Braddert who halted at the doorway.

Though Garn disliked the way the so-called lord treated those beneath his command, he hadn't exchanged a single word with him. That would now change. "Such a callous action of slaying one of my men had better have sound reasoning involved with it, Braddert," he said with a casualness he didn't feel. He'd purposely left out the lord part of the proper address. Such an affront should throw the man and any soldiers loyal to him off-balance by raising their ire.

To his credit, Lord Braddert said nothing.

Ignoring the rotund soldier, Garn regarded the two men, *his* men, who stood protectively in front of Lord Pomp. "You two, however, have no recourse. By betraying my trust, your executions will be as slow as I can make them."

Their long swords held at the ready, neither man reacted, each face as blank as when they had entered. He'd admired them for their competiveness in the past. When had they gotten so…professional? Why had he not seen it?

Rising above the three men's shoulders, Lord Braddert made an imposing sight. As he stood tall and muscular in his black plate mail armor, his dull hazel eyes fixed first on Pasquin aiding Drayne and then slowly slid to the hooded man. He spoke not a word, nor did his slack expression change.

Kara Laurel slipped behind Garn. "I shall try to let you know if I am able to switch protection barriers to the physical," she murmured.

Garn glanced back and forth between the Dark Users and his soldiers. Combating two fronts at the same time was not cautious fighting, and battling weaponry and magic together was foolish. Too many unforeseen occurrences could happen. A saying he'd made his daughters memorize rolled through his mind. *If one didn't have faith in the situation, one had but to change it.* Now he would follow his own advice.

The Alchemist's low, disdainful voice slid past Garn's hearing. "What do you truly hope to accomplish here, Lord Braddert? Had you thought to catch me unguarded?"

Drayne stood, pulling Pasquin to his feet. Huge blisters covered the black-robed man's neck and lower chin.

Lord Braddert's helmless head swung toward the robed men, but he said nothing.

The Alchemist's voice—not much higher in volume than a hiss—drew Lord Braddert's eyes back. "Your motive is of no concern, your death is. There is no escape for you or your men. Kill them all!"

At the command, Garn slipped into *Crow Flies in Deep Woods*—the form he taught and named himself for close-quarters fighting with a sword—and he reveled in the heightening of his awareness. The great sword's balance attuned with him, seeming to weigh the same as the wrist that gripped it.

His ears perked, sorting the minute sounds in the room: Drayne's quickened breaths, the ragged breaths of Pasquin's pain, the short breaths of Kara Laurel and the hooded man, and the bellows-like inhales of everyone else in the room. This triggered alarms in his mind; confronted with a hacking death from such a large piece of sharpened steel should have created a sense of wariness to those facing it.

Garn flicked a quick jab at Lynn's chest. Twisting his wrist, Lynn knocked his sword to the side. He took a half step backward to reassess; Lynn's move was clumsy at best and nearly too late. The captain of his guard was a far superior fighter. Why hadn't at least one of the three taken the opportunity to counter when he had made the move?

Behind him, the Alchemist drew a sharp breath. "Why are you not attacking? Do I have to do it myself?"

"I think the better question is why they aren't? Something's off," Garn replied over his shoulder.

The Alchemist's breathing quickened and then slowed. "Yes, I sense you are correct, though it does not alter the command. They *will* die.

Glaring at the newcomers, Pasquin's right hand burst into a ball of flame. The black flames flowed clockwise around his right hand without sound. "You dare attack Users here at the table of the ruling class? Your insolence will cost you!" His dark eyes brightened as a cloud of blackness streaked from his hand.

Lord Braddert grabbed Lynn and moved him in front of the cloud, ducking slightly to avoid overspray. "Too many have gathered here," he said, finally speaking from behind the eerily silent captain. Lord Braddert's voice sounded bored and listless. "Removal from this situation is prudent. Ensure my escape." He backed through the doorway pulling the soldier with him; the man's flesh sagged and smoked as it dissolved. Lord Braddert released his hold and vanished from sight.

As Lynn slumped to the floor without a sound, Grant and the portly soldier attacked.

Parrying Grant's quick side thrust, Garn spun, slid under the rotund soldier's hammer swing, and severed the arm swinging it below the biceps. Without much pause, he reversed direction and blocked Grant's downward chop to the back of his neck with a block over his shoulder. Spinning again, he moved with blurring speed, even for him. He sliced through Grant's leg where thigh met groin.

As Grant dropped, he turned toward the rotund soldier. A slight breeze warned him to leap to the side. Incredibly, Grant had swung at his head as he had fallen. Blood fountained from the gap of his missing leg as he lay still, only jerking in the throe of death once.

Bending calmly, the wide soldier fished his hammer from the hand that still gripped it.

Garn took a step forward and prepared to finish it.

A ball of black flame slammed into the round man's side and exploded, covering his upper torso with crackling flame. Swinging the great hammer back and forth blindly, the wide man advanced.

Garn blocked several wild swings, each one slower than the last. Finally, the soldier fell burning to the floor, the putrid scent of his flesh smoking the room. Silence descended, broken only by the occasional pop from the burning man.

Finally, the Alchemist spoke. "There is something amiss with this attack. I require your patience, Pasquin, now that I have decided you may live for a while longer. Your request for a meeting shall have to come later. Know that I shall expect it. For now, Lord Braddert has taken precedence. There is the small matter of enacting vengeance for your wounding…should you so desire it. Make your choice here and now if we are to finish it."

Pasquin gazed around the room. His dark eyes smoldered as his black eyebrows sank, his face twisting in rage. The light in the room dimmed, growing paler beside the promise of deep darkness.

Then, with a suddenness Garn found disconcerting, the light returned to normal. Pasquin turned to Drayne. "For the good of the citadel, I delay action for another time. Do you agree?"

Drayne gave a simple nod of his head and then turned to the hooded man. "We ask your leave."

The hooded man's golden eyes glittered with something indistinguishable, possibly disappointment. "My guard shall escort you."

Though he said nothing else, Pasquin's brown eyes were livid as he left the room, followed by Drayne.

As Garn made his way out of the room, the Alchemist's soft commands drifted to him. "Escort them to their chambers and assure that guards are left behind. Return at once to me, we have a shadow to root out of my domain."

Garn couldn't help feeling there were already too many variables beyond his control that stood in the way of finding his daughters and bringing them home. Now he had a shadow, an insidious something blighting his resources. He had no idea how to go about looking for it. He hated the helplessness the thought brought to him.

# ENFOLDED

Jade wandered away from the impromptu defense strategy meeting. She'd heard what she wanted to know after the first hour. According to the Valen and druid commanders, two additional concentrated retaliation attacks should send the aggressors retreating to the hills. At least, the leaders hoped so after the pounding the enemy had taken after Lore Rayna had led them to the southern outpost in the great falun tree. Between the Valens' ranged bow and magical attacks, coupled with Crystalyn's symbol bouts as she fed the Flow to her, the other side had sustained heavy losses for five days in a row.

With luck, the enemy would retreat to the Dark Citadel they'd spewed from soon. The past few days, she'd seen gobs of bloodshed; more than a young woman should have to endure in a lifetime. At nineteen seasons, she should be fending off, or flirting, with every buff boy who happened along, as Dad would say. Except, he wouldn't mean it in an amenable way, and he'd promptly intimidate all suitors into leaving rather quickly, nor would he want her flirting, she did that all on her own. She missed Dad.

Making her way across the rocking tree branches entwined in such a way as to provide a mostly flattened surface, Jade slipped from branch to branch with care; some gaps were large enough for to fall through for someone her size. The Valens would have no such risk.

Jade stopped to lean on the thin branches that acted as support railings for the bigger outpost platforms. The railings were twig-like and snaked a great distance from branch to branch. Having pressed herself against it for hours without a crack or creak of protest, she knew their strength exceeded their fragile appearance far beyond something made of deadwood.

Stretching away, the view was unmatched for any she beheld, including the Mountain back on her home world of Terra. Such an open view made her feel exposed though the ground was thirty stories below. It had taken them a good hour to reach the Life Watch Landing as the Valens called the second highest platform on the great falun tree.

The Weather Watch was another fifteen stories or so higher and was not much larger than an eagle's roost or so she'd been told. Jade took Lore Rayna's word on it; she had no desire to experience it firsthand.

Though sunlight would soon fade outside the tree, the great forest of the Vale was darker under the thick fern-like branches, even though the northernmost outpost blazed alongside one of the great falun trees. The Valens and Light Users there were forced to expend precious energy extinguishing them with coats of ice and stored basins of water. Slowly the Users and Valens' efforts gained momentum as darkness crawled toward them.

Yet, Broth and the Valen scouts had reported the enemy waited in force in that darkness, moving stealthily toward them.

Crystalyn joined her at the rail, clasping her hand with her own. Jade gained some small comfort from the touch. Her sister's hand had grown soft, losing the many calluses she'd garnered from her former indenture at Ruena Day's warehouse. It seemed their only servitude lately consisted of three things: traveling, battling, and running for their lives. If not for the task of locating Dad, she would wonder if coming back to Astura was the best choice for them.

Beside her, Crystalyn fidgeted. "It shouldn't be long now, get ready," her sister said, her voice hushed though high with excitement. Or was it anxiety for what they were about to do? Jade hoped for the latter. Crystalyn seemed to rely on her magic symbols more frequently, and the Dark Users' aggression toward the Vale gave her an almost unlimited number of excuses to use it.

As high up as they were, the wind gusted with constant force, adding a shiver to her vertigo when the platform swayed. Strangely, there wasn't a single creak from anywhere around no matter how hard it blew. A strong feeling of reverence permeated her senses with the revelation—coming from the tree, or the Valens who attended to it, she couldn't say.

A torrent of luminosity, brilliant with its whiteness, lit the shadows beyond the trees in the east. Throughout the area, rows of armored men and women halted with surprise. This time, huge canine forms as large as Broth stood beside each dark-armored warrior. Some rows back, many dark-robed figures' hands bloomed with a red or black glow of their own.

Crystalyn leaned forward. "Here we go!" she hissed, her voice rising with the last word.

Jade reached for the frothing river of the Flow, sensing its powerful, raging essence through the vibrancy of the living wood at her feet. Even now, after so many interactions, she was afraid of the power it contained. The slightest overdraw could destroy them and everyone on the outpost. Jade offered a tiny conduit to Crystalyn.

Crystalyn drew immediately, pulling the Flow through their clasped hands at a high rate. The path of the Flow from her feet to her hands built friction quickly, pain rising along her arm. Jade slowed the Flow to a trickle and then closed the connection altogether. Crystalyn had drawn a great amount, even for her.

Crystalyn had four symbols hovering in front of her, black on one side and white on the other. Each of the four patterns was circular on the outside. The front two had entwined doubled lines inside the circle that surrounded a vague shape of something in the center. Before Jade could get a better look at the shape and the final two, Crystalyn sent them streaking toward the battlefield one after another.

Striking in rapid succession, the first two landed beside each other, enveloping the feet of nearly three rows of the dark forms. Briefly, the symbol's blue radiance brightened with a golden light— the shape in the center now visible as a circle with a tree inside— and then the ground heaved, throwing dirt, debris, and bodies high into the air and then raining down upon the rows behind just as Crystalyn's third and fourth symbols hit.

Two narrow but tall vortexes of dark wind spinning ferociously followed, sucking all inside as they traveled through the ranks growing smaller as they went. Many a glowing sphere, along with the hand and body of the Dark User attached to them vanished into the cyclones.

Arrows showered the dark shapes outside the cyclones and the already fading eruption symbols with chilling accuracy. Even at night, the Valen archers were masters with bow. Yet, even they needed light to locate a target. As the white light dimmed noticeably, the shapes took on shadows making the enemy appear to multiply. Looking like a string of security lights, a row of red spheres with random gaps between them bloomed behind the nearly gone cyclones, only large enough now to maim.

Crystalyn squeezed her hand. "We have to go," she said calmly, but her tight grip implied otherwise.

Jade had no thought of disagreeing. The splinters were coming. With so many hands glowing red on the battlefield, a storm of them was on the way. "Go ahead. I'll follow."

Crystalyn was having none of it; instead of releasing her hand so they could run faster, her sister tugged her to a trap door at the far side of the platform. The first of the splinters struck where they'd stood, lighting the railing and the platform behind it with a faint red glow. The pungent smell of smoldering, living wood filled the air.

Crystalyn let go of her hand when a radiant white symbol, the size of an amulet, formed in the air in front of her. "The Valens seem to get by with the dim luminescence this tree emits, but I'm not going down this ladder without something brighter," she said. "Stay close."

Grasping the wooden poles extending out of the hatch, Crystalyn started down. "Don't lose your grip, you won't survive the fall," she said as her head vanished below the platform. Obediently, the symbol followed.

Jade kept close and moved as fast as she dared. The symbol's light was weak but made the climb doable. The ladder ended on a smaller platform a few stories down. She hurried over to Crystalyn at the next railing and clasped her hand as the amulet symbol dissolved. The shadowy twilight closed in again broken only by the dim, green radiance of the great falun tree's living branches— enough to make out the railing in front of her. The rails were all newly cultivated for them, or so the Valens had claimed. They had no need for a barrier.

At the rail, Crystalyn gazed below. "Where's the signal? It's going to get dark soon. I can't tell how it's going down there," she said quietly. "The last time I spoke with Broth, he didn't know how Atoi or Hastel were doing. Now he's not answering my queries at all. I don't like it."

Jade stared outward but up at the sky. The clear night sky dotted with countless stars and planets made her wonder if their struggles repeated on some other world. "I hope they're okay," she mumbled. It seemed so peaceful on this platform compared to their frantic climb a few moments ago. Crystalyn again clasped her hand and she knew the thought for the illusion it was. Their work of killing anything moving toward them was not complete. Sadly, not even close.

Almost as soon as she finished thinking it, the fading light of the meadow below lit with a sparkling white light. A surge of the Flow racing through their clasped hands gave Jade small warning. Then a beautiful, but deadly, earth eruption symbol streaked toward the meadow below. Two more of the glowing black-and-white symbols with the tree shape in the center left the platform before the light began to fade.

They sprinted to the next ladder down, repeating their frantic, dim-lighted flight to a small, four-person platform, at least for normal-sized persons. Jade doubted even two Valens would have room to move about on the perch together.

When the valley lit below, Crystalyn fired off four of her symbols, three earth eruptions and a full black one that was hard to see clearly, even though it too had a translucent radiance.

The black symbol halted a Valen's height above a large group of the opposing force, settling into a spin as if it were a great pinwheel in the sky. Rolling from vertical to horizontal, the spinning symbol shot radiant droplets that steamed on contact with chilling accuracy. The entire front row and parts of the many behind thudded to the ground never to rise again.

This time the light did not fade, getting brighter to the south of them and above.

The symbol Crystalyn had out, a complex green and white one, vanished. "We have to go now," her sister said. Her voice was soft with fatigue. Letting go of Jade's hand, she looked up. "Broth has shown me much of the Vale is burning, including the top of this great tree. He is uncertain of any survivors."

Jade followed her sister's gaze with her own. An orange glow grew brighter from where they'd been. Large, bare feet and legs appeared on the ladder. The Vale woman, Lore Rayna, slid down beside them, rocking the small perch precariously.

Lore Rayna appeared not to notice the swaying though her expression was concerned, judging from the way her golden eyebrows fell close to her odd, glowing eyes. "We cannot save our ancient grove, an evacuation has been ordered. Durandas and those who use the Flow are holding the flames back for now, but we do not have much time."

"Yes, I was just informed by my *Do'brieni*. I'm so sorry, Lore Rayna," Crystalyn said. "Broth and the other two will meet us at the base."

Climbing back on the ladder, Lore Rayna's glowing eyes illuminated the small landing as she regarded them. "Go then, do not tarry. Make for the town of Brown Recluse. Hastel knows the way. The Lore Mother and I shall meet with you after we have saved as many as we can." Her last few words echoed down to them as her feet vanished through the heights above.

Crystalyn stared after her as the light of the battlefield faded around them. "I hope Lore Rayna knows what she's doing. I couldn't stand it if something happened to her."

"Do you want us to go after her?"

Crystalyn mulled it over, worry furrowing her brow. "No," she finally said, her voice unhappy. "I'll have to trust she's not going to do anything too heroic. I'm worried about Broth and the others too. The Dark Users have used the shadows in the east as cover to encircle us though they are as trapped down there as we are here. Ironic, isn't it. I need to blow a hole for us to run through after all the trouble we had getting here. You go first; let's get to the ground while we can."

Jade put a hand on the first palm-sized handhold the Valens had coaxed the tree to grow about an arm's width apart. So much for the battle going as well as the Vale's commanders had thought. Perhaps, they had been portraying an optimistic outlook all along. Then she had a thought. "Shouldn't you climb down first? Your light will help."

The small light flashed into existence beside Crystalyn's head. "Good thinking," Crystalyn said. "It won't be long. I don't think we're that far from the ground now," she said, beginning her descent.

Jade waited for her sister to move out of sight before putting her feet on the lower knots. The soft whir of flapping wings behind her was the only warning she had. Scaly, inhumanly strong arms enfolded her and swept her into open air.

# BONFIRES

Camoe knocked a soldier's pike thrust to the side. He followed through with a flick of his sword, jabbing under the dark helm shaped as a spiderbee's alien head, feeling the softer flesh of the throat. He nearly missed deflecting a crossbow bolt aimed for high on his side in the process, spinning with a back swing of his sword at the last moment.

Several badly launched Dark User cones slammed into his personal barrier and then deflected outward. Two of them detonated near the bowman hiding behind a remnant of a sparkle fern bush. Man, bow, and bush exploded, clearing the area for the moment.

The enemy did not seem to mind the loss of a few of their own from attacks originating from their side. Some of the human druids and Valen kind on the battlefield elected to have physical protection installed and not magical.

In the past, he had thought as they. Having someone hacking at oneself with a sharp or blunt weapon seemed to trigger the instinct for protection. His solution was to learn how to defend and counterattack with his weapon of choice, whether long sword or spear with master skill, freeing his barrier for protection from long-ranged magical violence.

Gauging the flow of battle, he was alarmed that the light would soon fade in the Vale and his men were tiring. Worse, they could not hold the enemy back. There were too many of them. He fought down a growing sense of panic; he had to sound the retreat now before the enemy sent them into a complete rout. He opened his mouth to shout for his first in command to relay the order.

The twilight of the meadow melted into an image of Durandas in the war room of the southern outpost, cutting off the din of battle with stark abruptness. The head of the Circle of Light's left eye glowed with the bright white of the contacting. Behind Durandas, the great *flor'e'falun* had pulled its branches wide, giving him a dizzying window of view to the conflicts below. A winged creature he knew too well flew by carrying someone dear. "Durandas! A maimwright has Jade! Behind you!"

Durandas whirled.

Camoe gazed at the scene outside the outpost, his fear mounting. With wings wholly inadequate to carry weight beyond its own, the creature struggled to maintain altitude as Jade fought. Each of her kicks and squirms caused a noticeable decline in the thing's altitude. Nevertheless, it did not have far to go; already it had flown over half the force assaulting the Vale, making for the rear as it banked. The army moving toward the great falun tree halted. A widened area opened in a wave toward the rear.

A sense of hushed watchfulness descended on those below, and then a burning shape of a man, half the size of the tree, stepped upon the field. The ground shook. Raising a giant foot high, the shape took a lurching step forward. The ground shook again when the foot met the ground. Slowly, it raised its other foot.

Durandas turned to him, his words already ringing in Camoe's mind before he had faced him fully. "*The Vale is lost beyond all hope. Send the bulk of your men here to the base of the southern outpost; I have a mission for them. I will pass the leadership onto someone else. I want you to take a few of your most trusted and go after the anomaly vessel.*"

"That burning dark creation is coming for you," Camoe said

aloud.

*"Yes. We have given it all we have without allies. We shall evacuate and make for Brown Recluse. Find the anomaly, make haste, my trusted friend, losing her may have far-reaching repercussions."*

The image melted back into the war-torn meadows, the screams and cries of the wounded and dying loud in his ears after the silence of the contacting. He looked around, getting an assessment of the damage. Only a third of his company remained. He was heartened to find most were his best. The ground shook.

"What is that thing, Master Druid?" Peers asked, pointing with his longbow toward the lumbering man-shape. The dark creation's upper torso burned with a blazing fire, but it did not seem to have any effect on the thing's navigating. Perhaps its yellow-orange eyes could see through flames.

Briefly, Camoe wondered if Burl might have been able to see through flames with his like-colored eyes and then discarded the notion almost as soon as it formed in his mind. It was irrelevant now that Crystalyn had destroyed Jade's companion. *Blast it!* Burl was his companion too, though he would not admit it to anyone. Someday he might confide in Jade, but for that to happen, he had to get her back from the rank clutches of evil by staying focused.

The golem moved straight for the southern outpost. The ground shook.

Camoe turned his back to the advancing giant. "It is something we shall not contend with right now. Go to the runners; tell them to sound the retreat to the outpost. Once there, all shall follow the Lore Mother."

"But not you," Peers said.

"No and neither are you. Once our brethren have begun moving, you and Kerna meet me at Fissure Rock. Circle wide and avoid enemy eyes."

"As you command, Master Druid," Peers said, moving away

at a fast trot.

Camoe joined the fighting on the left side long enough for the enemy to shift to the right. "Long Draught, Tarn, Girth, you three shall come with me. The rest of you assist with moving the line back to the great falun, the Lore Mother shall lead you from there." Camoe turned his back on the company of warriors. There were many questioning and worried looks, but no one spoke up. He was thankful for it. They were all good-trained men and women who likely knew he had no time for explanations. He wished he could take them all.

Circling wide and making hardly a sound, they made their way through the thickest foliage still living. No one spoke. Soon they came to a slight incline. Moving uphill, they topped out with some effort. The flora growing on it had been nearly as dense as a bramble twister had.

Fissure Rock waited alone and forlorn at the peak of the little knoll. Camoe did not have to command his men to encircle it and keep a vigilant watch. Again, the thought flitted through his mind. They were good warriors and knew what to do.

Less than half a bell of daylight remained when a soft rustle forewarned of Peers and Kerna's arrival. Peers, the shorter of the two, carried his knives in many sheaths on both sides of his kell vest.

Kerna's dark skin tone and shorn black hair helped hide her athletic body in the shadows of the thick foliage and dwindling daylight. She carried her longbow, and a quiver of arrows peeked over her shoulder left bare by her uncustomary leaf dress. The flora dress surprised him until he recalled she studied under Lore Rayna and had gained the living dress only recently after bonding with the leaves.

Camoe kept his voice low. "From this point on, we travel with stealth, exercising deadly intent, considering anything moving as the enemy. If we cannot move beyond them spotting us, we dispatch them. Kerna, with her night sight, shall scout for us first. We make for the enemy's rear camp with all haste. Does anyone have questions?"

His answer came as a mark of their training; Peers melted into the foliage after his mate Kerna. Camoe had not brought them along due to their union but for their skills. He had selected only the best of his finest warriors for this journey, hoping they were enough yet fearing they were not.

Taking a last look around, he was nearly overwhelmed with sadness. A mere half dozen of the great falun trees survived in the vale, and one, the southern outpost, blazed. He feared they all would soon have the same fate of the rest, crackling as they burned or lying broken and shattered from concerted precise strikes of the Dark Flow.

The once clear and flowing Serenity Stream moved sluggishly, fouled by the dead and muddied by the tramp of many feet. He suspected the enemy had performed some vile deed to the Silver Pools under and feeding Misty Veil waterfall, the precious life-giving water that flowed from the heights above the Vale.

At least Kara, or worse, Maialene, was not around to view the destruction; she would not have had the strength to bear it, not his daughter. She was, and always would be, a daughter of the Vale. As for Kara, he had no idea what her feelings were now. Her departure so many seasons after he returned Maialene to the one root of the Vibrant Vale still ached.

His sadness deepened as he slipped into a patch of the few remaining greenery left on the outskirts of his beloved Vale, but he had no time for it. Someone else he cared for was in danger. This time he would ensure a better outcome than Maialene.

Taking longer than he expected, he finally spotted Kerna standing motionless at the edge of the small clearing the animal trail led through, her living dress obscuring her form well beside a sapling falun tree. Peers stood a little beyond his life mate, the shadowy, too-straight lines of his swords crisscrossing at his back giving him away.

Without slowing, Camoe motioned for speed as he moved their direction. Breaking into an easy jog, Kerna's long legs put distance between her and Peers as he burst into an easy run behind her. They slipped along the path making no sound.

Camoe did not glance behind. His warriors covering the back trail would keep up.

They ran, staying with the animal path until it veered too close to the enemy. Then, swinging north, his silent group wove among evergreen pines. Skirting the thickest patches of deadfall, they soon headed south and slowed. The rear command of the enemy was not far, and twilight was nearly upon them.

Peers and Kerna waited prone and motionless behind a rock outcropping. Dropping with a practiced ease to his belly, Camoe crawled the last three man-lengths. Raising his head with care, he gazed at the enemy's layout.

Below, nestled beside Serenity Stream, dark canvassed pavilions glowed from candlelight within, and fire pits dug in common areas provided flickering light outside. Armored soldiers grouped around the pits, and robed Dark Users clustered away from them. Every band avoided three larger, guard-patrolled tents centered at the rear.

He had seen enough.

He backed away from the edge, his two scouts slipping soundlessly with him. At the trail, he looked at each of his five best warriors. They were so much more than just his elite team. Each one was family. They were with him through his dark times. Things were about to get dark again.

How could he ask what he must of them when he suspected

most, if not all, would not survive? How could he not ask? They were the *best*, and Jade needed them. He knew how to ensure they would volunteer. "From this point forward, the danger will grow higher than any of you have experienced. I cannot ask you to go on this rescue with me, nor shall I command it. Make your way to the Lore Mother at the Southern Rim. Tell her to keep moving without me." He hated his subterfuge as soon as the words left his mouth.

"Hold on," Peers said. "I cannot speak for everyone, yet Kerna and I are with you. Elevated danger or no, our place is with you."

Kerna nodded vigorously, her clipped black hair hardly moving. "My life heart has the way of it."

Long Draught, the largest of them all, grabbed Camoe by the shoulder and gave him a gentle squeeze for all his size. "You have but to lead my friend. I will follow."

Girth, chuckled softly with little mirth. "When is the danger not great around you? You draw it to you like shadow hiding from the sun. This is why I follow. It never gets dull. I go with you." He folded his arms at his chest. For all his width, Girth was nearly as strong and as fierce a warrior as Long Draught. Camoe would gladly have him along.

They all looked to the last member of the group, Tarn—another druid of the order of the Green Writhe though much younger—who seemed resigned. "I suppose what we are after is down there inside the enemy's camp?"

"*She* is down there."

"So there is a human life involved?" Tarn asked.

Camoe nodded slowly. "Yes, there is someone important to our entire existence and very dear to me."

Tarn grinned. "Then how could I ever refuse such a worthy adventure? Lead on, my friend, darkness is coming."

Camoe led. Hoping to circle around and move stealthily into

the camp of the enemy, he would infiltrate the two larger tents from the open ground at the rear, cloaked in the shadows of twilight. It was a hasty plan that tasted sour in his mouth from working on his friends' nobility.

Flowing through the forest with only the faint whisper of a passing breeze, he put the matter from his mind. Warriors were what he required to get this job done, not friends. The fate of Astura may depend upon it.

# SOMETHING BIG IS COMING

The ground shook. The leaves on the thick, green foliage trembled darkly in the twilight. Even the knots on the trunk the Valens had coaxed the great falun tree to grow, which Crystalyn now gripped, shuddered faintly. A dull boom in the distance heralded another approaching tremor, two counts sooner than the last. *"What shakes us, Do'brieni?"* His response was immediate but laced with uncertainty. *"The enemy has made way for something to pass through from the rear, a tower moving on its own power."*

Though her link mate's thoughts raised her anxiety, Crystalyn tried to remain calm. "Everyone prepare, something big is coming," she said aloud, wondering what it was. Something moving about the land large enough to disturb the earth a great falun tree had sunk its roots deep into was a cause for concern, but she didn't want to frighten the others. Least of all Jade.

Three and a half meters from the bottom, the tree provided an extra-wide knot, enough for both feet. She paused and looked around while there was still some natural light. A group of Valens and warriors squatted below, eyeing the meadow. Crystalyn looked, but she couldn't make out much beyond indistinct shapes.

Another ripple quaked past, stronger this time. Her fingers were tired from gripping the knots worn smooth from much bigger hands than hers, but her legs needed a short rest. Some of the stretches to the next knot were long, almost longer than she was capable of, but she'd done it on the climb up, so she knew it was possible.

Hastel and Atoi stood vigil at the tree's huge base as Broth had assured her. Surrounding her friends, other Valens stood guard beside dozens of druids; all faced outward, weapons readied. *"Have you found many others yet, Broth? There's too few here, I want as many as I can get when we punch through."*

*"I bring nearly the same amount that is already there. We are close. Know that most have wounds, some severe."*

*"Well done, I wish we could look for stragglers, but the time has come to make our move as soon as you arrive."*

*"I understand. Take note, the enemy attacks as we flee. Lives are lost. The tower is gaining ground on us."*

*"Stay safe, my Do'brieni. I need my link mate with me."*

*"I am coming."*

Crystalyn checked Jade's progress. Leaning back precariously, she got a better view around a gentle inward swing of the giant tree. Jade hadn't climbed down to there yet. If her sister didn't hurry, she'd have trouble finding the handholds without light. Not to mention, Jade would also face the danger of the top of the great tree burning.

Afraid to call too loudly with the Dark Users so close, Crystalyn climbed up to the inward bend, feeling each shudder vibrate through her fingers, and then sent her light symbol up underneath the small, wooden landing. Jade was nowhere in sight. Alarmed, Crystalyn called out, keeping her voice low. "Jade? What's taking you so long? We have to keep moving."

Her calls went unanswered. Poking her head through the landing, her alarm grew to fear. The landing was empty.

*"Do'brieni!"* she screamed into the link.

*"I am here."*

*"Jade is missing from the bottommost landing. I'm climbing higher .She*

*may have went to help Lore Rayna."*

*"Have a care; the flames are spreading at the top, you may have to move those at the base."*

*"I know the bloody tree is coming apart, and something is coming. I can't find—"*

The Lore Mother dropped onto the landing from the ladder, and Lore Rayna climbed down after. Above them, the feet of a robed man came into view. Her face smudged with something black, likely soot, the Lore Mother reached for a knotty handhold. "Keep going down, Crystalyn. We have little time," she said.

"I know. Where's Jade?"

The Lore Mother hesitated. "Keep moving. We shall talk on the ground."

Crystalyn frowned, her anger growing. "Did you not hear—"

Broth's thoughts sent fear through her mind. *"I have seen her, Do'brieni; your sibling has flown past! Oh, no, Do'brieni, I fear!"*

*"What do you mean flown? How can she fly?"*

*"A maimwright has her."*

Crystalyn hadn't yet encountered a maimwright, but it didn't sound good. "What is a maimwright?" she almost shouted at the Lore Mother. "One has Jade."

The great tree shuddered. A loud *crack* boomed through the shadowy twilight above. A branch with a platform still attached fell past.

"Hurry!" the Lore Mother roared.

With her thoughts as numb as her fingers had grown, Crystalyn coaxed her arms and legs downward, scrambling awkwardly for handholds and footholds. Finally, her feet touched the ground, and she backed away from the trunk as the ground shook again. The tree shuddered. *Something big is coming,* she thought dully, staring at the tree's base, waiting for the Lore Mother. The Lore Mother was going to speak to her. The Lore Mother would clarify the situation.

Crystalyn's mind lurched. Suddenly she was afraid, afraid for Jade. *Oh, my Jade!*

Climbing down barefooted, the Lore Mother strode past her. "You there, get everyone together, we have to get moving. The great *flor'e'falun* valiantly struggles to hold but has not long before the top of it collapses. We do not want to be near when that happens. The Mighty One wishes to wait and topple on the enemy, though the fires have weakened it beyond all hope of repair. I cannot say how long our beloved falun has left." The Lore Mother spoke the last with tears flowing openly down her face

Crystalyn went to her, clutching her convulsively with a fierce hug. Pulling away, she asked again, her thoughts in turmoil. "What is a maimwright, where is my Jade? What do we do?"

The Lore Mother's tearful face looked down upon her, her voice cracking with each word. "If a maimwright has her, it is bad. So bad, we shall likely never see her again. I am so sorry, my daughter."

Crystalyn gaped. Fear lanced through her. She shut it out with a thought. *I'm not ready to give up on my sister and neither should the Lore Mother no matter what she believes.*

*"I am coming, Do'brieni."*

*"No!"* Crystalyn shouted into the link and then calmed, sending feelings of iron control through the link. *"Track where that thing takes my sister, then work your way to where I am. Do not let the enemy see you."*

*"I shall do as my Do'brieni commands, though I cannot track it from the ground if it flies from sight."*

If her commands bothered Broth, nothing of it leaked into the link; only a fierce determination mixed with…fear passed through. Not a fear for himself, but fear for Jade. Crystalyn quelled her stabbing fear again.

A giant burlap-textured foot and leg squashed a bush nearby. The ground shook. Sharp cracks of breaking wood rent the air as a great body, blazing with flame, grappled with the tree.

Durandas dropped from the trunk. "Run!" he roared.

Crystalyn ran.

# STOIC I STAND

Garn found it hard to curb his excitement. After months guarding the Alchemist during his rise to great lord of the Dark Citadel, they had finally left the bloody confining fortress under the plateau behind. The forest they had gated into had come as a welcome relief even though there was an armed force, the hooded man's army, working hard at destroying it. Right away, he'd wanted to do something to stop it. Too many ancient trees were burning, some toppling in flames, and good people were dying.

He was one man and powerless to stop it. He hated the Alchemist, the hooded man, for it. It was another reason in a long line of reasons for him to destroy the man. If only he could find his daughters. He would not hesitate to kill the *great lord* then.

The camp was set up a short distance from the base of a magnificent waterfall that added humidity and mud to the sodden, formerly grassy area the army had trampled when claiming it as a command base.

Garn kept watch as the three of them strode around the inside perimeter of the camp without challenge. The hooded man and even Kara Laurel were well recognized. As for himself, he noted several lingering glances fell upon him, though no one, not even the couple of generals the Alchemist had accosted with his demands for the whereabouts of the high commander, dared ask for an explanation of his presence. The men in this camp were all seasoned and knew him for the bodyguard he was, though they would not know how much the role scathed him.

The Alchemist found the person he sought at the western side, the side the fighting waged the strongest, though the small table they halted at was set a few rows back from the men doing the killing or dying.

"There you are, *General* Liam," the Alchemist said softly, yet his voice carried through the din of battle. His words jerked the horned helm of a big man around to face them. The fact that the hooded man had emphasized the man's title had not been lost to Garn. The man must fancy himself above his station by referring to himself as high commander.

"Great Lord, it is not safe for you here at present. The enemy has rallied for a last, desperate magical assault. Please, withdraw with me behind my iron wall. The Vale people's arrows or magic cannot penetrate the Flow-resistant barrier I have the black robes maintaining, nor can their arrows harm the iron." The raspy voice behind the helm bespoke a man leaving behind his middle years.

Garn eyed the battle, trying to look at everything, not just the burning magical creations, larger than any other dark creations—as most soldiers referred to the things—he had yet to lay eyes on. Most creations owed existence to the most adept Users for menial chores in the kitchen, stables, or sewers for the necessary chores no one else wanted. He supposed having one's head and torso lit with fire would constitute a task none wanted.

The rest of the battle was mainly small pockets of resistance from behind the bigger tree trunks. Magic Users flew flaming birds and shot arrows from bows amidst those within range as they marched into a main force on the left flank pushing them slowly back. General Liam had the battle won. The opposing side had a few hours, at most.

The Alchemist gestured for the man to lead the way to the

sphere, not once taking his golden hourglass eyes off the man. Garn joined them, catching sight of poorly concealed glares from soldiers and messengers as they strode or trotted past, going about the many endless tasks of warfare. The hooded man had garnered far-reaching hatred outside his own, for reasons he could only guess.

Moving past several sheets of glowing black iron forming a wall and partial roof supported with metal, they entered a lounging area. Logs hewn into crude chairs surrounded benches, and a large stump of a tree used as a map table claimed most of the space.

General Liam removed his helmet and gauntlets, setting them on a bench, and indicated everyone to sit where they would. His black hair was matted and moist with sweat, and his eyes—as dark and hard as agates—did not look like he was among allies.

Garn chose a place between the high commander and his charge to sit. Kara Laurel sat close beside him in silence. She'd been quiet since the hooded man had retrieved her from her rooms. Something must have passed between them, but she had not taken him into her confidence, a normal aspect of her personality.

"I expected you would arrive today," General Liam said without preamble, his eyes dull. "Half the main force is finishing off the plant people." The ingratiating tone of voice at the battlefield had vanished.

The Alchemist stiffened. "What? Where are the rest of them? And the reserves, what have you done with them?"

General Liam's jaw rose, and his lips twitched once, quelling what Garn suspected was a normal mannerism for the man, a sneer of disdain. "I sent them to the south. Their leaders are exposed, and the outlander is with them. I shall finish them all to the last one."

"The prophecy vessel? Call them back at once, you fool!" the hooded man said, his voice a snarl.

Kara Laurel spoke right after him. "Crystalyn is here? What have you done? She will kill them all, you blasted imbecile!"

Garn was stunned. *My daughter? How would she destroy a regiment of soldiers?*

General Liam's blank eyes grew duller. If he was upset, he mastered it well. "That is a dangerous word to use in reference to one such as I. They cannot possibly win. They are a defeated, ragtag force of a mere five hundred or so. I have five thousand soldiers and over three hundred Users, they will fall."

Kara Laurel stood, tall and imperious. "You are a *great* fool! They have their greatest Light Users, Interrupters, *and* the outlander! Call them back before it's too late!"

The Alchemist rose. Though shorter than anyone present, his soft voice and muscular stature exuded command. "Do as I decreed. Do it now, or I will order you executed."

Garn was on his feet before the hooded man had spoken his second word.

His movements stiff and jerky, General Liam also rose. His broad head swung back and forth between Kara and the Alchemist several times. He turned away, calling for a messenger.

Garn gazed at the two he had accompanied here. The Alchemist's golden hourglass eyes followed the dark-armored general's route; Kara Laurel looked ready to burst into an indignant flame. *What do they know?* he wondered.

General Liam hobbled back before long. Garn wondered if he had taken a recent wound, though he hadn't noticed the limp before now. "I have sent my three fastest. They should intercept the regiment in time."

Kara Laurel tossed her head of red hair back, rolling her eyes as if seeking divine help. Her hands became fists as she glared at the general. "You should have sent all you have with the promise of silver to whoever gets there first." Surprisingly, the Alchemist spoke no word to silence her.

Though his eyes remained dull, General Liam's chin rose slightly. "That is not for you to decide. You are nothing but a lackey User, and a Light User at that. No one has understood why the great lord would have need of such filth," he said, advancing toward her a step, his hand on the hilt of the curved scimitar sheathed at his side.

Garn stepped in front of her, drawing the great broadsword from the sheath on his back in one motion. If any fighting would happen, it would involve him. A strong push on his shoulder moved him unexpectedly to the side before he could plant his feet.

"I do not require protection," Kara Laurel hissed. "Not from this one, nor any of his kind. They have a mistaken assumption I shall tolerate their harsh words and glares. Such a supposition may prove fatal."

General Liam stopped, his expression as solid as stone. Turning, he advanced toward the Alchemist. Startled at the move, Garn's leap was a second longer than it should have been. Kara Laurel was faster. A bolt of white shot past Garn, striking the general between the shoulder blades, rippling outward along his shoulders and arms. General Liam stumbled but kept going as white flames burned along his neck and shoulders.

The Alchemist pulled a potion from his bag, a sneer of disdain on his mouth, the only part of his face visible. Then his lips drew slack. Suddenly he scrambled backward out from behind the wall.

A crowd of soldiers had gathered outside of it. "Do not let him touch me! Do not make contact with him!" he shouted.

The general shambled toward the Alchemist, his pace steady.

Garn could not wait any longer. Leaping, he lopped off the general's right arm at the elbow, even though the man hadn't drawn his weapon.

The general paused, glancing over his shoulder at him, pushed past a soldier, and continued his advance. The soldier stiffened and then moved out of the way, leaving the crowd behind. General Liam's pace slowed.

The Alchemist's hands blurred with a flash of movement.

Two starred blades bloomed in the throat of General Liam. He straightened abruptly. Blood streaming down his neck, he toppled slowly face forward to the ground. Several men rushed toward him.

"No one touches him!" The Alchemist's shouted command was too late. One of the soldiers rolled General Liam onto his back. Eyes glazed, the once imposing man stared back dull and lifeless.

The Alchemist's long finger pointed at the soldier kneeling beside the general. "No one touch that man. Destroy him now!"

The soldier looked wildly around and then sidled backward when no one made a move for him.

Unfortunately, he stepped closer to Garn. He thought about letting the man vanish in the crowd, and then recognized the unmistakable similarities to Lord Braddert's soldiers. No signs of pain and single-minded pursuit. Garn dispatched the man with a quick, almost bloodless swing to the neck. "No one touches the body, either part." Garn said. "Kara, burn them both, every piece."

Kara Laurel looked at him, the frown on her beautiful face revealing her puzzlement, and then her eyes widened. Perhaps she'd recalled the strange attack at the Obsidian Table.

Kara Laurel's white fireballs caused the circle of armor ringing the dead men to widen as the flames rose higher on the two men.

A large man wearing the red hammer insignia of captain on the chest of his dark armor backed only as far as he had to from the two growing pyres. "What is this? My man only checked if the blasted general lived. Why did you kill him?"

The Alchemist ignored the question, looking to Garn and Kara Laurel. "Did either of them have contact with anyone? Did I miss something?"

Garn opened his mouth to mention the jerky movements of the soldier, but Kara Laurel beat him to it.

"There was one," she said.

"Where?" the Alchemist asked. The tone of his voice was urgent and annoyed at the same time. "Why did you not destroy it?"

Kara Laurel pointed to the Alchemist's right. "He left to the north, going through the crowd. We would have ended him had we known."

The Alchemist did not appear to hear her. The crowd's anger had grown. Many voices grumbled an ominous "There are only three of them," and "They killed General Liam!"

Flowing into *Stoic I Stand,* his best defensive stance, Garn prepared for battle, a battle he would not have willingly entered had he a second choice. Seasoned warriors outnumbered them so heavily he did not bother to count the odds. On his left, Kara Laurel's delicate right hand burst into white radiance.

Suddenly the Alchemist stood at his right, his golden eyes blazing with an inner, amber light enhanced by the dark hood. He swept the crowd with his odd, feline orbs. "Your general, *my* General Liam, was doing what *I* commanded for this army in service to *me!* The general attacked your leader without provocation." The Alchemist's voice though low, reverberated throughout the crowd and the muttering quieted. "I do not believe this was something he would have done on his own. There is something here, something in our midst, something sly and powerful, wishing to control those with authority. It is now hiding among you, lurking inside one of you. Who has noticed a difference in the normal way their friend or companion-in-arms is acting?"

The hooded man's words had a profound effect on the crowd. Their proximity to each other widened. They parted, glaring with suspicion at one another. The captain ignored his men, his dark eyes fierce. "How do we know what you claim is true? It sounds as false as a night woman's lies!" he bellowed.

The crowd's silence was thunderous.

Without warning, a vial shattered on the man's armored chest, splashing upon his neck and chin. "What is this?" he asked, wiping at his chin. Then he screamed. Wisps of oily steam billowed from the man's chin, neck, chest, and now his hand.

Garn would have turned his back on the scene—he'd seen the effects of the flask's contents—if not for the crowd and an insidious creature to watch for.

Groping at his throat and chin, the captain's screams soon became gurgles. He spun, reaching with one hand toward his men. The men backed away. He fell to his knees and toppled face forward to the ground, his hand still outstretched. The Alchemist strode beside him, his eyes fixed on the crowd. "Stand aside and point the way toward anyone who has left your ranks recently or meet the same fate as our dear captain."

Though there were many glares, the line parted, opening a wide swath in the center.

Behind the hooded man, Garn strode through with Kara at his side. He kept a vigilant watch on those on his side, trusting his Light User companion would do the same. No one made a move toward them, though the crowd turned as one, following their every move.

The Alchemist halted in a small meadow, the grass beaten to humid soil by the tread of many booted feet. Three multi-roomed tents—command pavilions—were set in a half-moon formation. Smaller, one- or two-man tents of the soldiers ringed the entire area.

His biceps bulging under the gold band, the Alchemist pointed at a soldier steadying another soldier who had mounted a black horse. "No one leaves, stop that man!"

Letting go of the mounted man, the standing soldier gave a jerky swat to the horse's rear flank and then turned to face them. His blue eyes dull, he groped at his side and wrenched a hammer axe from a sheath. He started toward them.

"Don't let anyone leave!" the Alchemist shouted again.

Kara Laurel strode to one side lining up a view of the horse and rider galloping toward the main force besieging the Vale. The soldier turned with her. Kara Laurel raised her hand. A glowing bolt of white streaked away from it. Awkwardly, the soldier shuffled into the bolt's path, and a barrier the shape of his body dispersed it. The soldier continued toward her, eerily silent.

Kara Laurel moved to one side again, but it was taking too long. Garn slipped a dagger from the sheath at the small of his back and threw it, sinking it to its tiny hilt in the man's right eye. The soldier crumpled.

The way clear, Kara Laurel fired two glowing bolts of white that streaked toward the fleeing rider, but the horse and rider had reached a regiment of men pushing a catapult. Thundering into the group of men and pushing at a sharp angle, the great warhorse trampled men as Kara's bolts slammed into the hapless soldiers now ringing the rider. Pushing through, the warhorse broke out of them and vanished behind the catapult.

The Alchemist's golden eyes shone bright within his dark cowl, his hands balled into fists. "You failed, Kara, go after it. Kill it before it wears someone else."

Kara gaped. Then scowling at Garn, she turned and ran for

the nearest horse. Her long bare legs carrying her across the meadow quickly, she paused beside a support soldier and pointed to a horse. As the man untied the big horse, she grabbed the reins and vaulted upon its back. With her yellow kell skirt showing much of her legs, she urged the horse into a gallop.

The Alchemist stared until she vanished from sight amidst the army marching sluggishly toward the great burning trees. "Come, we shall find what has happened to my campaign here with that…aberration in command." He set off toward the three command tents.

Garn stayed at his side. He had questions. Perhaps the hooded man would relinquish some of his knowledge if he were careful how he phrased his inquiries as they walked. "This aberration, it's the same as whatever attacked us at the Obsidian Table, is it not?"

"It is my belief."

"Do you know what it really is, where it came from?

The hooded man hesitated, stopping at a fire pit beyond hearing of a group of soldiers heating a meal.

The setting sun left a surreal red tint upon a half-circle row of tents they faced. A guard stationed beside the largest stuck his head inside and then turned toward them. A young woman pushed the flap aside and obediently followed the guard.

Coming to a decision, the Alchemist continued. "Many years ago, in the arrogance of my youth, I thought to best a known evil. I believed it possible to steal the power of the Stair of Despair and make it my own. In my great conceit, I was…overcome."

Garn wasn't certain he'd heard right. "You were beaten unconscious?" he asked.

The Alchemist's soft voice grew softer. "Nay, I was enslaved. The entity—I know not what it was—gorged on my mind, as a carnivore would feed on an infant. Only a stroke of luck allowed me to break free before becoming a permanent part of its great mind, a single tiny speck in the vastness of immense superiority. Enough talk for now. Come, we shall eat."

Garn barely heard the Alchemist's words. The guard had moved closer, giving him a good view of the person he escorted. The young woman trailing the big man was his daughter Jade.

# IN HER POWER

Jade's stomach lurched with fear. Someone rustled the rain canvas outside the tent where the maimwright had dropped her half an hour ago. She'd stumbled inside before the guards outside could stop her. Likely, it was where they'd wanted her to go, but she didn't care, as long as she got away from the beast. Jade shivered. The thing was vile and reeked of decaying meat. Somehow, it hadn't snipped off pieces of her for its meal, not yet. Were they keeping her here until the thing got hungry? What did they want with her?

A guard wearing the armor of the Dark Citadel poked an unadorned full helm inside, startling her. She jumped. "Come," he said softly, his voice a near whisper floating out from the helm, though his tone brooked no argument.

Jade followed the man's wide shoulders through the tent flap and stayed back a couple of paces after getting a whiff of his armor. He must have had an extended stay in the field with no time to bathe. What did it matter? She was probably going to slaughter. Her legs grew weak with the thought.

Outside the tent, the sun quickly fell, the moon rising bright in the twilight before dark. The dark-armored man took her to a small group of people clustered around a large kettle set upon a rock beside a fire. Stopping, he stepped behind her and pushed her gently forward, showing her to those who attended a meal.

A pair of gold bands tightened upon a muscular man's biceps as he stirred a bowl. The stirring stopped, and he looked out from under a black cowl cut high on his torso that left his midriff bare.

Jade felt certain she'd seen him before. His golden eyes, hourglass in shape, reminded her of Broth's so much it was uncanny. Though only when the warden's mood was amicable were his eyes golden. All at once, she recalled hiding in a secret passage and overhearing a conversation between a hooded man and Darwin Darkwind months ago, Crystalyn beside her. The hooded man had planned to sap the Flow from under the Vibrant Vale with his alchemy worms.

The worms had a major weakness she needed to expose to someone, but who could she tell? She was a captive. What *did* they want with her? The situation was bad, but Crystalyn would be coming for her. She had to keep focused and stay alive until then.

The voice of the man with the hourglass eyes was a soft hiss, though it carried. "Where did you find her?" he asked the guard who had brought her from the tent.

"A shadow creature brought her, a winged wright. General Liam seemed to expect her and ordered her put in his tent under guard."

His golden eyes never leaving hers, the hooded man opened them wider. "The winged wrights serve only the Dark Master, or so the belief goes. Perhaps such a conviction was cultivated by the Dark Disciples, those who fancy themselves true believers of the Great Master," the hooded man mused.

The hourglass eyes finally moved their golden scrutiny from her as he regarded the soldier behind her.

Jade almost cried out with relief as he pulled the dark cowl lower, the golden eyes fading from sight altogether. "Captain, you are now General Karnas," he said, his words a soft hiss. "Ensure that you, the captive, and thirty of your best veteran warriors have eaten, and then command them to prepare for a mounted journey to the citadel. Travel at top pace, bring her without incident to my chambers, and await my return. I shall finish this campaign. Once the last great tree has fallen, expect me beyond the Dark Gate."

"Yes, Great One," General Karnas said, gripping her arm with a gauntleted hand.

The hooded man's black cowl swung toward a big man standing off to one side. He wore no armor, only leather pants and a vest; the color was either black or brown, but she couldn't be certain in the fading light. In his hands, he held a bowl. "My personal guard, one of my greatest, shall accompany you and your men. Perhaps you shall understand now her value is higher than your own. Do not fail to keep her from harm." Though soft, the hooded man's tone of voice held the promise of unimaginable violence.

Maintaining his grip on her arm, Karnas bowed deeply. "As the great lord commands," he said. Straightening, he pulled her toward another campfire, one of many burning in the night. In the distance, the night horizon lit with a red glow as the great Valen trees burned. Jade's stomach fluttered with an almost overwhelming sense of loss.

Striding on her right side, the big man spoke. "You can let go of her now." His voice had a familiar tone to it, gentle but clear, vibrant like her dad's, even with his ailing heart. Thinking of him caused her heart to race; she hoped he was still alive. Astura was too violent for an organ as weak as his was.

General Karnas removed his hand. "If she runs, you shall have the honor of retrieving her then."

"If she runs, you can count on it. No other of your men will need to lift a foot or a weapon."

The shadowy full helm of General Karnas swung toward her. "All the same, *if* she runs, all my men and *I* personally will chase her down."

The big man didn't respond. Instead, he held a bowl out to her. "Here, you should eat while you can, keep your strength high."

"Thank you," Jade said quickly, taking the bowl. Another pang of worry for her dad welled up in the pit of her stomach. Her father would say something similar, a gentle reprimand. She tried to keep the half-full bowl steady as they walked. There was no spoon; she'd have to drink from it.

Passing by the tent General Karnas had gathered her from, they stopped at a line of saddled horses tied to a guide rope. General Karnas bellowed names to an attendant to fetch 'his men' for him. The attendant trotted away, presumably to get them.

Raising the bowl to her lips, Jade took a tentative sip trying not to spill. An unfamiliar broth and something soft slid down her gullet, but she didn't care what it was; she was famished. She drank the rest and handed the empty bowl back to the personal guard of the hooded man. He handed it to an attendant who rinsed it from a flask he carried and then stored it in saddlebags. Untying the black horse, he handed the reins to the big man and another to General Karnas.

Mounting up, the big man stretched an arm to her. "She rides with me," he declared as she took his hand.

"You will slow us down, she gets her own horse. You can have the reins," General Karnas said.

As the big man let go of her hand, his arm slowly receded. "Agreed," he finally said.

Jade lowered her hand, looking around. She was suddenly unescorted. Did she dare run?

"Someone put the girl on a horse! Gently, treat her better than your own daughter or I will impale you upon my sword!" General Karnas bellowed.

Strong arms lifted her onto a tall horse. A dark land of

shadows in the moonlight, the ground seemed so far away. The horse jolted forward. Jade clutched the saddle's pommel as it moved behind an even taller horse the big man rode. A dark form handed him the reins.

All at once, there was a flurry of activity as men climbed upon skittish horses and General Karnas rode back and forth calling out to each man. Jade began to wonder if she'd have been better off with the maimwright and then shuddered at the thought.

After much shifting and moving about, they finally moved out, thumping the meadow with hooves two horses wide and a long string behind. General Karnas rode in the forefront next to a horse and rider she didn't know.

"Hold!" General Karnas suddenly yelled, raising a shadowy arm. The dark form of a man stood in his path.

The hooded man folded his thick arms at his stomach. "General Karnas, a word with you."

"Blast! I nearly rode you down, My Lord!"

The hooded man did not respond. Instead, the dark hood swung toward the man escorting her on his big warhorse. "You are my greatest experiment. Continue to prove your value. Protect the anomaly, get her to the Dark Citadel, and you shall have many such missions from me. No longer shall you be limited to traveling with only me," he said. He strode back the way they'd arrived.

"Blast it!" General Karnas swore again, pulling his horse around. "Keep them moving, Captain Bozlun, I will catch you." He rode after the shadowy form of the hooded man.

Jade was surprised. How could a man be an experiment? She couldn't wait for daylight and a chance to study the man.

They rode in silence, the thud of nearly thirty horses behind her thunderous in her ears. At meadow's end, the experimental man dropped behind her as they climbed a moist trail single file that wound through evergreen trees switching back and forth close to the roar of falling water.

The land around her grew slowly brighter as they topped out at a pine and aspen meadow. There, General Karnas rode past her to the front. Slowing beside Captain Bozlun, the general gestured to the trail ahead. "Keep going, I want to get through Broken Gap before we rest the horses."

"As the general commands," Captain Bozlun replied with a nod.

General Karnas nodded slightly at the man, a small smile on his lips.

With a start, Jade realized she could see the two leaders' interactions as they both turned to face the trail ahead. Looking first behind her, she found only the grim and grizzled faces of two black-haired soldiers; she quickly turned back in her saddle.

Glancing to the side, she discovered the experimental man riding alongside her. Thin brown hair and blue eyes reminded her of her dad, but there the resemblance ended. Where her father was overweight and weakened from congestive heart failure, this man's muscles bulged with strength and vibrancy. He rode easily upon the tall warhorse. The worn hilts of two swords peeked over his shoulders rocking forward and back, riding easily, as he did in the saddle.

Though she'd never tried it riding before, Jade slowed the cyclone spinning around him. Focusing intently on the stormy gray cloud, she forced his rotation slower. The three images inside rotated leisurely around him. A great silver sword encrusted at the hilt and pommel with prismatic diamonds, a disembodied brain, and an empty vial stoppered with a black cowl rotated around him…past her *father*. One of her dad's images had changed but there was no doubt now.

The rotation tugged hard at her mind. Jade let it go. Released, it twisted back into the gray cyclone spinning around him.

Shocked, she gaped at her dad as he turned toward her. Glancing forward and backward casually, he tightened his grip on her reins and coaxed his warhorse ahead, closing the distance between them and the general, only to slow abruptly before getting too close. "So you know," he said, looking to both sides of her but not at her.

His words sent joy racing through her, but he wished to keep it secret, as he should. The general would separate them the moment he found out. "How is it possible, Dad?" Her excitement grew when she called him that.

"Try not to smile, Jade. Remember we don't know each other, and you're my captive until I can get you safely out of here."

Jade curtailed her excitement with difficulty while watching the two riders ahead. At differing intervals, first one, then the other, shot a glance behind them keeping a watch on the two of them. She kept her voice down. "I'm trying, Dad. It's just that you're so healthy and so…young."

"The hooded man's power as an alchemist is great. His potions have enhanced my physique. Let's save that for when we escape. Until then, these men cannot find out about us. Now that I've finally found you, I don't intend to let anything separate the family any longer, Astura is too dangerous. Where is Crystalyn?"

For all her excitement, Jade grew worried. "I don't know. We were escaping a fire from the southern outpost built upon a great falun tree when the maimwright grabbed me."

Her father shifted in his saddle, seeming to keep a lookout into the trees ahead and behind them, before settling on the trail. "That must be the group Kara Laurel went after."

"Who's Kara Laurel?"

Her dad glanced surreptitiously behind him. "Never mind for now, it just means we have less time to get away than I thought. We leave tonight, prepare for it."

"Dad, Crystalyn has changed here. She and I have found—" Jade clamped her mouth closed when General Karnas suddenly turned in his saddle, gazing first at her and then at her father. Signaling the men behind them to close the gap, he watched until satisfied with their compliance to his command. Jade could hear the dull thump of added hooves not far away.

Jade forcibly kept her eyes ahead, a frown of terror fixed upon her face, she hoped. Captivity had just gotten better and more frustrating at the same time. Her father—her *too young father*—was planning to help her escape, but she couldn't ask him anything. Blurting out questions would put them both at risk. Something she'd do everything in her power to avoid now that they'd found each other.

# UPTURNED SOIL

The sentry died with barely a gurgle. Camoe lowered him to the ground, a soft thump the only indication something was amiss. No one would hear the soldier's lone death; the guards on either side had been slain just as quietly. He waited until Peers and Long Draught coalesced out of the shadows beside him. He did not have to look behind to know Kerna's wonderful vision perused the area they had cleared. Girth, with his axe, would keep watch over her and their planned escape path.

Moving hunched over, they slipped through the meadow without a rustle in the spongy grass. Over halfway to the two darkened tents already lit by flickering torchlight from stands placed on each side of the entrance, they came upon two soldiers in the third sentry ring lying dead, side by side, in the grass. Tarn lay on his belly not far away and gazed at the tents. They dropped to the ground beside him.

Camoe kept his voice low as he took in the surroundings. "Have you seen a young woman yet?" The armored shoulder of a soldier stood out prominently beside the smaller of the two tents. Three people conversed beyond a fire too far away to overhear.

Tarn turned to him sharply. "We came here after a *young* woman?"

The astonishment in Tarn's voice surprised Camoe. "Yes, she has auburn hair."

"There is someone else here you know well with that color of hair. Look past the fire where those soldiers are cooking," Tarn whispered.

Leaning toward Tarn, Camoe looked, allowing his eyes to adjust to the dimness of twilight. A hooded man with gold bands on his bare biceps spoke with a man and a woman. The gold bands identified the Alchemist though he had not met the man in person. The Green Writhe had transacted with the man in the past, not all of it good.

The other man he did not recognize, nor would he forget if he had—his thinning hair, going white, seemed out of place for his toned physique.

The woman shifted her demure stance; the ruby light of twilight illuminated her features with an orange-red radiance. Camoe's breath escaped him.

He did know the woman well, though he was not certain how he felt about it. He should have deduced where Kara Laurel had stolen off to after Maialene…though he decided it did not matter. Not now, not with the mission. "Stay focused, look for a young woman, find her," he hissed, his voice more abrupt than he intended.

Silent, they waited for darkness.

Kara Laurel suddenly dashed away from the two men. Briefly, Camoe wondered where she was going.

The two men strolled to a fire where several soldiers stood in a line leading to a large cook pot. The two men did not stand in line. The soldier ladling from the kettle grabbed the bowls from the nearest waiting soldiers and handed them to the two men.

An armored soldier strode away from a large tent, going over to the hooded man without deviation. Camoe's breath caught in his throat. Jade followed him. *Thank Onan, she still lives.*

The soldier moved Jade in front of him, and after a time, he relinquished his hold on her arm. Someone placed a bowl in her hands, and the tall man with thinning brown hair escorted her back toward the tent she had come from.

Camoe touched Tarn lightly on his back, signaling a withdrawal. Tarn did the same to Peers, and Peers to Long Draught. As one, they crawled backward away from the torchlight, melting into the shadows to a place out of sight of the activity of the fire and away from the unwanted eyes of the sole remaining guard at the large tent.

Camoe drew them all close, huddling together. "Our target is the largest tent closest to the guarded perimeter where they will keep her after she is fed." He gripped Tarn's shoulder lightly. "Go now and use the next half bell to cut a *quiet* entrance in the back, it should be full dark by then. Do not go inside until I give you leave." Tarn slipped from his grip and faded away.

"Long Draught, you shall have to wait at midpoint. Find a depression and become a false layer of meadow grass. Should you have no choice, remove any sentries coming to relieve those that were on patrol, those half-spears you carry should do the work quietly. With luck, we still have a couple bells before that happens. I want each and every one of us well away from here, by then."

"Leave it to me," Long Draught said. He too slipped into the shadows.

"Peers, we shall wait a quarter of a bell, permitting Tarn a head start, any concerns?" Silence answered his question. His respect for his companions grew. All of them were aware the longer they remained inside the enemy encampment, the greater the risk of discovery, yet no one had bothered to voice the concern. They were professionals and better followers than he deserved.

Time passed excruciatingly slow.

Finally, Camoe judged they had waited long enough. "Let us

begin, Peers." Slipping into the shadows, Camoe moved from grass clump to grass clump, depression to depression, crawling whenever the blanket of darkness was unavailable, most of the way. With the fall of the sun, the moonlight grew brighter. While the light of a full moon made for great viewing of the enemy, it also left him feeling exposed.

Fifty steps from their destination, he stood, walking boldly to it from a rear angle. Trampled, likely intentionally, the lack of cover left him little choice. Peers stood and strolled with him.

They made it to the relative safety of the shadows at the rear of a tent. Tarn allowed the curved piece of canvas he had cut to fall on the ground as soon as they arrived. Light brightened the ground around the cut.

Drawing his sword, Camoe signaled Tarn to wait ten counts and dove inside. After rolling to his feet, it took but a moment to know he was alone. Two candles mounted on the center pole illuminated every corner of the square, fair-sized tent.

Peers sprang inside behind him, a dagger clamped in his teeth.

Disappointed there was no Jade, Camoe padded to the tent flap and looked out. The blackness outside was too deep to see through. Then the darkness shifted as someone raised the tent's flap and stepped inside.

Camoe wrapped his arm around the person, his sword pressing against a thick neck. "Make a sound and you die," he whispered, putting his lips close to a black hood. The man froze, presumably feeling the metal of his sword at his throat. A gold armband glinted by candlelight as the man dropped his arm to his side. "Go to the back of the tent. A single false action shall result with your death."

Taking delicate steps, the man complied, stiffening a little when he noticed Peers standing guard by the hole. Camoe shoved him over to it, a vague idea forming in his mind. "Tarn?" he called with a whisper.

The reply came just as quietly from outside the tent. "I am here."

"We are coming out but not alone. Watch for treachery."

"Aye."

Camoe glanced at Peers. "Stay close. If he makes a sound or deceitful move, silence him, even if you have to take me first."

Peers answered by pulling both swords from his back sheath, holding one in each hand, to add to the one in his teeth.

Satisfied, Camoe lowered the man to his knees and pushed him through the hole. Forced to put one hand awkwardly on the man's back, he kept his sword somewhat in place as they crawled through without incident, glad to be on his feet again. The man seemed to want to cooperate, which made Camoe suspicious.

The candlelight leaking from the tent vanished as Peers came through.

An elbow slammed into Camoe's stomach taking his breath and hunching him slightly forward, gaining the hooded man a small opening between Camoe's sword arm and his neck. Wedging a hand between them, the hooded man slipped from his hold and dropped an object to the ground at Tarn's feet. It broke with a soft splotch.

Sucking in a breath, Camoe rammed the hilt of his sword into the back of the hooded man's head as he turned to flee. He collapsed in a heap.

Coughing quietly, Tarn bent over the fallen man. "He is breathing but unconscious."

Camoe cursed low in his throat. "We cannot kill him and leave him here; I need him alive until he reveals the anomaly's location."

"What anomaly?" Peers whispered.

"I mean the young woman," Camoe said softly. "Both of you get under his arms. I want it to seem as if he has swallowed too much drink. I shall take the lead, attempting to make it appear we are tossing him into the forest to sleep it off."

Tarn and Peers lifted the comatose man to his feet and put a shoulder under each side. "That is a flimsy assumption if we are seen," Tarn said. He coughed lightly.

"Then pray to Onan they do not see us," Camoe said, striding boldly back the way they had come. His two men followed, dragging the hooded man between them. They were two of his best, as close to friends as he could have with the way life had set him on the solo path after losing Maialene.

Keeping the tents between them and the fire, they made it halfway across the meadow before losing the cover the tents provided. Without breaking stride, he risked a glance behind. No one stood at the campfires, and the soldiers guarding the large tent had vanished. *What is going on?* He did not need to know; as long as no one had discovered the man missing, whatever was happening provided a welcome distraction. Still, the faster they got to the trees the better.

Long Draught stood up almost under his feet, materializing tall, as if an aspen tree had sent a stalk nearly seven hands high shooting from the main root. The four-bladed half-spears he carried sheathed on his back added to the effect. "The burden shall lie with me from here," he whispered. Bending at the waist, he folded the hooded man over a shoulder and dashed for the trees. Camoe and his two companions raced to keep up. As it was, they slipped into the evergreens at the same time, well behind Long Draught.

"I see no pursuit," Kerna called softly as he passed her. She fell in behind them.

Long Draught slowed and then stopped a short while later

where Girth waited watching the open meadow leading to Long Falls. They grouped around him. "He's coming around," he said.

"Has anyone packed hemp cord with them?" Camoe asked. "Kerna? Girth?"

"I kind of need what I have," Girth said, patting at his waist.

Kerna passed a fair length to him. "All of you except our round one have not learned. How often has the need for it arisen during our journeys?" she chastised gently.

Camoe tied the captive's hands together, handing the slack to Long Draught. "Set him down. He may be able to stand."

"I can stand," the hooded man hissed. "Do you not realize how foolish your actions are tonight? My generals will not rest until I am returned and all of you hacked to death."

Long Draught and Girth chuckled, Tarn choked, and Kerna snorted at his words. Only Peers was silent.

Camoe cared not for the threat. "Your generals shall arrive too late to save you, it requires little time to kill a man. For now, I offer you continued life as long as you cooperate. I shall even consider releasing you for the outlander young woman in your possession."

The hooded man raised his head high, his hourglass eyes glinting strangely bright in the moonlight. "So, druid, you too have knowledge of her great worth." He laughed. "Yet you are too late. The anomaly has been sent to a secure place."

In one motion, Camoe drew his sword and set the tip at the man's heart. "You risk much elevating my ire. I shall ask you only once. Where have you taken her?"

The hooded man stepped forward, the tip pressing into his cowl. "Thrust quick and deep, druid. Her location dies with me."

Girth moved beside Camoe, his axe free from its sheath. "Cut out his tongue or let me kill him. His voice and his life has little value to us. The young woman shall be tracked regardless of the deceptions that flow from his dark mouth."

"What do you speak of?" Camoe asked.

"A regiment of horses passed through the north end of Silver Meadow over a half bell ago. A young woman and a man with two long swords strapped to his back rode behind the Captains Karnas and Bozlun," Girth replied.

The hooded man's flinch of surprise was only discernible as a small vibration through his sword. Camoe sheathed it and turned his back upon the hooded man. "Bring him. If he slows us down, even a little, kill him."

He took the lead. Slipping cautiously into Silver Meadow, he found what he sought almost immediately. The upturned soil from the tracks of many horses passing through was easy to spot. From the distance between the horses' tracks, he judged them at a full gallop.

With the fires burning his beloved home flickering in the night behind him, he set off at run.

He did not have to look back to know his companions followed.

# FOUND

Crystalyn brought out another symbol, one of the ones under the heading Elemental Style, which she'd read in the black-lettered book, tier three of *The Tiered Tome of Symbols*. A glowing, green circle, half the size and width of a shanty wall, hovered before her. The white maze-like pattern inside it wound around many circles, both big and small. She had yet to use it, so was unsure of the effect, though it felt airy to her.

Avoiding the crown of thorns encircling the sphere at the top of the black crystal candle, she gripped it by the base with her left hand, releasing the symbol. The candle thrummed, adding the immense power that only one of the greater artifacts could accomplish.

Streaking into the burning dark creation lumbering toward them, the symbol's many circles spun with wind. Turbulent tunnels, big and small, struck the magical creation with gale after gale. The dark creation bent backward and then snapped apart at the thighs, falling upon the army behind it. Fanned by the slowly dissolving symbol, the flames spread in a growing circle incinerating dark-armored and dark-robed men and women alike.

Fighting down her disgust with her own destruction, Crystalyn sent another flying into the second, and last, dark creation entangled in one of the few remaining falun trees. Her wind tunnels blew the creation and flames out into the silvery meadow twilight, away from the severely charred tree and into the army.

The black candle artifact had grown uncomfortably hot with the power thrumming through it with each release. She put it in her pack and turned to face those behind her to issue the command to move out. Suddenly, weakness raged through her. She dropped to her knees and then her hands in the soft earth.

Broth's comforting presence found a way into her mind. *"I am here, Do'brieni. Draw strength from the link, use mine."*

Gratefully, she drank greedily from his great strength, sensing him weakening as fast as she had. Crystalyn forced herself to stop when enough strength returned to remain conscious. Even so, it was a while before she could speak. "Will that slow them? Can you escape through the southern pass now?"

A pair of legs wearing supple kell leather stopped beside her. "You have created a path to salvation for us all? Are you not leading us through, my daughter?"

Speaking with the stilted formality of a native of Astura, the woman's vibrant voice was familiar and unfamiliar at the same time. She'd heard it, though she couldn't recall where. Pushing away from the ground, she made it as far as her knees.

A shoulder slipped under hers, lifting her to her feet, supporting her. She found herself staring into the deep-green eyes of...Sureen Creek, *Mom!* "Mom? You're alive. How?" Nearly swooning, she clutched at the woman.

Broth's great surprise mirrored hers. *"This female human's scent has similar spoors as yours."*

*"She's my mom!"*

Sureen smiled. "Let us make our escape first. Then we can talk longer. Can you walk?"

"I think so. I hope it's not far."

Her mother's smile faded. Shifting her grip on a staff topped with a clear, white stone, she tugged at Crystalyn's shoulder gently with her own, helping her move, the sword hanging at her mother's side digging into hers. "It is some way, I'm afraid, and it is going to be close with who arrives at the pass first."

*"Someone comes."*

Atoi's dispassionate voice cut through Broth's thoughts. "Two riders gallop beyond the right flank coming toward us."

"Leave them to me," Hastel said, drawing his axes from the sheaths at his side.

That they came from that particular flank didn't surprise Crystalyn. She'd expected them to try something from there; the right one was the enemy's strongest. Though why send only two?

Leaning low in her saddle, the second rider chased the first. Closing the distance between her and an armored rider—male from the look of him—the woman's long dark hair streamed behind her.

Without warning, the first rider's hair burst into a bright white flame that quickly crawled down the man's face and torso. From there, the flame jumped to the horse, where it, too, burned with a ghostly light.

Eerily silent, the horse and rider rode toward Crystalyn, seemingly impervious to the fire. A few gallops from reaching her, the horse's legs buckled. Mount and rider crashed to the ground. Skidding to a stop, man and animal lay quiet and still.

The woman riding the horse behind the hapless man and horse, someone Crystalyn recognized, nearly rode past, pulling back on the reins at the last second. The white fire crackled as it burned down emitting a sickly black smoke into the air. A gust of wind whipped it away.

The Lore Mother came forward. "Kara Laurel, what have you done?"

Crystalyn had her own question. "Why did the Dark army let

you ride past them?"

"I did what needed doing, and they did not let me go easily," she said. With a grimace, she kneed her horse, coaxing it to turn around. The bolt of a crossbow protruded from her lower thigh, and blood streamed from below her yellow kell leather skirt hemline, filling her boot.

Atoi laughed.

The Lore Mother cursed. "Blast it all! That needs a bandage until I can remove it. You are strong, Kara; every equine step must hurt something terrible." Striding toward the wounded woman, she paused at the still smoking corpse. "You have not explained this mess."

"Nor shall I. Not until we have fled somewhere safe. Please, accept my word on this," Kara Laurel said. The melodious tone of her voice grew commanding. "No one touches these corpses or they shall meet the same fate," she added loudly, her head swiveling back and forth.

About to step closer, the Lore Mother hesitated, and her luminous eyes brightened as she gazed at the woman astride the black warhorse. She opened her mouth and then clamped it shut.

Positioning a yellow bag from her side to her lap, Kara Laurel coaxed the tall black horse to step around the Lore Mother and then halted beside Crystalyn. "Can you run? The time for walking has past," she asked, ignoring her mother, though she supported her.

Sureen spoke first, the tone of her voice flat. "She cannot, at least not far. She's expended herself attempting to save five hundred wrongly attacked souls. Perhaps something you may have been a part of."

Kara Laurel frowned at the woman whose strong arms kept Crystalyn upright.

Confusion permeated Crystalyn's thoughts and little else. She struggled with the belief her mother lived, yet the evidence was there from the beating heart she felt through her kell leather shirt.

Abruptly, Kara Laurel brought the sturdy warhorse to stand beside a flat-topped boulder spotted with lichen. "Help her mount behind me. Quickly, we have little time," she commanded, her voice cold.

With Sureen's support, Crystalyn managed to climb the rock and awkwardly throw her leg over the big equine's back and settle upon it. The horse sidestepped abruptly from the additional weight. A small cry of pain escaped Kara Laurel's lips from the sudden movement. Crystalyn felt badly for her, but she had no strength left to heal her.

"Can you delay the enemy's advance, Sureen? I shall aid where I can, though I fear it will help little," Kara Laurel asked, the tone of her voice softer.

Sureen held her petite head high. A stray strand of her light brown hair flattened against her chin, but she appeared not to notice. "I am still weakened from a Circle of Light endeavor. A duty you seem to have neglected for some time, but I shall do what I can."

"Then I shall interrupt the Flow for you both," the Lore Mother declared, placing one hand on her mother's shoulder and another on Kara Laurel's unwounded thigh, her elbows drooping toward the ground.

The warhorse stood quietly as if it knew what was about to happen.

Weak, Crystalyn watched the ground beneath dissolve away to translucence, as if the earth was only an illusion created to disguise the great river of power frothing below.

Two hollow tubes formed from the Lore Mother's elbows to the ground, filling with the glowing whiteness of the Flow. Her glowing eyes brightened. "The conduits are in place. You may begin," the Lore Mother said.

Slipping her left hand into the bag, Kara Laurel brought out a yellow crystal carved with the delicate hands of a woman pressed together. With the reins gripped in her right hand, Kara Laurel raised the crystal slightly as it vanished inside a white glow.

The clear orb on Sureen's staff burst forth with a golden brilliance.

A nearly invisible wall, several yards wide, shimmered briefly in the morning light before fading to transparency. A tall coil of golden flames spiraled to life behind it.

The conduits faded. As if liquid, topsoil and meadow grass flowed into place hiding the great river from view. The Lore Mother's glowing eyes dimmed, as her head turned to Crystalyn's mom. "One is curious as to why you placed your golden coil after Kara's shimmer wall? The normal technique puts it at the forefront to aid in hiding the walls location. Once touched, that part of the wall trap is sprung and its explosive effect used up. The enemy can get past by using the corpses as a location guide where to cross."

The golden glow atop Sureen's staff winked out. "Most Light Users who install a shimmer wall are not as adept as Kara; hers cannot be viewed until activated. With my coil behind it as an added obstacle and distraction, I hope to catch their front line unaware. They may well all contact it at the same time."

Crystalyn's stomach churned from her symbol use, and already the wide back of the warhorse had begun to cramp her thigh muscles from her instinctive reaction to maintain a grip, however small. "How long will it hold them?" she asked.

Her mother moved closer. "Not long, I'm afraid. Soon, they will work their way around it. We should go. Kara and you have drained yourselves with such powerful using. I am growing to that point. With Durandas and Lore Rayna leading the refugees, there is no one to cover us."

Hastel sheathed his axes in one fluid motion. "You have what little help I can provide."

Sureen smiled. "You do not give yourself enough credit, innkeeper."

The glow vanished from Kara Laurel's hand as she drooped forward in the saddle, the reins falling slack under the warhorse's long black jaw.

Crystalyn wrapped her arms around the woman. "She's lost consciousness. Hand me the reins, Mom."

Sureen froze, looking up at her in surprise for a heartbeat. Then she passed the reins to her, her green eyes moist. "She needs a healer."

Crystalyn turned the big black horse toward the fleeing refugees, feeling its powerful muscles as it tossed its head. "I'll find Lore Rayna and see if she can do a minor strength infusion while slowing the blood loss until I can heal her completely. Then we need to go to the front and come by a plan for the refugees. Blindly running will get them all killed. Can you three catch up?" she asked. The growing group of Valens and humans, mostly druids, still had some ways to go before converging on the narrow southern pass leading out of the once Vibrant Vale.

*"Broth, find Lore Rayna. Lead me to her quickly!"*

"Do not burden yourself with concern for us, we shall follow in good time," the Lore Mother said. She slapped the horse on its rear haunch. The black stallion galloped away, throwing Crystalyn back from the saddle. She barely had the strength to hold on. Atoi ran beside her.

Broth leapt ahead. *"Follow, my Do'brieni. The Vale people's scent is like no other."*

Glancing over her shoulder as long as she dared, Crystalyn watched the Lore Mother's eyes blaze bright as she and her *mother* turned to face the advancing army, the top of her mother's staff already aglow with a golden radiance.

Hastel pulled his crossbow from his back. Lore Rayna's longbow would reach farther had she been there, but the one-eyed warrior would do what he could to protect the two. Perhaps he had some of his exploding arrow-tipped flasks left to use. The damage those caused was comparable to her symbols. She could only hope.

Crystalyn returned her attention to guiding the big warhorse. His gallop was strong and powerful. Even so, her anxiety elevated for the Vale and her friends, making her want her meds.

It took all her self-restraint to not look back and see how they fared. Now that she'd found her mom, Crystalyn struggled with leaving her behind. *What had she been doing for so many seasons?*

Though her mother didn't know it yet, she was going to help her get Jade back. Along with anyone else she could scrape together, refugee or not, providing anyone escaped from the thickening smoke of the Vale.

# RUBY GLIMMER

The sand swirled. Darwin glimpsed the outline of a dark arched opening now and then through the dust and minuscule grains of red sandstone rock twisting in front of it. A whirlwind of gravel and powdered rock blocked the way to the hole in the rock.

The Red Rock woman, Railee, stood with the reins of her horse in her hands. A black silk cloth swathed her head and face. Only the deep gray pools of her eyes were exposed. Her admission of her race soon after mounting for the expedition had not surprised him. Though it was a common belief Red Rock people were red of skin, he knew better than to heed the words of commoners.

Still, Railee's complexion was light, odd in a desert environment where uncovered skin tanned a deep brown or darkened to a deep red, or worse, a searing bright red.

Whatever the color of her skin, the Red Rock woman had led them to this unpleasant impasse. He was not pleased. Even though she had taken care of his baser needs thrice on the three-week journey through the blasted desert, he would not hesitate to destroy her if she thought to deceive him. "What is this, woman? Why have you not mentioned we would encounter such a prominent barrier?"

"Your displeasure shows by calling me woman instead of using my given name," Railee said. Not looking at him, she hurried on as if afraid of raising his ire. "The wind door requires great strength with the Flow. Do you wish it opened?"

"Do not think to test my patience, woman. I have not endured such heat merely to gawk at the destination. Proceed."

The desert warrior woman eyed him, a frown marring her smooth face briefly. "The wind door is two-handed. How the wind door came to be this way is beyond our knowledge. No one, not even a Servant of Eons—one of the Infused—can say why the Ancients created it so."

Her words strengthened his interest. "Go on."

"The wind door not only requires sufficient strength of the Flow, it demands two hands at the same time. Two *right* hands or two *left*. Whichever is used, it must be the dominant hand."

"Obviously, my right hand has the strength. You, too, use yours for the sword. Together, we will open it."

Railee gave him a bold stare. "There is one other thing."

"What is it?"

"The door requires those seeking entrance to share an affinity for each other. You killed Bronz, my life mate, the one who mingled the Flow by my side. Yet, now I hold allure for you. Do you have this for me?"

"Yes, yes, let's go inside. I've waited long enough."

From behind, Malkor barked his raspy laugh full of disdain. "You have forgotten you address a great lord, woman. Such questions have no place falling upon a Dark lord's ears. I shall have you beaten for it."

Darwin's ire matched his impatience. "You will do what I command, nothing else. Perhaps I shall have your bared backside strapped for not recalling it. Now, go find Long Sand, inform him you are going to lead the way inside once we have cleared it. He is to bring up the rear."

Malkor's bow was abrupt. "I shall do as my lord commands,"

he said.

Darwin turned his back to him. Even angry, Malkor would do as instructed. His servant had remained loyal for his lifetime; he had spoken much worse to the red robe. "What is required from us to open the wind door?" he asked, keeping his tone milder than he had when speaking with his servant.

"Stay as you are, and I shall show you." Backing suggestively up against him, she held her right hand out, palm up. "Clasp my right hand with yours; try to put your left at my waist. We'll have to try it that way."

Ignoring the pain of moving his left arm so far outward from his stomach, he succeeded in awkwardly putting it on her lower stomach. "I can draw from the Flow in this position," he said.

She nodded, rustling against him. Her left hand rose to slip under his. "Once we begin, we cannot stop or we die. If our affection for each other is not prominent, one or both of us may perish. Are you prepared to try?"

The firmness of her body pressing against him, the scent of her, stirred his desire even in the blistering heat of midday. He had the suspicion the woman intended it all along. "Show me what to do," he said hoarsely, his voice drier than he liked.

Much stronger than he had expected, Railee drew from the Flow, pulling deeply, a stream of white interlaced with light yellows. As Darwin added his black torrent inside her conduit, it entwined around hers, and her Flow wrapped around his, flowing upward; they formed a radiant twisted pair. Their interlocked right hands burst into an interwoven ball of black and white twice the normal size of someone using the Flow.

Two interwoven bands of the Flow flowed forth from their hands, striking the bottom of the whirlwind, and again moved upward. The height and width of a small doorway, the ribbon of the Flow held the maelstrom at bay. Though it churned, the whirlwind vanished into the wide band and then reappeared, coming out of the other side and continuing its destructive path.

Slipping past his crippled arm, Railee tugged on his good hand. "Let's go. Our streamers won't last long. Don't let go until we're through," she cautioned.

Darwin stopped, halting her forward momentum. "Will it close when we pass through?"

"Yes. Our allure for each other is not as entwined as I had hoped. We have to go now."

"No! There is Guail and the clan. They cannot remain outside."

Railee swallowed. "Then we wait and hope our…your desire for me grows over the next month! If we fail once, it will not open again."

Darwin glanced at the hole. Dust sifted out from within it, getting denser as he looked.

"Do not trust her, Master! Let us wait and go together," Malkor said from behind. A quick glance revealed his manservant stood not far away. Punishment for his insubordination would come later. "Malkor, you go first, now!" he shouted.

"No, we haven't the strength for another!" Railee screamed.

Dashing without caution into the roiling darkness, Malkor vanished, leaving a last glimpse of his red robe billowing out behind him.

Releasing his hand, Railee tried to pull away, but he kept his grip, squeezing tighter. Striding past her, he hunched over and pulled her inside. The translucent white of her Flow illuminated the way. Twisting vertical at first and then horizontally, it spiraled through the whirlwind holding the raging whirlwind above and to the sides at bay, though not for long. Already he had to shuffle sideways or risk touching the Flow, which would likely unravel it.

Bending farther, he moved as fast as he could, his back

protesting with twinges of pain. He couldn't crawl and maintain his grip on her hand. His mangled arm assured that.

Railee resisted, the pull on his good arm growing stronger.

Ahead, an absence of the roiling chaos spinning around them beyond the twisting barrier of the Flow indicated they'd reached midpoint. Bending yet farther, putting heavy strain on his ankles, he staggered into the eye of the maelstrom, pulling Railee with him.

The light from the Flow winked out, plunging them into semi-darkness. Rock and gravel colliding within the fury of the whirlwind sent tracers of brilliant multicolored light flashing by in long lines.

Darwin let go of Railee's hand and straightened. Gently, he slipped his palm under her chin and urged her to stand. Once she had, she wrapped her arms around him fiercely and cried. Her low sobs were loud with the deathly quiet inside the storm. Pressing her close, his good hand rubbed the small of her back.

After a time, Railee loosened her grip, pushing back a little to look him in the eyes. "Do you not know what you have done? The wind door does not move away, it be tethered to this precise spot. You have doomed us to die the lingering death of thirsting. We have a scant few days at most."

Darwin glanced around, avoiding looking at one spot too long. The whirling lines were hypnotic. "Do you think Malkor made it through?"

Railee shuddered, her small firm stomach quivering beneath his arm. "I am uncertain. Methinks he may not have had the time." Pressing back into him, she shuddered again.

Despite their predicament and the probable loss of a friend and servant, his body responded to the innocence of the move. So did his thoughts. She was at her prime, lean and strong, the most desirable to him. He shook his head to clear it. "There must be another way. Surely the Servants of Eons come and go; a door may open at any time."

Railee shook her head, even before he stopped speaking. "The servants are solitary. Even so, should a wind door be opened, we wouldn't know of it. Each one is attuned to those who have an attachment to each other, they could pass through us, and we would never know."

She slumped against him, her dejection evident with her quivering. All of a sudden, he wanted her, *had* to have her. "As long as we are alone and going to die a slow death, we should make use of our togetherness. We may not have the energy later."

"A single jump into the stormy abyss will end the threat; we do not have to wait." Railee looked toward the churning whirlwind, but she made no move to walk way. Her hands slid to his hips.

He kissed her then. She responded by opening her mouth and pressing her lips to his. He tasted the saltiness of her tears. He pressed hard against her. The allure of her was strong…he broke off the kiss and clutched her hand. "Open the wind door, let's do it again while we're so close!"

"My energy is gone! It took all I had the first time, I am sorry."

"Open it now or I combat it with as much Flow as I can gather."

Railee shook her head sadly, such a lovely move in itself. "Do that and it will destroy you; your Flow will be sucked from you at an uncontrollable rate. You will become a pillar of Flow, burning as a bright dark flame until consumed," she said softly, desirably.

His need ascended a notch. "Then help me. What do we have to lose? We die here or we die trying to escape. Which is it, Railee?"

Squeezing his hand with a firmness that surprised him, Railee opened a conduit.

Using the path she provided, he joined her, pulling in the

sweet succulence of the Flow. Coated with an ever-deepening blackness, he drew it in. Weaving through white until entwined, the coupled Flow raced through him as it flew through Railee and gathered at their outraised, embraced hands. He'd never known such power, not the first time they had come together to open the wind door, not in his whole life. He exulted in it. *This* was true power. *This* was what he had spent his life searching for, unimaginable strength. *This* was where he was most alive, brimming with the great power of the Flow.

He wanted to draw it all in, always more. He would pillar if he did. "Now, Railee! Release the power, open the wind door!"

Railee complied. Twisting from their hands, the Flow ribbon climbed a story high in the maelstrom, parted it, and held it at bay.

"Run!" Railee screamed.

Slipping his arm around her waist, he ran.

Though it was awkward with their hips touching, they made better time, as if they leapt along a floor in some macabre dance.

Keeping the door open was harder, this time. The Flow streamed from his body reservoir at alarming rate, nearly draining him before going far. Forced to slow, he drew deeply from the river of power. The ceiling dropped steadily closer.

Siphoning from the river, Railee slowed notably.

Darwin pulled her along, pushing with the strength of adrenaline. "Keep moving!"

Ahead, light beckoned.

Bouncing against each other, oftentimes painfully, like a pair of drunken seafarers trying to catch a departing ship, they ran. The light became brighter as the ceiling shrank closer. As one, they bent over and fought for some little speed.

Light bloomed all about, exploding into the shrinking tunnel before them.

The Flow bled from Darwin, dwindling like smoke through

his fingers. "Jump!" he yelled.

The tunnel gave way to a red stone floor.

Darwin found he lay painfully on his crippled shoulder. Droplets of blood spattered the floor below him coming from somewhere on his head, the part of him that throbbed eye-cringing pain with every new beat of his heart. After a time, the throbs subsided.

Someone rolled him over.

Malkor squatted beside him, an odd look of relief—and disappointment perhaps—on his narrow face. "My Lord, I thought you lost when the tunnel collapsed. Was the woman not strong enough?"

Offering his hand, his manservant helped him sit and then placed his hands on his head, healing him without inquiring if he needed it. Darwin did not object. He knew he did.

Railee was sitting up and fared better. Able to catch herself with both hands, she had kept her head intact, though her palms bled, and she rubbed at a shoulder.

Darwin waited for the jolt of energy that informed him the healing had neared completion. "Save enough Flow to heal the woman, she shall guide us."

Malkor reached for Railee, but she drew back. "I do not want his hands on me, and I have a name. It is not woman," she said, her voice quavering slightly with pain at the end.

Darwin made a conscious effort at keeping his voice mild, though her reaction grated on his patience. Stopping to replace bandages cost precious time. "Let him help you. It will be the only times he touches you, I promise."

Raising her knees, Railee wrapped her arms around them. "Very well, but I shall hold you to it."

Malkor dropped his arms to his waist. "If the *woman* has not the desire for healing, then I will abide by her first decision." He stepped back, his hands going to hips.

Angry, Darwin stood quickly. A wave of weakness left from his recent restoring rocked him, making his words come harsher than he intended. "You will abide by my command, *servant*. Heal her. Or you will wish you had not healed me."

Malkor's eyes narrowed, making his narrow face seem skeletal as he lowered his head slightly. The shadows from the hood of his robe, in conjunction with the red light of the ruby glimmer shards mounted on the arched tunnel ceiling, darkened his features. "As the *master* commands the lowly servant, I shall obey," he said, his nasal voice a hiss.

Darwin waited for the initial shock of the healing, the stiffening of Railee's backbone, and then he turned his back on the pair, studying the way forward. Bored round the height of two men, the tunnel cut through the red sandstone for some distance where a darker opening indicated the presence of a larger area.

Malkor shuffled beside him, the drag of his shattered leg more pronounced. "It is done," he said, his voice waning at the last word. He sounded and looked tired.

Darwin imagined two heals had taken a lot, even from him. "You have done well, my loyal companion. Let us continue. Railee, will you guide us?"

The Red Rock warrior woman swept past. "Follow me," she said, her hips swinging with a pleasant renewed vigor.

Darwin was pleased. The destination loomed within reach, adding energy to his step from the mere thought of it. Railee, too, must have felt his exuberance or had some of her own. She set a quick pace, the light of the ruby glimmer shards making it seem as if they strode into the throat of a great sea monster.

Malkor shuffled behind, his one good footstep slapping the stone and the other scraping the sandstone behind him.

Darwin hoped his companion and manservant could keep

up. He did not want to have to come back for him once he acquired what he had come for.

# HER SERVICE

The rounded tunnel ended at a room created from an underground fast-moving stream that raged beside the slippery path of its older passage. The water vanished at the far end of a cavern the size of two pavilions. Lifting the strap over his head, Darwin removed his empty kell flask from under his black robe.

Railee put her hand on his wrist. "Not here, one slip would prove fatal. Such water will sweep one away in an instant."

"I am well aware of the consequences of falling," he snapped and then regretted his quick words when she jerked her hand away, as if shocked by the touch of him. He softened his voice. "I'm willing to take the risk, my servant requires it."

Railee glanced back the way they had traveled. "I appreciate his healing, but we are safe inside Slick Rock Caverns now. Should you choose so, your servant may wait at the cisterns in the next room. I will see he has sustenance brought to him as we leave the caverns and enter Red Rock."

Darwin pretended to consider. They were so close. Losing her guidance now could ruin it all. "I shall wait for easier access as you suggest. However, you should know, Malkor has other uses beyond healing. I desire him to remain with us for a while longer," he finally replied. He kept his voice low, though loud enough for hearing over the din of the fast-moving water. Malkor made his careful way along the slippery path to them.

Railee frowned but held her tongue as Malkor shuffled to them. Once he came close, she led the way though a rough-edged door that opened upon a carved cavern thick with humidity and heat. There, she paused, allowing a view of the room.

Twenty rectangular cisterns lined one wall. Sloped troughs flowed with switchback formations to seven pools on the opposite side. Brown- and white-skinned, the people of Slick Rock Caverns wore soft cloths or nothing as they sat about conversing or soaked in the pools. Only the first two of the seven tarns were empty, the water dark and pungent, and the flow from the troughs feeding them was but a trickle. Their guide continued past.

Climbing a set of three stairs at the third, Railee stopped upon a carved landing. Pulling her flask over her head by the strap, she thumbed open the stopper, letting it fall and hang by the string attached to the carved wooden pin fastened to the top.

Darwin dipped his flask in the streaming water before it burbled into the trough. Filling it, he drank slowly and in silence, following Railee's deliberate example.

Malkor paused with them, drinking noisily. Afterward, he splashed water onto his face and poured it over his head, letting it run down his back, soaking his red robes. A puddle of water formed at his feet.

Glancing behind them, Railee stoppered her flask and flung it over her shoulder. "We should move on."

Darwin agreed. A crowd had gathered. "What do they wish of us?" he asked, tilting his head toward the crowd.

Railee motioned for the Slick Rock Caverns people to continue with their bathing. Most of the throng dispersed, albeit reluctantly. "Wasting water here, even a single drop, is considered sinful and is a serious offense." Without waiting for a reply, she descended to the walkway. To the right and left, bored tunnels led deeper within the rock.

Darwin scowled at his longtime companion. "Stay vigilant, fool; their customs are not the same." He gestured for Malkor to go ahead so he could watch him. His manservant's progress was better; his limp appeared less pronounced, though his ruined leg would always slow him.

Their guide allowed them to catch up when she stopped to speak to two sheer-clothed women and a man. All three glowered at Malkor as he limped closer. "Please send someone. He will know what to do," Railee was saying when they came within hearing.

Malkor frowned. "Who will know?" he asked.

Ignoring the question, Railee set off for the end of the cavern, striding faster this time. Impatient with Malkor's hobbling, Darwin passed him, closing the distance to the Red Rock woman as she strode underneath an open-walled archway and into the blazing sun of midday. High cliffs of brown granite rose above the red sandstone on the three sides adjoining it, curving dome-like toward the center.

Darwin gaped. Cultivated fields spread wide before them. Wheat swayed gently there. In another, rows of vegetables sloped slightly downhill from the sandstone cliff, and a shaded area at the base of the granite cliff sheltered thriving fruit-bearing trees. He could hardly believe his eyes. The desert people were father advanced toward total self-sufficiency than most cultures on Astura.

Railee selected a trodden path that circumvented the fields by staying above them in the shade of the red cliff. A trough carved at the cliff base showed the simple efficiency of the irrigation in place using the underground river as the source.

Before they had traveled far, Darwin broke a sweat; the place was scorching after the coolness of the cave.

Once beyond the fields, they entered a hallway lined with statues serving as columns for a short but cavernous hallway.

Vented wooden doors hung on doorways lining both sides. The hallway ended at another huge archway. Beyond it rested an *oasis*. No other word for it would do.

Massive date palm trees, small leafed plants, and flowering cacti surrounded three pools of clear water fed from a small tributary stream coming, presumably, from the underground river on the far side. Carefully tended, the stream and the pools gleamed with granite lining, and red sand packed the ground of the paths between. Stone pots partially concealed behind plants or elaborate statues of nude or scantily clad men and women resided near at hand to water the trees and foliage.

Railee halted at the middle pool in front of a stone bench.

Joining her, Darwin glanced quickly around. No one was anywhere near that he could see; several people performed activities of some sort at the farthest pool, but that was all. He eyed his guide.

Motioning to a bench, Railee sat upon it. "Now we wait."

Darwin sat close to her. "Yet another delay? What is this? I dislike waiting, it make me…unreasonable."

Railee laughed. She rubbed her toned thigh against his. "Is that your way of saying your patience is finite?" Her fair features grew serious. "Visiting Slick Rock or Red Rock is to adhere to our ways; we are a touchy people, most notably the Servants of Eons. Shall I convince my contact to arrange a meeting?"

Darwin grew angry. "You have no direct connection to a Servant of Eons? You led me to believe you had." He reached for the Flow and then hesitated, searching her gray eyes for signs of deceit. He found none.

Malkor laughed as he shuffled up to them, though a wheeze spoiled the effect. "Your wench has been less than honest. Shall I burn her for you?"

Darwin eyed Railee in silence.

Her eyes widened. "You can't possibly be considering his offer!"

Again, Malkor laughed, rasping.

Darwin stood. "Let us hope your contact is prompt. I hate to wait."

Glancing at the path leading to the next pool beyond them, Railee bounded to her feet. "She is coming."

A woman clad with the brown kell form-fitted leather chemise and pants similar to Railee's, typical of a warrior woman in the south, strode through the palms and greenery separating the pools. Her knee-high boots protected her from cacti, and the long sword sheathed at her side rode with familiarity.

The woman's teal eyes lingered only a little on him as her contemptuous gaze quickly dismissed Malkor. She stopped in front of Railee, folded her arms under her ample bosom, and regarded the woman boldly for a long heartbeat. "Why have you sent for me, Sect Sister? What do you seek this time?"

Railee's reply came quick. "I have need of your diplomacy, Sister Sorrna. I would have you convince Naa'thon of our great and urgent need for a private rendering."

Sorrna jerked as if slapped, her arms unfolding from her stomach, and coming to rest on her hips. "You ask much yet offer nothing!"

Railee inhaled deeply, looking down at her boots. Exhaling slowly, she turned to Darwin. "I offer one liaison with him, the strongest here." She shook her head of flowing light brown hair from side to side.

Darwin frowned. "What is this you offer? What do you speak of, woman? *I* decide what *I* do, and only me."

Sorrna considered him. "He has good build, but his crippled arm brands him weak."

Railee smiled and then raised her voice. "Knock her from her feet, Darwin. Do it before she can kill you. Show my sect sister the value I have placed on you!"

Darwin was confused. "What val—"

In one fluid motion, Sorrna drew her sword and slashed at his chest.

Darwin bounded backward, the sword slicing through his black robes. Slipping his right hand through the wide gash, he pulled his long sword from its sheath on his left hip and parried her backswing, though it was a near thing.

The woman had precision, balance, and speed. All marks of a seasoned warrior, an expert with her weapon. He wasted little time drawing upon the Flow. When she lunged, he pushed her sword hard to the side with the flat of his blade, putting his weight behind it. Then, as she spun away, he kicked her in the side, staggering her farther away.

Stabbing his sword point first in the ground before him, he released his smallest squall of dark wind. A twisting blackness, not unlike the whirlwind at the entrance but on a much smaller scale, spun from him.

Twisting into Sorrna, the black squall picked her up and carried her spinning to the center of the pond. There, it slowed, unwinding gently. Hanging in stasis as she rotated to face them, Sorrna blinked once in surprise and then dropped heavily, vanishing beneath the surface still gripping her sword. A plume of water splashed high, marking her entrance.

"Blast you, we need her!" Railee cursed. Unbuckling her sword and letting it fall to the sand, she ran and dived into the water.

Malkor laughed.

Darwin gave him a sharp look.

Malkor's laughter dissolved.

Darwin picked up Railee's sword and leaned upon it beside

his own. "We still require her service, both of them, it appears," he said.

Sorrna surfaced first, inhaling deeply. Railee popped up beside her, blowing water from her mouth. Side by side, they swam to shallow water and climbed out, Sorrna's sword now secured in her sheath.

Twisting her light brown hair into a ball, Railee spat water and eyed him, her gray eyes clear. "That was not what I meant for you to show her, but it will do."

Admiring the polished red coral handgrip briefly, Darwin picked it up by the hilt and offered it to Railee. "Then she will help us?"

"Aye, she will, after you fulfill her payment demand," Railee said, taking the weapon and slipping it into the sheath with a practiced ease.

Darwin eyed Sorrna. Water dripped from her curly wheat-colored hair though she took no notice, returning his gaze openly. No flecks from seasons of heavy Flow use crossed her corneas. Yet Railee had no flecks either, and she had opened the wind door. "Name the price. My merchant will pay whatever you ask," he said.

Sorrna frowned, her eyes seeking Railee.

Railee grinned. "You are to provide the payment."

Now Darwin frowned. "What does she require from me?"

"Your seed," Railee said matter-of-factly.

Darwin gaped at them both. Finally, he asked, "When?"

"Now," Railee replied. "Payment has to be made in full before we can go farther. Do you agree to fulfill this service?"

Malkor cackled, long and loud. "I pay my master's debts."

Neither woman acknowledged the comment.

Darwin looked to his servant, gesturing at a nearby clump of foliage surrounding a large tree. "Go behind that palm until I call for you."

Malkor's mirth faded. "As you command," he said, executing a stiff bow. Scowling, he walked away.

Railee moved to block Malkor's view, turning her back to him.

Her smooth brown-skinned face devoid of expression, Sorrna sat on the bench, removed her boots, shimmied out of her wet kell leather from her waist down, and then lay back.

Not caring how rough he was, Darwin paid for her service quickly. His patience had worn thin; too much delay had occurred as it was.

# RENDERING

Sorrna paused at a set of double wooden doors reinforced with wide bands of beaten black iron on the top, bottom, and center. Mounted on the center one, the doublewide band had plenty of support for the twist handle. "Await my return," she said, the tone of her voice imperious. Slipping through the door on the right, she left without a backward glance.

Perhaps she had sensed his impatience since leaving the pools and following her deep into the maze of hallways and stairways, passing through an endless array of empty stone-benched rooms before finally leading them here. He had come to believe the circuitous route intentional to confuse memory of the way.

Darwin refrained from counting the passing seconds. *It shall only lengthen the delay,* he told himself.

When Railee sat gracefully on the smooth sandstone floor—the color of blood not yet dried—he lowered his body near her awkwardly, using his good arm. She was an enigma to him. He thought she had fallen for him, but her callous act of giving him to Sorrna made him wonder. That and she made no move to come closer. Perhaps she stayed with him only from the fact he had given her no choice.

He could not stay long on the floor; the coolness of it leached into his bones, while its hardness softened his buttocks, making them less of a cushion for his spine and causing his back to ache. He stood. The door to the room swung slowly open.

Sorrna poked her head and shoulders out from the doorway. "Follow my example, and bow to each of the Twelve. Failure to demonstrate subservience shall result in ejection from the Cavern of Ages."

Darwin glanced at his companions, his eyes lingering briefly upon Malkor. "Ruining this meeting is to die here with me." No one met his eye, though Sorrna's long lashes fluttered as she turned and led the way inside.

Though it was no match for the Gap of Thundering Darkness at the Dark Citadel or even the wash and bathing pools there, the cavern dwarfed him with immensity. The abundant white crystals that stabbed upward, downward, and outward from the curved walls for several stories were impressive. It was as if he walked through a giant geode.

Infused glimmer shards placed with a deft hand reflected light from the crystals dispersing luminance about the great dome with perfect brilliance. Only the backsides of the towering obelisk-shaped clusters of crystals remained in shadow.

A rough-cut path led to the center, though not to a crystal as he expected but to an object. He counted twelve red-robed figures surrounding it. Darwin glimpsed a great dark cube as the figures turned, those in the back moving to the front and sides, packing shoulder to shoulder between two mammoth crystal clusters on each side.

Sorrna stopped a short distance away and bowed to each of the figures. Railee took over as soon as her sect sister did, bending at the waist with elegant ease. Malkor watched him, waiting. Darwin thought about it. The bloody Servants of Eons should bow to *him*.

He could make them. In all likelihood, he had the superior

strength. Perhaps. The servants were a secretive lot; there was little common knowledge of their inner workings, and the Red Rock people had thus far shown some manipulation of the Flow.

Coming this far, only to lose what he came for, was unacceptable.

Darwin bowed to each one as quick as possible, his moments jerky from long disuse. He ensured Malkor did the same with a wave of his good hand.

The wall of red robes parted, allowing a thirteenth hooded figure to step through, and then closed ranks. Three dominant colors graced the robe, black on one side, red on the other, and gold centered between. The figure kept the tri-colored hood lowered, like the others.

"I have brought them as you requested, Lore Master Naa'thon. Do you wish a private audience?" Sorrna asked. The tone of her voice was hushed with reverence.

The three-colored hood rose imperceptibly. "You of the Red Rock sect shall await their return." The low hiss of the voice that drifted from beyond the hood had the creak of age, as if the door to an ancient ruin was pried open for the first time in an age.

The sect sisters left without comment.

The red-robed wall parted. Naa'thon's long-sleeved arm rose, pointing to the gaping hole left by the red robes, offering the way forward.

Though Darwin's excitement arose with the destination so close, he knew a moment's hesitation. A power emanated ahead, a power like no other; it called to him and repelled him at the same time.

He squashed his trepidation and stepped forward. Power was what he came here for, though of a different sort. Power was all he truly desired, had always wanted. Power would ensure he destroyed those responsible for shattering his arm, his perfect body, his manhood.

He strode boldly into the blackness, passing through a line of obelisks larger than the topaz gateway with barely an acknowledgment shunted to the back of his mind. A crystal cube, nearly as tall as he, pulsed brightly a dark red and then faded to murky darkness, brightening to a radiant glow a heartbeat later. Malkor stepped through followed by Naa'thon, and the wall of robes closed behind.

"Behold the Lore Stone," Naa'thon said. The tone of his voice resonated with power, power matching the stone. "You are granted a sole request for knowledge from the Rock of Eons for the following seventeen seasons. Afterward, you may fulfill a service deemed worthy, though considerably harder than first use. Have you an inquiry prepared?"

Darwin looked deep into the stone. Countless capillaries filled with a radiant redness from a large sphere were embedded in the center. The cube grew brighter as the substance reached the tips. He opened his mouth to ask his heart's desire, which had burned black and festering within him from the vile day Lord Charn had nearly killed him. What artifact did he require to ensure his dominion over the Dark Citadel, what power would he need to become the greatest, the great lord of all?

He closed his mouth before uttering a word. Once asked, he could not inquire again for seventeen seasons. Even if the request was granted now, a need would surface again. A question on retaining such power would soon rise. Inevitably, someone would challenge him.

Such a binding was unacceptable. There might be another way, a method to bring the knowledge along for seasons with no limitation for his queries. "I would ask how to instill in my manservant, Malkor, the knowledge of a lore master?"

The Lore Stone brightened and stayed bright.

Naa'thon's red hood swung toward him. Darwin thought he viewed a flash of amber hourglass eyes as the lore master did so, but he could not be certain. "Your wisdom in asking this question is worthy of the Lore Stone, though surprising for one seeking only one goal. Your manservant would have to undergo a rendering is the answer."

Malkor's strangled choke was loud. Darwin ignored it. "Will you perform such a deed?"

Naa'thon's deep hood swung slowly from side to side. "Your inquiry is spent. You may ask again after seventeen seasons have passed, providing your service is sufficient."

Darwin's anger erupted. "I *cannot* wait, I *shall not!* Either you tell me or all here can consider this cavern a tomb." He drew deeply upon the Flow, pulling in as much of the dark sweet substance as he could stand. The wall of red robes turned as one and faced them.

"Wait!" Malkor's nasal shout echoed loud throughout the cavernous rock, reverberating back and forth from crystal to crystal. "Tell me how to perform a rendering as a lore master, what service do I have to achieve?"

Naa'thon's red hood fell forward slightly as his shoulders slumped. "Once initiated, such a thing cannot be halted. Is your certainty with this course of action absolute?"

"It is. Bring whomever you wish for me to service, and then render me a lore master," Malkor said his voice a sneer. "My master has no time to waste."

Naa'thon hesitated. "You have the power of healing strength, yet the rendering cannot be healed," he finally said, his dry and hollow voice echoing as if from afar.

"I have no concern to heal, get on with it," Malkor snapped.

Naa'thon motioned toward the wall of bodies. Two red robes stepped forward. "The service requirement is higher for a rendering than any other; it is paid with the blood of those making the request." Grabbing Malkor by his shoulders, the two robes pinned his arms behind his back and forced him to his knees beside the stone. Naa'thon produced a stiletto rounded to a sharp point.

"What is this?" Malkor squeaked, struggling.

"What do you think to do?" Darwin asked. "I shall not permit his death by your hands."

Naa'thon's deep voice boomed throughout the cavern, belying his great age. "Interfere and he dies!"

Malkor looked over his shoulder, his brown eyes wild. "Master, do not allow this!"

With speed and precision, Naa'thon pulled Malkor's head back by his stringy brown hair and stabbed the point of the round blade into the center of his forehead. He removed the stiletto nearly as quickly as he had supplanted it. Malkor screamed as blood gushed from the round hole; the two red robes forced his head to the stone. As soon as his forehead made contact with the crystal, Malkor stiffened, growing quiet.

Darwin was enamored; the bloodstone stored power, immense power, and it stained his mind with the reek of it. He lifted his good arm and reached for the radiant, pulsating cube.

"I would not advise such an action," Naa'thon said softly. "Without a direct pathway to the mind, the Lore Stone will create one in the flesh through first contact for the rendering, always much larger than it requires."

Darwin lowered his hand. Even the two red robes had stepped back.

Though his head never moved, a tremendous spasm passed through Malkor.

"Is he going to survive the rendering?" Darwin asked, curious.

Reaching up with both hands, Naa'thon pulled his hood back, letting it fall to his shoulders. Patchy, nearly transparent, skin held a skull expanded grotesquely wide and elongated to the back. Eyes of blood red gazed from a slightly sunken face of great seasons. "As you can now view with your own eyes, most have not the mental capacities to accept what the Lore Stone shall bestow upon them. If his mind is strong and adaptable, he may live for an age beyond everyone he now knows."

Darwin quashed his inner alarm for his servant and friend.

# LOSS OF STEEDS

His great sword slick from the sweat of his palm and blood splatters, Garn tossed it from his bloody right hand toward his left. Spinning, he grabbed the familiar handle as it hung in the air and followed through with his *Bear Swipes Deer* stance, using the momentum of his spin and the sword form's downward slash design to cut into the beetle's carapace. His arm sank in the creature's oily black blood, splashing over his arm to the elbow. He gave a silent curse, wiping his free hand on his leg, though he'd covered it with the vile substance from his previous wipes. The boulder beetles tended to fountain when their hard shells were penetrated.

"Back up Garn, everyone!" General Karnas bellowed. "He seems capable of killing the blasted things without wearing himself down to a pair of dangling, useless arms. Most of you carry swords, not hammers, follow his example!"

Screeching, sounding as if two rocks had scraped together, a huge beetle barreled toward a soldier chopping at a beetle. Its mandibles opening and closing in anticipation, the big beetle came at the man from the back.

Jumping ahead, Garn cut the pincers from the thing with two quick strokes, keeping his sword well away from the scissor-like claws. He'd seen the mandibles slice through armor with ease. Without them, the creatures could only knock someone over and attempt to flatten them under their weight, which was unlikely as lumbering as they were. Most of the men wore plate armor that *should* withstand the smaller ones' bulk.

Garn let it go. Careening through its mates; it knocked them side to side, upending a half- dozen as it headed straight for the burial cairn Jade had climbed when the beetles had attacked. Captain Bozlun stood beside her, perhaps as protection, yet the bloody fool still had his scimitar sheathed.

Most of the beetles, even those assailing him, reversed direction, spreading out behind the big beetle, moving toward the cairn.

A sea of swaying blacktop boulders stood between him and his daughter. *Blast me! Why wasn't I watching how far I was getting from her?*

Garn leapt upon the top shell of a beetle and then jumped to another as soon as his boot made contact. In two strides, he was dashing across the bubbling black sea, using beetle shells as stepping-stones. Adrenaline rose with fear. He wasn't going to get there first.

A rock slammed into the lead beetle.

A quick glance showed him Jade had thrown it as she launched another. *Good girl*, Garn thought, pumping his legs harder. *I need more time.*

The huge beetle suddenly veered, taking the crowd south with it.

With a few additional jumps, Garn landed at the base of the cairn. He scrambled to the top, heedless of the sharp clatters of sliding rock as he spun to face the enemy at the cairn's top, keeping Jade behind him.

Captain Bozlun moved to the edge, away from him. "They return to their lairs."

Garn took no chance. Though their spidery legs carried them

away at a fair pace, they could change direction at any time. He kept his sword raised until the last of the boulder beetles vanished inside the dark holes scattered on both sides of the narrow pass. Only then did he slip it into the sheath at his back.

Dropping the rock she held, Jade moved to his side. "You were amazing," she said, her voice low.

Even so, Garn shot a glance at Captain Bozlun. Though the man seemed absorbed with watching the pass, he kept their subterfuge, speaking at a normal tone. "My training included many sword forms designed for multiple foes."

"Well, the beetles certainly qualified as multiple." Jade spoke normally.

Garn was proud how fast she caught on. "I must commend you, my lady. Throwing those rocks was quick thinking."

Jade flashed a smile.

Captain Bozlun's snort of disdain was loud. "One has to wonder why those you protect would have to make such a feeble attempt at defense. Is not a guardian's place but at his charge's side?"

Garn took a step back, putting himself between Jade and the captain. "If you wish to state something of importance, do so, or remain silent."

Captain Bozlun's brown eyes hardened. "You dare speak so to me? I am captain."

"So you are, but you are not my *captain*. I answer to your great lord."

"As long as you ride with my regiment, you ride under my direction," General Karnas said, climbing the low end of the cairn. He halted beside Garn, though he regarded his soldier. "*Captain Bozlun*, you, however, follow my command. Retain your provocations for your men, or I may choose another to carry your title. This man saved many lives."

Open-faced, the helm Captain Bozlun wore was a good fit. It remained in place as he inclined his helm forward and then back with a sharp jerk of his neck. "Noted," he muttered.

General Karnas paused. His full helm made his face unreadable. Two black steel mesh screens allowed him a wide vision, and a slit cut in the helm at the mouth permitted vocals, which gave the illusion of interacting with a machine. Yet the general carried the air of living command, which exuded partly from the helm's blankness, from the *look* of no expression whenever the black metallic eyes fell upon him. Garn imagined the dark polished steel had its original design intended for such a purpose. "Adhere to your duty. Gather a report of the men and horses lost, organize the burial," the general added.

Again, Captain Bozlun inclined his head, slower this time. "As the general so commands." Navigating a rocky path, he half-slid, half-strode, to the bottom and then made his way to a large group of soldiers already piling rocks on one side of the pass, creating a wide pit—the final resting place for the fallen.

General Karnas removed his helm. Close-cropped white hair topped his flat nose and sunken, but lively, light blue eyes. A groomed, silvery-gray beard added a wizened look to the man. He regarded Garn with a sweep of his eyes, avoiding looking at Jade, which he found curious.

"You fought well for a mercenary. Every other I have known fights only for a single paid service and does not work well in groups. Several of my men owe their lives to you, though they are not even aware of it," the general said, the tone of his voice and the look in his eyes speculative.

Garn watched for the minute signs of subterfuge in the man, a tic at the corner of an eye, a quick glance away and then back, perhaps a subtle rigidity in the stance. There was none. "Your soldiers owe me nothing. Battling those creatures required every man. Most were unprepared with how to accomplish a kill, however. Have they not fought them in the past?"

General Karnas strode to the top edge of the cairn, gazing upon his regiment as he spoke. "There has never been a need. Rock beetles are docile creatures, content to feed from the fungi growing on and around rocks, in damp shady areas. This type of behavior may well be a first for them, and it troubles me." Looking over a shoulder, he set a sharp eye upon him. "You, however, fought the beetles with some success. Tell me, are such attacks a common occurrence where you hail from?"

Garn met the man's gaze, recalling a job not long ago the Alchemist had taken him and the henchman Codar on, before moving into the citadel. That one had consisted of a one-way escort into the desert for the previous owner of the Old Town Coliseum's topaz gateway. That man's eyes—someone he would likely never know the name of—had been much the same color and vibrancy as General Karnas' eyes.

Codar had extinguished the spark from them on the hooded man's orders, another reason, of many, to kill the man. "Not these kind, sand beetles are quite numerous on the outskirts of Gray Dust; they are a higher threat there. They travel at greater speeds. The white ones are the deadliest," Garn replied.

General Karnas gave a slight nod. "So I've heard. All the same, the black ones are a nonaggressive species. Something drew them from their lairs…or should I say *someone*." He turned, sweeping a meaningful eye upon Jade.

Jade's round green eyes grew wide. "Me?"

Garn was surprised. "What makes you say that?"

General Karnas continued to regard her even as he replied. "They moved straight for her until we got in their way. As some died or were hit with grievous injury, they broke off the attack, charging for her once again."

Garn knew he was right, though he had to scoff it off and keep the man from asking too many questions. "Perhaps. It might be the reason the great lord wishes her taken beyond the Dark Gate, without harm. I would not think to question the great one, nor will I fail my charge." Garn spoke the latter sentence in a milder tone but with conviction.

General Karnas eyed him again and then placed his helm upon his head, sliding it over his face with a practiced ease. "No need for the stark reminder. I, too, gave my word to the great lord. She will arrive safely at the citadel, or we shall all die protecting her. For now, desert man, know that you have garnered some small measure of my gratitude."

Garn was spared a reply as a soldier trotted up, halting below the general. He wore black chain armor with no helm. "Captain Bozlun sends his report, General."

An imposing figure, General Karnas stood at ease, his gauntleted hands resting casually on the pommels of the two long swords sheathed at his hips. "Before you begin, soldier, answer this question: Has Captain Bozlun viewed the state of your report personally or has he commanded it passed on through you?"

The soldier's face paled, seeming odd for a man of his stature. Most all in the regiment of soldiers were tall and sported obvious muscle. General Karnas had chosen the best. "He directed me to you, Sir."

"I see. What are our losses then? Speak, man, don't keep me in suspense."

The soldier flushed, returning color to his skin. "Nine men and two steeds have perished, my lord."

Garn was again surprised. "Only two horses? Are you certain?"

With his dark eyes fixed on the general, the soldier ignored him.

General Karnas shifted his stance, his back gaining some rigidness. "Are you daft, man? Our friend asked a question."

The soldier jumped at the harsh words and then gave a slight bow of his head. "My apologies…friend. Horse Master Jerrol led the mounts back the way we came when the first of the boulder beetles struck."

Garn nodded. "Jerrol is to be commended. The loss of horses is a delay I cannot allow."

The soldier shifted his weight from his right to his left foot. "There is something else I detest to mention, but duty requires it."

"Out with it, man, we have much to accomplish before day's end," General Karnas commanded.

"A horse and rider are unaccounted for."

"Who?" Garn asked.

The soldier looked to the general, who waved impatiently. "Scot, Sir."

"How well do you both know him?" Garn asked.

"Less than a season, Sir, though he's performed exemplary with his duties until this point," the soldier replied with no hesitation this time.

Rage had darkened the general's features. He controlled it with difficulty. "Scot saved my life more than once. I personally chose him for several missions, though it means naught now. Desertion and cowardice is punishable by death. Send two men to bring him back, kill him if he resists. Bring me his sword either way."

The soldier bowed. "It will be done. There is one final matter, Sir, if you will. Captain Sammon died protecting the horses. Captain Bozlun wishes to salvage his plate armor."

General Karnas began his trek down from the cairn. "We shall reclaim the plate for certain, Captain Adonal, but I think you shall don it. Your new designation has a nice sound to it, does it not?" he asked, striding past the soldier. "Come with me. We go to inform Captain Bozlun that our newly promoted *Captain* Adonal is going to don plate armor. I *do* like the sound of that." The general's words drifted in the air after them.

Garn motioned Jade to join him at the edge. His daughter seemed so frightened, the shock from the revelation the beetles were hunting her apparent in the brightness of her eyes and the slight quiver to her lips. It was all he could do to restrain himself from giving her a reassuring squeeze. Someone was always watching.

They started down the mound. The regiment would be mounting soon. Though he was careful not to show it, he wasn't happy with the amount of steeds remaining in the company. It meant the number of men he had to contend with was still high, though the unexpected desertion removed three others for a time. He would've preferred to insist upon leaving men behind from the loss of steeds to ride rather than have them die.

Now he would have to find a way to kill them.

It was a distasteful part of his job with keeping Jade from the Dark Citadel. He would not allow that to happen, even if he had to let her see the cold violence he was capable of, and soon. Nightfall was coming.

# EVERYONE ALIVE

Afraid that fatigue had made her hear wrong, Crystalyn stared up at the Valen man. Sweat glistened on his hairless bare chest and arms, but his breathing was steady even though he'd run uphill to the old quarry. "Why are they withdrawing? Have they caught on to my ruse?"

Whipping his long golden hair back and forth, he shook his large narrow head. "We do not believe so, *Sarra'esiah.*"

"There's that word again. What does it mean?"

Sureen answered. "It translates roughly as 'Star Savior' in the common tongue. To the Vale people, it likely means 'savior beyond the stars.' or something similar." Her mother stood beside her, next to the fallen evergreen tree the Dark Users had broken two days ago. *Has that many days passed already?*

The adage she'd penned from medical school slipped into her mind. *Wear the right emotional mask and people will respond.* Crystalyn put on her stern instructor face. "I am no one's savior, Vale man; I cannot even get through to rescue my sister with that bloody army in the way. What do I call you?"

The Valen's blue eyes were troubled, the corners of his broad mouth pulling down as he frowned. At least, they were normal and not glowing like some underground white phosphorescent plant or something, just big. "RaCorren, *Sarra'esiah,*" he finally said.

Atoi laughed. Lying prone below the ledge overlooking the

valley, the little girl clamped a tiny hand over her mouth to keep the sound of her mocking laughter from carrying below.

Crystalyn sighed. "Fine, RaCorren. Do your scouts have any idea why the enemy hasn't chased them to the meadow below the cliff? How are we supposed to bombard them with arrows and magic if they don't go where they're supposed to go?"

RaCorren's fine eyebrows drooped with puzzlement. "The enemy withdraws, *Sarra'esiah*," he repeated.

*"Is this true Do'brieni?"*

*"The enemy has pulled back to the Vale."*

"I suppose it's possible they only wanted the Vale from the start," Hastel mused. He spoke over his shoulder, keeping his vigilant watch hidden inside the dying, but still green, branches of the fallen evergreen. "This is the second time the Vale has sustained an attack, though not like this, it cannot survive, too much has been put to the fire or blown apart. The Vibrant Vale is no more."

Concealed under the tree, Crystalyn stared at the blackened forest of the great faluns; most had burned through the night. Now within the golden evening light of spring's end and summer's beginning, the great falun trees smoldered, sending great plumes of gray smoke to blanket the land. All were hundreds of seasons old. The sight sickened her to no end, elevating her ire and impatience. Two days, and she still hadn't found a way to Jade.

Crystalyn had brought those capable of long-range retaliation to the old quarry with the hope of weakening the enemy and allowing Jade the opportunity to escape, while delaying pursuit as the refugees slipped over the mountain ridge, something the enemy may not expect. An unnecessary hardship now, it seemed.

Her anger grew alongside a frustrated sense of running out of time. Jade was in danger, lost somewhere down there. At least Durandas had someone going after her. She'd been heartened when he'd told her, though no word had come since that contacting. The First Light did not believe it safe to attempt another exchange so soon. When she caught up to the white-robed man as he led the refugees away, *that* was going to change.

Even though she knew frequent attempts ran the risk of Dark Users breaking into the contacting, perhaps implanting something vile, like the mind worm she'd cleaned from Lore Rayna; she'd done it once, she could do it again. Crystalyn shivered thinking about it. Never was too soon to have to battle one of those again, but she would if it meant reaching her sister. Why had they pulled back?

"Why destroy the Vale?" she snapped to no one in particular. "Why not overrun it and keep it as a stronghold? Was the Vale so great a threat that the Dark Citadel felt compelled to ravage it to the ground at such great expense? They've taken heavy casualties and not just in lives lost. Those burning creations must have cost a lot of the Flow to create."

"Each one drained the life from thirteen Interrupters," Kara Laurel said, the tone of her voice grim. Carefully keeping her bandaged thigh from touching the ground, she slid down the small slope to the quarry pit. Blood spotted the white gauze at the center as she picked her way forward, though none leaked down her bare leg.

As soon as they'd found Lore Rayna, Hastel had pulled the bolt from Kara Laurel's leg unceremoniously while she was unconscious. Lore Rayna had then given what healing she could. Now it was up to Crystalyn to complete the healing, but she'd been too busy causing a retreat, it seemed.

Pushing a branch out of the way with her staff, Sureen joined Kara Laurel as the woman halted near Crystalyn. "What do you know about Dark Users and their Interrupters? Where have you been, Kara?" Sureen asked without preamble.

Kara Laurel opened her mouth to speak, but Crystalyn held up a hand. "RaCorren, do you still possess the strength to carry a message?"

"My strength has not yet truly been tapped, *Sarra'esiah.* Your wish is my command."

Crystalyn quelled a sigh and swallowed her admonishment. It would serve no purpose. The Valen regarded her with obvious adoration for some reason; it shone deep inside his intelligent gaze. "Do you know where Durandas and the Lore Mother are positioned for their attack with those that can still battle?"

"I do, *Sarra*—"

Crystalyn interrupted. "Good. Tell Durandas to prepare his band of refugees to exit the Vale from the south draw. If he cannot guarantee safe passage through it, he is to send word immediately, for we will work our way down from here once you leave. After that, but only if the way is clear, send a trusted messenger to Lore Rayna and the wounded. Get them moving toward us. Can you do this?"

"Yes, *Sarra'esiah.*"

"Then go, make haste. May the One watch over you."

RaCorren bowed deeply and then vanished downhill moving faster than she would've thought possible for one of his great size who descended a steep mountain slope.

Crystalyn returned her attention to Kara Laurel. "It's time you revealed what you know about the vermin ransacking the Vale. Make it quick. We shouldn't stay here long." As much as she hated to leave the view the quarry provided, there were many people to get to safety.

Brushing at a dirt clump on her yellow skirt, Kara Laurel left it alone after she only succeeded in smudging it. "For now, I cannot say how I know; you must accept what I tell you. The attack was staged not for the decimation of the Vale people or even the great falun trees."

Atoi was suddenly beside her. "What else could they want there? The Vale people hold little wealth."

Kara Laurel went on as if she hadn't heard the little girl. "The Alchemist sent his army here for one specific purpose. He came for what was under the falun trees, under the Vale itself. He came for something below that was there tens of thousands of seasons ago when the Vale was young. *He* came for the source." Kara Laurel grew quiet, looking at her expectantly, her green eyes bright.

Slightly annoyed, Crystalyn took the prompt. "What source?"

Kara Laurel raised her chin, holding her head higher. "The source of the Flow for power Users, the Flow itself."

The quarry grew deathly quiet. Or had her heart thumping loudly in her ears blocked all hearing? Crystalyn quelled her rising anxiety with difficulty.

Kara Laurel glanced around the quarry, her gaze lingering a long moment on everyone, even Atoi. "The Alchemist has developed worms, Flow worms as he refers to them, introduced to the Flow, they feed upon it and proliferate. Eventually the Flow shall cease to exist as they multiply."

A man wearing gold bands on his large biceps and a dark hood covering his head intruded upon Crystalyn's mind, dredged from a memory she'd thought locked safely away. A conversation between the hooded man and Darwin Darkwind, her *Darwin*, clamored for attention. The worms had a weakness, one that had caused the hooded man concern. If only she could recall what it was. Sifting through the events of that dreadful day, she kept stumbling over losing the man she loved and failed to think beyond it.

Kara Laurel was watching her. "You have knowledge of this?"

Crystalyn stuffed the image of Darwin's broken body, a

distraction she couldn't afford, back into the cold dark recesses of her mind. "I know only a small part of it. The hooded man tried introducing the worms the first time the Vale survived such an attack last spring."

Sureen gasped. "You have met the Alchemist? Those who meet him do not survive."

Kara Laurel hobbled near, nodding her head full of hair. "Do you not see Crystalyn? He must not succeed this time. The Dark One believes I follow him, I have his complete confidence, but I must return before he releases the Flow worms."

Crystalyn's irritation rose. An early sign of her great anger testing the barrier of her will, she knew, but she didn't care. "Then why did you chase one of them down and incinerate him horse and all. The horse was only doing what it was trained to do, and we might've been able to take it for our own use."

Kara Laurel was shaking her head before she finished speaking, which added another spike to Crystalyn's irritation. "No. Listen carefully. I performed the hooded one's bidding to destroy the rider, and the *horse* he rode, for one urgent reason only. There is something unseen infiltrating the Alchemist's domain. It has an unnerving ability to infest a mind and gain control. No one, no corporeal *thing*, is safe. This entity appears to have the ability to infest and control the mind of anything living."

Shocked by the woman's words, Crystalyn's irritation grew from a stab of doubt. Could she destroy such evil before her own subversion? After all, her mind was already broken with hard-to-control anger, her mind affliction. Wouldn't that make it easier for the thing to take her? *NO!* She couldn't let that happen. Her mind *must* be her own, broken or not.

Kara Laurel's melodious voice broke into her reverie. "This thing is insidious and powerful. At least it was, pray that I managed to end it with the rider, though it seemed too easy. Even so, my mission has not changed. Defeating the Alchemist's dire plan is paramount to Astura. Have you sufficient strength to heal me?"

Sureen moved beside Crystalyn, their shoulders touching. She stared into Kara Laurel's eyes, her mouth tightening around the edges as she pursed her lips. "Do not trust her. There is much more she's not revealing."

The woman stared back at Crystalyn, her face smooth and her light green eyes unblinking.

"Do not forget how she repaid our aid last time, mistress," Hastel said, sliding down from the overlook.

Atoi's bejeweled dagger appeared in her hand. "Jewel ends all concerns. Let me end this one for you, mistress. How do we know she is not this evil she speaks of?"

Atoi rubbed a thumb on a brilliant ruby embedded in the bone white handle. Perhaps it truly was bone. Crystalyn almost sighed. Atoi wouldn't understand. The entity she hosted couldn't comprehend the subtle nuances of allowing one's instinct to determine the course of action. All it knew was how it could kill. Though that wasn't entirely right either, the Dark Child had shown great sophistication on several occasions. Atoi was a mystery of duality. "Put it away, it will make healing her harder. I'll let you know when to use it. Such a time is coming, I fear."

Reaching behind his back, Hastel pulled his crossbow to the front and fitted a bolt. "Healing will drain you, won't it? What's to keep her from trying something with you too weak to stop her?" he asked, raising the weapon.

Crystalyn did sigh this time. She couldn't stop herself. "Fine. Keep it pointed at her if it makes you feel better. Why do you all see her as such a threat? She's never actually done us harm."

Steady, Hastel kept the crossbow leveled. The scar across the bridge of his nose wept a little from his frown. "She's admitted to working with the hooded man."

"Listen to the warrior," Sureen said.

Crystalyn was mildly surprised. "You've heard of him also?"

Hastel's gaze flicked to Atoi and then away so fast, she wasn't entirely certain she'd seen it. "Why should that surprise you?" he asked.

Crystalyn knew a hedge when she heard one. Asking a question to avoid answering one was a tactic she'd used on many occasions, but she let it drop. A bloody Dark army was not that far away.

Imagining the silver-white symbol with its simple spider-webbed pentagram pattern brought it hovering in the air before her. "We have little choice with trust. The threat of the Flow worms is too great a risk not to take her at her word. Kara Laurel will have this one chance to show Astura where her loyalties lie."

Kara Laurel inclined her head. "You shall not regret it."

"My symbol works better if you are lying down." Having never tried it on someone upright, Crystalyn didn't know for certain, but it sounded right.

Using a branch for support, Kara Laurel eased her body to the ground, accepting Sureen's hand under her shoulder. Neither Hastel nor Atoi made a move to help the woman.

Combining the golden symbol with one she'd read under the heading dilutions in the tier one book of the *Tiered Tome of Symbols*, the symbol reformed. Intricate gold and silver lines wound back and forth filling the symbol with a hedge maze with no beginning or end. The symbol glowed faintly silver and gold in color. Crystalyn flipped the symbol horizontal over the prone woman and let it sink into her, attaching her awareness to it.

The wound was easy to find. Damaged muscle and sinew beckoned her from the muscular system immediately under Kara Laurel's skin. This time she wouldn't have to conjoin with her circulatory system. Had the crossbow bolt even so much as nicked

Kara Laurel's main artery, the woman would have bled out in mere minutes.

Once she reached the deepest point, Crystalyn fused a portion of her symbol there. Unraveling it, she began working her way back out, pulling ligaments and tying sinew together as she filled the hole with symbolic gauze. Having already begun to close over from natural healing, it filled quickly.

With only one tenth of her symbol used, she reached the top. Crystalyn let the symbol dissolve, which snapped her awareness back to her. Though she'd expected it, the speed of the transfer created havoc with her sense of self for a heartbeat or two. Her brain readjusted, and she found herself bent over Kara Laurel's leg.

Crystalyn pulled the bandage off. Only a red bruise remained, already fading. A wave of fatigue dimmed her vision for a time, long enough she grew frightened it wouldn't return. When it did, her anxiety lessened but little.

Kara Laurel had sat up. When Crystalyn sat back, the woman stood, her green eyes wide. "Your symbol magic is always a sight to see. However, I do not wish to experience it firsthand again. Your presence is so…powerful. Why do you have such great anger?"

Crystalyn didn't care for her healing showing that side of her. Having Kara Laurel curious and asking questions constantly was a scenario she didn't want.

"It's an affliction of the mind," Sureen replied, before Crystalyn could tell Kara Laurel to go on with her mission. One question from the Circle woman answered always led to many more. "She has had it since childhood," her mother added. Bending over, she examined Kara Laurel's wound briefly before straightening, and turning to Crystalyn. "Quite interesting. There is no mark visible. I do not doubt she will not have even the slightest limp. How about you my daughter, can you walk?"

Crystalyn grew irritated with her mom and then wished she

hadn't. Her head throbbed. "We don't have the leisure to sit around waiting for me to gain strength. Besides, Broth will support me, won't you, *Do'brieni?*"

Broth rose to his four paws and came close, offering his broad back. *"Lean on me, Do'brieni. Together we shall descend."*

Crystalyn draped an arm over her companion's front shoulder gratefully, rising to her feet. *"Go gently, Do'brieni, I've overtaxed myself again."*

"Are we to go then?" Atoi asked.

"Yes," Crystalyn replied.

Atoi dashed beyond the fallen evergreen, vanishing from sight.

Turning to follow, Hastel let out a great sigh. "I was going to say I'll take the lead. Instead, I'll settle for finding you the gentlest path down. Atoi will be waiting somewhere below when we get there."

Sureen waved her staff. "Go next, Kara; I shall come last and watch the hillside above."

Kara Laurel smiled briefly and then followed Hastel without comment.

Crystalyn nudged Broth to begin, but her mom gripped her shoulder, making her pause.

As soon as she gauged Kara Laurel had moved beyond hearing, her mom spoke. "I would hear your plan. What of the refugees, where are we to go with them?"

Irritated, Crystalyn shrugged out from under her mom's firm hand. "There'll be a meeting with the leaders once we've secured a place away from the Dark army. I don't trust the situation. As I asked, why retreat when they had us in a rout? Did they get word of my trap?"

Her mother frowned, which looked odd on her usually serene brow. "That would mean someone has contacted them."

Crystalyn smiled, but she had no mirth. "I imagine it would."

Her mother looked troubled, and then her brilliant green eyes, so like Jade's, hardened, unlike Jade. "Then we will flush out whoever has done such a traitorous act from our company. There are methods that may do it. Shall we begin?"

Crystalyn wondered what methods she meant, but there was a burning question foremost on her mind. "Once you've told me why you abandoned your family for so many seasons…we thought you dead."

Sureen, her mom, set the end of her staff on the ground, gripping it with both hands. Her lips thinned as her mouth tightened. She seemed resigned and saddened. "The story is long and fraught with my great dereliction. My selfishness caused many lives to have been lost, or so I was informed. Yet my decision would remain the same to this day. For now, will it suffice you to know I did not leave you willingly?"

"When you vanished from your room, Dad put all he had into finding you, forsaking everything else. He lost his indenture as head of security for the king, and worse, his health. His heart is failing. He may not live much longer."

Her mom's lips twitched, and her shoulders slumped. Then she straightened. "You must believe I never meant for him, for any of you, to have such turmoil placed upon you."

Shifting his weight a little, Broth leaned against her chest. His deep breaths pressing gently against her gave her comfort. "Didn't you care for us, for him, at all?"

Letting go of the staff with one hand, her mom reached for her. Partway there, her arm dropped her to her side. "You would not comprehend. I have done what needed doing."

"Oh, I understand enough, enough to know you weren't there during some bad times, and we grieved for you. Dad is somewhere on this world, did you know that? How long do you think it will take for his heart to fail *here?*"

Her mother's eyes widened with shock. "Then it *was* him," she breathed, her voice barely a whisper.

Crystalyn's anxiety rose steeply, though she wasn't certain why. "What are you saying?"

"I have seen him, not long ago."

Crystalyn relaxed a little. "That's a good thing. It means Dad's still alive."

Her mother shook her head slowly from side to side. "It is not what you think. The hooded man has him."

Crystalyn's anxiety rocketed. A glaring thought rolled around in her mind. *Now I have two to rescue.* How was she ever going to keep everyone alive?

# ARRANGE AN ESCAPE

General Karnas raised his dark gauntleted hand. Garn slowed, as did the men riding abreast behind him and his daughter. The general's hand fell downward, pointing toward the ground as he brought his horse to a standstill, pulling slightly on the reins with one hand. A billow of gray dust coated a thicker layer to the horse's underbelly, stirred from his black stallion's great hooves.

Stopping, Garn hopped from the back of his dark gelding, gathered the reins from Jade with his own, and then helped her dismount with a hand under her shoulder. He headed for an open spot beside the general, trampling across dry dusty plains of the foothills they'd encountered after leaving the green canopy of the mountains surrounding the Vale, a full day and night's ride beyond Broken Gap.

A dark shape halted in front of Garn, blocking his way forward. Captain Bozlun sat upon his horse. Though he spoke to General Karnas, his agate eyes fixed him with a hard stare. "Why do we stop, General? The dangers and pestilences of Bracken Lake and Serpent Gorge are close. Silent Blade is only a half bell's ride; the men could use a hot meal."

The general's harsh voice carried, coming from under the front shoulder of the great warhorse. "By men, I assume you mean yourself as well. We are going to bypass Gray Dust, have you forgotten our core command so soon? Stopping for a hot meal will only invite a night of carousing in the tavern after. Perhaps that was your intent?"

At the first words, Captain Bozlun's helm swung toward his commander. "Nay, General, but a mug of ale would not cause untoward harm. I will ensure my men stick to the rules of active patrol. No more than two mugs shall slip past their lips in one sitting."

"No ale shall pass any man's lips until our charge is safely guarded inside the great lord's chambers," General Karnas hissed. Tall and forbidding in his black palate armor, he strode toward Captain Bozlun's steed, his helm wedged under his left arm. As he strode past the great warhorse, the stallion's long tongue shot forth and licked him on the cheek. General Karnas stiffened. Then he spun on a metal-shod heel and moved back the way he'd come, his movements stilted, as if sudden cramping from too long in the saddle assailed him.

Captain Bozlun shifted in his saddle, looking after the general for a heartbeat and then behind him. "Make temporary quarters, we stop for a meal," he shouted down the line.

Garn heard a few groans, but the soldiers did as ordered. Seasoned warriors all, there were still too many to take on at the same time. Though he had a slim chance at success, he couldn't take a chance something would happen to Jade while he battled.

Hearing a town was close had caught his interest. Perhaps he could slip away with Jade and make a run for it with the hope the horses would outlast the others, providing he could get an idea which direction the town lay.

Leading both horses, Garn strode past Captain Bozlun making certain Jade stayed close to him by keeping a hand on her elbow. He was disappointed to note General Karnas striding toward an earthen mound close to the lake, his movements unbalanced. *He must need some privacy,* Garn thought. Too bad, he'd wanted to question the man about how long it would take to reach the citadel, though he'd have to exercise delicacy with how he asked. He didn't want the general getting suspicious of his motives.

Captain Bozlun rode up. "Take your mounts to the picket soldiers. They will allow them to graze on the scant grass of this hillside while they can. The land gets sparser from here."

Garn was surprised. The captain had offered information without his asking. "How long of a ride is it from here to reach the citadel?"

Captain Bozlun studied him from horseback, saying nothing for a time. Then abruptly, he dismounted. "Give the reins to me," he said, holding out his free hand. "I will take them with my own."

Garn passed them to him.

Jade reached for the halter on Captain Bozlun's horse. Nearly jerking the reins from Bozlun's gauntleted grip, the big warhorse snorted and shied away, his eyes wild.

"Here now! What's got into you?" Captain Bozlun demanded, pulling the three horses together with a strong downward tug on the three reins. Without another word, Captain Bozlun headed toward a cluster of dark-armored soldiers.

"You didn't answer my question," Garn couldn't help saying before the soldier had gotten far, though he didn't expect a reply.

Captain Bozlun stopped, turning back, his curly hair springing back into place from the sudden sharp movement. "I suspect General Karnas will lead us south to Serpent Gorge and Serpent Falls, over to Black Bottom Ferry, and then follow the edge of Bracken Lake passing under both Silent Blade and Gray Dust. The route is longer and fraught with greater creature peril, but it will avoid the lawlessness of the settled areas and possible human attack from someone trying to aid the one you guard. Yet, I loathe following such a course. Even barbarians shy away from the Serpent and the dark water it flows into; it will cost us an extra day.

Two days and three nights' ride should see us at the Black Gate…elite fighting man, providing you keep a sharp eye on your…charge." Turning, he walked away leading the three horses. One, the horse Bozlun had ridden, was too weary to hold his head up.

"What's wrong with his horse?" Jade asked softly. "The poor thing looked tired, is he older than the rest?"

"I don't believe so; the man must have ridden the animal harder than needed. I have no respect for a man who treats his horse poorly," Garn replied, watching him go and wondering at the enigma of the man. Captain Bozlun had shown respect by calling his weapon mastery elite, yet the veteran soldier had made it obvious he didn't trust him by taking his and Jade's mounts. Normally the two horses were high-strung, yet they followed as docile as sheep. Perhaps they sensed something in the man.

He gave up trying to understand and glanced around. The hillside was a flurry of activity. Soldiers led horses to sparse patches of greenery or dug holes in the hard earth with spiked hammers and thickheaded axes, while others lined the holes with rocks. Half a dozen others circled a set perimeter in pairs, working saddle cramps out of muscle while patrolling the outskirts of the thirty-soldier camp. Not all were male.

Some of the paired soldiers *were* a pair and walked simply for the short time of spending a semblance of aloneness together. Garn searched for a possible escape opportunity there but didn't see one. They were too well trained and kept their eyes upon the task.

"Three days—" Jade whispered. "I can't go back to the Dark Citadel, I won't."

Garn completed his visual inspection of the camp. No one wandered near them, though several cast looks in their direction now and then. "Did you hear the captain mention Gray Dust?"

Jade glanced his way sharply before catching herself and looking down. Good girl. Those watching would think he'd said something to make her afraid. "Yes, I did. How will that help us?"

Standing in the open was bound to draw added attention. He pressed her elbow gently in the direction of the farthest fire pit, the one closest to the horses. "Walk slowly but steadily, Jade. Gray Dust is the town I first arrived at on Astura; I know my way around it a little."

Jade glanced quickly around and then put her head down once again. "We're not going there, I heard the captain."

"They're not, but we are, as soon as I discover which direction the town is and night falls, things will happen fast, prepare for it. Be ready to gallop when I say. We have to flee by horseback. Right now, they are unaware you know how to ride a horse. I intend to take full advantage of that."

Jade flashed a quick smile and couldn't keep her deep-green eyes from shining briefly, so alike her mother's that the sharp pangs of grief and guilt tightened his chest. Whatever it took, he would make good with his promise to his daughter, unlike how he'd failed to protect Sureen.

On his knees, blowing the flame higher inside a nest of sticks and dried grass, the cook looked up when they halted at the fire pit closest to the horse picket line. Flint and a small piece of steel lay on the ground beside him.

Garn bent over a pile of kindling beside the pit and added tiny sticks to the flame, advancing its height slowly. The cook, a soldier Garn recognized as handling himself well during the fight with the rock beetles, grunted appreciatively and dragged a pair of saddlebags closer. Opening the largest, he removed its sole content, a wide black pot that he filled to the brim with water from two leather flasks.

When the flames leapt higher, Jade added a few wrist-thick

branches, and the fire blazed, crackling with exuberance. Her survival skills had improved. Garn was surprised, though he shouldn't have been. She'd had to survive on Astura for months; they all had. Training her a little at the farm back on Terra had helped, though he still didn't know where he'd developed the skills himself. Not even the scientists had claimed a working knowledge of it, only reading about it. He missed those days.

When the flames lessened, the cook set the pot in the pit, letting the steel handle fall away from the flames and bang against the side. "It won't be long now, less than a bell for the water to simmer and heat up the stew. Why don't you two stretch your legs around camp? I'll call you first when it's ready," the soldier said. He sat a tee-handled hook, made to lift the cook pot for safe turning, on a bag and rummaged through another.

Garn motioned to Jade, and they strolled the perimeter passing close by groups of dark-armored soldiers clustered around the horses, standing together in twos or threes or keeping watch alone, staring outward at a certain area. He hoped to overhear the larger groups' conversations as they walked and perhaps get an idea about the direction Gray Dust lay from where they were.

He was sorely disappointed. The moment they came within hearing distance, conversation stopped, continuing again after they passed. Completing a full circuit and starting a second, Garn kept his voice low; the presence of the lake had given him an idea. "Prepare to mount quickly, Jade, the time to make our move may come sooner than expected."

Jade nodded, though fear scrunched her auburn brows briefly. "Will you have to kill?" she asked quietly.

Garn almost glanced at her. "Only if I must."

"Where did you learn to fight, Dad? After watching you with those beetles, I'm not at all certain Camoe is a match for you, and he's the best fighter I know. Crystalyn has said Hastel is good too, and I believe her."

Garn felt like smiling but refrained. How had it come to discussing battle prowess with his youngest daughter? Something else occurred to him. "I've not met them, though I am certain I will. Are they someone you girls are mixed up with romantically?"

Jade's face paled. "By the Great Father, no! Camoe is older than you are, I think. Hastel is a scarred and bitter fellow. He follows Atoi around as her self-appointed protector."

"Atoi?"

"She's a little girl, perhaps ten seasons…but not. You've never met anyone like her I'm sure. Crystalyn will tell you all about her."

They were nearing another group of soldiers. "We'll talk as soon as I get you out of here. For now, let's gather information."

This time the soldiers ignored them, going about their conversations as if the two of them had lost flesh and bones and floated by without corporeal substance.

A tall man with long brown hair had his back to them, but his hands moved with constant gestures. "I tell you Rall, Gray Dust has a master infuser now. Jard had dwelled there for some time working the glimmer shards, infusing them with the Flow, and he's gotten better." Garn slowed. Two names caught his attention—the town and the infuser.

"Jard is old, it takes strength to infuse something beyond a glimmer shard," a narrow-faced soldier scoffed. "Infusers master that level of infusion by middle adulthood or they never do."

"Do you not know where the general got his sword infused? No? Well, if he lets us ferry to town, I'll show you." The soldier turned, staring off in one direction. "I imagine he'll stop there like we did on our way to the Vale. Besides, the town's in the way of our going to the citadel. What would he have us do, wind our way along the blasted Serpent Gorge and follow the lakeshore after? It's too long and too risky."

They moved beyond hearing, but Garn didn't mind. He now knew which direction the town lay and where they were going. East.

Now all he had to do was arrange an escape.

# BIG SISTER

Storming around the small fire centered inside the little grove of aspens, Crystalyn glared at the Lore Mother and then swept a lingering gaze across Durandas for good measure. "What do you mean she's out of our reach? How *dare* you say that to me?"

Durandas winced. "The wright dropped your sister at the enemy's camp. A regiment of the Alchemist's men are now taking her to the Dark Citadel."

Crystalyn threw a scathing look at the white-robed man. "Then why are we still here? Point me to the closest gateway, I'll visit this Alchemist at the Citadel in person and convince him to return Jade."

The Lore Mother frowned; her fine white brows scrunched together, her aged hands going to her hips. "You cannot go around strong-arming everyone on the planet."

Donning her empress mask, Crystalyn smoothed her face. *Wear the right emotional mask and people will respond.* How easily the litany came to her lately. "I'll ask nicely, at first. If he's disagreeable, I'll change his mind, quickly."

The Lore Mother sniffed. "Even with your power, you cannot take on the entire Dark Citadel and hope to win."

Durandas raised a palm. "Ladies, please. Let me finish. She is not yet at the citadel. A company of dark soldiers is taking her there by horseback."

Crystalyn was elated. With only that many out in the open, the people she had with her now could surround them. "Good! We have a better chance of getting her back from them. How many is in a company, fifty, sixty soldiers?"

Durandas shook his head as he folded his arms inside the wide sleeves of his robe, and his long white hair flailed from side to side. "There is not much over forty in a regiment, but that is not what I am attempting to convey. My man has already gained much on your sister's situation. He has taken the Alchemist hostage to exchange for her, if needed. All they have to do is catch them, and they are close."

Hastel whistled, long and slow. "That's impressive. Many have tried to detain that one, none survived."

Atoi spoke, her voice resounding as if from across a great chasm. "The hooded one's place has not yet been ordained."

Crystalyn eyed her. "What's that supposed to mean?"

The little girl regarded her as if noticing something about her for the first time. Standing out on her pasty face, Atoi's deep-green eyes glinted bright. Broth sat on his haunches beside the little girl.

Through their link, Crystalyn asked, *"What do you know about this man, Do'brieni?"*

*"My people know little, only that the Dark One, as he's known in many places, is rumored to rival the late Lord Charn with power and foul deeds."*

Crystalyn considered her little group. "All right, everyone; summarize what you know of this hooded one. Broth hasn't much knowledge. And Durandas, how *close* is close?"

Watching for scouts and message runners from the grove's perimeter, Lore Rayna spoke first while glancing over her shoulder from time to time. "We know that after Lord Charn's prolonged absence from the citadel, the Alchemist personally killed or had those wishing to command it assassinated. He is the great lord there.”

An acidic thought surged into Crystalyn’s mind, making her nauseated. “And I let Kara Laurel return to the wolf’s den when there’s no need. The alpha male has been removed, the threat of the Flow worms have been contained.”

The Lore Mother removed a hand from her hip, gesturing toward the smoke-filled valley. “That is by no means a certainty. The Alchemist’s Dark lords and generals could still perform the deed. Kara Laurel should rank high with them and may convince them to wait or even abandon the process. You have done right.”

Crystalyn regarded Durandas since the Lore Mother’s face was so hard to read with her glowing eyes, though the set of her mouth spoke volumes of the pride she harbored. “I take it you both will vouch for her. Is she an agent of the Circle of Light still?”

Durandas cast a pointed look around the little grove.

Crystalyn swallowed a scathing retort. Instead, she sighed, letting it draw out to show her patience. “You can speak freely in front of Atoi and Hastel, they have my complete trust. You’ll have to speak for my mom though; I’ve not interacted with her for six seasons, and that was before reaching adulthood.”

Hastel’s chest puffed at the compliment.

Atoi seemed as unconcerned as always.

Shifting her grip on her staff, Sureen stood silent; the white stone topping her staff reflected the sun’s last rays.

The Lore Mother’s radiant gaze turned to Durandas. “Tell her everything. She must now know.”

Durandas bowed to her briefly, his long white hair flowing over his blue eyes. Pulling it to the side, he flashed a hard look up at the Lore Mother. “As you will have it, Second Light. The consequences lay upon you alone.”

Crystalyn’s patience dissolved. “Blast you, get on with it! My sister travels further away the longer we delay.”

Durandas flushed, noticeable even in the waning daylight. "Very well, Kara Laurel is Third Light of the Circle of Light for those of you who are unaware of her esteemed position. She is only required to report to the two of us here on the Circle, which made it easy for her to vanish from Surbo right after you left, Crystalyn. No one had the slightest knowledge of her location until recently, when she attacked and killed many of our warriors."

Crystalyn's ire grew, building momentum. This time, she didn't bother to push it away. "You bloody Circle idiots with your blasted secrets!" Stepping forward, she confronted Durandas. "Why didn't you tell me this before I let her go?"

Thrusting her staff in front of Crystalyn, Sureen eyed Durandas. "Speak truthfully. Tell her why you believe Kara Laurel did what she did. We shall decide then if you have the right of it."

The Lore Mother moved closer to the First Light.

Scowling, Durandas pulled his hands from his sleeves and clasped them together. "We have the right of it. Kara Laurel was charged by the Writhe to infiltrate the Alchemist's domain, something she volunteered for after what happened to her daughter, Maialene."

Spinning her staff vertical, Sureen rammed it into the ground. Then she leaned heavily upon it. "Are you saying Kara Laurel is a member of the Writhe, she's one of us?" She regarded the Lore Mother. "Did you know this?"

"Yes, only the First Light and I have known."

"Blast you both and your bloody secrets!" Sureen swore.

Crystalyn's anger plummeted, displaced with confusion. "So what if Kara Laurel is part of the Green Writhe, does it matter?"

Sureen gazed at the First Light and the Second Light with narrow eyes. Neither one seemed to want to look at her. "It matters. The whole ideology behind the Green Writhe, as these two well know, stems from a strict adherence to the belief of working toward the greater good of Astura. To help fulfill such a large task, members have to know some aspects of individual missions to assist each other. It is a lifetime commitment, thus there is a need for a group of elite warriors called the Green Watch to monitor *every known* Green Writhe member. Not knowing who those members are defeats *my* warriors from eliminating them should they stray."

Hastel choked. "This is not something two of us should hear. Let's go, Atoi. You can help me with the care of the warhorse." Hastel strode away, trailed by Atoi. The little girl followed without protest.

Crystalyn turned to her mother. "Is this why you abandoned your family, left us believing you were murdered or something, to come here and watch over these…these fanatics, Mom?"

Sureen straightened as if struck, though she kept her eyes upon the Lore Mother and Durandas. "Perhaps one of these two is better suited for a reply."

Durandas' shoulders drooped. "Sureen's involvement is as long and complicated a story as any in our history. Selfish acts of bravery are central to it; I shall not do it the injustice of a short telling. For now, please accept that your mother did not return here willingly and with prior knowledge. The Green Writhe employed the desperate measures of sacrificing a gateway to bring back the greatest commander the Green Watch has ever known."

Crystalyn glared at the white-robed man. "What kind of answer is that? Never mind, don't bother with a reply. Once Jade is safe with us, you will tell me the whole story." With difficulty, Crystalyn smoothed her features and reinstalled her empress mask. "From now on, I expect straightforward answers with involved explanations if needed from each of you or I'll send you away. Am I understood?"

"You cannot mean that!" the Lore Mother protested.

"Oh, she means it all right. I stand with her," Lore Rayna said. Leaving her post, she moved beside Crystalyn and folded her arms under her ample bosom.

Crystalyn's respect for the big woman swelled. The vines making up Lore Rayna's living dress didn't know what to do with the woman's abrupt movement at first, shifting to the bottom of her breasts before crawling back to something resembling decency. Like Crystalyn, Durandas averted his eyes.

"Lore Rayna, no!" the Lore Mother exclaimed.

Sureen pounded her staff on the ground. "Crystalyn has spoken. Are you going to abide by her declaration and speak freely?"

Durandas and the Lore Mother exchanged a look, and then both bent at the waist, slightly. "Ask what you will, but know that time slips from us faster than even the Surbon Codex hinted at," Durandas said.

Crystalyn was glad for an "ask what you will" response, though his cryptic words had her curious, something he no doubt intended. "What do you mean?"

"This being Kara Laurel chased, we have known of it. Or rather, we knew of the possibility of something rising stronger than anything Astura had yet contended with, the codices simply referred to it as the corruption in the south. It was not until you and your family's arrival last spring that dark hints of it became greater than abstract references inside a scroll."

Crystalyn's annoyance flared back. "What are you getting at?"

"It is our belief your sister woke it when she passed close to it while fleeing the Dark Citadel."

"Why? What would this thing want with her?"

"If only we knew, dear," the Lore Mother interjected. "Our best scholars have pored over the slim passages in all three codices though only conjecture has come from it. Recently, the monks of

Brown Recluse claim to have deciphered some of the idioms written into a copy of the Virun Codex about the threat."

Crystalyn had heard plenty for now. "Then it has become even more imperative we find Jade. I'm not going to wait to discover what that thing wants. Once she's safe, I'll deal with it." Crystalyn looked up at the big woman next to her. "Prepare the refugees to travel on their own. Gather only your best warriors, we leave tonight."

"Yes, mistress," Lore Rayna said.

"Wait!" Durandas protested. "My man has assured me his band was only three bells behind the regiment two bells ago."

"What man?" Crystalyn asked more harshly than she intended. "Didn't you just say we had no time?"

"Camoe Shadoe and his best druids are nearing them. Jade will be rescued as soon as the regiment halts for the night."

Crystalyn was relieved. Camoe had protected Jade like a daughter not long ago. But her irritation with Durandas was still there. "Why didn't you mention Camoe in the first place?"

Durandas' looked away. "I was not aware you had met him."

"I haven't. Nevertheless, my sister has and thinks highly of him. Where will he bring her?"

"To Brown Recluse, it is the closest safe place from the Vale."

"Then we go meet them halfway to Brown Recluse if we must. My order still stands, Lore Rayna. We leave tonight, only now we'll bring the refugees with us," Crystalyn commanded. She quashed the urge to yell at everyone to get going. Moving such a large group at night would be tricky, but she was determined to see her sister safe and by her side where she belonged. *Hang in there, Jade. Your big sister is coming.*

Crystalyn would rescue her sister by gathering the help to accomplish it. Even if she had to heal every refugee still fit to fight.

# PALE BLUE

Serpent Gorge flowed true to the name, and Jade grew lethargic from following it back and forth before the first hour had passed. The soldier they'd overheard speculating about where General Karnas would lead them next couldn't have guessed more wrong and more right. As soon as he'd returned from his three-hour solo outing, the general had led them to the gorge. Something he had not thought Karnas would do.

Now Jade could see how one could lose their mind to the gorge's winding ways. Though the general had cut past the longest curves in favor of a straight run, they'd lost hours—most of the day—going this way. It made no sense.

She wouldn't complain though. The longer it kept them from arriving at the Dark Citadel, the better it was for her. The place gave her the shivers whenever a stray memory happened to crop up. When she had been alone in an enemy fortress the size of a plateau, the flickers and the dominion wraith there had come close to consuming her soul before Crystalyn had found her.

Today was different. She wasn't alone. Her dad was with her. Casting a furtive glance his direction as he rode beside her, Jade marveled anew at the strength he possessed, how easily he handled the big warhorse, and the great sword strapped to his back. Gone was the wheezing and pale skin of congestive heart failure. Her dad was in better shape than she'd ever known, and he'd promised her an escape soon.

Staying alert with the infernal twisting route of Serpent Gorge as a guide was taxing, but she'd manage somehow. Her dad, her freedom, and perhaps her life depended upon it.

Slowing from a gallop to a trot, General Karnas rode down a short embankment and onto a narrow grassy area between a steep ravine and a rocky tributary. Halting, he signaled for a dismount.

"Serpent Falls is the last clean water before Bracken Lake," Captain Bozlun bellowed. "Water and graze your mounts for one bell, fill your flasks. We ride through the night."

Her dad led her horse past the captain, stopping a few horse lengths from the two men before dismounting. He held her horse as she put her feet on the ground. She was happy to do so, glad to feel the cushion of the green grass growing underfoot, likely the last for a while.

Those of the regiment riding behind them thumped past, coming to a halt in a line stringing toward the Even Flow River and Serpent Falls. The river's current flowed noticeably faster as it vanished over the fall, the roar of it reaching her ears even from where she stood. Jade wondered how long a drop the river plunged, but she didn't wish to walk past so many soldiers working with their horses to find out.

Lifting her warhorse's front leg, her dad inspected its hoof as he spoke quietly, the reins of his horse secured to a wrist. "There is a ferry crossing coming up soon, we make our move as we start loading upon it. Do exactly as I tell you, don't hesitate a moment."

Jade seized her horse by the halter as she patted it affectionately on its soft jaw. Slipping her hand under the bridle, she stayed close enough to hear his words.

Dropping the leg, her dad moved to the other side and repeated the procedure. "Stay alert; I'll have to take the four who carry crossbows out first."

Too terrified to speak, Jade nodded though he couldn't see her. Violence was bad enough; however, premeditated vehemence made her stomach flutter from the first thought.

Checking all four hooves, her father untied the reins of his horse from his wrist one-handed, handed them to her, and then bent to inspect a front hoof.

General Karnas strode toward them, stopping to watch her dad as he rubbed his thumbs along the hoof feeling for signs of an embedded object or cracking of the hoof. Leaving without saying a word, the general tromped to Captain Bozlun.

Her father set the horse's leg on the ground and straightened to his full height. "What was that about?"

"I don't think he feels well, he seemed a little gray."

"Perhaps he is. That may work to our advantage at some point. Right now, we should let our mounts graze. We're going to need them."

Going toward his men, Captain Bozlun strode past. Chewing on a green stalk of something, he eyed them with distrust but kept his silence, which suited her; the less they knew of her, the better.

Jade led her horse to a clump of grass. The horse lowered its long neck and clamped on bunches of the yellow-green stalks with its strong teeth and versatile lips, tearing it close to the ground and then chomping happily away. Jade gave it another pat on the jowl and then looked around.

Some of the soldiers had their horses' legs raised, though not all were going as well as her father's inspection had. Three men dropped a hoof quickly or risked agitating the horse further. One man sat on the ground holding his stomach as he gasped for breath. He was lucky. A backward kick from a powerful haunch could kill a man instantly.

Captain Bozlun strode along the line of soldiers, bellowing at the soldier on the ground. Behind him, light blue and translucent, something winged arose from the edge of Serpent Falls.

"Da…um, excuse me. What is that?" Jade asked, pointing. Two others joined the winged creature, the size of a large bird. Spider-like legs hung from the bottom of an oval body.

Glancing where she pointed, her dad let go of his horse's hoof and straightened. "Bozlun! Behind you!" he shouted.

Lovely and alien, the lead creature zipped to a soldier woman, its wings a blur. The woman had drawn her sword, slashing as soon as it came within range, but it passed through, having no effect. The creature's forelegs gripped the woman's shoulders as the rear of its body curved toward her and then impaled her deep into her stomach as if she wore no armor. The translucent stinger filled with red liquid. The woman screamed and then stilled.

"Leechers! Recall your training!" Bozlun shouted.

Jade screamed. Swarms of the creatures arose from below the falls.

Her dad was at her side. "Mount up, Jade, hurry!" Grabbing her by the waist, he flung her onto the saddle. She tightened her grip on the reins as he pulled the horse around. "Go the direction your horse is pointed, top speed. I'll catch you," he shouted, slapping her horse on the rump. Her horse leapt into a gallop, racing headlong toward a deep ravine. Several glances behind made her wish she hadn't looked. The woman hung limp in midair, the many legs of the creature gripping her by the shoulders as it lifted her weight with ease.

Thundering past General Karnas, the great warhorse charged into the ravine. Forgetting to grip with her legs, Jade rose from the saddle. The stirrups caught on her toes and slammed her back into her seat. Pain vibrated through her pelvis, but she pressed her knees tight and held on, concentrating on the narrow path ahead. Somehow, the big horse had found an animal trail. Gripping the pommel, Jade leaned back and gave the black gelding free rein, trusting in its footing though she struggled to stay seated, the jostling growing in duration and frequency.

Following a cliff edge of dirt and flat rocks, the trail angled steeply downward away from the lake below the fall. Notably smaller on the opposite side, the bottom of the ravine came into view. Where the gulch emptied into Serpent Falls, as it became a fall of its own, motion caught her eye. A pair of the translucent creatures flew into the mouth of the gorge.

Though it put her downhill, Jade lay forward, hunching low in the saddle and hanging on with everything she had. A stumble and a fall now would kill her, yet better that than letting the bloodsucking creatures impale her.

Arriving at the bottom, the warhorse slowed, leapt across a rushing stream, and clopped up the other side, lunging forward. Leaping uphill, it strained its powerful equine muscles. Jade could barely hold on, her arms and back jarring violently with each powerful thrust. Though only a dozen leaps topped them out, Jade's grip grew watery, her hands numb, as they leapt upon a plain of yellowed brush and dusty ground, racing toward Bracken Lake.

A quick look told her all she needed. Their wings a blur, all three creatures angled toward them, flying at an incredible rate in a tight formation. A clinical description of Crystalyn speaking of her frightening encounter with the creatures flashed through her memory. Jade tried to turn the horse away and add distance between the spiderbees, but her fingers refused to let go of the pommel while her arms refused to raise the reins. Fright mingling with despair, she rode on. It was going to be close.

*"Jade, can you hear me?"*

Jade flinched. Her sister's urgent voice rang in her mind, echoing down from somewhere above. She looked up. Only blue sky met her stare. "Crystalyn? Where are you?" she asked aloud.

*"Coming to get you, tell me where to come."*

Glancing over her shoulder, she lowered her head, matching her dark horse. She willed it to go faster. The spiderbees had gained upon them. "I don't know where we are; spiderbees are after us. We're galloping toward a dark lake."

*"Bracken Lake?"* a new voice said, permeating her mind with warmth. Surprised, she nearly lost her grip on the pommel. The voice had sounded like her mom's had. But it couldn't be; her mom was gone, missing a long time ago.

*"Who's us?"* Crystalyn asked.

"Dad! Dad is with me, and he's changed, Crystalyn, he's strong! We've escaped from the soldiers, and once he kills the spiderbees, we'll meet you in Brown Recluse. You don't need to come get me."

The voice that sounded like her mom spoke. *"The contacting is closing!"*

Crystalyn's voice in her mind rose with frustration. *"No! Jade, make certain Dad uses wood against the spiderbees, it's the—"*

*"Are you there?"* The silence of her own thoughts reverberated through her mind. Briefly, she wondered why the contacting had closed and then decided she couldn't worry about it. She had her hands full with staying on the big warhorse.

Ahead, the first vestiges of Bracken Lake sprang into view. Incredibly, the warhorse picked up speed, all four legs tapping the ground at precise intervals for maximum speed. Forcing her terrified muscles into action, Jade bent her knees and raised her rear slightly out of the saddle, letting the stirrups handle the shock she flowed into the ride. Though death flew toward her and raced beside her, she felt exhilarated. The horse gave all it had, and so would she.

Bracken Lake loomed larger on the horizon; a wooden pier came into view. Its great lungs bellowing heavily, the warhorse responded to her gentle pull on the right rein and adjusted their headlong flight toward it minutely. Jade dared not look to the side. Not yet.

Sounding like a zip cycle back on Terra, the drone of wings overrode the labored breathing and hooves thumping the ground of the warhorse. Jade looked. The original three had nearly caught them. Worse, behind them, the sky had spotted with azure; dozens more were on the way.

The warhorse's front hooves clopped upon the dock, slowing at the halfway point. Tied to the end of the dock, a flat-bottomed ferry floated languidly on gentle waves. For the first time, Jade wondered what she would do when she reached it.

Two ferrymen leapt from the boat and ran toward her. Pulling on the reins, she slid the black gelding to a halt before crashing into them and running out of pier.

As he ran past, the tallest man yelled in her direction, "Here, take this!" and tossed a coil of rope to her.

Jade caught the rope, swung her leg over the mount's broad back, and dropped to the pier. Turning around, she dropped the reins, her fingers slack.

The three creatures flew onto the pier, slowing to bend oblong bodies and position stingers forward. Behind them, seen eerily opaque through the wings and body, her father raced. Clouding the sky at an angle to overtake him, the swarm drew closer, the drone of it growing in volume.

On silent wings now, the three bee-like creatures separated. Two singled out a ferryman, and one flew for her.

The tallest ferryman waited, standing with his side to the creature, with the rope held coiled at his chest.

Jade was transfixed, viewing the scene through the body of the creature flying for her. Spider-like, its four front legs rising in anticipation, the bee creature glided at the man. When the creature was a horse's length away from him, the man whipped his arm forward, releasing the coil. The tip struck the creature, popping it with a wet-sounding splotch. A small puddle fell to the pier and dissolved into a puff of white steam. The man spun toward her. "Use the rope!"

Forelegs raised and stinger readied, a spiderbee glided in for a landing on her shoulders. Jade swung the coil of rope, swatting it away. Popping wetly, the creature splashed her face and hands with a blue gel that slid to the dock and dissipated on the wood. Both men flashed a brief smile and then turned to face the opposite end of the pier.

A great ball of pale blue made the sky behind her dad murky. Though the flyers had failed to intercept him, the swarm had gained.

Galloping onto the pier, her father urged the great warhorse on, pulling on the reins the moment before reaching her and throwing himself from the saddle before the horse fully stopped. He ran to her. "Are you hurt?" he asked.

Jade hugged him. "I'm okay."

Returning the hug briefly, he shouldered her arms loose. Turning, he pushed her behind him, reaching to draw his sword.

Jade gripped his hand, stopping him at half draw. "I don't think that works against them, take this," she said, flinging the rope over his shoulder.

"There are too many!" the shorter ferryman shouted. Sprinting up to her, he grabbed her hand and pulled as his companion ran past. "We have to run for the ferry, our nets are there!"

Jade removed her hand, glancing at her father.

Slipping the rope from the ferryman's hand, her father walked away from her, away from the ferry. "Go, I'll hold them off. Run!" he shouted.

Jade ran, looking back.

The pale blue ball descended toward him, separating into dozens of creatures, each stinger held at the ready as they dropped from the sky. *There are too many!* Her steps faltered, but she was at the ferry.

Jade jumped onto the boat beside the shorter ferryman. "Help Jarl untangle the net, hurry!" he yelled.

Tugging on a pile of rope at the bow, the taller ferryman, Jarl, worked at spreading it apart.

With her and the shorter ferryman's help, the net unrolled quickly across the deck. As the short man clipped the net to rings on the decking set in a circular pattern, Jarl squirmed under it and raised a short pole, slipping it into a tightly bored hole. "Under here, miss!" Jarl shouted.

Crawling under and sitting beside him, Jarl handed her a pole slightly shorter than the one holding the net. Jade took it and fearfully checked on her father.

Both ropes a blur, her father spun them in a tight overlapping ball, whipping them around him like blades on a hover engine, as he moved toward the ferry in leaps, his feet barely touching the deck. Falling from the sky like giant drops of blue rain with greater frequency, the pale creatures burst into white mist, surrounding him with a white haze.

"We have to help; he's not going to make it!" Jade screamed. Standing, her head touched the top of the net.

The shorter ferryman pointed above her. "Look! It's too late."

Jade spun, looking up. The top of the ball had broken away and dropped toward them.

"Use your wooden pole, but don't let them touch you with their stinger. They can fit it through a square of net," Jarl said. Thrusting through one of the squares, he jabbed a creature and then withdrew the pole under the netting.

Going to her knees, Jade stabbed upward at first one, then two, of the pale stinger creatures. The creatures dived, raining down in ever-growing numbers. Her world became an endless series of upward jabs. For every winged creature she burst, two took its place. Her arms quickly grew tired, but she couldn't quit.

For every one stabbed, two hit the netting and burst, adding watery weight to it before dissipating to mist. So many slammed into the netting, the center pole swayed dangerously, the squares stretching, drooping closer toward her. Still they came.

No longer able to jab, Jade held her pole upright letting the translucent creatures impale upon it, until it, too, became heavy. On they dropped. Propping the pole against the deck, Jade wrapped her arms around it and leaned it against her shoulder.

The netting drooped against her skin, which frightened her and gave her a second breath. Quickly finding a knot in the squares, she wedged the pole in it and lay back. Stingers stabbed through and then burst, each one dragging the net closer and closer. Jade despaired. A stinger would eventually—soon—impale her. The net was so heavy from the weight, the pole bent. *You fought so hard, Dad, I'm sorry.*

The weight of the net lifted from her. "Jade, are you okay?"

Jade blinked. Her dad stood above her, offering his hand. She stared at it in surprise. Struggling to her feet, she wrapped her arms around him. "Dad! I thought we'd had it!"

Her father chuckled once, softly. He patted her affectionately on the back with his right arm. "I believed it over too, and then I suddenly found none were attacking me, they concentrated on going after you."

Jade disengaged from her father and took a step away, looking him over. The vibrant tanned pigment of his left hand had vanished, replaced by a washed-out gray, and his arm hung limp at his side. Her breath caught at her throat. "You're hurt!"

Her father flashed a brief smile. "It's nothing I cannot live with. One of the buggers nicked my arm with a bloody stinger."

"The paralysis will not last long," the shorter ferryman said. His swarthy grizzled face had the look of one rarely indoors. Taking hold of the net, he laboriously rolled it toward the center pole his companion removed. "I am Surn, proprietor of Black Bottom Ferry. My deckhand is Jarl. I thank you for your aid with the leechers; all would have been lost if not for your battle prowess, citadel soldier."

Her father jumped upon the pier, gathered the reins one-handed, and led the two horses down the wooden ramp, halting beside her and the ferry owner before speaking. "Nay, it is we who owe our thanks to the two of you. I am called Garn, and this is my…charge, Jade."

Surn's dark eyes flicked to her briefly and then returned to his task. "I am puzzled as to why the swarm broke from the attack. They would have overrun us in a quarter bell, no more."

"I am uncertain, though they lost a quarter of their number. Perhaps that was too many," her dad replied.

Jarl glanced skyward. "I've never seen such a swarm. Never before has the pole net failed."

"It didn't fail. Your wonderful setup saved us all."

"Perhaps it did at that," Jarl agreed, but he looked troubled.

"What cost is the ferry from here to Gray Dust, and how far is it?" Garn inquired.

Surn answered without looking up. "Gray Dust is a two-bell ferry ride; one would think a citadel man would know this. There is no cost to you and you're…charge. The rest of your patrol shall cover it easily."

Confused by the comment, Jade followed her dad's gaze, back along the pier. The dust cloud beyond it indicated riders coming at a fast pace.

"Our time is limited. What cost for the two of us to make the crossing first, with the cost of the others riding toward us you'll lose out on?" her dad asked next.

After tying the rolled net and pole to rings on the deck, the ferry owner stood gazing at them for a while, his dark eyes unreadable. "Even if you have sufficient coin, I am contracted by the White Lands and Virun to make a certain amount of crossings a day. The two of us only have sufficient strength for three, which means I fill it with passengers or leave at certain bells. This is the third scheduled for today. We depart in half a bell. Your companions will arrive long before then."

Jade opened her mouth to plead, but a sharp glance from her dad stopped her cold.

"We are in your debt and defer to your ways. Please, advise us of any assistance we can give to make the journey easier," her dad said. He gave a small bow. Jade didn't even know he knew how.

Surn's answering bow was deep. "Nay, my lord, as I have stated, we are indebted to you. Simply care for your mounts, we shall handle the rest." Letting his deckhand finish clipping any unsecured item in place, he strode to the moorings to await the new arrivals.

On an impulse, Jade slowed the aura spinning around the ferry owner, gazing at the three images as soon they slowed enough to view. All three contained the same dark image. A tentacle groped about from a patch of darkness and then vanished, leaving only shadows behind. Startled, Jade let the images go and they whipped away, spinning into the gray misty cyclone around him. *What do they mean?* she wondered, dissatisfied with her useless ability. All it ever provided was riddles without answers. Utterly inadequate, it helped no one, least of all her.

Jade crossed the ferry to stand beside her dad and wait for her captors to arrive.

They did not have to wait long. Soon, the clatter of hooves tromping on the pier rang loud in Jade's ears. "What are we going to do now?" she whispered.

Her dad barely spoke above the din racing along the pier. "We let them launch, there are but nine of the general's men left not including himself and Captain Bozlun. Midway across, I'll finish this, stay alert."

Jade wasn't certain she liked the coldness of his tone, but what choice did they have? The hooded man's commanded escort wouldn't let them go simply by asking. She felt tears building pressure from deep inside, which she quelled with difficulty. Why was everything bad on this world always after her? Pushing down another a bout of tears rising strong, her eyes searched the sky for a pale blue glint.

## BLOODY ROCKS

The pace set by the Vale refugees was maddeningly slow. Crystalyn chafed at yet another delay. Crossing the Even Flow River had cost hours yesterday. RaCorren's recent request was the third pause asked for and barely after midday. How many rest stops did the people need in one day? Her first inclination was to deny it, but then a thought occurred to her. She could use the time to gather information, something she should have done several stops ago.

Crystalyn glanced sidelong at RaCorren as he strolled beside her warhorse, walking beside her as if out for a daily jaunt in the woods. They'd left the Vale behind a day ago, yet he showed no sign the distance traveled bothered him. One would think she'd have gotten used to the Valens' prowess with slipping through forests at will.

"Your request is granted with a condition," she said to the towering Valen liaison, getting his attention. "Send someone to fetch Durandas for me. I'll await him at the hill's farthest edge, we stop there for thirty minutes, uh, half a bell, no longer," she said, pointing to the top of the small mountain they climbed. One of these days, with repetitive use, she may get used to using the Asturan designation for the passing of time.

Without missing a step, RaCorren bowed low. "Your command is my wish, *Sarra'esiah*," he said. Straightening, he darted between a mixed group of Valens and human druids who strode with their families, those who remained.

Crystalyn tracked his progress by his great mane of golden hair until the crowd swallowed even someone of his tall stature. Apparently, he intended to perform the task personally, which shouldn't have surprised her. For reasons unknown, he had taken it upon himself to attend to her since leaving the quarry.

Giving up on fathoming what motivated a Valen, she urged the warhorse to gallop the rest of the way up the hill. The great horse needed little prodding; its powerful muscles required flexing. A slow day of trotting had done little for them. At the final, steepest part of the slope, a log lay. Instead of going around, Crystalyn sailed over it, exhilarating in the feel of all four legs leaving the ground and a perfect, almost gentle landing on the other side.

The Lore Mother stood at the top beside her mom, neither woman looking happy, as she rode up and dismounted.

"A leader should refrain from foolhardy chances at an accident," the Lore Mother said.

"So should my eldest daughter," her mom said.

Crystalyn patted the warhorse's front dark shoulder affectionately, the color giving her an idea for a name. Saying it aloud, she tried it out. "Murk is strong and surefooted, I was perfectly safe." The horse gazed at her placidly. He seemed to like it, as she did.

"I was speaking of the horse. We do not have enough to go around," the Lore Mother drawled.

Crystalyn glanced at her sharply. Her luminous eyes were as equable as the horse, her face smooth. She changed the subject. "The refugees desire a rest. I've sent for Durandas, when he gets here, I have a task for the two of you."

"What of me?" Sureen asked

Looking around, she found Hastel nearby, beside Atoi. She gestured to him to watch Murk. As the dark horse cropped a clump of green mountain grass, she left the reins hanging on the saddle horn, turning to the two women. "Glad you asked. I've been mulling something over for a while. Walk with me, both of you."

Warmed by the sun radiating brightly above her right side, Crystalyn climbed toward the peak. Round and wide at the top, the view was only hill sloping away. Crystalyn walked downhill until the area below spread out before them, the two other women coming up to stand one on each side of her.

The forest thinned. A hillside, sloping down, waved with tall stalks of grass and sagebrush, swaying gently from a light breeze. In the distance, the ground leveled and uniform fields claimed great squared chunks of land. "Tell me what to expect from here," she said quietly.

The Lore Mother waved an age-spotted hand at the expanse below. "This particular hill, known as Barren Mount, slopes gently to the Great Plains to the east. The route is a good one. The refugees shall have an easier journey to Brown Recluse."

Leaning forward, her mother glanced at the Lore Mother. "Barren Mount is southeast of the Vale, is it not?"

"Yes," the Lore Mother said.

Crystalyn grew alarmed. "Isn't that taking us away from Jade?"

"It was necessary to deviate from our course to avoid Silent Blade," Durandas said from behind them. He halted beside the Lore Mother. "Many of those from the Vale would be an easy mark for the filth that frequents the town. Bypassing it in exchange for a slightly longer though safer route is well worth it. What did you wish to speak with me about?"

Crystalyn kept her face smooth with difficulty. How many days' distance between her and Jade had he cost her by not consulting with her? She was ready to throttle the man, but she needed his talents first. "I want to speak with Jade."

Durandas clasped his hands together. A frown crinkled his forehead between his bushy white eyebrows. "A contacting of that magnitude would drain me for bells. We still have dangerous lands to pass through."

Crystalyn had grown tired of excuses. "Perhaps I used the wrong word. I *have* to speak with Jade."

Durandas' frown deepened. Folding his hands behind his back, he paced along a narrow animal path that followed the ridge a short way, and then he turned back, his white robe brushing through the clumps of grass. "I distinctly recall we agreed contacting your sister may put her in grave danger."

"The time has come to take that chance." Crystalyn put her hand on the Lore Mother's shoulder and squeezed gently. "Will you help him complete the contactings?"

The Lore Mother patted her hand and nodded as she spoke. "'Contactings' imply more than one, dear."

Crystalyn smiled. Though she knew it cruel, keeping them off-balance made for easier manipulation. Besides, she should exercise her authority when appropriate. "Right after Jade, we contact Camoe."

Pacing to a point on an animal trail that only he knew as the boundary, Durandas froze in mid-step. Then, pivoting on a heel, he spun to look at her, his blue eyes bright. "You ask much from two old ones."

Crystalyn's anger spiked, but she quelled it. "The Lore Mother grows old, *you* grow younger every time the two of you use together. Do not make the mistake of thinking I don't know how the symbiotic, parasitic relationship works between a User and an Interrupter."

Durandas blew out a breath. "Very well, I shall make the

attempt though I cannot speak for the Lore Mother. It is dangerous and requires her to make her own decision."

"The prophecy vessel is right," the Lore Mother said. "We may learn much by ascertaining Jade's location. This is a good place to attempt it away from the others. Join me, old one," she added, sitting cross-legged on the wildlife trail, likely made from the small herds of deer and elk they'd spotted along the way.

Durandas flashed a small grin as he sat facing the Lore Mother on the path he'd only moments before been pacing. "I shall take focal point." Reaching into a pocket of his white robes, he removed the leather strap with the glowing white stone tied in the center. Making certain the contact stone touched his forehead, he tied it in the back.

The Lore Mother set two larger green crystal orbs triangularly away from the white stone of his leather strap.

The warm scent of her mom wafted into her senses as she leaned close and spoke softly into her ear. "Are you certain this is wise, daughter? The Dark Users have developed a stronger ability to break into these transmissions."

The Lore Mother's aged head swung abruptly toward them. "Prepare to sever the connection at the first sign of a Dark attack, Sureen. Crystalyn, you may begin picturing your sister in your mind and calling her name. We are ready."

Crystalyn thought of Jade, how her auburn hair always had a stray lock that insisted upon covering an eye, her habit of sucking her bottom lip into her mouth, and how she looked up to her for protection and friendship. Only three days had passed, but she missed her little sister badly already.

The Lore Mother's glowing eyes flared bright.

His blue eyes vanishing behind their own burst of white radiance, Durandas sat transfixed. Triangulating from the white stone on his forehead to the two green orbs, an image stacked upward. Three-dimensional, the image formed quickly as countless cubes making the image stacked faster and faster from the ground up.

Inside the triangle, Jade bounced in the saddle of a great warhorse galloping at top speed. Shrubbery and bare ground passed by in the background too fast to make out the landscape. "Can you hear me, Jade?" Crystalyn asked aloud.

The image of Jade galloping through a faceless background continued uninterrupted.

"You have to make contact for the contacting to triangulate," her mom said. "Give it a light touch. We both shall, you on one side, me on the other. Think about your sister, I shall think about my daughter."

Crystalyn set her palms on the top surface and tried again recalling the way Jade sometimes pulled her bottom lip into her mouth when worried. "Jade, can you hear me?"

Jade started. Then she looked up. "*Crystalyn? Where are you?*" Jade's voice reverberated through her mind, as if from a great distance.

Crystalyn nearly cried out with joy and then spoke aloud. "Coming to get you, tell me where to come."

Glancing over her shoulder, Jade's eyes widened with fright. She lowered her head, matching her dark horse. "*I don't know where we are; spiderbees are after us. We're galloping toward a dark lake.*"

"Where is there a dark lake, a huge one?" Crystalyn asked aloud.

"Bracken Lake?" asked her mom.

Crystalyn's focus remained with her sister, as Jade tightened her grip on the saddle horn. "*Who's us?*" Crystalyn asked silently.

"Dad! Dad is with me, and he's changed, Crystalyn, he's strong! We've escaped from the soldiers, and once he kills the spiderbees, we'll meet you in Brown Recluse. You don't need to come get me," Jade said aloud, the tone of her voice even. Then she glanced fearfully behind her again.

Her mom's urgent voice broke in. "The contacting is closing!"

Crystalyn's anxiety nearly stole her speech. "NO! Jade, make certain Dad uses wood against the spiderbees, it's the—" Vanishing, one by one the blocks picked up speed and disappeared in reverse order as fast as they had stacked.

Durandas leaned back on his hands, the glow of his eyes winking out. "That is as long as I dare if you want to attempt a second contacting. You should tell Sureen what you wish to communicate with Camoe. I do not believe he has the sense of your mind. Please assure it is brief." His eyes burst into the familiar radiance. The three-dimensional image stacked into the triangle faster this time. Contacting someone she'd never met might not work, but she was determined to try.

Crystalyn thought about what little she knew of the druid from Jade's descriptions. At first, Camoe had wanted to kill Jade, believing her a creature made by dark magic. Then he'd helped her escape the Dark Citadel, saving her life numerous times with the help of a magical creation made by a Dark User. Crystalyn owed the druid much for saving the one she cared most about in the world.

A three-dimensional image filled the triangle, vivid and life-like with rich detail. Garbed in the brown and green kell leather of the forest, a silver-haired man with matching close-cropped beard ran nimbly along a well-beaten trail. Behind him, a tall smooth-faced man with four long-bladed spear tips poking over his shoulders followed. The tall man led a muscular man wearing a black half cloak by a rope tied at the wrists. A wide man wearing a great axe strapped to the side of his brown kell leather brought up the rear.

Crystalyn concentrated on the man leading the procession. "Camoe Shadoe, I would speak with you about Jade."

The silver-haired man slid to a stop, those behind halting abruptly. His firm but soft tone carried a promise of violence into the recesses of her mind; he was one who knew how to dispatch an enemy with proficiency. "*You have but one opportunity to identify yourself before I sever this connection.*"

"I am Jade's sister, Crystalyn."

"*Why do you hide from my view?*"

Crystalyn shrugged though he'd just admitted to not seeing her. "I'm not certain why you can't see me, but I can you. I'm Jade's sister, and I have knowledge of her whereabouts."

Camoe glanced up, his blue eyes fading to light gray. "*How do I know you are truly her sibling?*" he asked, his words ringing softly in her mind.

"There's something you both know, but others may not. When Jade fell into the underground grotto into the water, you started a fire to keep her from freezing to death."

Camoe's eyes darkened as his eyebrows rose. "*What happened after the fire burned low?*"

Crystalyn wracked her memory. Only one thing stood out from Jade's retelling of her harrowing escape. Though she didn't think it what the druid searched for, she mentioned it anyway. "Something bad sniffed outside your hiding place."

Camoe smiled, lighting his now dark blue eyes briefly. "*Yes, I suspect they were Dark hounds. I greet you, elder sister of Jade. What is the nature of this contacting?*"

Though Jade had spoken of it, Crystalyn found the druid's eyes unnerving for some reason. One would think it wouldn't bother her after spending time with Broth and his marvelous hourglass color-changing orbs. "How close are you to catching up with Jade?"

*"Judging from their speed, we are only a few bells behind. Have you had* word of her?"

"Yes, I have. She's nearing Bracken Lake. Is a more direct route available from where you are?"

Camoe looked off into the distance. *"Yes, there is such a route. Our time of overtaking them would halve…your sister's faith in you is not without merit,"* he said, looking up. Then he froze.

Gaps of blackness pockmarked his face, bursting through the background surrounding him. Tendrils of darkness popped out along the top, writhing like stalks from an underwater plant disturbed by the passage of something immense.

Crystalyn jerked her hands from the triangle as the foulness of the tendrils permeated her mind. Darkness profound and absolute engulfed her. In the blackness, an immensity moved, slipping close. Sliding around her mind, it squeezed, compressing upon her the sense of unrelenting dominance birthed from an ancient arrogance.

Its indomitable will knew only subversion for it had not known thwarting. The blackness within the darkness had no concept of it, which raised her ire. Thwart it she would.

Crystalyn envisioned her golden symbol and wrapped it around her awareness as the immensity struck, beating down upon her with wave after wave of arrogant domination. Resolute, she held strong. No one, no *thing,* would do that to her. She fought back. Expanding her symbol, she pushed outward, pressing the arrogance back, bit by minuscule bit.

Abruptly, the dominant will popped. Behind it, the immensity recoiled in surprise. Swelling, it expanded beyond the boundaries of her comprehension. Slowly, almost serenely, a great axe swung out from the vast immensity. Picking up a sense of speed as it fell, the axe chopped into her symbol, bursting it into immeasurable pieces. The great axe rose and again descended. She could not stop it.

A powerful concussive *ting* resonated through her mind, and the colossal axe halted abruptly, frozen a hair's breadth away from the sense of who she was and what she knew of herself. A thin barrier of intense azure rippled but held firm.

A voice raspy with ancientness and long disuse boomed from out of the immensity. *"You dare to interfere in my domain? Consequences shall arise from your action."* The axe withdrew. The immensity receded.

Crystalyn found herself looking at the pale face of Atoi, her passionless emerald eyes staring up at her unblinking. A sudden, powerful scene opened inside her mind.

The first of three oblong winged shapes closed the distance between it and the dark child-like shape fleeing across a brown desert of sand. The winged shape stretched four giant legs downward, the shadowy hooked ends of its claws opening and closing with anticipation of prey within grasp.

The child shape veered sharply toward a formation of red and brown rocks. As the shape turned, Crystalyn saw an oblong object cradled at the waist shimmered with darkness. A second winged shape swerved to overtake the running child. Beneath a large pile of sand, a shadowy opening swung into view.

The winged shape arrived first, pulling up to hover in front of the enticing darkness. Crystalyn willed the child shape to go faster. The tiny shadowy child sped up, racing under the grasping claws at the entrance, merging into the darkness.

Crystalyn gaped at her tiny companion, a string of questions burbling from her mouth. "Was that you? Did you help me? What did the winged beasts want with the Dark Child?"

Atoi stared, her dispassionate face uninterested. "What?"

Crystalyn's anger rose. "Don't tell me you don't know. You had to have been the one who stopped that monstrous axe and then projected such a strong image to me. Broth would not have done it without an explanation." "*Isn't that right, my Broth?*"

"*I sent no image, Do'brieni.*"

Broth's assurance only elevated the ire. She wanted answers from the dark thing; it had interfered to show her something of importance. "Is there something under the brown sand we should know about?"

Atoi gazed at her unrelenting.

"What happened?" her mother asked.

Ignoring the question, Crystalyn took a step toward the little girl. Bending face to face with her, she spoke as clear as she could. "Tell me, *blast you!* Or I'll leave you here for the bloody Dark Users to find. What attacked me? What were those dark shapes in the desert? Where were they?"

"Here now, mistress. Let's have no threats," Hastel said, leading the horses closer to his charge.

Slowly and deliberately, Atoi turned and faced southward.

Hastel stopped moving, his one eye blinking in surprise. "Blast!"

Crystalyn hated to ask the question foremost on her mind, but she had to. "Is that the way I should go?"

Atoi stared at the southwest without moving. Beyond her, a gentle slope led toward cultivated fields.

Crystalyn sighed. "I suppose I have my answer."

Her mother moved beside her. Crystalyn drew comfort from her steadfast presence. "Are you certain you can trust her? Can you believe the Dark Child she hosts?"

Crystalyn wasn't certain she had faith in anyone but herself and her father and sister. "Jade is safe with the one I know I can trust, my dad. I will meet them or send for them as soon as the refugees are safe. After I've discovered what the Dark Child has to show me."

Her mom smiled. "Your father is the best thing for her." Her face smoothed. "And what of me, can you not trust me?"

Crystalyn kept her own face smooth. "I'm not certain I even know you, not yet. But I do have something which will go a long way toward earning my trust."

Raising her head of rich brown hair, her mother compressed her lips. "What must I do?"

"Go to Jade, help Dad protect her."

Her mother's eyes flashed a bright green, a sign of her quick anger, which Crystalyn now recalled. "I do not wish to leave you, *my* daughter. *My* youngest daughter is safe with your father. He has certain capabilities, even he is not aware of."

"I am a survivor on this world, Mom, but you wouldn't know, I have friends who fight for me. Jade, however, has to have help. Something is always after her. Why, I don't know. Your being with her would ease my fears. I've seen the power you draw from the Flow."

Her mother stared. "You can see it? Have you tried to access it?"

Crystalyn pushed her impatience to the side. "You're changing the subject. Will you go?"

"I shall go to them by way of the Vale and combine two…requirements I am to fulfill, though I truly do not wish to leave you. Her mother's gaze flickered to the ground behind her. Her smooth facial features remained serene. "I imagine I should aid with your healing of those two before I depart."

"What two?" Crystalyn spun around, making her question rhetorical.

The Lore Mother and Durandas lay crumpled on the ground. Though their chests rose and collapsed normally, her guilt at not thinking of them ascended with her rising anxiety. Even now, a mind worm could be assaulting them as it fed upon their neural processes. Once she saved them, and she would, she'd send them both back to Surbo to help fight the assault on the capitol city of the White Lands.

Recalling her golden symbol, Crystalyn attached her awareness to it and sank into Durandas.

# MISSING

Camoe's inner vision sprang back to normal. He had halted the company by simply stopping for the contacting that had stabbed into his mind, coming with greater insistence than normal. Durandas had provided the means to communicate, but Jade's sister, Crystalyn, had spoken. Oddly, he could not see her through any part of it but he had little doubt of her identity, not with her having intimate knowledge of Jade. Another strange occurrence of the contacting bothered him. It had ended abruptly. Either Durandas had used a fledgling Interrupter or Dark Users had found them and severed the connection, which meant they were getting better. The connection was not long.

Whatever had happened, the information Crystalyn imparted was grand news. Jade's father had broken her free; he now knew she was closer than expected. After navigating through Broken Gap, a short run down the mountainside and across the foothills would put them at Bracken Lake in a short time after nightfall.

He had thought to inquire how badly the Vale fared just before the contacting had ended, but he was better off not knowing. He had a mission he would see through until the end, regardless of how safe her sister believed his charge to be.

An undertaking he had jeopardized by halting the men out in the open. He signaled for the group to move behind a large pile of slate rock slabs. Though it would slow them, they would draw far less attention from unfriendly eyes.

He continued along the trail alone. Ahead, round dark shapes skittered about. Wary, he slipped from the shade of a boulder the path wound around to a sparse recess of scrub weed growing at the mouth of Broken Gap. He waited for the others, watching the frenzy within.

Kerna, Peers, and Girth trotted up on silent feet, followed by Long Draught pulling the prisoner behind him. Wheezing, Tarn came last, though he kept as silent as he could by muffling the sounds with his fist.

Moving beside him, Girth frowned as he gazed ahead. "What are they doing?"

Camoe slipped his long sword from the sheath at his side, glancing at each of his companions as he spoke. "They are gorging on their dead. Many boulder beetles perished here though most consider them harmless. Yet, something slaughtered them, or they attacked a disciplined force. I imagine it was our quarry. Keep a sharp eye as we move through."

Peers slipped to the front. "Aye, something is amiss in there." His hushed words hung in the air as he moved into the gap.

His scout's words added a cloud of foreboding Camoe disliked. The bouts of true sense that assailed him, the divinations of Flow threads attracted to him as possible future occurrences, usually came riddled with a sense of impending doom; there was no getting away from it. As the fifth generation of a long line of essence druids, he had to live with it. All he could do was follow close to Peers and hope he spotted danger before it found them.

Halfway through the narrow pass, Peers slowed, finally coming to a halt at a rock cairn piled chest-high with slate. Several open-faced helms adorned the top but no weapons or plate armor. Those were too precious to leave behind. A wide path of dirt and buried slate surrounded it, indicating a recent construction.

The beetles had vanished, leaving behind partially eaten corpses of their own kind, the oily black blood staining much of the gray limestone.

After a quick perusal of the area, Camoe put his sword away. The signs of battle told the story. Several soldiers and two mounts had perished. It was hard to determine how many beetles had met their demise, though that did not concern him. From the way the string of corpses led from many of the holes to the rock cairns, the boulder beetles had initiated the attack, which concerned him and made him uneasy.

He was heartened to discern that patches of human blood had not yet baked black from sun exposure. Perhaps he could help Jade and her father after all. "Peers, Kerna, keep watch farther along the gap; we have gained on our quarry. They rode from here less than a bell ago. Stay alert, something frenzied these creatures, and I want advance warning should it still lurk near."

Giving a slight nod, the life mates ran ahead.

"Not all rode away." The hooded man's quiet statement echoed softly around the pass. "One has to wonder why a carrion scavenger would attack a large force of men," he said, his silky voice echoing Camoe's thoughts.

Long Draught gave a sharp yank on the rope, reeling the hooded man to him. His long arm pulled the Alchemist close. "No one gave you permission to speak," he said, quietly but firmly. Where the Dark One's voice was pleasant, Long Draught' soft tone promised quick and decisive repercussions.

The Alchemist's golden hourglass eyes fixed steadily upward at the man gripping him.

Camoe could think of none better at guarding a lone prisoner than the tall druid. Satisfied, he strode away. Climbing an old cairn, he squatted for a closer view of the top. Four sets of tracks were prominent in the packed dirt between the rocks. Of those, one set was smaller and by itself. *Jade.* The disturbed earth had very little soil sloughing from the edges, backfilling the prints. They *were* gaining on her captors.

He moved to a mound of piled slate at Broken Gap's bottom, gazing at the hooded man over the top of it. "Regarding your question of the beetles' attack, had you genuine curiosity? Or do you wish to tell us something of importance? Speak freely."

The hooded man's broad chin lifted, and his pale lips thinned.

Camoe counted four heartbeats of flagrant pause and accorded it to the man's arrogance. The Alchemist's first words confirmed it.

"You still do not know with whom you speak so to, do you, *druid?*"

Two strides brought Tarn behind the hooded man. Two well-placed kicks at the back of the Alchemist's knees put him kneeling painfully in the limestone and dirt. His two longest daggers suddenly rested on the shoulders of the black-hooded man, the blades resting against the bare skin of his neck, the tips of them crossed. "You would do well to show respect for Camoe. He is our leader and your captor. He alone decides when and *if* you shall continue to draw breath," Tarn said softly, his voice full of menace. His deep cough racking his muscular frame only slightly diminished the effect.

Though one of the long knives drew droplets of blood because of the coughs, the hooded man smiled.

Tarn's cough deepened.

The hooded man's smile broadened.

Camoe started. He hopped upon the cairn, staring down on the hooded man. "Your darkness is well known, *Alchemist*," he said, speaking over Tarn's wet-sounding hacking. "What foul concoction have you infected my man with? Tell me or I shall have him squeeze his blades closed."

The Alchemist's smile faded.

"Blast you, evil one!" Girth cursed.

"Befouled blood, soiled earth, and the stink of rot, what have you done?" Long Draught asked with a string of curses, the tone of his voice clipped. Squeezing and loosening his grip on the rope, his prominent biceps expanded and contracted, he looked like he wanted to pull the hooded man to him but was leery of Tarn's daggers.

The Alchemist swallowed slowly. "Breath bane is a base ingredient of the poison, gray petra spore is used in part. Though how many parts shall remain with me."

Camoe could not keep a frown from his face, though he regained composure quickly. "Are you toying with me? I shall consider commanding Tarn the opportunity to squeeze his blades together…slowly. Your brain shall not have time to shut down and protect you from pain. You shall feel the sharpened steel from two sides as they meet."

The hooded man's chest expanded as he straightened his back, powerful and muscular even kneeling. "Give your man the command to lower his swords, or you shall get nothing from me."

Camoe kept his tone even. "'Nothing' is exactly what you have provided thus far. In truth, I no longer believe you possess knowledge worth gleaning, and I cannot allow such vileness as yours to continue staining the world unchecked. That leaves only one alternative."

The Alchemist froze.

Tarn coughed into a shoulder.

Camoe folded his arms to his chest, looking down at the man. He chafed at the delay, but knowledge gained, even from a duped, untrustworthy source, may save lives later. "You have intelligence and some natural ability to read intent, I believe. Tell me, what is my *intention* if you do not offer some value to our quest?"

No longer smiling, the Alchemist drew breath. "I have created a remedy for the lung rot your man has acquired."

"Give it to him."

The Alchemist stood slowly, raising the swords with his broad shoulders as Tarn's coughing worsened, drawing a drop of blood at his lower neck. The hooded man's frown was brief. "If you desire my death, tell your man to finish it or remove them. You attacked *me* at *my* camp," he said, his golden eyes brightening in the morning sunlight.

Camoe was sorely tempted to give the order to rid Astura of the Alchemist's blight upon the world; the disease of him could be vanquished right here. The hooded man had committed atrocities simply to progress his wicked experiments. The Green Writhe knew about his carnages for seasons, yet they had done nothing to stop him. Perhaps now was the time.

Tarn stood at the ready. A simple flex of his druidic friend's muscles would end it. Then Tarn would die. Camoe was not prepared to make such a decision yet. "Put away your steel. Let him continue to draw breath, for now."

Tarn did so without question. Covering his mouth with a shoulder, he hacked into it, eyeing the Alchemist.

"Give him the antidote to whatever foulness your flask contained," Camoe said softly. He was nearing the end of his patience. Jade moved farther away the longer they stood in one place. Now that they were close, they may catch them before they reached the ferry.

The Alchemist smiled. "He shall have it as soon as we get it from my chambers at the citadel. You have my guarantee you shall all have safe passage once the remedy is administered."

"You take me for a FOOL!" Camoe roared. "Kill him."

His hands bound, the Alchemist scurried away from Tarn as he raised his long knives again, but a pull of the rope flung him back. In desperation, he attempted to shoulder Tarn, who pushed him away easily. The druid prepared his swing. "Wait!" he yelled. "There is another method!"

"Hold!" Camoe shouted.

Coughing, Tarn lowered his weapons.

"Passage root will open the airway and slow the effect, prolonging his life until the remedy is retrieved. Once we have traveled close to the citadel, I can send someone to get it, eliminating the need for you to go there. Is this sufficient for an agreement?" the Alchemist asked.

Camoe glared at the man. "Passage root is a simple herb used for head and sinus ailments. Do you dare still toy with me?"

The Alchemist's chin rose. "If I say to use it, do so, or do not. His life becomes yours by the decision. I carry the herb always."

"Then we shall see," Camoe said.

"I'll get it," Girth volunteered. "We haven't yet taken the time to discover what else he carries. It's time to *remedy* that."

"Do not touch me," the Alchemist snarled. Pulling away, the rope bit into his hands and jerked him around to face the man holding the rope. Long Draught yanked hard again, tugging him close.

The whistle of a blue mirral shrieked along the gap. *Peers.* "Find cover!" Camoe shouted. Jumping from the cairn, he dropped behind a large slate boulder. The mangled carcass of a beetle lay on the threshold of one of their dark holes, but he had no time to worry over the possibility of attack from below.

Something big sped along the gap from the bottom.

Scraping both sides where the gap narrowed, a monstrous dragon lion clawed toward the only living thing visible, the

Alchemist. Clattering upon a pair of boulders, the long snout of its great lion head bit at the dark hood of the Alchemist.

A sharp tug yanked the Alchemist from his feet.

The powerful jaws of the creature clicked together, snapping upon empty air. Snarling, the dragon lion raised its head and raked the ground with its powerful lizard-like hooked claw. The Alchemist rolled to the side.

Then Long Draught was there. A half-spear in each hand, he sank the one in his right hand into the heel of the dragon lion's claw. Half the bladed end protruded through to the other side.

The claw jerked away, taking the spear with it as the dragon lion reared.

Hampered by his hands tied together, the hooded man gained his feet and shuffled backward until bumping into a boulder.

Long Draught reached under his left shoulder and pulled a third half-spear from its sheath.

Camoe dashed to the top of the largest rock cairn and hopped upon a nearby boulder pile, scrambling along a jumbled outcropping. A thick slab of limestone slate jutted outward, teetering precariously as he crept upon it.

The dragon lion's tail whipped back and forth, slamming into the crumbling slate rock walls as it roared with frenzy. The outcropping rattled and shook from vibration.

Camoe shuffled away from edge, using his weight to balance the slab. The next whip of the dragon lion's tail would fling him toward it. Drawing his sword, he braced for it.

Girth appeared at the dragon lion's left foreleg, his great hammer held high.

"Wait!" Camoe yelled.

With all the force of Girth's considerable weight and strength, the hammer blurred and then slammed upon the dragon lion's three-toed foreleg. Blood sprayed around it.

The dragon lion roared and then leapt the only way open to it, its lashing tail striking the outcropping. The slab fell away, launching Camoe as he wanted, but the trajectory was wrong; changed by the dragon's leap, he would pass by, flung too far. He swung his sword, hoping to slice into the softer fur of the lion's head where it joined the hard scale of the reptilian body.

Twisting harshly in his hand, Camoe's sword glanced off the hard scale below the neck and wedged under the plate below. Slamming into the beast, he lost his footing though he retained his grip on his sword. Drawing his long knife, he caught a glimpse of Long Draught on one knee, his half-spears held high. Then the dragon lion's wide back covered him from view.

The jolt of the creature's weight as it thumped the ground nearly jarred his grip free. The dragon lion bucked, roaring with rage and pain. He held on by stabbing his long knife below an ear. Roaring weakly, the dragon lion careened from side to side, clattering against rocks, trying to dislodge him. A pile of slate toppled covering the place he'd last seen Girth.

Surging forward, the dragon lion stumbled and fell, its lion snout digging into the rocky ground.

Refusing to let go, Camoe ran in front, as the beast slid to a halt.

Thrashing fitfully, its powerful hind legs clawed at the stone and then grew still.

Finally daring to release his hold on his long sword, Camoe looked around, his alarm growing.

Long Draught, Girth, and their hostage, the Alchemist, were missing.

# DEPTHS

Garn kept the horses calm at the ferry's center simply by being near. Though both of the stallions didn't like standing on bobbing wood that floated on water, the warhorses were veterans of previous rides and only moved to maintain stability. Having a smooth ride helped, for which he was grateful. The source of the ride's smoothness, Black Bottom Ferry's owner, stood with his back to him centered at the boat's front keel. Statuesque, Surn had one arm outstretched toward unseen land and the other palm down toward the water. Garn had been surprised to discover he was a User, but he should've known. How else would the ferry acquire the power to move on Astura? Surn must have some strength too. Their steady progress across the long right fork of the lake had not once faltered.

"He does well for his chosen profession," Captain Bozlun said from behind him.

Putting his daughter behind him, Garn turned. Captain Bozlun and General Karnas gazed at the two of them calmly. Where Bozlun's brown eyes glinted with vigor, Karnas' contrasted with his dull eyes of light blue, reminding Garn of the leechers more than he liked. The general's gray complexion indicated the man was sick or getting over something that made him ill, almost as if a spiderbee had leeched some life from him. "That he does, but I'm certain you did not seek me out to discuss the ferryman.

What is it you wish to speak of?" Garn wanted to know.

"How did you and my escort package survive the leechers when so many of my men died?" the general rasped. Struggling for volume, his voice came out as a wheeze.

"My sister calls them spiderbees," Jade said. "Are you unwell?" she asked the general.

General Karnas ignored her question, not even deigning to look at her.

"The general has assured me he is as well as ever," Captain Bozlun answered.

Garn replied to the original question. "The leechers…spiderbees…are impervious to normal weapons. According to the ferryman, the spiderbees' only weakness is real wood."

"Yes, that is right," Captain Bozlun said. "Yet you do not carry wooden items. Except for the hardwood cross bolts, none of the men do. There has been little need. Leechers have never swarmed in such a capacity before, preferring to seek out one or two hapless souls traveling alone or to drink from the animals of the wild."

Garn regarded the general though he spoke to the captain. "The boat we stand upon was our salvation. The ropes they make for netting is woven from wood not plants. I used them. The ferrymen have had a run-in with a few spiderbees in the recent past."

His gray grizzled face staying passive, General Karnas' dull eyes showed nothing of his thoughts. "I commend you on your survival perseverance. We shall take command of the 'package' from this point. Consider her under my personal protection. You shall report to Captain Bozlun."

Jade made a small sound.

No one looked at her for which Garn was thankful. He had

to stop this now. "I am truly sorry, general. You seem like a good commander, but I do not take orders from you or your man. There is only one man whom I follow, and *his* orders were clear. The 'package,' as you so elegantly described, is deliverable to Lord Alchemist's chambers by his personal guard. You know as well as I do who that is. Do you wish to risk his ire now that we're close to finishing this?" Reaching over his shoulder, Garn gripped his sword and backed away, shouldering his daughter with him. His arm had some feeling returning but no muscle control yet. Given a choice, he'd take control over feeling, but the two had to work together.

General Karnas' hand went to his weapon, a long sword hung centered at his waist at a forty-five-degree angle. "Though I am certain you understood my *command,* I shall express it one final time. Release her unto me and report to Captain Bozlun."

Captain Bozlun stepped in front of Garn, his back to him. "Are you certain of this, General? He does have our lord's support."

"Move away, Bozlun. *I* am your lord, you shall do as commanded," General Karnas rasped.

Garn backed slowly starboard; his daughter's hand on the small of his back informed him she moved with him. The nine soldiers spread out on each side shuffled to ring him. He couldn't have that; a 270-degree radius was better to guard than a 360-degree radius. He preferred his back to the water.

As Garn slid his sword from the sheath, the nine drew weapons. Five raised swords, and four leveled crossbows. The bows didn't concern him, but he worried a stray bolt might hit Jade. Her hand pressed against his back. He stopped. He sensed more than saw brackish water on either side. They'd reached the ferry's edge. "Stay behind me and keep low," he told his daughter without taking his eyes from the nine.

"Hold!" Captain Bozlun shouted. "No one makes a move, or I—"

The *splotch-schalunk* sound of sharp steel puncturing flesh and ending at bone cut through the air with stark clarity.

Captain Bozlun hunched, bending toward General Karnas.

Quick and decisive, the extended ping of steel scraping metal armor accompanied General Karnas withdrawing his sword.

Captain Bozlun collapsed to the deck.

Sword in hand, General Karnas advanced, and the tone of his voice was now strong. "If anyone even nicks the girl, they shall meet the same fate as the captain. Kill the mercenary!"

Garn flowed into *Beaver Builds a Wall* stance, blocking a cross bolt with the flat of his blade and then following through with a curved parry. A sharp *ring* echoed dully across the ferry as Garn smacked away sword thrusts to either side hard enough the two men winced. Wary, the two stepped back, waiting for an opening. He blocked a second bolt and prepared to give them what they waited for, drawing them closer.

General Karnas charged, chopping wildly. He shuffled back and forth clumsily, swinging hard as if he believed sheer brute force would end the fight in his favor. Though surprised by the moves, Garn parried easily, slicing across the older man's forearm. Blood streamed down his arm and dripped from his elbow. Not slowing, General Karnas hacked and thrust. Garn's parries caught them and the third cross bolt.

Nonetheless, the general's unorthodox attack was eking away at Garn's strength; the wild swings took much concentration and muscle to stop. The powerful commander had created a distraction he couldn't afford, adding an element of danger outside his control. The five soldiers brandishing long swords were shuffling close. A subtle look would signal the move to come at him as one. He hoped they worked well together. The stance *Wind Blows in the*

*Rushes* worked best with a well-ordered simultaneous attack.

As Garn fended off another flurry of blows from the general, Jade called to one of the crossbowmen circling for a back shot, a man nearly within his quick-strike range who hadn't long to live. The man stopped shuffling for position when his daughter shouted something about plate armor. The man would live a little longer. Yet it was time to end this.

Deciding on the best position to have General Karnas' body fall for fast removal of the rest, Garn would have missed the danger reaching for him, if not for his daughter's scream.

*****

Jade was frightened for her father. Surrounded by men and women with swords and crossbows, the maniac General Karnas thrust and chopped at him. Even though he bled from a wounded forearm, the general still swung with great vigor. Jade worried it was too much for her dad. What would he do if they attacked at once?

To make matters worse, three of the four with crossbows had bolts redrawn as they maneuvered for a shot. The fourth cranked on the drawstring with less than half the distance to the trigger latch remaining. Then, she would drop in a bolt and point it at her dad. She had to help him. But how?

Reading the aura revolving around someone was her only ability, useless when it came to aiding in a battle, fighting for survival. Or was it? Perhaps she could discover something to stay the hand of those attacking, at the least, glean *intent*. Perhaps then, she could call out a warning.

As one of the three crossbowmen slipped around the left perimeter working for an unguarded back shot, Jade slowed the rotation around him and shuffled through the three images, marveling how easy such things came now.

The first image, a scaly beast with the head of a lion was no help and frightening to look at. She hastily moved on to the second. A golden-haired woman wearing a blue dress twirled a parasol at the end of a pier. She might have a use for that one, but she didn't get the feeling the woman was the soldier's companion. The third image contained what she hoped. Black plate armor hung on a rack. Jade let the images revolve back into the cyclone raging around him. "You with the crossbow, slinking to the side," Jade called. "If you harm the hooded man's guardian, you'll never receive plate armor."

The man froze and then frowned. "How could you know that?" he mouthed. Then, looking behind her, his eyes widened.

Something dark and slimy pinned her arms to her chest and lifted her from the decking.

Jade screamed.

She lost her breath when the thing tightened its grip, squeezing with suffocating force. Jade felt herself ascending at a rapid rate. Quickly, the ferry shrank in size as she rose upward. Monstrous black tentacles dropped upon the decking, tilting the boat violently with their great weight.

Now, she descended faster than when she'd risen. The tentacle loosened its hold slightly. Jade barely had the presence of mind to gulp air as she plunged underwater.

*****

The ferry listed sharply starboard. Garn twisted his legs, getting his feet sideways as he slid toward the edge. Digging his sword into the wood, it further helped slow his slide, allowing him to come to a complete stop a few inches from dropping into open water. A black tentacle stabbed from the black depths, seeking to wrap around him. Garn sliced through it. The stump withdrew as the severed half flopped on the deck and then rolled into the lake.

Garn's heart caught in his throat. One of the bloody squirming things had his daughter, carrying her down toward the lake.

Gasping for breath, Jade crashed into the lake's surface and vanished beneath, pulled from sight before he could react. As one, the tentacles withdrew, plopping into the water. The ferry bucked, rocking violently portside. Sliding backward, Garn kept his balance as the boat righted itself.

Both hands gripping his upraised sword, General Karnas stumbled past him, screaming manically, "You shall not have it for your own!" He stepped from the ferry and sank.

Garn had no time to wonder. Sheathing his sword, he drew his dagger, wedged it between his teeth as he dashed across the decking, and dived into the lake where he'd seen his daughter last.

Though not frigid, the water was cold and dark. If not for the large bubbles of air floating toward him, he may have soon lost his way. Fanning his arms and pumping his legs, he swam, giving his all. The bubbles rose larger as a murky shape moved below and then stopped.

As he closed the distance, he made out a cluster of tentacles, none moving. His daughter squirmed in the center, a large tentacle wrapped around her. Garn swam to her and pulled the serpentine thing loose. Taking her by the waist, he pushed her upward and then followed when she swam on her own, glad he didn't need his knife. Like a giant black corral forest, the tentacles swayed gently in an underwater current.

Passing the longest tentacle in the forest, a clearing of the murky water revealed General Karnas enfolded at the tip, his sword missing from limp hands. Beyond him, Surn floated wrapped in a tentacle. The gloomy water closed in again hiding the scene in a cloak of obscurity. Garn swam on, his lungs burning to draw breath.

Above the water grew noticeably brighter. Jade struggled but kept moving up, and then she broke the surface. Garn surfaced beside his youngest daughter, grabbing a ragged breath and then two.

Drawing in deep breaths, Jade smiled as she treaded water. "Have I told you how are amazing you are? I love you, Dad," she declared. Abruptly, her smile faded, and her eyes rolled to the whites as she listed to her side.

Then she vanished.

Garn blinked, confused. *Jade?*

Something horribly strong wrapped around his waist and pulled him down into the murky depths.

# OVER THE EDGE

Prying the scales to one side with his dagger, Camoe then swung his sword as he would an axe, cutting deep into the dragon lion. Hacking into the breast of the beast, he chopped and chopped, hewing huge chunks from the carcass. Panting from his efforts, he raised his sword high above his head once more. The grip slick with blood, he shifted his hold, preparing the downward swing.

An unsteady hand held his wrist in place.

Coughing, Tarn pointed at the dragon lion with a dagger. "You have found what you seek," he managed to say, his voice hoarse.

Long Draught's familiar leather wristband lay wrapped around a hand frozen forever clenched on the handle of a half-spear.

Slowing his breaths, Camoe lowered his sword and checked his friend's pulse, though his underlying sense of Long Draught's vibrancy was missing. As he expected, there was no beat of a heart. Letting go of the cold wrist, he stood. "Look for Girth and the bloody Alchemist, I have no sense of them, but these rocks could have put them out of range," he growled at the three warriors who did exude the breath of life. Tarn's had grown worrisomely weaker.

As Peers, Kerna, and Tarn moved carefully around the pile of rock covering his oldest warrior—Long Draught had served him the longest—Camoe leaned against the corpse of the dragon lion and barely held back a flood of the black despair, an old familiar battle that seemed to want to stay with him. He would miss Long Draught's spears. Were all those near him destined to die?

The clatter of rocks nearby tore him from his reverie. Peers and Kerna held the half-conscious hooded man between them. Tarn followed, his complexion ashen. The Alchemist's hands still tied together in front, his arms bled from several raw abrasions, and a long gash down the left side of his head streamed with blood. "What of Girth?" Camoe asked.

Tarn shook his head. "He was badly damaged. Death came quick with much honor."

Camoe drew an extended breath and raised both fists shoulder-high as he leaned back looking upward. "Onan, please take my warriors under the shelter of your divine arms. They are good men."

He regarded the hooded man and quelled a sudden irrational urge to hack the man's bleeding arms from him. Deep down, he knew the prisoner had no part in bringing the beast upon them. Or had he? The group had run afoul of more than their fair share of nasty creatures of late, starting after the Dark One's capture. Coincidence?

Camoe held little stock in happenstance. Broken Gap had more than one odd occurrence for his liking. Normally docile rock beetles had attacked Jade and her captors, and the enraged brute at his back had released the life essence of two of his men. There was something wrong with that. Dragon lions ranged farther north, and this one had gleamed with the sheen of sweat indicating the creature had traveled far at great speed, as if called. Though how? Had the Dark Users developed control of wild creatures?

From the hooded one's past words, Camoe suspected the man had knowledge of whatever was happening or at least harbored some theory about it. It did not matter. Whatever information or suspicions the man concealed, he intended to pry from him even if he had to sort through the man's screams of pain. He was not too squeamish for torture; though he detested it, he would do what he had to. "Clean and wrap his head wound and any others detrimental to the Dark One's survival. Without Girth's healing, our warrior training shall have to suffice. I do not care if he scars, only that he lives."

No one moved.

In no mood for a lengthy discussion of his reasons, Camoe hardened his demeanor and emphasized his request. "Go on, do as I have *asked*, or I shall handle it personally."

Tarn coughed.

Peers exchanged a look with his wife.

Letting the hooded man hang on her mate, Kerna stepped to the side and reached into her leaf dress. The outfit accommodated her action by parting the length of her side. Her slender hand slipped a worn bag made from the sturdy leather of the kell from her shoulder. Camoe had not known she carried the bag. The living dress covered her smooth deep brown hip and toned front torso quickly.

Deftly, Kerna unwound the tie wrap strings from around two brass pins. Flipping the cover flap open, she removed a string-wrapped bundle of the leather, setting it on a flat-topped rock near her. "I see no reason we should help the Dark One, he has caused two of our number to go to the embrace of the Great Mother. But I follow your wisdom without question," she said softly, though her abrupt movements belied her words. Untying the bundle, she extracted a needle with black thread already inserted through the eye and a wad of cotton. As the kell leather flattened from its own suppleness and weight, clean rolled strips of the leather popped into view.

Camoe's ire softened. Kerna was right in a big way. Girth and Long Draught had given their lives protecting the group, even for the dark stain of evil they all knew as the hooded one. He should kill the man and be done with it. Yet his true sense of the future warned the man might have a use still, though he knew not what. *Blast the bloody foresight!* Camoe thought. When had it brought anything other than a vague knowledge of something unanswered? Camoe could answer his own question with a single word. Never.

Brusquely, Kerna swept the black cowl from the Alchemist, letting it fall upon his broad shoulders. Pushing his head to one side, she threaded the needle deftly along the gash. Blood streamed freely as she pulled the skin together, tugging the thread.

The Alchemist moaned, his eyes fluttering open.

Deftly tying the thread, Kerna bit through the remainder, wadded cotton on the wound, and wrapped it with a kell strip, knotting it at the back.

Peers moved from under the Alchemist, reaching for him as he sagged.

Weakly, the Alchemist pushed the offered hands away and straightened. Swaying a little, the Alchemist blinked rapidly, his golden eyes tinged darkly with red. Reaching a shaky arm to the back of his neck, he draped the black cowl over his head.

Camoe stood and restacked the slate rocks over his old friend. Working alone and in silence, he covered the corpse thoroughly. No scavenger would feed upon his remains. He turned to those who yet followed him. "Come, bring him. Let us leave this foul place." He regarded the prisoner. "Your knowledge has some use still; I expect to hear from you at first rest or you go no farther alive."

Peers picked up the rope and tied some of the slack around his waist. A sharp tug tested the knot above his braided belt. He avoided eye contact with the Alchemist.

Camoe moved close to the hooded man, his hatred for an old enemy growing with each step. "Keep the pace, or my warrior shall drag you like the rotten carcass you are, Dark One. No one slows us down, do you understand?"

The black hood rose slightly, revealing the grim line of lips drawn back with pain. He nodded without saying anything.

Camoe expected as much; the hooded man was no fool. The less he spoke, the fewer mistakes his weakened mind and body would give away. Now, while the Alchemist believed himself safe from interrogation was when he should fire questions at the man, but the gap exuded a sense of watchfulness, as if the entire ravine waited for the signal to strike.

Taking the lead, Kerna set a measured pace, her shorn head of black hair twisting back and forth as if she, too, expected trouble.

Camoe trotted at the back, keeping an eye on those few warriors left to him and the prisoner. Tarn's valiant, though futile, attempt at covering his mouth with his hands matched the Alchemist's stumbling as a cause for apprehension. No matter how quiet they moved, Tarn's increasing coughs forewarned of their coming. With his hands tied, the hooded man's staggers came with a likelihood of falling and bashing his head open again, but Peers tugged him along with no mercy.

Getting through Broken Gap came first, and coming up with a solution for the two other concerns would have to wait.

Winding around large limestone boulders and hopping over smaller ones, they passed numerous dark openings under and beside rocks pockmarking the rockslide on both sides of Broken Gap. As they ran, Camoe's foreboding amplified, the holes increasing with a sense of malice and the darkness inside them flickering.

The trail ahead widened, slowly growing less rocky. Kerna

increased the pace. Camoe discarded his first thought of calling for her to resume the same speed, as the foreboding built, pounding an impending sense of doom inside his skull. The bloody prisoner would have to keep up.

Kerna moved beyond a dark hole, the largest yet, burrowed beside a house-sized boulder. A great malevolence emanated from within, growing stronger the closer he got to it. The darkness lightened, shifting from abysmal blackness to ominous shadows, as Peers and the hooded man jogged past.

When Tarn passed, two large eyes, divided in half, opened. Seeming almost as four, the eyes glared redly as they swayed back and forth, coming closer.

Camoe burst into a sprint, roaring his fear. "Move! Run faster!"

A mark of their training, his band of warriors sped up and dashed into an all-out sprint without slowing to look for a threat. Camoe glanced over his shoulder. A dark round shape charged from the blackness, the claws on its six legs digging into the packed soil. Behind it, the rockslides roiled with shifting shapes.

"Blast you all! I said run! I shall not lose another this day!" Camoe roared. The line of warriors, and even the hooded man, gained a burst of speed. At top speed, the southern end of Broken Gap grew larger, the ravine widening and sloping into a respectable highland valley at the mouth.

Camoe risked a second look. The big rock beetle, larger than any he had ever came across, the red-eyed mother of them all, moved ahead of the scurrying ravine bobbing behind it, gaining ground with every bound of its six legs.

Judging the distance, Camoe ran on. "Keep going! They will turn back at the end of the slide, the openness frightens them!" he shouted, though he doubted his words. Rock beetles did not grow bigger than a wolf and throng after prey, not as these had.

Ahead, the Alchemist stumbled, making a desperate attempt to right himself. His shorter legs charged forward, trying to outrun his leaning upper body. With an incredible lunge, Tarn caught at the man's shoulder, righting him. They ran on, the eastern mouth of Broken Gap drawing near.

A strong canyon wind gusting from the bottom pushed at Camoe, siphoning precious speed, as he broke out into the open. The trail sloped downward slowly at first and then grew steep.

Slowing, he looked back.

Though the smaller beetles were motionless, grouped in ordered lines at the ravine's mouth, the red eyes of the mother beetle bore down upon him at full speed.

He jumped to the side, sliding in crumbling slate and grasping at his sword.

Leaving a rank scent of malevolence combined with something else behind, the mother beetle thumped past, oblivious to him. Ahead, Tarn rushed along the trail, one hand held at his stomach, the hooded man's affliction slowing him.

Though too late to be of use, Camoe dashed across the slate, a twinge of pain racing in the small of his back as he scrambled for footing. "Behind you!" he roared. The path intersected the trail, and he picked up speed on the downslope.

Tarn glanced over his shoulder. Spinning, he drew a dagger, sliding to a stop. The beetle bore down on him. At the last moment, Tarn stepped to the side, and with his left hand, he stabbed the long knife into the softer meat above the beetle's eyes.

The beetle shuddered, slowing but little.

Maintaining a firm grip, Tarn used the momentum of the beast's charge to wrench himself atop the black carapace, straddling it with his legs and holding on by one hand. Beyond him, Peers led the Alchemist to one side of the trail, turning to face the creature where the path vanished over an edge.

Shrieking with pain and rage, the beetle veered, targeting the two men. Tarn plunged a second dagger beside the first. Emitting an ear-piercing screech, the beetle veered sharply to the cliffside and then vanished over the edge.

Camoe ran to where he had seen his friend last, though the fear in the pit of his stomach told him he was too late.

# BLACKNESS

The blackness was back, rolling toward her awareness, her sense of self, like a dark fog of malice exuding supreme arrogance to all that dared stand before it. Jade stood before it, small and insignificant beside its great power. But she'd kept the darkness at bay before, even pushing it away by the force of her will, and she'd do it again. This would be the last of it. This time it was for good.

Gathering her will, she faced the hurricane storm of malevolence, confident in the knowledge she'd deterred the thing once and she would do it again, even without Crystalyn's help.

There was something horribly wrong. The darkness rushed in without slowing, pushing her back to her safe pocket, her tiny bubble of protection, almost before she could install it in the farthest corner of her mind.

How had it gotten so strong? The answer came to her with such clarity she knew it for truth even though it frightened her badly. Her body was dying, drowning in brackish water, and her willpower with it. As her body died, her brain lacked the strength to resist.

Arrogance, black and unyielding, pressed upon her, compressing her bubble inward and bearing down on her. Inhumanly strong, a dominant overbearing will clamped upon hers. With no strength left to fight it, she was doomed.

The darkness hesitated. Relenting a little, it flowed around her barrier setting up full control. Then it restored her eyesight to the bubble. Images flooded into her awareness and then opened up, becoming all-encompassing until she managed to sort it coherently. Images with sounds trickled in and then pieced together.

Black water melded into sandy shoreline from a distance above. The shoreline seemed to advance closer as the perspective changed. Her dad descended, a dark tentacle wrapped around his limp form. Releasing its burden on yellowed grass, the tentacles arose to eye height, squirming in place.

*"Search for structures intruding upon your domain made by man. Destroy them."* The command projected outward from the blackness. The inherent menace she sensed in the thoughts left her cold from the sheer brutality of it. Whatever thing had wrested control of her had a total disregard for all species.

The frightened little girl part of her wanted to babble incoherently, but her vocals, even her tear ducts, no longer belonged to her. She couldn't cry to relieve pressure, which brought pressure bubbling around inside her thoughts. She wanted—no *needed*—to scream.

Now she looked out upon Bracken Lake, the tree of tentacles withdrawing. Pulling itself deeper into the lake, it took its myriad of lidded eyes at every tentacle base with it. That many staring about was hard to look at, even though it was as if she viewed it through someone else's eyes.

As the creature submerged, Jade caught a glimpse of General Karnas' body gripped in a tentacle as another tore at his armor, his boots gone. Somewhere on the thing, it had a maw. Jade was glad she hadn't seen it.

The scene swung back to the shore. Her dad stirred, expelling water. Two hands reached out and pulled him on his side—*her hands*. Doing so allowed him to expel another round of water. To her great joy, her father lived. Yet the knowledge of it came with trepidation. Why had it kept him alive?

Her dad rolled onto his hands and knees, clearing his lungs and throat. Finally, he climbed to his feet, flashing a weak smile. "Praise the Great Father, somehow we survived that tentacle thing, and we're free of your captors."

A voice—*her voice,* changed and sounding different—spoke then. "Your neural functions were left intact for the purpose of ensuring the host, your offspring, is protected. If you wish for reunification, remain diligent with the task."

About to come close, her dad froze. His shocked look stabbed at Jade's emotions, adding to the pressure of her helplessness.

Her feet closed the distance between them as her otherworldly voice continued relentlessly on. "The One Mind will demonstrate the cost of failure." Her hand grabbed her father's forearm, and her vision changed, switching inward.

A translucent barrier hung before her, but it dissolved as they went through it. Images spun before her, slowing to a leisurely rotation, playing through as if a live holofeed. Side by side, her dad and her mom strolled through a lush garden. Flowering plants of all colors bloomed, exotic bushes spread intricate patterned leaves, and an earthen pathway led them onward.

The clothes they wore confused her. Her dad was dressed much as he was now, but his black leather shirt and pants were brown instead of black. Her mom's customary Terran outfit of gray silk suit shirt and skirt had vanished; in its place, she wore the supple brown kell shirt and pants of a warrior. In her hand, she carried a staff topped with a clear orb of crystal.

Had she a voice, Jade would've gasped with surprise when her mom spoke. "Are you certain you wish to do this, beloved? It is not too late for us to change our mind. I will tell them we have reconsidered."

"You heard the Lore Mother, Durandas, and the rest of the Elder Voice," her dad replied. "They have read the omens and believe our sacrifice will have the best odds of sending the land toward the greater good, only Camoe is against it. Is this not why we joined the Green Writhe?"

"You are right, though I wonder—"

"I do not truly believe fully in the rightness of my words, for I share your trepidation," her dad interrupted. "How can we know for certain we do the right thing, the *best* course for us and our future family?" Her dad put his hand lovingly on her mom's stomach briefly, a look of awe crossing his young face. "Perhaps we should tell them we cannot go through with this. I shall stand beside your decision, beloved."

Taking him by the hand, her mom pulled her dad to a stop, hope shining in her green eyes, so like her own. For a while, they stood gazing at each other. Then a look of resolve clouded her face. "We cannot, there is too much involved with this, so many have put so much into it."

Her dad's shoulders slumped with sadness. "As long as you know how much I love you, I shall bear it."

Sureen's smile was brief. "The precise act of what we have agreed upon with the elders permeates all things with the cries of our love."

Her dad's answering smile matched hers.

They walked off, moving slower, as if going to their doom. There were more images, but Jade found her vision shifted to the external, and she faced her dad. The horrified expression on his face disclosed he'd seen what she had.

"What are you? What have you done to my daughter?" her dad gasped.

"Your inferior human mind would not comprehend the

properties of the Over Mind though an attempt at a small explanation shall be attempted. Your offspring's ability and unique unlimited neural capacity permits the One Mind to read humanity without the necessity of assimilating all neural functions. The Over Mind now has the capacity to view memories. With this significant capability, the One Mind has only to consume those whose influence controls many of you, either with the great power flowing through this world or authority over another. The One Mind's capacity is now great enough to consume this world; no single mind will be hidden," Jade heard herself say, though her tone was alien, clinical.

Her dad gaped, his jaw dropping as he grappled with the enormity of it all. Jade had no doubt hers would've dropped too if she had control of it.

Reaching over his shoulder, her dad slipped his sword from the sheath on his back. "I am not certain my daughter is even alive in there. How do I know she hasn't fully succumbed to your evil?"

Her arm extended toward him.

Moving backward, her dad pointed his great sword at her like an accusatory finger. "Stay away or you'll force me to slay her to kill you."

The voice spoke then, the alien voice that echoed oddly along the beach. Gone was the mild, medium-pitched tone of a young woman moving into adulthood. In place of it, a woman's husky voice resonated through the air, sounding as if it originated from some cold and desolate place. "I am here, Dad. It's still me."

Though he tried not to show it, her dad was horrified. His mouth worked, but for a long while, no sound came out. Finally, he lowered his sword slightly. "So you say, but how can I truly know you still exist?"

The power controlling her hesitated, roiling with confusion. A flicker of many minds, people she had never known, shuffled through her thoughts. "You cannot," it finally said. "There is not a way to provide proof the One Mind has not consumed your offspring's memories and now speaks to you with them. You shall have to rely on what you humans refer to as faith."

Her dad raised the great sword again. "But how can I be certain, blast you!"

"The One Mind will now release the host's vocals for a brief period," the alien voice said, abruptly.

"Dad! Listen!" Jade shouted, louder than she intended. Having her voice returned to her was so unexpected. "I've managed to protect a small part of me in a tiny corner, but it's so strong!"

"Jade! Is it really you?"

"Yes. Listen, Dad, you have to make me a promise."

"Anything, Jade, tell me. You have my word."

Jade had to be strong, as strong as the strongest person she knew, Crystalyn. As strong as the two people in the image, her mom and dad, had seemed. "I don't know how long I can hold on, and this thing is so deadly. You have to kill me."

"No, Jade!"

"Do it now, Dad! I love—" Jade's words reverberated as silent thoughts through her little bubble of awareness. The alien, imperious woman voice rang throughout her mind. "Destroying your offspring will serve only to slow the inevitable. The Over Mind, the One Mind, shall prevail."

Her dad's chest rose and fell rapidly. Jade's wanted to cry over the agony in his blue eyes and the distress of his quickened breaths. He raised his sword high. "So you claim. My daughter, however, has resisted you. *My* beautiful, wonderful daughter, the noblest, most selfless living being anyone could ask for believes otherwise. You shall die with her."

The malice inside her recoiled, flickering through memories.

A moment passed. Jade's arms spread wide. "Then strike your descendent. The One Mind shall live on in the father."

Her dad lowered his sword and his head. "I'm sorry, Jade, I cannot," he whispered.

The black wind of the Over Mind's triumphant satisfaction rippled Jade's protective bubble.

# TRUE SENSE

Camoe eased the pressure of his sword tip from the hooded man's chest only when blood dripped below the man's black cowl, flowing down his bare stomach in tiny teardrop rivulets. "We go no farther, Dark One. With Tarn's ailment and the girl whom I sought to rescue by using your knowledge to aid her no longer a factor, there is no good reason not to push slowly through your flesh and watch the darkness fade from your eyes. Answer all that I ask quickly, or die."

With the bottom of the cliff at his back, the Alchemist attempted to shrug off Camoe's companions' grip on his shoulders to no avail. Experienced warriors, Peers and Kerna tightened their hold, ready to break a shoulder bone if necessary. The hooded one grunted with pain or distress when Kerna pulled his hood back, exposing his brown broad face to the shade of the cliff and the filtered light of early evening sun. After finding and burying Tarn, it had come to this.

Camoe respected the Alchemist's courage. One light push from him, and the great sword's weight would finish the rest. "Making me repeat the command is not advisable. My weapon of choice is getting heavier, my patience thinner," Camoe said mildly, though he seethed inside. The bloody Dark One had cost him friends.

The Alchemist relaxed, his shoulders slumping in defeat.

"Very well, choose your questions with care, and we may all yet survive," he hissed.

Camoe tensed.

Though the Alchemist pressed backward into the cliff wall as far as he could, the red drops increased. Pain glistened in his dark, golden eyes.

His movements more abrupt than he intended, Camoe sheathed his great sword. Running the man through would not serve his purpose at this time. "You believe this a game, Dark One? That belief may yet be your last. Speak or die. From the time of your capture, creatures of this world have come seeking your demise. What hunts you? What foul thing have you angered with your colossal arrogance?"

"This is why we have lost so much, for him?" Kerna asked. Her light-colored burgundy eyes glared at Camoe.

The Alchemist jerked upright with such strength Peers and Kerna lost their hold.

Camoe's sword was out in an instant.

Cursing, Peers and Kerna fought to reestablish a grip.

The Alchemist took no notice of them or the sword tip a finger's breadth from his heart. His hourglass eyes widened as he gazed off in the distance. "A great fool I have been," he said, the tone of his voice a fierce hiss. "Our pact is broken. It has sought my extermination!"

"What comes for you, filth?" Camoe snarled.

The Alchemist regarded him as if meeting him for the first time. A tint of red outlined his golden irises vanishing inside his dark pupils. "A power greater than anything the world has ever seen. Old when Astura was young, the ultimate embodiment of stealth and cunning has come; it is now fully awake and active."

Camoe prodded another hole in the man's chest, over his dark heart this time. "Stop speaking in riddles, Dark scum. What is coming?"

The hooded man snarled, "Kill me, and then destroy each other, go meet your deity. Death is preferable than allowing it to control you; you will only feed its power."

Camoe's patience fled. He raised his sword and then hesitated, giving the man one final chance for redemption. "Your next words decide your fate," he warned.

Though his golden eyes widened, the hooded man did not plead. His stance grew relaxed. "Four centuries and four decades ago, a friend and I traveled to a place of ultimate evil on a dare. We foolishly rode to the Stair of Despair."

Peers tensed. He shifted his grip on the hooded man, clamping tight. "The short version, Dark One, your life's story is of no concern to us."

The Alchemist struggled halfheartedly. Then he relented, his broad muscular arms growing slack. "As you wish. The White Lands, the Dark Citadel, the northern, western, southern domains, all of us face the greatest threat our world has ever known. Even with all of us working together it may not be—*unnnh*."

Kerna rammed her elbow into the hooded man's side before he finished. Collapsing to his knees with a groan, he pulled away from the grip Peers had on his arm. "What makes you believe we would ever join forces with you? You destroyed the Vale, our people, my friends. Do you carry the hope we shall allow you to live?" Kerna hissed. Drawing her long-bladed dagger, Kerna gripped the Alchemist by his stringy black hair, yanking his head back. Her dagger glinted with a stray ray of light against his throat. "I say we end this now."

Gasping, the Alchemist groped the air in front of the sleek woman. His left arm hugged his stomach. "Wait!" he croaked. "You have not heard what it is we face."

"We have listened to your lies long enough. I say kill him,

too," Peers said.

Kerna's hand whitened from the tenseness of her grip on the long blade, but she looked to Camoe, as did Peers.

The Alchemist dropped his hands to his sides. Raising his neck slightly, he allowed a much wider target. The hooded man's golden gaze fixed on Camoe.

Camoe lowered his sword though he did not sheathe it. The man should not live. He was a fool for insisting on keeping the Alchemist alive, no matter his instinct. If not for him, Tarn, Girth, and Long Draught would still be alive.

Jade was safe, and whatever rubbish the man spouted about the danger stalking the black plateau, he had no care for. Whatever had awakened and attacked the vile place they deserved, if it was true. The man had played him for a fool, answering nothing, even giving a life friend a slow death.

Camoe pulled his sword back, preparing to sever the hooded man's head from his shoulders and end the world of an evil stain.

The true sense, his druidic foretelling curse, struck him with the force of an upper canyon wind. Staggered, he lowered his sword and then sheathed it. The Dark One had a role unfinished with fate; killing him would corrupt it and destroy many innocents, more than the Alchemist would if left alive. *How is that for irony?* he asked himself. Everything inside him screamed against it; it felt so *wrong*. Yet such a powerful grip of the true sense was not something to ignore. He had once, at the cost of someone too dear to him. Thinking of it, he despaired, the grief and guilt still raw. His loving daughter's beautiful sweet smiling face flashed in his mind. *Maialene, forgive me!*

Underlying the foretelling, a foreboding as light as a midsummer breeze caressing the hair on an arm, the feeling Jade was not truly safe brushed against him. "Untie him," he said.

"What!" Peers and Kerna exclaimed as one.

"Do as I say!" Camoe said tersely. "We run from here. If he falls, he has to catch himself. I need him alive to lead us past the Black Road."

Stunned, no one moved.

Camoe drew his hunting dagger and sliced through the cords binding the hooded man's wrists, gazing into his golden, hourglass eyes. "Know this, Dark One, fate has kept you alive for now. As soon as I receive a different intimation, I shall eradicate your pestilence from this world."

The hooded man pulled his cowl over his head. "I would expect no less," he said, standing.

"Peers, stay close, keep watch. If he strays, kill him. Kerna, you have rear sentry. If Peers fails, put your arrows in the Dark One. His life is now judged by how well he keeps up, his complete cooperation, nothing less," he said, meaning every word. The foretelling be damned if the Alchemist attempted even the smallest escape. Dismissing his companions' looks of betrayal, Camoe set out at a run.

A jog of two bells brought them to a highland ranch overlooking pastures on a rounded hilltop. A rancher looking to be of middle seasons packed grease in the hub of a wagon. Camoe waved as he neared, stopping beside the wagon when he came close. "Greetings, Goodman," he said.

Wiping his hands on a cloth as he stood, the man regarded him with dull blue eyes in a plain sun-browned face. "I am a man, 'tis true. A good man remains a question yet. It shall depend on what you seek."

Camoe took a closer look at the man. Propped against the wagon wheel, within easy reach behind the man, a great sword rested in a worn scabbard. "I wish to hire four mounts, if you have them."

The rancher eyed him and the rest of the party before

returning his sharp, no longer dull, gaze upon him. "I have them, but they are not for hire. A rancher without horses cannot long survive."

The man was more than he wanted to appear, yet he had told them as much. It was subtle but a warning nonetheless. Camoe respected his courage and confidence even though there was no need. He was not a thug. "I have sufficient coin for two weeks, which shall include the return trip to you along with an added week extra for your trouble. Can you manage without them for a fortnight?"

The rancher raised his jaw, leaning slightly closer to his wagon and the sword.

The hooded man presented a cloth-wrapped bundle the size of his outstretched palm. "There is a better offer to consider. For purchase of the four animals," he said. Unwrapping the supple cloth of the kell, he revealed a rectangular glimmer shard, bright in the early evening sun. "You could acquire another ranch with twenty horses along with the hirelings to work it for you, with such a flawless shard as this," he added quietly.

The rancher frowned. "I do not barter with Users, no one around these parts would."

The Alchemist opened his mouth, but Camoe interceded. "He is no User, at least not with the Flow that I am aware of," he said, masking the truth. The hooded man led entire armies of Users.

"Then where is his weapon?" the rancher asked, his face flushed with suspicion.

"We are his weapon. You have seen he holds wealth. What other proof do you require?" Camoe asked.

The rancher's features cleared, sliding into his bland features with ease. "Very well, the glimmer is infused. I accept the offer."

Slow and shaking slightly, as if reluctant to part with it, the

Alchemist placed the shard in the rancher's palm.

As soon as his hand closed upon it, the rancher stowed the shard in his kell leather vest pocket. "Follow me," he said. Grabbing the great sword, he strode past a stable, halting at a fenced pasture beyond it. Half a dozen horses grazed peacefully. "Choose your four," he said to Camoe. "Select well, there are but three saddles."

"My life mate rides bareback," Peers said to the rancher. "As long as you have a bridle," he added.

The rancher's blue eyes glanced at Peers and then shifted to Camoe. "I shall include four bridles, three saddles, and an evening meal in the barter."

"That is generous of you. A night's lodging and a soaking bin is well within your means with what you have been paid," the Alchemist spat.

His right hand reaching up to his shoulder, the rancher gripped the hilt of his sword. "Do you wish to renege on your acquisition?"

"No one is reneging on anything," Camoe said hastily. "Please forgive the manners of my charge. He shall restrain himself from now on if he wishes our aid," he added, glaring at the Alchemist.

The man under the dark cowl turned away.

Camoe slipped through the gap under the top pole of the fence, moving for a closer look at the horseflesh the glimmer shard had purchased. A big black roan caught his eye first. A wine-red stallion and a bay-colored horse with a brown body, black mane, and tail, were next. The final horse, the buckskin with golden coat, black mane, and tail, he chose as a mount for Kerna.

"You have decided on the four," the rancher said from beside him. "I shall prepare them for your journey. The offer of a meal still stands; my life mate will have it heated within a bell."

Camoe had not heard the man's arrival. The big sword rested easily on his broad shoulder. "Though a home-cooked meal made with a woman's deft touch is sorely missed, I must decline your gracious offer. There is a need for swift travel."

The rancher nodded. "I thought as much. Allow me a half bell with the mounts. Then we shall meet in front of the cabin."

"How will you acquire another saddle? Gray Dust is two days away." Camoe asked.

"Three days. The two older horses you leave me with can pull the wagon still, though at a much slower pace. I shall purchase two more horses and let them drag the wagon and new saddles back," he said, striding away down the gentle slope to where the horses grazed.

True to his word, the rancher led the four horses from the back to where Camoe and the others waited under the shade of the wide front porch of the main cabin. He no longer carried the great sword; the long handle rode high upon his back. Four bedrolls lay strapped behind the saddles of the three that had them, two on the bay.

Anxious to get moving for reasons Camoe could only guess at, the foretelling hammered him with the feeling that a major event would occur somewhere soon and he and his party needed to be present for it.

Camoe met the rancher below the porch almost as soon as he came to a standstill. Taking the reins of the dark horse, he mounted, motioning for the others to do likewise. Interestingly, to a man and woman, each selected the horse he had picked for them without his having to mention it.

"Treat them well and they will carry you far," the rancher said.

Camoe stroked the dark horse's great mane. The tall horse shuddered but did not grow skittish, a sign of even temperament.

"Rest assured of that," he said. He had no doubt the horse would do well for him.

"The whole lot is prime horseflesh, from the Great Plains, I suspect. A surprising discovery to find pastured with a simple rancher this far in the highlands," the Alchemist said, his voice soft, though it carried.

Backing toward the porch, the rancher ignored the comment.

"You have done us a great service," Camoe said, urging the great horse into motion. It did not take much. The dark horse's powerful muscles bunched, springing into a trot. The horse carried him easily down the gentle slope of a faded wagon trail. He looked back once before the trail dropped him from sight. A woman, slender in profile, the backdrop of the evening sun highlighting her golden hair, stood beside the man watching them go. Camoe turned back to the trail ahead growing gradually steeper.

Leaving the highlands, they rode over the Great Road Bridge leading into Gray Dust. Camoe veered around, circling to the south at a full gallop, putting the place behind him in the dark of night. Riding until the sun rose in the afternoon, he rode to a secluded spot in a copse of trees, the last before the Black Road. "We shall camp here for the night. Peers, you have first watch, then Kerna. Awaken me for the last." Dismounting, he tied the black horse's reins to a green aspen sapling for the lush grazing around it.

The Alchemist sat his horse. "Why did we not go to Gray Dust? I control the topaz gateway. You know this. We would have already arrived at our destination."

Camoe untied the bedroll. "Yes, I am aware who controls the great gate. For that fact alone, I may not have chosen to follow that route. Such a thing would have many guarding it, and the temptation for betrayal of hostile assistance is too great." Holding the bedroll under one arm, Camoe gazed at all of his companions, hostile or not. "If you must know, since the highlands, the true sense has led this way. Do not ask for more explanations. I shall not have the answer." Turning his back on them, he strode away. Finding a flat grassy spot, he unrolled the soft mat made from several large pieces of kell. No one protested.

Tied to a pine tree limb, the bay horse stood still while Kerna rummaged through its saddlebags. Peers led her buckskin off to graze. "The rancher was generous," she observed. "There are enough foodstuffs for two in this bag for several meals and to break our fast in the mornings."

The Alchemist looked up from where he squatted, unrolling his bedroll. "For the amount he was paid, a tent should have been included," he hissed.

No one bothered with a reply.

Camoe gathered firewood thinking that no matter how much some people had it was never enough. Most days, led around by the whim of his cursed ability, he was glad for some small morsel to eat. What did the bloody true sense have in store for him this time?

# POWER OF HER SYMBOLS

Founded at the base of a nearly vertical cliff face rising over twelve stories, Brown Recluse thrived from the commerce of the lush wine, wheat, corn, and fruit fields it overlooked. The farther Crystalyn progressed toward the center, the more she admired the brown stone buildings built to last with large blocks of granite, trimmed with white marble columns at entrances and windows. The buildings were a much different style from the sun-faded wooden buildings and merchant stalls they'd passed on the outskirts. Fewer people moved about the opulent areas giving rise to her suspicion they were nearing their destination.

"Is that the place?" Crystalyn asked RaCorren, gesturing with her free hand toward a cobblestone courtyard of river rock set around a circular display of weathered bronze statues turning green. "Your people need temporary dwellings until we find permanence for them. I want to have the town leaders' assurances of this in writing before they change their minds."

RaCorren peered in the direction she'd indicated. "I believe it so, *Sarra'esiah*. Allow me to verify one of the bronze monks presiding eternally over the Patron Gather has a bald head, as the prominence's acolyte mentioned."

Crystalyn laughed. "It's a statue of a monk. Most of them will have a shaved pate."

RaCorren blinked. Then jogged ahead, giving Lunge Bite a

wide berth even though his tough kell leather would likely repel most nips from the big warhorse if the stallion chose to bite at covered skin. In short order, the Valen vanished around the monks, whose large backsides faced them. Lore Rayna took his place.

The warhorse Murk had nipped at anyone who came close once the little group had clomped into town. Hastel had promptly taken to calling the horse Lunge Bite after the first episode. Yet, the big stallion left Lore Rayna alone for reasons known only to the horse. The name was growing on her. "Is RaCorren always so accommodating?" Crystalyn asked the big woman.

With an abrupt movement that swung her long golden hair, a color Crystalyn envied, behind her, Lore Rayna's luminous orbs fell upon her above Lunge Bite as he tossed his mane of glossy black hair. Another color she coveted. "RaCorren is obstinate and demanding in all things, except when it comes to relations with you. What motivates this is beyond me. No one comprehends the actions of males, as it is."

"That's a statement I can agree with completely," Crystalyn said with a smile. Lore Rayna had proven to be a friend in many ways. It was good to have her around.

Lore Rayna's answering smile brightened her radiant eyes as they rounded a large circular rock the size of a Valen carved with the names of people she hadn't heard of.

When they rounded the statues, RaCorren spoke with a portly monk at the feet of a two-story bronze of a stern-faced man in monkish robes located in the center of the wide courtyard. Both men quieted at their arrival. "We have been honored with the revered of the monastery coming in person, *Sarra'esiah*. Please greet Prominence Shadoe, most high of the devout monks of Brown Recluse."

Caven bowed low, his wide girth of little hindrance. "It is

with great pleasure I greet you. Onan has blessed me with the exquisite radiance of the Divine Vessel."

Handing Murk's reins to Lore Rayna, Crystalyn joined them, keeping her face smooth. She had no idea what the proper response to the greeting was, but she knew someone who may know. *"Broth, how should I respond to such a formal greeting?"*

Broth slipped into view on the opposite side of the courtyard and halted not far to the side of the two men; his sleek feline body made no sound as he sat on his rear haunches. His now azure hourglass eyes inset on his wolf face took in everything and missed nothing. *"This human has no care for such courtly rituals. I do not know the reason for it."*

Crystalyn was relieved. She had no use for such pomp either, though a bit of drama now and then helped throw people off, particularly new acquaintances. Her old adage from acting school popped into her mind. *Wear the right emotional mask and people will respond.* She put on her bored and deplorably important face. "You may dispense with the pleasantries Your…Prominence. Contrary to what you've heard, I won't blow apart half your town in a fit of rage for informalities. Well, I shouldn't anyway. Not if I'm watered, fed hot food, and bathed, in that order. It *has* been such a long ride across those horrid dusty plains with naught but cold rations."

Prominence Shadoe grimaced as if something he had eaten had soured his large stomach, but he masked it quickly by flashing a thin smile. "Consider it dispensed then, my lady. Please, walk beside me so that we may accommodate your necessities as soon as I can arrange it."

Prominence Shadoe set a fair pace toward the south and east; Crystalyn had to scramble to reach the path beside him. For a portly man, he moved well. Her estimation of him rose a notch. "Where do you take us, Prominence? My companions led me to believe the monastery lay north and west from here on top of the cliffs."

The monk glanced up at the sprawling stone structures peeking majestically over a high wall that followed the cliff edge with a rectangle formation before vanishing around the ends. As a stronghold, Brown Recluse Monastery had high defensibility, both figuratively and literally. His blue-eyed gaze swung to rest on her, sharp and alert, as if he waited for something from her. "Please call me Caven…Caven Shadoe. The monastery is going through some tumultuous times, I am afraid. The safest places are not as they once were."

"Caven Shadoe. Camoe is—"

"Camoe is my brother, yes, as Jade Creek is your sister," he interrupted with a quick glance behind, checking for anyone within earshot. Crystalyn also looked. No one kept a close pace. "We must discuss a malevolence I believe seeks you both," he went on.

Crystalyn slowed and then dashed to catch up, his words taking her by surprise. "Which malice? There has always been someone or *something* after my sister and I since arriving on your world, it seems. I have come for the sole purpose of securing a writ of promise for the Valens. They need to camp in the fields outside the city until we find a home for them. You did hear what happened to their homeland, didn't you?"

Caven glanced at her, his blue eyes bright as he scrutinized her sharply. Abruptly he looked away and scanned the tall brick and wooden houses and wide brown granite streets they passed. He spoke in an undertone. "The vileness I speak of has its foul roots south of the Dark Citadel. It has lain dormant for countless seasons. The Order of Brethren, *my* order, has been content to observe and gather knowledge and arm ourselves against it. Now, with the two of you traipsing about Astura, it stirs. Prior knowledge of such power growing in strength is advantageous, perhaps crucial to survival, and not a thing one should take lightly. Do you not wish to hear more?"

The glare Crystalyn shot the portly man's way went unnoticed, lost in the folds at the back of his thick neck. The fact he had a pressing concern didn't justify speaking to her as if she were young. She was, after all, nearly twenty-three, but he was right. Awareness of a potential enemy beforehand may serve to keep Jade safe from harm. She could take care of herself but not her little sister; trouble flew at her with the accuracy of a dragon on the hunt.

Following Prominence Caven's example, Crystalyn perused the fronts and sides of the buildings, front foyers, gardens, streets, and well-groomed alleyways they strode passed. Though what she looked for, she only had a vague notion. Perhaps for things that stood out beyond ordinary, such as two cloaked figures who stopped moving along an alley as they passed by. Though their actions could be a normal occurrence at Brown Recluse, for all she knew.

When she looked in her guide's direction, his eyes, bright with expectancy, gazed at her. She smiled. "Yes, I do want to hear what you know. Go on," she encouraged, even though the conversation sounded similar to the warning Durandas had went on about. Perhaps the monk could explain it better.

Caven's smile was brief. "I had thought to wait for a…colleague before discussing the matter at length. His particular insight shall add much to the conversation."

Crystalyn gaped. Why bring the matter up until he had everyone present? There was no understanding the mind of a male.

Crossing yet another street intersection, the area they strode into had obvious differences from the one they'd left behind. Constructed solely of wood, some structures owed their assembly to whole logs nailed and caulked; others had fastenings of iron at the edges cobbled together with rough-hewn lumber varying in length, crude shanties at best. With no green gardens or statuesque courtyards to keep dirt in place, the dry-rutted streets and alleys stirred up the dust compounded by the additional townspeople they passed, even though Caven chose the routes less populated at every turn.

Forced to let a group of sun-browned men clad in serviceable leather swagger past, she fell behind Caven. The group's confident gait and bold glances made her think that, to a man, each one knew how to use the swords, axes, or bows that hung comfortably from their hips or were strapped to their broad backs. Their lingering stares turned to outright leering.

Swallowing something gritty and worrying Lunge Bite would get cranky from thirst, she hurried to catch up with the surprisingly agile Caven, pulling the warhorse along with her. "Where are you taking us?" Crystalyn demanded to know when she got close.

Caven swung into a nondescript alley that resembled a number of those they'd passed. "Somewhere we can talk without disturbance," he replied over his shoulder. Moving quickly, they soon came to the alley's midpoint. "And, we have arrived," he added with a flourish. He stopped at an unadorned wooden door faded from the sun. A man and a woman wearing half cowls pulled low enough to hide their features in shadow stood at each side. Both had long swords hanging from their right hips, the hilt grips scarred and pitted from use. They made no move nor uttered no challenge to stop them.

Though she kept her gaze on the two at the door, Crystalyn halted beside Caven, her ire rising. If his words were supposed to generate enthusiasm, she hadn't seen enough yet to judge. Why couldn't he simply tell her where they were meeting? Why all the secrecy?

Ignoring the silent warrior sentries, Caven rapped twice on the top, middle, and bottom of the door, bending slightly to perform the latter. The door flew open before he fully straightened. A wide muscular man of shorter height than the monk held the latch. He fixed a glare at the monk and Crystalyn and then looked behind them, his bushy brown eyebrows dropping lower still. "There is room inside for two or three *people*, Prominence, not horses, wardens, and Valens," he said.

Caven swung around, his gaze taking in her companions, and his face flushed. "I must apologize to my lady for my failure to consider space requirements."

*Wear the right emotional mask and people will respond.* Crystalyn slipped into her captain-commander mask. Smoothing her face, she widened her stance, clasped her hands behind her, and assumed an air of authority. "Let's just get where we're going and get on with it, shall we? Atoi and Hastel will stay with me. Lore Rayna, take care of Lunge Bite, please. He seems to tolerate you; anyone else is likely to lose a finger, or worse. Afterward, ensure that the rest of our little group has a meal and drink. Is there a place close by for her to accomplish these tasks, Prominence?" *"No matter what the man at the door may say, you're coming with me, Broth."*

*"Yes, my Do'brieni."*

The stocky man barring the way inside flashed a tiny smile, so small Crystalyn wasn't certain she'd seen it.

Caven gave a brief nod. "Aye, my lady. There is common access to the tavern from the main street at the front of this alley, though the local patrons will not appreciate some who travel with you openly."

Though she managed to maintain her smooth-faced air of importance, Crystalyn detested the implications of his words. "My companions are exceptional in many ways; you'd better have a good explanation for a statement like that."

Lore Rayna spoke, her melodious feminine voice booming without intending too. "He means I shall not have welcome in this inn—drinking establishment is closer in truth, I—"

His voice a growl, Hastel cut in before the big woman had finished. "We know what it is you want to say, *monk*. The town locals dislike our giant woman for manipulating the Flow; they hate anyone or anything having to do with any aspect of using. Is this not right, Prominence?"

Caven gave a brief nod. "Yes, there is history behind it. Their frightened disdain comes from a tolerance for Dark and Light Users in the town's early seasons. The repayment for such forbearance was near destruction of the town and seasons of enslavement at the hands of those most powerful. They do not know your group, but it would not make a difference if they did."

Pointedly resting his hands on the axes at his side, Hastel's one blue eye narrowed. "They don't have to get acquainted with us; all anyone has to comprehend is what happens right after a derogatory word with any member of our party. They get to meet Onan in person—"

Crystalyn brought her hand up, silencing whatever he was about to say next. "Keep your axes sheathed, for now, Hastel. We did not come to fight the entire town. At least, not yet." She eyed everyone else in turn, lingering last on Lore Rayna. "It is decided. Now go, see to the others."

"As you command, *Sarra'esiah*," Lore Rayna said, bowing slightly. Straightening, she walked away.

Lore Rayna's use of the Valen word surprised Crystalyn; it was the first time her large friend had.

The man in the doorway stepped aside. "Whoever is coming inside, please do so quickly. I fear we have already been the focus of many prying eyes, and my excuses will not fully alleviate suspicions."

Caven waved them into a small room where a rough-hewn wooden desk and a tall object covered with a dusty rug claimed most of the space. From the look of it, the rug had lain on a floor for many seasons before getting the duty as a covering.

Hastel filed in last. Once he was inside, the broad-shouldered man closed and locked the door behind him. Then he took a seat behind the desk, glancing at the group briefly. "Since the monk— *Prominence*," he corrected, prompted by Caven's scowl, "has completed the condition I required of him for my services, my identity shall remain hidden. As for each of you, I know your backgrounds, even the noble warden. I make it a point to research anyone leading a force that nearly held back an army of Dark Users.'"

Hastel's thick arms folded at his barrel chest. "Why is it so important for us to not know who you are?"

The man at the desk smiled without mirth. "Revealing that would nullify all this subterfuge."

With no other choice in the cramped room, Crystalyn sat on a rough-hewn crate carefully. The last thing she wanted was a splinter lodged in a hard to reach place. As she did, a name popped into her mind, one she'd heard from someone dear to her. "Why are we here, Craight? What do you want?"

Craight's blue eyes flared bright for a brief moment. "Your own network of knowledge is impressive, Crystalyn. Perhaps we can speak more of it after our business has concluded."

Caven stirred, shifting his bulk from one leg to the other. "Can we get on with it, Craight? I granted your request for inclusion with this meeting for the sole reason of your promise of having information of great value to the leader of the Vale…what do you call your fighting force?" he asked.

Crystalyn stared. "We are not a fighting force; we are a band of refugees from the Vale."

Caven nodded as if she'd agreed with him. "Your word choice is partly why I wanted to meet with you. With a little outfitting from the resources available to me, your people could fight back. Also, please consider not referring to them as refugees. Such a name aids the Dark Users with denouncing them as a force in this war. With over five hundred Valens at your command, you are formidable still."

"Bringing them here to fight in your Hundred Season War wasn't my intention, not after fleeing the Vale running for our lives, and I'm not their commander," Crystalyn insisted.

Thumping his muscular arms on the desk, Craight leaned forward. "Are you certain? The reports I've read have the Valens naming you *Sarra'esiah*, is this true?"

The small of her back starting to ache, Crystalyn shifted her weight with care. "Yes, they think of me as their savior, so what? Such a notion is harmless, though misguided. As long as they followed and left their burning homes to those destroying it, I've allowed it."

Caven exchanged a quick look with Craight. "*Sarra'esiah* has a longer meaning in the old Valen, the Alterran tongue, as the Valens were known as in ancient times. The closest translation known comes across as 'Our Lady Savior of Intricate Light.'"

*"This revelation has little surprise, Do'brieni. The plant people have an exceptional ability to discern extraordinary nature."*

Hastel gave a low whistle.

Even Atoi stared, her green eyes pensive.

"Stop it, all of you," Crystalyn said, pushing a black cloud of rising irritation from the forefront of her mind. People always seemed to expect so much from her. "I get to decide what I'm going to be, not what everyone thinks I should. Let's get on with why we have need for this meeting, Prominence. The *refugees* require a place to regroup and heal. Your city of Brown Recluse has space outside its walls. My, *our*, intention is to set up temporary dwellings at the base of the south and east walls where several cleared fields converge. This will ensure minimal movement of the wounded and lessen the impact on cultivation. Will you help?"

Caven nodded before she'd even finished. "Yes, of course. The monks shall provide assistance; there is no further need for concern."

"Good. You have my thanks. Though I am curious why you sent for me when handling this at the walls would have sufficed," Crystalyn said.

Caven glanced at Craight.

Craight glanced quickly left and right though no one but the five of them occupied the room. "My…agents have discovered the whereabouts of someone who it is believed you search for. As a goodwill gesture toward a future relationship, I wish to share this information with you. Do you accept?"

Crystalyn grew irritated. "What kind of *relationship*? How do I know your *free* information has any value until I've heard it first?"

His muscular forearms resting heavily on the desk, Craight clenched and then unclenched his hands, though his face remained impassive. "The value of my words is for you to decide after hearing them. Darwin Darkwind roams the town of Shimmer in the south. At least he did until a few days past. He has since vanished into the Shimmering Sands Desert. Does this information hold *value* to you now?"

The mention of Darwin caused her stomach to flutter. "Yes," she managed to hiss after he stared at her for a time.

Craight smiled. "Good, then I shall reveal what little is known. After a few days of no contact, he suddenly resurfaced as the head of a caravan owned and operated by a shrewd and not well-liked merchant. Perhaps you have heard of Guail?"

Crystalyn dismissed the name. "No."

There was no indication if Craight was surprised or disappointed. He could've been watching a holoflick for all he revealed. He continued. "Far into the harshness of the desert, the caravan set up camp at an old resting place for long-forgotten kings. What he searches for is unknown."

Silence followed his words. Hastel broke the silence. "Whatever it is, if he's involved, it can't be good."

"The question is, why choose such a desolate place? What would he want there?" Crystalyn asked.

Craight shrugged. "Our researchers believe it is a place of power, though exactly what, they cannot say. With the expense of such a massive undertaking, the gain must be great indeed."

"Agreed—" Crystalyn began.

A loud rap sounded at the top of the door they had come through, followed by two centered knocks and one low.

Frowning, Craight pushed away from the desk and stood. "What is this? Not many know today's code. Have you invited someone else here, monk?"

Caven wore his own frown. His thin white eyebrows had scrunched together, and his blue eyes narrowed with suspicion. "I told no one. There was no need."

The rapping came again, louder this time, the door resounding in the same sequence, top, center, and bottom. Though it was the same as before, the pounding seemed wrong somehow, too demanding.

*"Darkness comes!"* Broth howled in her mind.

"Ignore it!" Crystalyn shouted though she was too late.

Craight wrenched the door open. "Blast it all Dolph, Sera! What in the bloody—"

A brown-robed figure glided past Craight's wide body, slipping inside. A larger second form shoved the bulky man to one side, charging in with sword drawn. A black cloth wrapped around the head and face left only the eyes bare.

The robed figure reached Crystalyn as a symbol loomed in

her mind, but it vanished as she gazed at the face under the hood. Dark eyes had bulged to grotesque spheres. Covered with a black cloth, the person's head and forehead split in the center and then peeled away, dropping onto both shoulders. A man-shaped darkness detached from the person under the robe, slipping out from them as one would clothes. The skin of the person sank to the floor, deflating without a sound.

A scream of terror froze in her throat when the dark figure wrapped around her. Dank malice as thick and oily as tar permeated her spine, chilling her limbs and slowing her heart rate.

*"Do not succumb to it, Do'brieni! You are strong! I am here."*

A fleeting thought drifted into her lethargic mind that she had to fight back, somehow push the vileness from her as one would let go wrongful dark desires, urges of blackest violence known to hurt, but it slipped away.

The foulness oozed along her spine. Sliding upward, it befouled her nerve endings by overriding motor control as it assimilated her neurons with a flow of darkness.

The foulness had rancidness behind it, an evilness that had permeated the planet from an age long past, when its reign was absolute. If not for an even older alien interference, something not of this world, Astura would know only darkness, its darkness, brought upon the planet by the absolute power it wielded, the True power. Avenging that other worldly intrusion upon its mastery burned strong within the evilness; the power of her symbols would help regain dominion measurably. For the alien entity stalked the dark domain still, skulking with such cunning and strength the master had grown wary.

Despair came with the revelation of the Dark Flow. She hadn't the ability to fight such power, and soon she wouldn't know she should.

The overpowering mind behind the dark thing raised a great

axe. After its fall, her mind and actions would no longer be her own. The axe reached the top of the arc, and the vast power grew in glee.

White-hot pain tore through her instilling darkness of a different sort.

# GENETIC INFUSION

The white light Crystalyn followed, simply from the sense of warmth and gentleness it exuded, led her to the luminous upside-down eyes of Lore Rayna. Concern creased the big woman's inverted broad forehead, indenting a deep gouge at the bridge of her nose between her fine golden eyebrows. Then Lore Rayna smiled, and those wondrous eyes brightened. Her facial features smoothed, flushed with the vibrancy of youth and genuine happiness.

Crystalyn smiled back.

"Our illustrious leader awakens," Atoi said from somewhere close by. She sounded disappointed.

Crystalyn tried to turn toward her, but her neck refused the command; something rigid hampered it.

"Please make no attempt to move until I give the word," Lore Rayna said. "A head binding was deemed necessary to quicken the healing and perhaps save your life. Though you seem to accept healing remarkably well."

Fear made Crystalyn want to retch though she quelled it thinking of her training. "My neck is damaged? Is it broken?"

*"Ease your fear. No fractures occurred."*

Crystalyn sent her gratitude flowing through the link knowing now he'd taken some of the damage from her.

Lore Rayna's tone was clinical. "It is not as far as I can discern. However, I wish for complete assurance. Though he likely saved you, the prominence's blow cracked open your skull, and the possibility of added damage to your weak human neck is high."

Caven spoke from the far side of the room. "Please forgive me for such a hard swing. I feared I was too late and you had succumbed to the Dark Man. If not for the quick action of your man with his blocking axe, I may have killed you with the next blow as Craight advised. Forgive me as well for not coming closer; I…cannot, not until the healing is completed."

For a long moment, Crystalyn was confused. The tone of the stocky monk's voice contained revulsion, though she knew not why. Then she thought of something, something in particular her big companion was one of the few capable of. "Is your splint your hands?" she asked Lore Rayna.

The pressure at the sides of her head lessened slightly when Lore Rayna shifted. "What is this splint you speak of?"

"Have you hardened your hands and fingers?"

"Oh, yes! It's so unnatural, my eyes refuse to look at it, and my mind shies away from the thought of it," Caven lamented.

"Nonsense," Crystalyn said. "Lore Rayna is the most natural being I know. You did know she talks to plants too, didn't you?"

"Yes," Caven replied. "They all do that, the entire race. It is not so alarming when a whole population whispers at foliage, but it is quite unsettling to have them change into one."

The pressure against Crystalyn's ears grew stronger on one side, nearly painfully so. "Come here, Prominence," Lore Rayna commanded softly. "Touch my living flora, feel the smoothness, revel in the wondrous art of the *flor'e'form* at its highest. Perhaps, should you carry an inherent affinity, you may even glean the beat of my heart underlying the hardened oak," Lore Rayna said, the tone of her voice soft and mild.

Caven's choked cough shot across the room. "Please, though what you suggest is intriguing, please, *please* refrain from such ardent detail. Wood should not have a heartbeat, living or otherwise." His words sounded strained, going small at the end.

Lore Rayna laughed, and Hastel's deep guffaw joined her. Even Atoi's tiny tinkle rounded out the end as the jollity quieted.

Crystalyn smiled at her companions' mirth though she sensed the subtle traces of forced tension relief. They'd been worried about her very much, it seemed. However, she wasn't certain about one of them. "Atoi, come here, please."

Luxurious black hair covering a tiny head above a ghostly white face popped into view on her left. Overlarge, brilliant green eyes, so like Jade's, regarded her with only a trace of curiosity. "What is it you wish of me?" she asked.

"Did you not want me to heal?" Crystalyn asked. Her own curiosity held more than a trace of desire to know, considerably more. Had the little girl wanted her to die? She'd believed they'd become friends.

Atoi blinked. "Those going to stand before Onan exude an inner light I wish to understand."

Crystalyn gazed up at her tiny companion. Then she, too, blinked. "I'm not certain I know what you mean, or perhaps, I'm afraid I do. Either way, it is not important right now. Do you still insist on a desert trip after leaving here?"

An odd frown creased Atoi's normally impassive face as the little girl cast a quick glance at the rest of their group. The little girl once more gazed down at her, and her fine black eyebrows dropped with annoyance. "The catalyst shall have an outlet." The voice that issued from Atoi's mouth reverberated from the depth of an unseen chasm.

Crystalyn bit back a sigh. "That's as cryptic as it gets. Just once, can't you be more specific, Dark Child?"

Atoi's deceptively innocent eyes gazed at her unblinking, her face as smooth as a statue. *And nearly the same pallor,* Crystalyn thought.

A slight feeling of warmth traveled up her spine from her lower back. Gathering at her neck, the warm feeling grew more insistent, heating as it moved from one side to the other until almost causing pain. Then, with a shocking abruptness, the feeling vanished. The rigidity that flattened her ears to the side of her head softened and then pulled away.

Inundated with new vigor, Crystalyn sat up without asking if it was safe for her to do so. The room they now occupied wasn't the same as the one she'd entered with her companions. Wider and longer, the room contained a double set of rough-cut liquid-stained tables and chairs stacked at one end making room for her recovery. An open doorway behind her revealed a partial view of Craight's blocky desk, and a closed door in front of her led farther inside the building.

Her companions had gathered on her left, except for Caven and Broth. His back to everyone, the portly monk stood beside the tables and chairs, staring, presumably, at a plain wall devoid of decorations. Broth lay with his great head on her legs; her hand automatically stroked the soft fur between his feline ears. The building's owner, Craight, was nowhere in sight. "Okay, someone tell me how I…how *we all* survived an encounter with that *thing?*"

*"Not you, Broth, I know you were there."*

*"Aye, my Do'brieni."*

Hastel offered his broad hand to her, which she accepted readily, gently slipping her legs out from under Broth. He pulled her gently to her feet as he explained. "Apparently, the creature's sole weakness is with wood. Reacting faster than I would have believed, the monk clubbed the darkness, as it forced its vile way into you." The one-eyed man paused to swallow, his face lighter by several shades.

Crystalyn felt a surge of nausea herself as she recalled the black thing's oily touch.

"The monk's first swing burst the dark shape, popping it like a festered wound," Hastel said. "Doing that, he also cracked you in the head. When you collapsed, his bloody friend Craight shouted for him to finish you as he sprinted outside pursuing the second assailant. I put a stop to the monk as he raised the chair for a second, final blow—"

Lore Rayna's gasp came as a booming hiss.

Hastel hurried past the interruption. "Atoi slipped into the tavern through that door"—he flipped his long curly brown hair toward the door in front of her—"and brought the Valen healer. Still, it was close…too close for my liking."

Her hand going to her head, Crystalyn touched the damp stickiness of blood drying in her hair as she took in the situation, letting Hastel's narrative settle in. Caven's shaven bald pate shone, his head bowed as if in prayer. It was a source of irritation; she deserved an explanation after he'd brought her here. Yet the man refused to look at her. "Was this all a ruse, Prominence? Did the two of you set that foul creature after me?" she asked halfheartedly, not fully believing it, but goading him would get a reaction.

Prominence Caven straightened. The frown that creased his forehead looked odd paired with his wide blue eyes. "If you knew me, you would not have spoken such a thought. Your sister trusted me without question."

Crystalyn kept her face smooth though she wanted to smile. The goad had worked better than expected. "Therein, your words are my dilemma. I do not know you, nor am I my sister. Jade is the trusting sort. I find it safer to hold new acquaintances a pike's tip away until they've proven themselves. Now that you know where you stand, let's talk about how I almost died. You called that creature a Dark Man, but what is it really? Where did it come from? Who sent it, if not you?"

*"Broth, do you have a sense of the monk?"*

Caven's scowl deepened and then cleared. "I have failed at a proper accounting, it appears. Please accept my apologies. As the prominence for the Brown Recluse monks, I have had little experience with justifying my actions for many seasons. The position requires rigorous vows, bound with the Flow upon acceptance, that cannot be broken. Most on this world know naught of it. However, I would venture to say a goodly portion of the company you keep do. Nevertheless, this is not the place, nor have we ample time, for an in-depth discussion. The presence of another Dark Man in the city constitutes urgency."

The floorboards creaked with the weight of Lore Rayna moving beside her. "Your vows do not release you from giving us an explanation for attempting to strike the *Sarra'esiah after* the destruction of the Dark Man. I am not happy to hear of it. Of all humans, you would come last for suspicions of treachery."

Caven's eyes rounded with shock. "Please do not think the worst of us, nature lore woman. Even though the dark shadow dispersed, Craight thought her lost; it is likely he still has the belief. No one has ever survived a Dark Man's touch that we have heard."

*"The human male exudes suspicion more than remorse, Do'brieni."*

"Have you not perceived the Vessel?" Atoi asked. Her small voice carried with distinction, perking every ear within hearing.

In the midst of a frown, Caven froze. Then his face smoothed, and he gave a slight bow to the little girl. "I must ask for forgiveness, Ancient One. Though the event happened fast, I should have waited for an irrefutable indication of possession before again raising the chair."

Without waiting for a response, he turned to Crystalyn and lowered his head. "Forgiveness must come from you first, Vessel of Prophecy, I nearly destroyed the one chance of eluding destruction."

*"The human male's remorse has increased, though for the thought of harming you, or nearly destroying prophecy I cannot say."*

Crystalyn grew irritated with the whole conversation, spoken and unspoken. "Or, more likely, you may have missed your chance of killing off the one who could possibly destroy your world. As long as we're on the subject, don't call me vessel. Atoi is the only one who uses that term. I don't seem to be able to stop her from saying it."

Caven stiffened as if she'd slapped him.

Crystalyn would have, if she thought she could get away with it. The monk was getting on her nerves. "Don't look so surprised, Prominence. Though I hail from Terra, I'm aware how much of your so-called prophecies pertain to me. Please, keep in mind the codices are only cryptic words written inside dusty old tomes and a few scrolls. They all contradict each other in various little ways."

One corner of Caven's mouth rose with a sheepish grin. His smile was brief. "Pardon me, Lady Crystalyn. I did not wish to insinuate ignorance—"

The door opened. Craight backed inside it talking to someone beyond it. Crystalyn caught a glimpse of a nondescript man sporting a scraggly black goatee. Patrons sitting or standing at a bar filled the background. She caught a glimpse of RaCorren looking in, concern mirrored in his blue eyes. "Deal with it," the blocky man said. "I have business. If you haven't resolved it in half a bell, speak to me then."

The man glanced into the room, his brown eyes hard. "What's going on, Craight? There are plant people strutting about the tavern demanding food, and you say to let them, but Cook cannot keep up with it. Now you have personal business with one of the glow eyes. The townsfolk will talk; likely, the old women's tongues are already wagging. What happened to Staunch the Flow does not serve Users?"

Lore Rayna made a move to step forward.

Crystalyn extended an arm out in restraint. "Wait. We don't know all that is going on here." The tenseness she felt from the woman pressing against her lessened slightly.

The muscles on Craight's arm holding the door latch bulged. "How the townspeople react and who I serve is my concern. I will defuse the situation soon since you seem incapable of it," he growled.

Closing the door in the man's face, he turned to Caven. "I'm probably going to have to eliminate my longest-running barkeep; I hope we know what we're doing. How long are those from the Vale going to populate my tavern?" His agate eyes shifted to Lore Rayna. "The naturists are hard, if not impossible, for me to convince good folk they don't use, particularly if one of them chooses to dress with ferns."

Crystalyn dropped her arm to her side where it found her hip, matching the one already on her other side. "The Valens are in my care. I'll leave them only when convinced they have a safe place outside your city walls. Your townspeople will find the cultivation and harvesting of fields has just become easier with more abundance of everything they grow. And, for future reference, Lore Rayna's dress is morning glory leaves, not fern."

Craight smiled briefly. "It is glorious whether morning or night. Please do not mistake my words, the dress has had my admiration since first sight of it, she certainly has the body for it. However, for simple-minded sharecroppers, merchants, tailors, beggars, and the numerous other people eking a living here, the beauty of it is lost to them. They see only the power of the Flow manipulating the One's creation."

As she glanced sidelong at her companion, Crystalyn's face flushed. Lore Rayna's hands had landed on bare hips before the distraught dress could cover the gap, long slender fingers and all.

If Lore Rayna noticed, her words had no indication of it, as she gently pulled her hands from under the leaves. "The Great Mother, in her infinite wisdom, has provided a way to converse with the sustenance of life to those who choose to listen."

"Hold!" Caven said loudly. Taking a deep breath, he continued in a softer tone of voice. "As much as I would prefer it, we cannot afford a virtuous discussion; the ruling council of monks and the Order of Brethren await a report. Soon, they shall send runners to investigate the delay. What have you found with the second assailant, Craight? What knowledge have you of the Dark Man?"

Craight leaned against the wall, folding his arms at his chest. Leaving his hip pointed slightly outward, his longsword dangled within easy reach. Splotches of something burgundy stained the hilt. "The Dark Man's companion was likely human though my network has little evidence to support it. He or *it* escaped after fleeing into the maze of the Sour Warrens south of Brown Recluse for those who do not know. I failed to even gain a look under the cowl; it could have been a woman for all I discovered."

"He was a man," Crystalyn said. "The two of them were watching as we passed a street on the way here," she added quickly when both men looked at her sharply.

Accepting her explanation, Craight went on speaking. "We know little of the Dark Men as they are called, only that they are vile creatures sent from the Dark Plateau, somewhere under the Dark Citadel. Even Caven's Order of the Brethren, his supposed *secretive* ruling class of all monkish orders he freely mentioned, have limited experience with such evil."

Caven continued when Craight quieted. "He speaks truly. After the attack on your sister, I poured much of the monk's and the Order of the Brethren's extensive resources into discovering all we could about them. Nearly a season of poring over old tomes, even meeting with dark monks in secret, provided little. Your sister herself discovered their only weakness, though it is a great one, of wood dispersing the darkness. That alone caused much of our research to focus on the Dark Citadel where wood is scarce and used only for the convenience of a door lighter than stone. Only after painstaking research, and an infiltration, did we come to believe the Dark Man did not originate from within the citadel."

Crystalyn was almost hesitant to ask. "If not the Dark Citadel, then where?"

Caven exchanged a brief look with Craight.

The broad-shouldered tavern owner then gazed at each being in the room, one at a time, before his brown eyes came to rest on Crystalyn. "This one is puzzling, changing all that we have known. The brown robe and the warrior that got away were nomads, rovers of a desert they rarely, if ever, leave. Their garb and swarthy features mark them as the Shimmering Sands clan, a particularly remote sect."

Crystalyn sputtered getting the words out. "But…but didn't you say Darwin went there, may still *be* in this Shimmering Sands area?"

"Yes," Caven and Craight said in unison.

Hastel whistled softly.

Crystalyn rounded on Atoi. "Is this why you want me to go there?"

Atoi gazed at her, her white face smooth and impassive.

"So that means—" Hastel started.

"Going there is likely a trap," Crystalyn finished. "So why would they make the attempt today and show their intentions early?"

Only Broth had a response. *"Perhaps the Dark Man had instructions to attack and possess at any opportunity."*

Crystalyn agreed. *"I believe it so, Do'brieni."*

"What does it matter?" Crystalyn asked aloud to no one in particular. "Darkwind is up to something, I know it, and I'm the best hope of discovering what it is and putting a stop to him. There is another thing, you should know, all of you. I got a sense of the Dark Man's desires, or at least the power controlling it. There is something moving in this world it is wary of, an alien power. The entity that sent the evil hungers for my ability along with an unknown factor in the desert. I must go there."

"Huh? What would it want in the desert? The same thing Darkwind searches for?" Hastel asked.

"That is my guess," Crystalyn said.

Caven's silver eyebrows drooped. "I must send more stealth monks, this matter has just risen beyond high priority…" he said, trailing off.

Lore Rayna's arms left her hips and folded at her chest to the consternation of her dress. Flashes of white skin testified to the fact. Her face darkened. "I do not trust this as a wise decision, *Sarra'esiah*. Darwin Darkwind has proven a fearsome foe in the past."

"Precisely why he must be stopped," Crystalyn said. "Now if only we had some way to get there quickly."

Again, the two men exchanged a look. Then Craight pushed away from the wall. "Come with me," he said, moving toward the back office.

Crystalyn nearly stepped on his heels as he strode past the crude desktop to the object covered by a frayed rug.

Grabbing an edge, Craight whipped it away with a flourish. "Behold your access to Red Rock. I shall have it infused with traces of his manservant's essence," he said.

"What do you mean, 'infused'?" Crystalyn asked.

Caven exchanged a glance with Craight before gazing once more at Crystalyn, his face unreadable. "During a stay here or elsewhere by a collection agent, trace samples of Malkor's genetic makeup were harvested and stored, frozen in the vaults under the monastery. Using the Flow and a master infuser, we can perform a genetic infusion to this, of his manservant," he said, pointing. "Darwin is too careful; we have yet to gain but a single source."

"My respect for you monks and your capabilities has risen substantially, "Crystalyn breathed, staring in wonder at the instrument offered to follow the pair.

"I am no monk," Craight said. "Far from it."

Crystalyn barely heard. A pair of beautiful red crystal obelisks awaited activation.

# FAILING STRENGTH

Darwin loathed the heat bearing down upon his head and rising up in shimmering waves from the hostile terrain. He abhorred the abrasive sand rubbing against his body whenever he moved; it burned an itch the length of his mangled arm he dared not scratch, even inside. Without the protection of his black robes, his skin would blacken and peel even though he had always sported a natural tan.

There had been no sating his thirst after ordering the merchant Guail to whip the caravan bearers into entering the blazing heart of the desert after exiting the wind door, the way back through it easy. The cyclone twisted one way, sweeping him out the entrance, almost as soon as he stepped in it.

Now perhaps, enduring such hardships would pay off; the workers had discovered the entrance to another tomb. The discovery meant venturing outside the shade of his tent. Though nightfall would come soon, the heat before then would be crippling, but he would go out in it. Such trivialities could not keep him from the artifact.

Had they truly found the right ossuary at last? Grabbing a flask of water, he eyed a round-bottomed glass phial of torch oil. Lifting it from his makeshift crate table, he stuffed them both in the large inner pocket of his black robes.

The round scar prominently displayed in his forehead,

Malkor stood at the tent's outer foyer regarding him with expectancy, waiting for him to give the order. This time he would know some certainty. There was no *for certain* when it came to the artifact. "What makes this one different from the others? Are there words carved in the granite, perhaps above an access of some kind?"

Looking odd on his narrow tanned face, Malkor's twisted smile did not reach his blood-streaked brown eyes; eyes that Darwin suspected were changing slowly to match the hourglass ones of Naa'thon's. He hadn't mentioned it to his servant, nor would he. Allowing the man to discover it himself would lessen the course of adjustment from the loss of his birth orbs. "Again, you surprise me, Master. Were you expecting this? There is…something chiseled above the entrance," Malkor said, wiping drool from the corner of his mouth, which was a side effect of the drooping lips he had acquired from the Lore Stone, and likely temporary. Naa'thon had had no such problem.

His manservant's lack of knowledge to some of the questions he had asked after the infusion surprised and suited Darwin greatly. It meant the bloody lore masters did not know everything; they only knew what the Ancients had left behind in the Lore Stone. Even as advanced as they were, great wisdom still had limits with how much one could retain.

From Red Rock, Malkor had led them unerringly to an excavation site left behind by the Ancients, likely the same advanced race who had made the Lore Stone. Perhaps, even the great gates. Yet they had not included all, leaving out the old scrolls written in a long ago forgotten language, which he had learned to decipher. Poring over the old and brittle papyrus in the vaults under the Dark Citadel had paid off, which made him smile inside; the less anyone knew of his intentions, the fewer betrayals. "What words have you found?"

"I do not believe they are words, only pictures: Two arms, vertical from the elbows with the hands raised toward the sky, a beautiful woman wearing a strange headpiece, and a cluster of stars."

Darwin smiled, barely containing jubilant laughter. They were getting close, the words proved as much, and they were exactly that. Well, picture representations of them—Kai, Neferet, and Akhu—Malkor had described them well.

"You have knowledge of the meaning, Master?"

Darwin opted for a bit of fun. "Are you saying my knowledge is greater than that of a lore master?"

Malkor's painfully bloodshot eyes reddened.

In a few weeks, Darwin suspected no trace of the color flecks in his servant's eyes would show inside his corneas. Eventually they would darken to the color of blood in one's liver, nearly black, when the infusion had fully set in, as Naa'thon's had.

Malkor cringed. He glanced quickly upward and around as if searching for unseen eyes fixed upon him. A look of revulsion, or fright, flashed in them. Darwin couldn't tell which. "Master is aware knowledge flows into my mind still. Interrupting it shall be as difficult as it was gathering the lore that brought us here. As then, I shall have the great risk of the flow of knowledge overwhelming my mind along with the empathies of countless others. Should you desire it, I shall make the attempt again."

Not the reaction he expected, Darwin spoke quickly. "Nay, Malkor, the pictures have meanings, which are known to me. They state rather simply, 'power of the sun,' 'beautiful,' and 'soul of divinity.' At least, I have interpreted it that way.'" He did not want his servant to end a gibbering husk before the artifact was indisputably his. Even then, the man had his uses.

"What you seek is here, Master?"

"I believe so, though I am reluctant to say for certain. Once we break into a room of light absorption, I shall rejoice. Now, I wish to observe these carvings. Lead the way."

Malkor pulled the canvas flap to one side, holding it open for him. The blazing light and inferno heat of the Shimmering Sands Desert, southeast of Grit Eye Oasis baked him, siphoning moisture from his exposed skin. The tan sands of the desert radiated heat, nearly strong enough to sear his lungs even though the sun drifted to the horizon. He pulled his black cowl farther over his face.

"This way, Master," Malkor said, his voice drifting out from his hood pulled low, as he raised a bony finger and pointed. "It is a bit of a hike around that large dune. Do you wish a palanquin arranged to carry you?"

"No. Let the workers continue to dig, all of them."

The red hood swung in Darwin's direction. "Dig where, Master? The entrance is exposed," he said.

Darwin prodded his servant's shoulder, getting him moving. They could not stand around talking in this heat. "You decide. As long as no one sees what we do."

Malkor shuffled forward without comment, the red hood now bowed.

Darwin followed, glancing out from under his hood. The glittering sand dune rose to the enormous monstrosity he had yet to view in any of his travels. Fortunately, they strode at the base of the wind-smoothed pile following a well-traveled path as it wound to the far end of the bank. The grand excavation swung into view.

Railee waited underneath the front shoulders of a huge carving of a warden, her face wrapped with a cloth—her *shroudin*— left only her eyes exposed. She had corrected him so often now for the Red Rock peoples' name for it that the facial covering came to mind easily. He touched the one she had given him, hanging at his neck, reassured by the softness of its presence there. Had he thought about it, he would have pulled the *shroudin* to the bridge of his nose the moment he stepped from the tent, which may have helped keep his lips from cracking.

Matching his pace as he moved past the ancient carven behemoth, Railee strode in companionable silence beside him, comfortable at his right side as they passed a row of two-story columns.

As they entered a tall doorway the workers had broken through with the aid of the Flow—traces of which he could feel resonating—he glanced sidelong at the warrior woman. Her longsword sat as a single entity with her right hip, a mark of her familiarity with the weapon. More than that, the sword accented her shapely hips. For now, he was happy to have her on his journey. Perhaps he would send for her tonight, or even better, take her as soon as he had the artifact.

Striding by the dim light from sparse wall sconces of flickering torchlight, they moved along a straight and level hallway. The torches sent shadows racing toward them and then springing away as their booted feet scuffed the reddish-brown limestone making up the flooring. Dust from a past age billowed, disturbed only a bell ago by the brief passage of workers lighting the torches. Darwin was not pleased. "From now on, Malkor, no one shall traverse this hall without your direct supervision."

"As you command," Malkor said. He spoke over his shoulder without breaking his odd stride. His shuffling gait of dragging his mangled foot a half step behind did not slow him so much now that he had learned how to force his body to work around the handicap.

"Have you great fear of thievery?" Railee asked, her voice deadened by an obstruction. "As of yet, I see nothing of value."

They had reached the wall and intersection, the very one Malkor had come for him for. Darwin regarded the carvings lit by three wall sconces, one to each side and one above, which reflected light downward from a large disc of white rock fixed in the tan limestone ceiling. "Not thieves, such daring is easily and quickly dealt with, but workers. They are difficult to come by. This tomb, for it is one, may have ancient guardians whose power is unknown. Of a certainty, it will contain…safeguards. Your sword shall need all the quickness and precision you have within you before we are through."

Railee's step softened, her well-formed upper torso swiveling to both sides as she searched each hallway leading off into the darkness. No light illumed either one.

Wisely, Malkor had sent the workers away as soon as they had reported the ancient writings. As described, the picture glyphs were there. They sent a thrill into the pit of Darwin's stomach. Carved with an expert's skill and a sculptor's eye, Kai, power of the sun, Neferet, beautiful, and Akhu, divine soul, looked down upon him, the paint as colorful as if daubed yesterday. The power of the sun and divine soul especially excited him. The great artifact he had studied and had many scour Astura for fit the description. Might it possibly be inside?

The white disc above the painted carvings caught his focus. The fact that the Ancient Ones had expended considerable effort to hang such a large piece of heavy stone, likely marble, inside a ceiling of large, brown-blocked limestone made it significant. Devoid of markings, the disc hung starkly white, shimmering with faint translucent orange brilliance brought on by the torchlight.

Railee drew close, her gaze matching his. "What is it? What purpose would it serve there?"

Such questions spoke aloud next to his wondering thoughts raised alarms, though he knew not why. He glanced around, trying to look everywhere at once.

Gripping the rightmost torch base, Malkor smiled at him, his long face grotesque, made more so by the flickering shadows underneath it. "Perhaps better light may illuminate the answer, Master," he said, lifting the torch from the sconce.

"Leave it!" Darwin screamed as the torch came free.

An audible click preceded the thunderous sound of stone scraping against stone. Darwin dove to the side and collided violently with Railee, his momentum carrying her from her feet as light vanished.

He landed on something firm but softer than stone. Railee. As he bounced from atop her, she grunted with pain, the breath whooshing from her lungs.

The hard stone floor banged into Darwin's side painfully. Gasping for breath, he rolled onto his back and stared at blackness absolute. Stale dust coated his throat and filled his lungs causing a hard cough. Panic rose within him as his breaths came in shorter gasps. *Breathe slower, calm yourself. You do not want to die in the dark inside this blasted tomb, you great fool,* he thought, adding an inner sneer of disdain at his cowardice.

After a time, his coughs and racing heart slowed to an occasional splutter and quickening thumps. He lived.

Darwin sat up and fished inside his robes, quelling a second bout of rising anxiety. Finally, his hand closed upon the flask of oil. Detecting no leakage, relief flooded him along with added appreciation for the thick cloth of his robes. The Flow required a vessel, something to contain its powerful, precarious nature. Removing it from the protective pocket, he drew upon the Flow, trickling a sliver from the source, delivering as small an increment as he could muster into the phial.

Radiant light burst from the phial of oil. Squeezing his eyes shut, he turned away, giving his vision time to clear.

Railee moaned.

Darwin's eyelids sprang open. The Red Rock warrior woman lay on her back beside him, blood pooling from a wound on the back of her head. With reluctance, he transferred the phial to his crippled left hand, his grip far weaker than he liked, but he had little choice. He needed her strength to retrieve the spear. Fingering her thick golden hair with his good hand, he found the gash superficial though bleeding profusely as head wounds tended to do.

Railee moaned louder.

The fall had knocked her unconscious, but she was regaining it. Darwin worked at untying the *shroudin* from her neck for a short time, but the knot was tight. Worried about the amount of blood soaking her neck, he let it go and pushed her hair through the cloth ring, working it over her hair until it was high enough to pry over the bridge of her nose at her eyes. He coughed with the effort.

Satisfied he had helped curtail the bleeding, at least for a time, he stood and transferred the phial back into his right hand. Later, he might attempt a healing even though his ability was limited, unlike Malkor's exceptional skill, provided his strength proved sufficient to merit such an attempt.

Raising his arm, he waved the light slowly back and forth in a half-circle. The disc of heavy white marble stood ominous and large, blocking the way from floor to one-story ceiling. The massive, nearly luminescent, rock vanished somewhere above, rising into the chute from where it came.

The stone hewn taller than the carved roof gave him a sense of awe for its precise construction, but moving to one side had strengthened the feeling. At its narrowest point, a hand's width of space opened to darkness beyond. Whoever had designed the trap had left room for the transference of air, little else. Death would come slowly from the absence of a vital liquid, a fluid grossly understated and severely taken for granted at times, the most precious commodity in the desert, water.

The small leather flask in his robe pocket had become as important as the phial in his hand. Strict rationing would now be required, though the thought of its coolness flowing down his dusty throat made his mouth moisten. He could drink a river.

An abrupt coughing drifted from the darkness coming from beyond the left side of the disc. Darwin slipped his arm into the gap to the shoulder, squeezing his face next to the wall. Only darkness lurked beyond his light. "Malkor?" he shouted, though he feared it was only a worker.

Malkor's high-pitched voice floated from the darkness, the incredulous tone of his voice unmistakable. "Master! You're alive!"

"Alive, yes, though trapped as you. Listen carefully, we have to keep going deeper within and find the artifact; it is our one hope. With it, I do not believe even stone can block the way. Do you hear?"

"I hear, Master, and I shall obey. What am I to look for? You have not yet spoken of what we seek."

"You shall know when your eyes befall it. Do you have light or a vessel to contain a Flow sliver as I taught you?"

Malkor's nasal voice grew higher and thinner. "I have some light, the torch that created this catastrophe, Master, though I am not worthy of your help, of finding a way out. You would be wise to leave me here to die."

"Perhaps, but your dying will not find the artifact. Go. Search every room; find a way to map every weapon you find. Work your way to the final resting chamber. I shall rejoin you there. Whatever you do, do NOT touch any of it. I cannot yet reach you to save you."

"As you command, Master," Malkor, his nasal voice now normal, replied, the volume getting smaller at the end as he moved away.

"There is one other thing you must know," Darwin said, raising his voice.

"Yes, Master?" Malkor said, his voice gaining volume as he

came back. "What is it?"

"Stay alert, there will be…obstacles, some as deadly as this one."

"I understand," Malkor replied. "I shall not fail a second time."

Turning around, Darwin found Railee sitting. The warrior woman leaned forward, her hands cradling her head.

Going to her, Darwin bent, and holding the light close, he inspected the wound. The bleeding had slowed to an occasional drip along the bottom of his makeshift bandage.

"Great pain throbs in my head, nausea weakens my stomach, and I have no vision. Am I dying?" Railee whispered.

"You *should* live," Darwin said with a calmness he did not feel. He could not shake an urgent sense to keep moving, to continue the search for the Spear. He hoped his warning would be enough to keep Malkor's hands from it should he find it first, though the thought failed to inspire faith it would happen so. As bejeweled and shimmering as the old drawing and scrolls depicted the artifact to be, his servant would likely pick it up upon sight. "Your blindness is temporary. I covered your eyes to stabilize a nasty head wound."

Railee felt at the cloth covering her head.

"Leave your *shroudin* in place until the wound closes over. Until then, find my shattered arm, hold onto it, and let me guide you. We have to discover a way out before losing breathable air," Darwin said, lying only partially. He had no way of knowing when the workers would believe them dead and reseal the opening.

He braced himself as Railee gripped his rigid arm and climbed to her feet. He had to take more of her weight than he expected, nearly collapsing to the floor with her a couple of times. Once standing, she clutched his arm tightly.

When he stepped forward, her knees buckled. Only the

rigidity of his arm kept her from falling, though it was a near thing and caused the red haze of pain to speckle his vision, stealing his breath.

Gripping him tight, she shook with weakness. The blood loss from the wound must be worse than he believed. He did not want to leave her, but he had to get moving. The artifact resided somewhere in this tomb; it had to be here, perhaps close. He would come back for her…if the way out led back to her. He opened his mouth, the lie on his lips about going for help, when her grip on his arm loosened.

Straightening to her full height, Railee stood as tall as he was. "I am weak but able to walk if you allow a slower pace at the beginning," she said, her voice steady.

Even with her hair matted with blood and blinded by her *shroudin*, she was still beautiful. Even better, her strength appeared to be returning. She may yet serve him well.

Though he set a fair pace, Railee matched his stride with only an occasional falter as they moved along a narrow hallway for close to a bell. No side door or intersection appeared beyond the dust-speckled light of the phial. He found it convenient to have her blindfolded and dependent on him, controlling her every move with a simple tug of his arm.

He did not stop to admire carved and painted picture glyphs staggered on each side of the hallway when they came to them. He cared little for the pyramid-shaped buildings and bizarre clothing of the inhabitants, some few he recognized. None yet had the three markings pertaining to the artifact.

The frescoes marched on )and on, leading the way along the hallway he despaired of having no end. Railee's sudden stop swung him around by his crippled arm, bumping their hips together painfully.

"Did you hear that?" she asked in a whisper.

Darwin was annoyed. He had heard nothing beyond the thud of their boots for nearly a bell. "What is it?" he asked, not bothering to keep the impatience from the tone of his voice.

"A soft click, now there's a crackling sound. It's getting louder."

Now that she had mentioned it, he did hear a slight crackle, as if small bursts of lightning plunged into water with a last hiss. Out of caution, he drew upon the Flow and installed a physical barrier around the both of them. Looking up, he scrutinized his dome only to have his stomach muscles tighten. Circular, plate-sized stones dropped from the ceiling in two rows of six, followed by a red oozing liquid.

"What's happening? Why is it suddenly so hot?" Railee asked, the tone of her voice raising his fear.

Molten rock poured on his dome from four of the twelve holes, forcing him to add Flow to himself. He filled the vessel of his body, raising the level of the Flow within him to close to what he could safely handle—closer than he'd ever attempted. He poured it all into the dome though it would leave him spent.

His protection would not hold long against such a powerful natural substance. The lava slowed as he thought of its strength flowing away from them and pooling in several spots about the floor. Slackening to a dribble, it cooled quickly, hardening to a soft shell on the floor.

Once it halted from dripping above them, Darwin allowed his dome to dissolve. Heat hotter than the Shimmering Sands they had left outside the tomb assaulted him, evaporating the sweat from his brow. "Listen carefully, we cannot stay here longer, get behind me, and hold onto my waist. Stop moving when I do, immediately. Do you understand?"

Railee trembled. "I may swoon at any time, my stomach churns terribly, something is wrong," she said, swaying slightly.

"Stay focused or we die," Darwin hissed, swallowing a scathing retort that arose from her mention of weakness. Stressing her further would worsen the situation. One misstep from either of them and he would be hard-pressed to stop from falling in molten lava. He *could* remove her arm and go on, but his instinct nagged he would need her to survive more of the Ancients' vast cunning.

Railee's grip on his arm tightened, surprising him. Her lips pulled into a grimace. "My balance is off, I must remove the *shroudin*," she said her free hand at the back of her head.

"Leave it," Darwin said quickly. "As hot as it is, I fear the wound will tear open easily."

Railee dropped her hands to her side. "Yes, it would. The cloth is thick with dried blood, removing it now would tear it open."

"We must go now or die, woman. Can you do it?"

Feeling about his neck for his shoulder, she moved behind him and put both her hands at his waist. "Go," she said, her voice a croak.

Moving around a slow-moving peninsula of smoldering rock, Darwin chose his route carefully, keeping his charge in mind. Though he shied from the heaviest steam, his lungs burned, and he hacked.

Railee, too, coughed, gasping for air behind him as they progressed to the opposite wall where the lava flow thinned the most. Even so, at the narrowest portion, they would have to jump. Wide glowing red cracks surrounded square and rectangular chunks of cooler volcanic rock like weathered roof thatching peeling upward or mud flaking at the bottom of an evaporating pond.

Though it was a stretch, he would make it across. *Perhaps.* Expending so much of the Flow on the dome had left him physically drained, worse than he had imagined. He wanted to sit with his head in his lap, replenish the strength dwindling from his legs, and clear the lethargic fog growing in his mind. Again, he gauged the distance. Rest would come on the other side of the lava flow, *if* he made it. It was going to be close.

Behind him, Railee coughed, shifting the weight of her grip to his left side. "It's so hot and...I'm...not sweating anymore, my skin is clammy. How far do we...have to go?" she asked, her voice hoarse.

Darwin doubted the woman would make the jump in her condition. Though she weighed less, she was too large for him to toss safely.

He had his life to consider.

Firmly, he removed her hands from his waist. "Wait for my call, then walk forward, do not deviate right or left."

"Where do you go?"

Darwin kept his voice placid. "Do as I say if you want to live." Gathering his failing strength, he leapt.

In the air, he knew his trajectory and momentum were not enough to carry him beyond the molten stream. Desperate, he drew upon the Flow, installing a thin barrier on top of the red glowing lava.

Pain cascaded inside his head; he fought to sever the link to the source of great magic raging beneath as his feet touched the thin membrane of the barrier a short way beyond center. His feet sank, and his knees buckled with agony. He fell, sliding on his stomach and forearm, and blackness overran his consciousness.

# CRUMPLED FORM

Darwin woke to a faint red glow and a thumper headache, which he shunted aside. Ignoring pain was second nature to him now, something he had trained himself for seasons ago. Pushing away from the polished stone beneath him, he struggled to stand and comprehend why he yet lived.

Oddly, his barrier remained below him, glistening as smooth as glass.

Railee sat huddled where he'd left her, her legs drawn up and her arms wrapped around her knees.

Comprehension came to him. Rotating in a slow circle confirmed his suspicion. He had not cleared the lava with his foolish leap, nor would he ever without boosting it with the Flow. His heat-stroked brain had not thought of that, though his use of the Flow had saved him. He stood on the thin ribbon of his barrier.

But how? The barrier's protection should have dissolved when he lost consciousness. Perhaps it had. Squatting, he touched it, finding it cool and hard. Then it dawned on him. The barrier had insulated the lava, cooling it underneath, causing it to harden.

Awed by his luck, he made his way carefully along the path, stepping beside Railee. As he gripped her elbow, she tried to pull away. "Come, we have to keep moving," he said, losing patience.

Railee's head rose at the sound of his voice. Then she

wrapped her arms around his legs, hugging him tightly. "I thought you left me."

Darwin patted her back awkwardly with three soft taps. "Come," he repeated. "We waste precious time."

Releasing him abruptly, she accepted his help and stood, moving behind him as before.

"There is a step up here, can you accomplish it?"

Railee coughed before she spoke. "Please, let us go."

Darwin said no more on the subject.

They came to his footprints and the trough his body had created from the momentum of his slide. The now darkened phial lay on the smooth part of the barrier beyond it. Stooping, he picked it up. The Flow's luminescence had bled away, but the glass appeared intact. Drawing upon the Flow, even for the micro amount required to re-light it, was beyond him for a while; he would not have the strength to sever the link. Putting it in his pocket, he worked by the dim light of the glowing lava on both sides, though even that was fading as they came to the end.

"Have a care, there is a step down," he said.

Railee said nothing, only moaning softly as she made the transition from cooling melted rock to dusty granite flooring, the scuff of her boots swallowed by distance and darkness ahead.

Her silence suited him. Concentrating on shuffling forward took all of his energy.

How long they walked and what distance they traveled, Darwin had no concept. He stumbled through the dark, keeping the wall near at hand, his legs wooden. After some time, the last of his energy and drive dissolved. Dropping to his knees, he fell onto three limbs, his left hand holding his torso from the stone. He panted as hard as an animal.

A persistent ache in his back triggered an alarm in his mind, clearing away some of his exhaustion stupor.

A weight rested on him.

Time passed. Then he became aware that Railee lay on him, her head weighing on his back below his shoulder blades. Fast asleep or unconscious, perhaps worse, it did not matter, she could not remain there.

Raising and lowering his right side took a few attempts, but her weight finally slid from him.

Thudding to the floor, she made no sound.

Rolling clumsily, he ignored the pain of long unused muscles and put his back to the wall. Sitting, he drew his legs to him and slipped into a sleep befitting a tomb.

Darwin woke to the sound of his name. Or had he? His thoughts were sluggish.

A voice called from out of the darkness. "Darwin?"

The voice had the ring of familiarity. A small beacon of light caught his eye, growing brighter and larger.

"Please respond, Master," the voice called again, though with less volume as if despairing.

The name of the light's carrier came to him in a rush. "Malkor, come here," he shouted, struggling to stand.

The light froze and then grew more luminous as it moved toward him. Before long, he saw the light bobbing toward him. Malkor's narrow disconnected head and face came into view, the torchlight casting his emaciated body in deep shadows.

As his servant drew close, a fierce look of cunning twisted Malkor's features and then vanished so fast Darwin dismissed it as an illusion of the flickering light. His manservant looked as passive as always.

"Oh, Master, you cannot know how I begged to the Great Bane of Onan to find you. Every trap I disarmed coming here added to the fear I would discover your remains in it. Why have you not drank your water?" Malkor asked, tugging at his black robe.

Malkor had his utmost attention. "You defeated the traps? Alone?" he croaked. He nearly pushed Malkor's hand away waiting for an answer. As the first few drops hit the back of his parched throat, he was glad he did not.

Disappointingly, Malkor stoppered the flask. "You must ration our water if we are to survive. I only defeated some of them, Master, only the traps placed between us."

Darwin had a thought, which gave him a burst of excitement. "How could you perceive the precise way to defuse the Ancients' cleverness, even know where they were hidden?"

Malkor's jaw rose, a smug smile tugging at his thin cracked lips. "Trapped with little else to occupy my thoughts, I switched to my new ability, accessing the data streaming at a high rate into my mind. This time, I hit upon the secret to dealing with such a heavy flow. Instead of trying to interrupt the stream, believing it would cease or slow someday, though I know now it never will, I allowed it full into my mind. The data shall stream uninterrupted into my mind until I terminate, as even now, Naa'thon must have a constant—"

Darwin could not stop himself from interrupting, nor did he desire to. "If you do not halt it, how do you read it?"

"I have come to that, if Master will allow me to finish."

Darwin waved for him to go on, not entirely ignoring the slight of his servant's words. He would address them after they escaped the tomb.

"The key to the data is simple. One has only to request the information, where it is rerouted through my mind but not *interrupted*. Once I made the discovery, I requested information on the designing and constructing of this tomb. The builders are in here with me, so is everything they ever did in their long or short lives."

Darwin felt invigorated by the water and the news, not solely from the knowledge of having his suspicion confirmed. Acquiring what he came for was a very real possibility "An excellent revelation my old friend, let us continue to the artifact."

Malkor smiled and turned, offering a shoulder of support, which Darwin accepted. The light from his torch revealed Railee lying in the fetal position on the floor. "What of this one? Should I check for the possibility of healing?"

Darwin did not hesitate to reply. "Save your strength. One or both of us may require your energy before this is through."

Without another word, Malkor headed back the way he had come.

Darwin did not glance behind at the crumpled form of his former lover.

# SERIOUS FLAW

The ruby gateway dropped Crystalyn on the peak of a beige mountain—not quite red or brown. A heated wind loaded with warm sand picked at her eyes and tugged at the straps of her daypack. She closed her lids to mere slits. Though difficult to see through, it was better than scorching her corneas.

Holding her hand outstretched in front of her for some small protection, Crystalyn moved a safe distance along the dune's ridge from the drop point. Having the gateway plop the others in her space with her still in it was a danger they were all aware of. She didn't relish the thought of merging with Atoi, Lore Rayna, or— *Great Father forbid*—Hastel. Broth, she could probably live with should such an accident occur, *if* she lived through it. In ways hard to imagine, she'd already merged with her link mate.

The sand pummeled her painfully from all sides. Crystalyn turned her back to the worst of it, letting her pack block some.

A thought slipped into her mind she may have to expend strength casting her absorption symbol for relief if the others tarried much longer, but it proved not the case. Lore Rayna materialized and rushed to her side, and then Broth, Atoi, and finally Hastel came through the gate. The grizzled warrior growled something unintelligible—probably a curse—cupped a hand over his one good eye, and then made his way carefully over to them.

Turning his back to the wind, Hastel moved down the

leeward side. "Follow me, we have to get off this ridge," he shouted.

When they staggered below the ridge, the wind gave way to searing heat. Crystalyn almost wished for the wind to return, perhaps a cool breeze, even just a bit of shade under a tree with a blue pool of cold water to languish in. *What am I doing?* They'd just begun their desert trek and already she daydreamed of shade and water.

Hastel paused. Pulling the canvas with the map drawn on it from the kell satchel hanging at his waist, he unrolled it and gazed at it, glancing about from time to time.

"Well?" Crystalyn asked. Standing and baking in the heat wasn't good for them. Physical exertion at least got them progress as they sweated the moisture from their bodies. Already her perspiration evaporated on her skin, a sign of heat stroke.

Hastel looked up, gazing around again. "With no landmarks to go by—one dune looks the same as the next—it's hard to know for certain, but I think I've got a direction for the Valley of Forgotten Kings." Rolling the canvas tight, he pointed a direction to the right of the round cook fire in the sky.

"The tombs await at the rising sun," Atoi intoned in her otherworld voice.

Crystalyn glanced sharply at her little companion though her expression was as impassive as usual. No surprise there. "Are you certain?" She waited only briefly for a reply that wouldn't come. "Do we follow Craight's map or a child?" she asked her companions next.

*"I have no knowledge of this land. Such a place is unsuited for my kind."*

Lore Rayna hugged herself. The dress fared badly; some of the leaves had darkened to a sickly brown, rent with tiny holes or rips from the whipping sand, revealing white skin. "I do not care as long as we get there soon.

Hastel stowed the map in the satchel. "The child is more than that, she is the Dark Child. This map is rudimentary at best. As soon as we find Atoi's right, I'm going to mark which direction is north or any other, something the cartographer failed to note."

A quick glance away from the sun indicated east wasn't back to the dune's ridge, which she appreciated. Nevertheless, they would have to travel perpendicular with another large windblown pile of brown sand, eventually having to move over the top of it. There was no help for it. "It is decided then. Atoi, take the lead. Find the tomb with obvious activity as quick as you can. We can't have Lore Rayna wandering around naked in this bloody heat. Broth is struggling with it too."

Atoi dashed past Hastel. Crystalyn followed. Going with the dune, they trudged slightly downward for what seemed a mile, but in reality, only half that put them at the bottom. For every step taken, two were required in order to stay at the height the little girl set in the loose sand. Finally, they reached the bottom. There was no shade, yet it felt noticeably cooler.

Crossing a narrow furrow cut with the windy sword of time, Atoi started up the side of the higher dune.

"Hold!" Crystalyn called, studying the sandy furrow. The channel grew slightly wider and deeper before vanishing around a bend. "Let's follow this to where it changes direction; it looks like it may go the right way."

Atoi changed course without comment, the path swallowing her from view after a few quick strides.

Rounding the bend soon after her companion, Crystalyn was pleasantly surprised to find that it not only headed the right way, but the channel widened and deepened, sloping downward as it went. Farther down it, the sand gave way to a two-toned rock. Pale tan like the sand and a light red texture layer traveled along the channel in a near straight line. The air grew noticeably cooler with each downward step. Before long, they slipped into the divine coolness of shade.

"Though one is grateful for shelter from the nourishing, but overbearing, rays of the south, one wonders what purpose this odd path in the desert has," Lore Rayna said from behind.

Broth bounded past. *"The Valen speaks truly, Do'brieni. I shall scout the path beyond the Ancient One."*

Ahead, the passage curved slightly eastward. The light red layer at the bottom widened, growing darker as the rock above rose higher. Vertical lines scarred the layers at regular intervals from top to bottom. Crystalyn trailed a finger on them as she walked. "These marks have the smooth feel of chisel marks cut long ago. Perhaps we've stumbled upon an ancient waterway designed to bring water to a cistern."

"Aye, I do believe you have the right of it," Hastel agreed.

Lore Rayna's deep voice carried easily to her, though she had entered the waterway last. "Which would indicate—"

"Our chosen path will lead us down to the Valley of the Forgotten Kings," Hastel finished.

"Please refrain from doing that in the future, little warrior man," Lore Rayna said.

Though he strode a few paces back, Hastel's raspy voice sounded close. "Doing what, oh large woman warrior of the great naturist people?" Grossly exaggerated, the tone of his voice strove for innocence.

"You play at a dangerous game…little warrior man," Lore Rayna growled.

Crystalyn halted. "Would the two of you quiet down, please? We've come to ruin someone's unknown, but undoubtedly evil, aspirations, remember. At least, I think we have. Who knows what our little Dark Child guide has in mind for us."

"You are correct as usual *Sarra'esiah*, please accept assurance it—" Lore Rayna began.

"Shall not happen again," Hastel finished.

Though low in volume, Lore Rayna's growl reverberated down the channel.

Taking a quick drink from her water flask, Crystalyn shifted the wide leather carrying strap, getting it to ride on her shirt instead of her bare neck where the sand underneath rubbed her raw. Grateful for the shade, and invigorated a little from the splash of water in her system, she followed the gentle downward slope around a slight bend and then another.

*"We have arrived, Do'brieni,"* Broth sent. The warden sat on his haunches beside Atoi at the edge of a gigantic stone spillway. The channel sloped steeply into a wide valley strewn with large constructs of brownish red limestone half-buried in sand. The bloody same rocks she'd seen in the vision on the hill above the Great Plains. At least, they looked similar from this high up.

Far below where she stood, a town of plain two-person tents mingled with multi-roomed gaudy-colored cabin pavilions. Timber hoists and retaining walls withheld a mountain of sand from reclaiming a partial excavation of a grand structure guarded thousands of seasons by a massive statute having the head of a man and the body of a beast.

"Guess we know where we go next," Crystalyn said as Hastel and Lore Rayna joined those on the ledge.

"Aye," Hastel said quietly. The warrior's one blue eye moved with constant motion from side to side, gathering the details transpiring below quickly. "Two-thirds of those tents are mercantile design; even the cook stove areas will have shaded awnings. The rest are the functional nomadic shelters of desert dwellers, lightweight and sturdy. The nomadic peoples are warriors."

Crystalyn held back a sigh. "I thought as much. Yet we have little choice but to stroll through the front door. It's the only one uncovered."

"Aye," Hastel repeated.

Lore Rayna leaned forward. "How shall we get to the bottom of the channel?"

Crystalyn followed the big woman's gaze. They all did.

In its time of use, the waterway had flowed gently along the constructed passage and then raced down the steep spillway only to slow once more at the bottom as it leveled out.

"That's a good question. Ideas, anyone?" Crystalyn asked. Going back wasn't an option she wanted to consider. They'd have to backtrack at least two miles before the channel became shallow enough to climb out from and then another two back to the valley rim under the scorching heat. From there, who knew how long it would take to find a safe pathway to the bottom.

Atoi stared at the left side. "The stone is cracked and pitted at the edges where little moisture insulated it from the sun. One may have handholds enough to make the descent."

Crystalyn's initial excitement waned as she studied the route the little girl proposed. "Only if you have Lore Rayna's reach. Some of the handholds are quite far apart. Even then, she'd have to revert to her roots part of the way. No pun intended, my large friend."

Lore Rayna smiled, briefly.

"Besides, Broth couldn't do it. He's not made that way. Next idea."

*I shall return to the dune, follow the rim, and rejoin you at the bottom should you decide to attempt this path. However, I am against such an attempt.*

*No, my Do'brieni. We stay together.*

"I could carry the warden in *flor'e'form*, perhaps all of you at once, except then I have limited mobility, and I cannot hold the form for long, a half bell at best."

Hastel had turned away from the spillway. "How long of a reach do you have in that form?" he asked over his shoulder.

"Seven, perhaps eight, meters if I push my strength."

Giving a nod, he tilted his head back, looking up. "I thought as much. Therefore, that leaves you, Mistress Crystalyn. Please tell me you have a symbol in your arsenal capable of loosening that rock up there and getting it down here, intact."

Gazing up, Crystalyn found the rock he spoke of with little trouble, though rock was a misnomer—slab fit better. A huge chunk of limestone had broken from the main cliff wall where it lay overhanging the channel. A jagged crack gaped with darkness below it.

Crystalyn opened her mouth intending to say her symbols didn't function in the way he wanted, but then she closed it. The blackness within the crack drew her attention. *Perhaps, if it's deep enough, I might have something. Providing I get a feel for the right symbol.* "Everyone come with me. We have to be well clear," she said aloud, moving up the channel's slight slope.

When she judged the distance safe, Crystalyn wiggled out of her pack. Setting it on the ground, she brought out the *Tiered Tome of Symbols,* tier three, and opened it. Page after page, she flipped through it, getting a sense of a swarm from one with squiggly lines speared by diagonal lines inside a radius. Another symbol, drawn with interlocking squares inside a circular diagram, exuded coldness. Moving on, she paused at a simpler symbol depicting a ring of wider than usual forked lines that seemed to moisturize her skin as she looked at it. How would a water symbol help?

Going with an impulse, she brought it out to hover before her along with the one emanating coldness. Combining the two, she now had forked ends with square handles inside a radius that was black on one side and white on the other. "Here goes nothing and everything."

She sent it zooming toward the beckoning blackness. Most of the symbol hit outside the gaps, breaking apart and frosting the cliff face next to it with big splotches, but some of the symbol vanished inside the crack. At first, nothing happened. Then, a loud *pop* rent the air. Chunks of stone poured from the crack, widening it. Clattering into the channel below, the shards of stone formed a pile of dirt and rock.

A deafening scraping heralded the slab dropping heavily into the gap left in the cliff wall. For a brief moment, the slab hung there, and then teetering once like a boat sinking in deep water, it slid down the side and flipped onto the pile with a thunderous *SMACK*.

Silence fell with the dust cloud that hung in stasis above the slide, even as it slowly settled upon the pile.

Hastel cleared his throat, breaking the stillness. "That certainly did it," he said, the tone of his voice thick with awe.

Wicked laughter, echoing from a great distance, sounded from Atoi. "Now, what do you intend to do with it?" she asked. A short jump put her on the flat stone.

Ignoring the question, Hastel's head full of curly hair turned toward Lore Rayna. "Now it's your turn." Flashing their largest companion a brief smile, he joined the smallest of their group by clattering up the pile and stepping onto the limestone boulder.

Lore Rayna frowned at his smile. "Now you have use of me? What game do you play, little man?"

Crystalyn cut into the conversation, her anger growing, though there was little cause for it. *Calm yourself, Crystalyn. Another bout of dealing with your broken mind is the last thing you need,* she told herself. "Hastel has shown he can be a gentleman at times. Accept it for what it is and move on."

Lore Rayna laughed. "There is nothing refined about that man!"

Hastel chuckled. "Yes, I'm as rough as they come. Will you help us?"

Lore Rayna blinked. "What would you have me do?"

Hastel pointed to the spillway's edge. "Can you slope this pile of rubble that way with your special talent?"

Lore Rayna's arms and hands elongated as her skin hardened to the roughness of tree bark. The bark traveled up her legs to the upper thighs as all four limbs snaked toward the rocks. Branching out as they extended, each new branch limb slipped under and around a loose stone and roped it tight. Lifting and tugging with superb dexterity, her branched limbs adjusted the stones in a surprisingly short amount of time as if they weighed little.

Retracting swiftly, Lore Rayna's limbs returned to normal. The big woman moved closer to the pile inspecting her handiwork. "What comes next?" she asked, her orbs brightening.

Hastel tapped a foot on the flat rock, which teetered slightly downslope. "Join us on our little mound. You too, mistress, please, and your link mate."

*"Go ahead Broth; let's find out what he has in mind."* Broth leapt beside Atoi, his paws barely contacting the path of rock he chose.

Having an idea what may come, Crystalyn clamored up the pile and slowed at the top in order to step on the flat rock at the same time as her Valen companion. Hastel, too, took a step forward.

As soon as their combined weight rested upon the stone, the slab tilted and slammed onto the rocky slope. With a loud scraping groan, the limestone slid, rumbling toward the spillway. "Everyone hold on!" Crystalyn shouted." Dropping to her knees, she clutched at a crack too small to get her fingers inside.

Plunging over the edge, the massive rock listed at a sharp

angle, picking up speed.

"Blast it! There's nothing keep us on this!" Hastel roared.

*"I cannot hold, Do'brieni!"*

"Lore Rayna!" Crystalyn shouted as her feet slipped. She slid helplessly toward the stone's edge.

Something wrapped around her waist as a flash of brown heralded a pole wider than a spear dropping in front of her. Acting on instinct, she grabbed at the pole as two others fell into place on each side of it. Shifting her legs around, Crystalyn supported her body weight on the two of them, risking a quick glance over her shoulder.

Resplendent, Lore Rayna stood at the rock's center; the vines making up her dress had extended in as many directions, the ends roped around her waist at her navel. Like a vibrant willow tree, arched branches protruded from Lore Rayna's shoulders, arms, outstretched hands, and legs. Climbing higher than her golden head, the branches drooped to the edges all around the circular stone, supporting them inside a living cage.

The wind whipped past Crystalyn pulling harder at her hair as the bottom of the spillway came into sight. Though the slope had a gentle curve to leveling out, there was a serious flaw to riding a ton or more of rock down it. Sand had filled the channel long ago.

# WOLF FACE

Though Crystalyn braced her heels on the living cage and the vines at her waist cinched uncomfortably tight, the force of the impact catapulted her into a dense cloud of exploding sand. Darkness enveloped her as stinging wind rushed past. Banging something hard, her breath whooshed from her lungs. She rolled and slid. Finally, sand clutched at her side, pulling her to a stop.

Scrambling to sit up, she brushed grains of sand from the left side of her body. Her pack still rode on her back, intact. In no hurry to rejoin the desert floor, thick tan dust floated around. Straining to see through the surreal landscape, Crystalyn sought the flat rock they'd imprudently ridden down the ancient waterway.

Plowing into the sand-filled channel, the limestone monstrosity had gouged a deep rivulet in the ancient waterbed. As the desert grit had accumulated under it, the sand had won the battle of momentum by burying it half under its grainy embrace.

His sienna-colored fur standing out in the lighter-colored dust, Broth leapt over the rock, stopping a couple of meters from it. Her link mate's great head bent toward the desert floor.

Lore Rayna lay nude in the sand, her bosom still and her legs covered in sand from the knees down.

*"The tree woman has sustained grievous injury, Do'brieni."*

Crystalyn struggled to stand, ignoring the burning on her left hip, left arm, and face. Going to the fallen woman, she passed Atoi helping Hastel regain his feet. Both looked to be in fair condition.

It wasn't so with her large companion. Embedded in a massive abrasion, grains of sand stuck in Lore Rayna's muscle filaments and blood. The wound marred the right side of the big woman's beautiful face where her eyelid clung above her non-glowing eye by a strand. Her hair had turned a sickly brown, which was the least of Crystalyn's worries. Lore Rayna's breath came shallow. Her fingers had unnatural bends to them, yet she had suffered the worst injuries to her arms. Multiple breakages were apparent by the shattered bone shards penetrating her forearms in too many places.

Fearing her Valen friend's injuries were too great, Crystalyn brought out her golden symbol and combined it with one she'd read under the heading dilutions in tier one of the *Tiered Tome of Symbols*. The symbol reformed. Intricate gold and silver lines wound back and forth, filling the symbol with a hedge maze with no beginning or end.

Glowing faintly silver and gold in color, the symbol floated before her, and Crystalyn laid it horizontally over the prone woman and let it sink into her, attaching her awareness to it, though she sensed a difference this time. The warmth of her link mate's mental presence still resided with her though more tangible than she'd felt before. An image of his wolf face drifted about in her mind. She walled it away; there was no time for it.

First, Crystalyn swept the symbol past her Valen companion's internal organs, happy to find them intact. Then she tackled the worst damage by tying a portion of the symbol to each fragment of bone, however small. Pulling them together from the inside out, she fused them by phasing her healing symbol into every fracture, losing a fourth of it in the process. Sealing the puncture holes and knitting the skin closed on Lore Rayna's arms took another fourth. Straightening the big woman's long slender fingers required two-thirds of the remainder.

With less than a fourth of the symbol's original size left to her, Crystalyn traveled Lore Rayna's capillaries to the socket of her right eye and stitched the skin around it from there; then she concentrated on the organ itself. A wide tear on her Valen companion's previously unseen pupil and the crystalline lens behind it made her pause, and not only for the obvious fluid loss. She lacked the experience of healing the delicate complexity of an eye with its rod and cone cells that added color and depth perception as light passed through, though she had trained with it in medical school.

Broth's comforting presence sharpened, as if to say he had every confidence in her; he would see her through to the end simply by being with her. Gratefully, she drew upon the strength of his warmth and then continued the task.

The torn muscle holding Lore Rayna's lens in place was a quick fix. A small part of her symbol unraveled and reattached it, fusing it in place. The tear was trickier. Working her way deeper inside her friend from the cornea back, she fused as she went, though she needn't have worried about the fluid loss between it and the iris. The glowing substance of Lore Rayna's eye returned. Traveling from her spine and then the brain, the Flow flowed in replacing the loss of substance, the breach to the outside world gone.

Repairing the gash through the iris and part of the pupil took some ingenuity. The ring-shaped iris with its fine filament membrane and the adjustability of the pupil made it a delicate task of fusing many varying fibrous lengths, matching those on the opposite side of the break.

After the iris and pupil, the retina came with its countless layers of cells, causing anxiety. There were too many missing cells, and her now tiny symbol floated inside a cavernous space. She'd expended so much energy, weariness made her thoughts slow to come. Determined, she sent her symbol unraveling along the right wall of cells where it made it the full length before finding her awareness dangled by a single minute thread. She'd done what she could, but the left cell wall lay untouched.

Again, she needn't have worried. The cells reacted to the healing exceptionally well, multiplying at an incredible rate. Soon the little strand she clung to brushed the left cell wall. Releasing the symbol, her awareness snapped back to herself.

Blinking, she stared into the golden hourglass eyes of her warden friend and companion, the one being who knew her with an intimacy no one could match, nonhuman or not. Broth sat on his haunches beside her. She could almost swear her companion's wolf face held a grin.

# TREPIDATION

Pausing only to shift the straps from her pack higher on her shoulders, Crystalyn strode through the large bustling tent camp in the Valley of the Forgotten Kings boldly, hoping her little group didn't stand out. Most of the camp consisted of silk-robed or leather-clad armed men striding purposely on some mission known only to them. On rare occasions, a woman dashed by or darted out of tent only to vanish along one of the several packed walkways serving as streets. No one glanced overly long at them, not even with an enormous Valen and warden in tow.

In the center, erected away from all others, a large black tent came into view. "That must be the one," she said.

Hastel's curly, brown-haired head swung from side to side. "Of course, it is, but this is madness. Strolling in here midday. Why haven't they put us under guard yet? What are they waiting for?"

Atoi strode unconcerned beside him. "Methinks he waits to pounce upon us in his lair."

Crystalyn removed the sneer growing within. "Darwin? Not his style, he likes to stage a grand show, right out in the open. Something else must be going on."

"I have agreement with the human of one eye. A bold risk we take by traversing about in the light of day," Lore Rayna said. Her melodious voice held a note of tiredness. She'd lost a lot of her natural vibrancy to the heat of the desert. The sickly brown color of her hair added much to the effect.

Crystalyn felt much the same way after putting the big woman back together. Though she'd had to rest for two hours afterward and then lean on Broth for the remaining bell it required to reach the camp, she was still weak and in no mood for idiosyncrasies. "Why not just call him Hastel, Lore Rayna? It is his name after all. Daylight is why we couldn't afford to wait for darkness. You need shelter from the heat. The extra shirt and pants *I* brought along are doing a poor job of covering you. Your stomach is turning the same ugly red as your abrasions, and I am baking from my own weakness."

Lore Rayna paused, looking down at herself. "Water." She spoke the word as if angered, her frown adding to the intensity of her tone.

Surprised, Crystalyn stopped. "What?"

"Where?" Hastel asked, gazing around. "We need to replenish our bags."

"The brown-green woman speaks of her crawler wear. Her people refer to it as a liana sash. It thrives on water," Atoi said over her shoulder without slowing. The large black tent loomed not far from her.

Throwing her head back, Lore Rayna dropped to her knees. "I am a great fool and not fit to have been blessed by the Great Mother. I have failed the life bonding!" She wailed. "Someone bring water!"

The big woman's raiment had not fared well; a sickly brown strand of the vine dress the same hue as her hair wrapped around her waist, clinging there and quivering.

Though Crystalyn now understood her companion's distress, loitering in the desert heat would cause worse things to happen to her body. "Come, my Valen, we have to get to shade. Your dress needs shelter from the sun."

"I shall not move until water is brought! Someone bring water!" Lore Rayna roared.

A crowd gathered, silent and watchful.

A haughty-faced man stepped forward from the crowd. Although clad with no hood or cloth wrapped about his head, his face and skin remained light despite his bright red hair and clean-shaven face. The yellow robe he wore was open at the front, the suppleness of brown kell leather noticeable underneath. Two scimitars hung from straps near his waistline. "I have what you seek," he declared. Reaching in the front of the robe, he removed a clear hose clipped to the leather, offering the tube to Lore Rayna.

Crystalyn gaped. The hose glowed with the radiance of the Flow. She grabbed the man's wrist. "What do you think to give her?" she asked. The man's powerful muscles tensed under her grip. The pattern for her knockback symbol formed in her mind.

Lore Rayna laid a hand over hers. "Stay your concern, *Sarra'esiah*. I must have moisture."

"I believe it's only water, though some is reclaimed if I recall right," Hastel said.

Confused, the symbol dissolved from Crystalyn's thoughts. She released the man's wrist. "I'm afraid I don't understand."

"You are correct, warrior," another man said, waddling forward from the crowd. Short of stature and wider of frame than average, he wore gaudy silks of bright colors denoting him a merchant. His small blue eyes regarded Crystalyn from a pudgy face. "The Sands nomads have developed an advanced method of filtering out the impurities of body fluid using the cleansing properties of the Flow, thereby recouping water. Nothing is wasted." He turned to Lore Rayna. "Go on, Valen, have your drink. They do not offer lightly."

Grabbing the tube between her thumb and forefinger, Lore Rayna put it in her mouth. Her big laryngeal—as Crystalyn recalled the term for an Adam's apple from nursing school— was prominent and shifted up and down as she drank. Crystalyn suppressed a shudder at the thought of reclaimed fluids. "Who are you?" she asked the merchant instead.

The little man bowed low and then straightened with a speed and grace belying his rotund stature. "Guail, the premier purveyor of northern comforts in southern extremes, at your service, and this"—he waved an expansive arm toward the nomad—"is Long Sand, sand reader for the Clan of the Searing Sun."

The merchant's name she'd heard before, in Brown Recluse. Crystalyn moved beside Lore Rayna. On her knees, the Valen woman still had to bend to drink. Crystalyn nodded to the sand reader. "I am Crystalyn and these are my companions, Lore Rayna and Hastel." She glanced around for Atoi, but the little girl was nowhere in sight. Some of the crowd had dispersed, continuing errands.

Countering a tug from Lore Rayna, Long Sand widened his stance. "Might I inquire what has brought you to this remote encampment?"

Crystalyn was reluctant to answer. "I...we come for someone," she said.

Guail spoke, his beady eyes wide. "Then the master has sent for you as we suspected. Speak no more; it is well known how he prefers to keep his own counsel." A look of cunning cleared the wariness from his eyes. "I'm certain *he* will want to see you right away. Are all of you required? Perhaps, even the Dark Child?"

Saving Crystalyn from coming up with a reply, Hastel spoke. "How does that fit into 'say no more'?"

Though slight, Guail bowed again. "You are right, warrior, please forgive my asking. I simply wished to allay doubts to my master's safety. However, he has proven to not need such concern in the past."

"You should seek to gain experience from what has come before," Crystalyn said.

Guail's face flushed.

Crystalyn laid a hand on Lore Rayna's shoulder. Her pulls on the tube had slowed. "Have you finished? We shouldn't delay much longer."

"The revered one has not returned to his tent since leaving this morning," Long Sand said.

Guail glanced sharply at Long Sand. When the bright-haired sand reader failed to look his way after a few breaths, he kept his sunken gaze locked with Crystalyn.

Crystalyn was alarmed. Had she come too late? "Where has he gone?"

Another sharp tug from Lore Rayna pulled Long Sand a half step closer. Though he had the look of overbearing confidence mixed with great arrogance, his long face and nose complimented his rounded jawline. "Our…clan leader entered the Shrine of the High King not long ago."

A saying her father had told her a time or two came to mind. *Maintain an expression of stone during interrogations. Give nothing away.*

Though excited at the news of closing in on Darwin, Crystalyn made a conscious effort to keep it from showing. "Then we go to the tomb. I assume it's that imposing mound of sand and rock overshadowing this camp?" she asked, nodding beyond Long Sand's shoulder.

Guail folded his arms at his wide belly, puffing out his chest. "The great lord has forbidden all but the diggers to enter the shrine. You may wait for his return inside his tent."

"What did you call him?" Crystalyn asked.

"You are a bloody fool, Merchant," Long Sand said simply.

Guail flushed, the skin on his face deepening almost to the maroon color of one of his layers of silk as his beady eyes narrowed. "Hailing from a land of greenery and moisture, I expected a Valen wouldn't know the nomadic clans' courtship rituals involve the sharing of one's water," he said with a sneer.

Lore Rayna spit the tube from her mouth.

Several armed men in the crowd laughed. The women mixed among them scowled.

Red of face, Lore Rayna stood to her full height of eight hands. Moving too quickly, the shorts she wore tore at each hip several inches, and the shirt ripped slowly between her breasts with each breath.

Crystalyn groaned. She was running out of outfits she'd brought from her home world of Terra.

Again, the men in the crowd guffawed.

Hastel's axes swished as he tugged them from the leather-wrapped steel rings on his hips. "The next laugh dies in the throat of the one emitting it. No one laughs at a companion of mine."

Lore Rayna glanced down quickly at the warrior, her light brown-haired head swinging toward him at his words. Her eyes brightened.

The soft *schlepp* of many weapons leaving the safety of sewn leather scabbards lined with wood caught at Crystalyn's hearing. Some of the sounds had come from behind.

Crystalyn reformed the knockback symbol in her mind, though she feared she'd expended her strength healing Lore Rayna. With that handicap, and the fact she couldn't discreetly remove the black crystal candle artifact from her pack, now really wasn't the time for a brawl. "Put your axes away, Hastel, blast you! Sometimes, I swear, you're too fast at drawing them."

A quick glance over his left shoulder informed anyone paying attention that Hastel had also heard the sound of weapons drawn. Gripping the half-moon heads of his axes, he stabbed both handles into their ringed holders without taking his vivid blue eye from the crowd.

"Seize them now!" Guail shouted.

Strong arms grabbed Crystalyn's arms, forcing them roughly behind her back.

Broth's growls came from behind a ring of warriors.

*"Broth!"*

*"No worry, Do'brieni. They have surrounded me, but they do not attack."*

Three men and a woman grabbed Lore Rayna but not for long. Her arms and legs hardened, and her hair brightened to a vivid green. Tree-like branches without the leaves shot from her hands, slamming into those trying to pin her arms behind her. Her branch-like hands knocked her would be captors roughly to the side.

The nomads took no chance with Hastel. The pommel of a sword thumped into his head and dropped him to the ground where he stood.

Crystalyn froze. In one fluid motion, Guail had pulled a dagger from a silky sleeve and held the edge at her throat. "Stop resisting or she dies!"

Lore Rayna batted the last warrior, a woman, away and turned to Guail. A mound of sand bulged upward in a line, moving toward him.

The burning sensation of pain followed by wetness flowing down her cleavage indicated the knife had taken a bite. Crystalyn hoped it was shallow.

"How deep do I have to go to prove my determination? Stand down, Valen, or your leader dies," Guail said softly, pressing the dagger deeper.

The burning started anew.

Scowling, Lore Rayna grew still as several warriors closed upon her.

The arm around Crystalyn's neck relaxed.

Crystalyn formed her gray-shaded knockback symbol, set to a star pattern, with its white outline in her mind. Bringing it out and already reforming it into three concentric circles at chest level, she sent it behind her. The first of the three slammed into Guail, flinging him and the biting dagger away. The second and third circles hit those racing to his aid from the crowd.

Adding a touch of complexity, she formed another and combined it with a second aggression symbol, changing the white outline to gold and the gray to silver. Sending the now golden stacked circles soaring behind her again, they generated a thunderous boom.

Freed, she gazed about gauging her next round as her anger mounted. Though weakness raged within her, a third symbol hovered in the air before her, the intricate pattern of her smoky garlands, one of her strongest for aggression. She was prepared to do damage this time; her drained mind and body would accept no less.

Long Sand's deep voice trumpeted loud and concussive. "Hold position, you bloody sand adders!"

Thirty of the forty-two warriors she counted shuffling toward her in a tightening circle stopped in their tracks. Twelve kept coming, moving with fluidity unnatural for men.

Long Sand leapt in front of Crystalyn, a scimitar gripped in each hand. "Halt, you blasted vermin! This is your final command. Continue this path and I shall kill you all personally," he said. Even though he did not shout, his voice carried.

The warriors split, circling in silence, coming to a stop only when they surrounded Crystalyn, Long Sand, and Lore Rayna.

Graceful, as if a beast gauging the moment of attack, Long Sand spun on a heel. Slow and deliberate, his fierce gaze fell upon the ring of warriors. "Think carefully, you bloody imbeciles; can you not see how strong a User she is? Is the merchant's promised payment greater than your own lives?"

No grizzled, clean-shaven, or permanent hairless face looked her way. Strangely, all looked at Lore Rayna.

Crystalyn stepped out from behind the nomad warrior, expanding her symbol to twice its size, as she, too, made a slow deliberate circle. As she passed, one by one, the mercenaries fixed on her, their eyes bulging. Her anxiety rose as a thought occurred to her, nearly stunning her with the implications. "Lore Rayna! Use your wood! They're all Dark Men!" she screamed.

Broth growled.

*"Don't touch them or let them near you, Do'brieni! They are too strong together!"* Crystalyn boomed into the link.

*"I cannot come to your aid without attacking them!"* Broth protested.

*"Stay back!"* Crystalyn warned.

Six of the twelve heads split down the middle, dropping on shoulders like one would peel back a hood, the first of the Dark Men started to emerge. The rest raised long swords in unison, preparing an attack on Lore Rayna.

They were too late. Already the Valen woman's arms had elongated with the *flor'e'form*, her legs hardening. Extending and branching out into three forks, each of Lore Rayna's hands elongated to a sharp point, impaling all six in the throat.

Three of the emerging six stepped from a deflating body. The trio of dark shadows converged on Crystalyn. Long Sand's scimitars slashed outward, passing through two of the shadows. The third dispersed into wisps of black smoke, dissolving right after. The first two soon followed. Then, Lore Rayna's branches dissolved the last three before they had fully detached from the host.

As Lore Rayna's arms and legs retracted, Crystalyn flashed a grateful smile at her friend. Then, putting a hand to her neck, she stopped the flow of her blood.

Long Sand's blue eyes were wild as he turned to her. "There is more to you and your group than any would have imagined. What has that blasted merchant infested his men with? I beg an answer, though please put your…weapon away," he said.

Crystalyn dissolved her symbol, not bothering to point out he still had weapons drawn. "They are known only as Dark Men, shadows that ride inside men, destroying them in the process. Their weakness against wood was discovered not long ago, that's about all we know."

In one fluid movement, Long Sand sheathed his scimitars. "What do they want with you? How did they get…inside those mercenaries?"

Crystalyn gave a one-handed shrug. Though she had a strong sense some power wanted hers, she didn't want to discuss it at length. "You'll have to ask your 'blasted merchant.'"

Long Sand bowed. "I shall at that, if he still lives. Please, allow me to send for a healer for you and your man." He strode to the comatose form of Guail, lying on his side some way forward on the path of sand.

Crystalyn checked Hastel's breathing was normal, and then she joined the sand reader who spoke with two of his men. The men sprinted away as she came near.

"The healers should soon arrive," Long Sand said. He prodded the gaudy silk back of the merchant with the toe of his boot, smearing it with sand. "Did you kill him?" he asked.

Failing to find a pulse in the thick folds of the merchant's neck, Crystalyn checked for it at his wrist, finding a strong one there quickly. "He is unconscious, though he will wake soon, like the others struck by symbol. This time, they live."

Long Sand gave a slight bow. "That is well, I suppose. The shifting sands foretell the merchant still has some use. Had I not seen this, I would not have hesitated to kill him where he lay."

Abruptly, Long Sand bowed low, intoning, "We, of the Searing Sun clan, have accrued a debt of deep service to…" He straightened. "What clan do you hail from?"

Crystalyn thought for a moment. Only one name fit. "Creek Family clan," she finally said.

Again, Long Sand bowed. "The clan is honored to serve you. The Clan of the Creek Family has only to express a desire and the Searing Sun will see it done."

"There are but three of us, no, four, I suppose. Wait! Did you say your *whole* clan?"

"As the highest ranking leader present, I speak for my people. For three seasons, it shall be an honor for the Searing Sun Sect to serve you."

"Thank you for your offer, Long Sand, but consider it declined. Not one of us requires subservience. Take care of your people, I'll handle mine."

Long Sand's clean-shaven face darkened, and his hands clenched and unclenched above the pommels of his scimitars.

The scowl Crystalyn masked was partly from symbol fatigue as she thought of her present weakness, only one step shy of the shakes, but mostly from impatience. Why couldn't they just get on with the search to find blasted Darwin? "What is it?" she asked the nomad.

"I believe your refusal has given him and his entire clan offense, mistress," Hastel cut in, the tone of his voice weak. One hand covered the blow to his head. "Refusing now will make an enemy of every last one of them, even the non-warriors and the children…for three-fold the seasons." Removing his right hand from his head, it joined the left one fingering the heads of his axes.

"This clan shall find I block the way," Lore Rayna said, the tone of her voice ominous.

Long Sand gripped the pommels of his scimitars.

Throwing back the hoods of their robes, the ring of warriors advanced as if signaled. Perhaps they were.

Crystalyn gaped around. "You're all bloody serious, aren't you? Has this entire blasted world become battle hungry? Okay, serve me. I have a request. Take me to your revered one."

Raising a hand, Long Sand motioned to the advancing clan warriors. They dashed beside him, lining up on either side. Again, he bowed low, as did the warriors, in unison. Straightening, he smiled. "As I said, it is an honor to serve, follow me." He turned to a tall woman, slightly shorter than Crystalyn herself, on his right. "Ensure the merchant has a guard of twenty sect mates, the strongest. When he wakes, bring him to me at the excavation site after we exit the tomb. As for his hirelings, those unconscious, give them the opportunity to don an oath veil. Bestow a swift death upon them should they refuse. One final command; supply everyone here with something wooden to use as a weapon in case more of those dark creatures are walking about in the skin of mercenaries or clan."

Smoothing away a look of revulsion, the woman bowed. Then she gathered nineteen other men and women warriors and jogged to where the rotund man lay.

Four nomad warriors led the way to the revered one, Long Sand behind them. The five that remained fell in behind Hastel bringing up the rear. Though still weak, Crystalyn's strength built quickly as she moved, glad to have finally neared the end of this hot and dry desert search.

Yet she had trepidation that grew worse as they came within the shadow of the hulking tomb blocking the sun with its palpable presence. How would she react upon first sight of Darwin? Would she hug him or destroy him?

It bothered her that she didn't know.

# HAND OF THE ENEMY

Moving from a patch of green banana fern, Sureen dashed through a small opening, making it to a lightly singed clump of red oak brush. Nearby, a falun tree smoldered, massive even with its charred top half-gouging a large furrow in the meadow beyond its roots. Marveling how a forest fire could burn with such intense heat and still leave patches of flora unscathed, she plotted the way forward. Most of the army had vacated the Vale, but a significant force occupied the southern entry as three mounted guards rode the perimeter.

Hidden under shrubs or inside green fabric half-tents erected in the spotty patches of tall grass, shadowy scouts watched the forest and the Vale's trampled meadow. So far, she'd marked them before they'd seen her, and she'd managed to avoid trip wires both mundane and magical strung with clever hands or created by an adept using the Flow. Her training with the Green Writhe had allowed her to slip past them barely.

The devastation of the Vale sickened her; the great trees had grown for hundreds of seasons, perhaps a few into the thousands, nurtured, as they grew old, by the Valens. Or likely, the trees taught the people of the Vale how best to care for them.

A flicker of movement caught her eye. A figure squatted at the base of the oldest tree in the falun forest, the southern outpost. *Kara Laurel!* She couldn't believe the fool woman was still in the

Vale so many days later. How had they not caught her and killed her?

Smothering her impatience to charge in and confront the woman, Sureen scanned the area with a cautious eye. Tethered to a seared sapling behind the woman, the black warhorse grazed. No other mounts were even close to the area. Her quarry was alone. A grim smile crept upon her. Kara Laurel had much to answer for.

Stooping low and keeping to the brushes and ferns, she worked her way to the back of the tree. Leaning her back against it, she took a moment to gather the Flow, filling her body and the white crystal on her staff. Kara Laurel would not return to the Circle of Light for judgment willingly. Hopping over a mossy root, Sureen rounded the great dead tree.

Kara Laurel waited with her arms folded at her chest, her smooth face serene and unreadable. Dried blood splashes coated her arms and the midsection of her yellow dress. "There you are. I suspected the Writhe would send you. Know that I am not disappointed."

"The Green had no part in this. I come by my daughter's command alone."

Kara Laurel raised a fine auburn eyebrow. "Your daughter trusted me, allowed me to roam free, to help the Vale. What did you have to do to convince her otherwise?"

Obtusely, Sureen scanned the small patch of greenery behind Kara. Nothing out of the ordinary caught her eye. "My daughter is intelligent. The supposition of your trustworthiness was hers alone and needed no persuasion."

Kara Laurel's arms dropped to her side. "There was a time when you would have defended me in all things, no matter if you knew but little of my motivations. Have you not missed me?"

"You changed, Kara. Your daughter's death made you indifferent to those who love you. Let me help you, it is not too late."

Kara Laurel's shoulders slumped, her smooth face losing composure as the corners of her mouth drooped a little. "You cannot, there is only one who can, one that has fought valiantly, unaided and with great sacrifice."

The brief glint of something shiny drew Sureen's eye. Empty flasks shelved on a thick root lined the wide tree limb before it vanished underground. Rings of moist spots pocked with tiny holes darkened the soil from the base outward. Anxiety flowed into the pit of her stomach switching to fear with a dawning comprehension. "You have not returned to the Vale to stop the Alchemist. You came to aid him."

Kara Laurel smiled. "You are as observant as always, my once companion. We were close before discovering our life hearts. Were we not? Try to understand me now. Allow me the faith you had in me, the love we shared. The Alchemist has found the way to harmony, the path to end all troubles of the land. Finally, *we*, all of us, our *world,* shall be free of turmoil! Think of it! There shall be no fighting, a quick death to atrocities, and a resolution of conflicts. At last, all shall be equal throughout the land."

With every word Kara Laurel spoke, Sureen's alarm grew. She reached for the Flow and found…*nothing!* The great frothy river had vanished. "What have you done?"

Kara Laurel's smile was radiant, her most lovable. "Please, consider, dear heart. No Flow means no one person can dominate another, the war shall end!"

Keeping her face serene, though her rising panic made her desire to scream and gibber, Sureen focused on the source of her irritation. "Have you lost all your sensibility? The war shall go on. Only now, the soldiers shall hold dominion over the populace. Those with the most weapons and best armor shall rule. Those like us, especially the beautiful ones, woman or man, will become submissive to the most proficient sword."

Kara Laurel dropped her hands to her side. Standing straighter, she moved close, putting her hands on Sureen's shoulders. "The great lord has foreseen that and taken steps to ensure he leads the greatest force. One that I, that *we* with high stations are a big part of, join with me. Together we shall have the life we dreamed of when we were young," she said, her green eyes intense. They still contained the Flow saturation. A flicker of white mist mixed with light blue pulsed across her corneas as they had for seasons past. Yet, the signs of her addiction seemed less dense, as if the blue had faded to gray and the white was growing obscured by the dark green surrounding her pupils.

Stepping back, out from under the shorter woman's hands, Sureen swung her staff, carefully placing the blow at the side of Kara Laurel's head with the handle. Even if the Flow was unreachable, damaging the white crystal was unthinkable, and killing the woman was not her intent. Not yet.

Kara Laurel collapsed. The thud of her weight striking the ground echoed softly through the flora.

Standing over the woman she had once thought to spend her life with, Sureen squashed a growing remorse. The woman had changed, had become dangerous. "You are a fool, old heart of mine. There is one thing you and your precious 'great lord' have not foreseen. Your chosen path shall make my daughter the most powerful being on this world, quite possibly two," she said quietly.

Going to the warhorse, Sureen caressed the large jowls on its great black head gently, calming it. Riffling through her saddlebags, she found the coiled hemp she hoped she'd brought, which added a smile to her lips. Securing the woman to her horse and transporting her back to her daughter was now achievable.

The clop of a hoof and the creak of leather forewarned her as she turned around.

Four men, two with bows drawn and arrows nocked, sat atop horses similar in stature to the one behind her; all wore black plate armor. The graying, grizzle-faced man closest to her leaned forward in his saddle. "Bring me the rope," he commanded, outstretching a hand. "The great lord's favored User expected you would not come easily." The tone of his voice was gruff yet seemed to hold no animosity.

Having no other choice with her power gone, Sureen strode to the hand of the enemy.

# FOOTPRINTS LEAD

Flush with the energy of a fresh healing, Crystalyn climbed the seven steps leading to the columned entrance of the tomb of the high king long forgotten. A magnificent four-story carving of a warden came next for her to marvel at as she walked by. Atoi slipped from the shadows of one of the wide columns. Matching her stride for stride, the little girl seemed to float along with little effort beside her. If Long Sand noticed the girl's intrusion, the sand reader gave no sign as he led the way inside. Slowing a little, Crystalyn leaned closer to the tiny girl as she walked.

"Where did you slink off to?" she whispered.

Atoi's green eyes, huge in her small, too-white face, regarded her for a short while before shifting to the path ahead.

Crystalyn ground her teeth and then clamped her jaw in place with a conscious effort. The noise overrode the sound of their footfalls. As they moved on in silence, the gaping blackness of the crumbled doorway grew large, nearly as tall as the two columns rising two stories beside it. From there, a short walk along a dimly lit hallway brought them to a massive disc of marble blocking the way forward.

Long Sand gazed at the stone. "After the revered one and his lore master was seen entering, a loud rumble brought sect warriors dashing inside, and this they discovered. Our shouted inquiries have gone unanswered. I fear the worst, for no way around has yet to appear."

"Your revered one, this Darwin, he has a lore master?" Hastel asked.

"Yes, it is a recent occurrence. Before our side journey to Red Rock, the man was but a Dark User of the red robe."

"Malkor," Crystalyn and Hastel said in unison.

"Yes, that is the revered one's designation for him, before and after the change," Long Sand said dismissively.

Crystalyn didn't like the sound of the 'change' the nomad spoke of. "What *is* a lore master, should I be worried?" she asked.

"Probably," Hastel replied. "A lore master is a walking library with access to knowledge dating back to the Ancients, perhaps longer."

"Great! That's all we need, having Darwin able to access knowledge spanning to the beginning of time," Crystalyn said.

"I do not believe he could go back such length," Long Sand said. "Even Naa'thon, the master lore master could not."

Crystalyn smiled at the nomad. "I wasn't serious, but never mind that. We can't have the two of them running around developing whatever twisted plan Darwin has in mind. I'm going to stop them. Do you have an objection to that?"

"As I have mentioned, there is no visible path around the white stone," Long Sand said.

"Then we make our own," Crystalyn said. Plopping her backpack on the rock floor, she removed her last and best kell silk shirt, handing it to Atoi.

Slipping the jeweled dagger from the slit in her dress, Atoi cut the shirt into wide strips without the need for explanation. Once completed, Atoi passed them around, offering one to Long Sand. The tall nomad waved a dismissive hand, bringing out his own. "Had I known you required shrouding, the sacred material would have been brought. We carry additional; their importance is of the highest value during a storm of sand."

Holding a remnant of her beloved finery, Crystalyn groaned at the nomad leader's words. Then, holding the silk strip at the bridge of her nose below her eyes, she covered her mouth and chin, wrapping it at the back of her head and tying the ends. She was ready for what she had in mind. *A delicate touch here girl or we all die,* she told herself.

*"Do'brieni, are you well? Your anxiety has risen."*

*"The 'well' part has never been determined when I'm involved, my Broth, though my broken mind is slowly mending, I think. Isn't my mind affliction less than when we first met?"*

*"It has seemed so, yet I grapple with confusion."*

*"How? Think to me, my Do'brieni."*

*"Where anger and anxiety had dominated the flow of the sense of you, wonder, worry, decisiveness, conjecture, and a host of others come in a jumble without order."*

Crystalyn laughed with delight. *"My dear, dear Do'brieni, you are a treasure beyond compare. I would guess those of your White Wolf clan males linked to a human would know our minds are complex and chaotic. Adverse emotion explodes havoc throughout them. You are used to my broken mind. Don't worry; such a mind is still here."*

Confusion flowed through the link.

Crystalyn laughed with affection.

"What is your source of amusement?" Long Sand asked.

"Don't let it concern you. She does that," Hastel said.

"I shall attempt to recall this at the next occurrence," Long Sand said.

Gazing carefully at the circular hole bored through the stone roof, Crystalyn found where the edge had chipped and a small crack ran upward. "Everyone, move away from the disc," she warned.

*"You too, my Do'brieni,"* she sent when Broth sat on his

haunches beside her instead of leaving with the others.

"*Together we are stronger, Do'brieni.*"

"*You sound like my father and sister.*"

Broth was pleased. "*I am aware.*"

"Okay," she said aloud, "promise me you'll spring away if this goes awry."

"*Have no concern, Do'brieni.*"

Crystalyn let the matter drop. Seeing what she was doing was critical or she, too, would move back, taking him with her. Bringing out the interlocking square and the forked line symbols, she combined them. If it worked once, perhaps it would again. Sending the symbol up, it stuck to the rock. The crack dimly glowed with a blue radiance. Dribbling small amounts, she fed more of the symbol into the crack, thickening it bit by bit. The symbol brightened. Then a loud *pop* warned her to cover her eyes. Pebbles of sharp stone pattered around her, clattering to the floor.

"That's it? Do you have to do it again?" Hastel asked when the dust cleared.

Her symbol had shattered an opening large enough to serve her purpose, she believed, though bigger would've been better. "Lore Rayna, can you get me up there?"

A pair of branches snaked past and climbed the disc, entwining as they went.

Crystalyn laughed with delight. "You're amazing, Rayna!" she said.

"Many thanks, mistress." Spoken quietly, the tone of Lore Rayna's voice sounded humble, though there was a sharp note of pride.

*She should be proud,* Crystalyn thought as she climbed. The entwined branches made for wonderful handholds and footholds, as good as any ladder. Near the top, she peered over the disc's rim. A faint red glow revealed a hallway and a wall on the left. She needed light. Bringing out the two symbols again, she combined them, the blue radiance illuminating the way. She sent it hovering over the right half. A second hallway branched off into darkness. Moving the radiant blue symbol in a slow arc around the disc, she dissolved it when it came near and climbed down.

Atoi dashed past. "I want to see," she said. Scrambling up the branches, her hands and feet were a blur of motion.

"Atoi!" Crystalyn yelled. "Oh, never mind. Be careful, there's little light."

The tiny girl vanished over the lip.

"Has the way been found?" Long Sand asked.

"There is nothing to see," Atoi said, her disappointed voice drifting downward before her small head appeared above the top of the ladder.

"Not yet, Long Sand, but we're going to do something about it," Crystalyn replied. She turned to Hastel. "Give your sturdiest axe to Atoi; I need a starting point for my ice symbol."

Drawing the left one from his hip loop, Hastel scowled as he handed it up to the little girl. "Both axes are the same, though they're unique. I forged them myself along with designing the sheaths. Be gentle with this one, little one. They've been a part of me for a long time, you know that."

Reaching down, Atoi accepted the axe, her features as compassionless as always. "What do I do with it?"

"Break a piece of the roof leading above the hallway with the red glow. I will join you when you tell me it's done."

Atoi slipped away.

Turning to Lore Rayna, Crystalyn raised her voice for all to hear. "Can you hold a while longer? After I climb up and give an 'all clear' shout, Hastel, and Long Sand, if he chooses, will follow. The openings are too small for you or Broth. Will you stay with him until we come back?"

Lore Rayna's luminous, lidless orbs blazed in the dim torchlight adding a green glow to her hair. Strangely, the color seemed a permanent part of her now, though Crystalyn found she liked it. For many moments, the big woman spoke no word as the sharp cracks of steel against stone rang out from atop the disc. "Is this wise? Little is known of the sand reader, and trusting a nomad is always a risk," she finally said, not caring if the man overheard, for he looked at them.

*"The naturist has sound reasoning, Do'brieni. Nomads have proven dangerous and untrustworthy through much of our histories."*

*"There is little choice, Do'brieni. I would rather keep an eye on him than have him stay behind with you."*

*"As you wish, though I have objections."*

*Long Sand won't betray anyone with me watching him.*

Broth grew silent. A sullen feel of dislike leaked into the link that she chose to ignore.

"I shall continue on with you," Long Sand announced. Stepping up to the ladder, he climbed it with ease, vanishing over the rim as Atoi had.

Hastel paused beside Lore Rayna. "We'll return as soon as we can. If there's trouble, don't try to take them out by yourself. Hold them back until I get here, all right?"

Lore Rayna smiled. "I shall endeavor to keep one alive for you."

One hand on the ladder, Hastel grinned. "That's all I can ask."

Crystalyn gazed at her companion. "*If* something happens, Broth will send word to me. Find a place to stay out of sight and wait for us, and we'll come at a run. Darwin can wait."

"Only if they skulk about in large numbers, *Sarra'esiah*. A dozen desert scurries would not justify the effort of calling."

"No, my dear one, do not battle alone. Go back to those

large columns, stay out of sight, and hydrate in the shade. Both of you keep watch on the entrance. Can you do this for me?" Crystalyn asked.

Lore Rayna looked away.

*"Have no fear, Do'brieni. It shall happen as you say."*

"It shall be done as the *Sarra'esiah* commands," Lore Rayna said, her eyes upon her once more.

"That is well. Your dress hasn't quite recovered. This will help," Crystalyn said as she climbed the ladder. She was glad the dress had been able to absorb moisture from the big woman's skin and appeared to be on the mend. Lore Rayna wasn't herself without it.

Long Sand stood watching Atoi and Hastel work, both axes trading blows with the blunt end. "That will do," Crystalyn said, eyeing their handiwork. "Everyone stand beside me. Turn away from my symbol."

As her companions complied, Crystalyn brought out the symbol and repeated the process of her slow freeze, amazed anew at the power of ice when the shattered limestone shards caused her to wrap a protective arm across her face.

Though more jagged, the hole on the far side of the disc was twice the size as the one she'd made before. Going over to it, a quick look revealed a drop similar to the climb up, though nothing she couldn't handle safely. On her hands and knees, she backed over the edge, gripping it firmly as she slid down hanging by her hands. From there, the drop over half her body length was still jarring, but she managed to come away with her ankles and legs intact.

As soon as she moved away, Long Sand landed with barely a stagger and then Hastel, whose grunt sounded as loud as his impact with the stone floor. Crystalyn worried about Atoi. The smallest of them had the farthest to fall, but she needn't have worried. As delicate as a finch, Atoi slipped to the floor without the smallest scrape left behind.

Sauntering past the two men, the tiny girl headed along the hallway. Crystalyn took one last look at the disc. The jagged hole gaped invitingly above, imploring her to return to the two companions, to escape the gloomy mustiness of an ancient resting place for a king long forgotten. She turned her back to it. There was no leaving now, not that way, at least not all of them. The distance to reach it was too great without the benefit of a living ladder.

The dim red glow originated from several piles of molten lava skinned with dragonscale-like flat plates as it cooled. Atoi deftly worked her way around the hottest piles and scampered over the coolest. As if they'd stepped into the desert sands in midday, heat dried the perspiration on Crystalyn's skin as she followed, trusting in her littlest companion's ability to move around in low light. Toward the end of the still steaming elongated rubble, the little girl paused, her wide eyes seeming to glow eerily infrared as she looked back. "Our quarry came this way," she said, her voice echoing dully in the tomb.

Jumping over a molten crack, Crystalyn hurried over to her. Wider than a person, a smooth walkway had an imprint of a body atop the lava the width of a person. Oddly, the surface was smooth though the lava moved unhindered underneath fed from two molten streams plopping from slits in the roof. "Judging by the heat and the lava still falling, we're not far behind," Crystalyn said. "We'd better cross before the path softens. I don't want to wait for the flow of magma to slow and cool."

Atoi dashed to the other side, her leather boots leaving no mark.

Hesitant, Crystalyn tested the path with her toes first. As smooth and hard as tempered glass, the surface seemed adequate to hold her weight, so she ran across as fast as her little protégé had, which made little sense; should the odd bridge fail, she was as good as dead.

Ahead, away from the dim glow of the chamber, the hallway closed in with blackness. Bringing out her symbols, she combined them. The luminous blue light lit the area beyond Atoi who waited farther along the hall. Crystalyn liked the radiance of the blue better than the white she'd used back at the southern outpost in the Vale. She looked for the two others accompanying her.

Strolling behind Long Sand on the glassy smooth bridge, Hastel paused briefly now and then, glancing up and down. "How is this possible?" he asked. "Fast cooled with the Flow, do you think? Even more puzzling…will someone tell me how melted rock is contained in a heated state? Wouldn't it eventually cool or melt through?"

"The Flow was used here, but not as you believe. Overlaid on top, a thin layer, too fine for the eye to view, shields the heat. It is clever, truly, using a shield in such a manner. *If* that is, in fact, how it was accomplished," Long Sand muttered.

Crystalyn took a closer look at the path, opening herself up to the great river of power underlying the world of Astura. As Long Sand mentioned, the Flow ran atop the path but in so thin a stream she'd nearly missed the glowing white strands running through the membrane in the east-west direction like normal. She turned away. How Darwin had managed it was a mystery she had no time to solve, not with him so near. "Come, I get the feeling we're almost there," she said, eyeing a pair of dusty footprints leading away into darkness.

Her blue symbol illuminated the hallway from side to side, allowing for an increased pace, which Atoi set without needing to be told. The little girl flitted along, barely stirring up dust at the blue light's edge. Crystalyn plodded behind at a near run, sneezing occasionally from the musty smell of the fine powered sand. The dust had formed during an age so long ago no one could recall whose tomb they desecrated by their intrusion.

Atoi slid to a halt. "Someone lies here," she said, the tone of her voice matter-of-fact, as if she'd opened a door to allow visitors into her home.

At the little girl's feet, a leather-clad woman lay on her side. Peculiarly, a *shroudin* covered her ears and eyes. A quick inspection revealed the necessity; a seeping head wound wetted the back of her head, matting her long hair to her pale neck.

Without giving it much thought, Crystalyn replaced her ice symbol with the golden-illumined healing one and sent it sinking into the woman, attaching her awareness to it. Finding and sealing the gash came fast with limited effort, and most of her symbol remained. Replenishing the woman's dangerously low blood was another matter, though they had the same blood type. How could she do it?

She'd have to resort to a more mundane method. Dissolving the symbol, her comprehension snapped back into herself. Her head reeled as weakness flowed through her from the effects of what she'd done. Still, she managed to recreate her ice symbol for light. "Long Sand, I need a hose from your water flask, just the tube," she said.

Long Sand produced a dagger from somewhere underneath his yellow robes and the black leather underneath. He sliced the tube from near his abdomen, pulling it through fitted holes in his attire. "One hopes the length is adequate, my lady," he said, handing it to her."

"It will do well," Crystalyn replied, flashing him a weak smile.

Pulling her pack to the front, she sat beside the woman. In the outside pocket where she'd put it and nearly forgotten it, she found the medical cylinder waiting, her mental crutch from not long ago. As she'd recalled, it was almost empty. Breaking it in half, she dumped the three medical loads inside on the floor. Slipping a cylinder end over each tube end, she reversed the valve action on the side. "Does anyone have a rope, something to put around my arm?" she asked.

Hastel removed a retaining strap from his crossbow, holding it outstretched. "Will this work?"

Crystalyn held out her arm. "Yes, very good. Tie it off at the base of my bicep and get it tight, we need to start the flow of blood, not stop it. I have to find my vein. With hers, I'll just have go with my training. "

Hastel wrapped it around her, tying it off with the expertise of experience with wounded.

Probing the woman's limp arm with her fingers, Crystalyn finally balled the woman's hand into a fist, sticking the sharp end of the cylinder into the back of her hand. She hoped the vein would hold and her makeshift equipment would provide enough volume. She poked the opposite end of the cylinder into the prominent vein of her forearm. Once she activated the valve with a press of her thumb, the tube flowed red. Her arm grew cold.

Atoi sat beside her. "What happens when your blood runs dry?" the little girl asked, sounding genuinely interested.

"First, I'll turn pale as you or her. If I allow it to go on too long, my organs will shut down, I'll die."

Atoi leaned over the comatose woman. "Her paleness has transferred to you. Are you now dying?"

With her free hand, Crystalyn gripped the woman's wrist, gauging her pulse, the strength of her heart pumps. Though weak, they were steady. She'd done what she could; the rest of the healing lay with the woman's desire to live.

Thumbing the button, Crystalyn closed the valve, deactivating the transfusion. Removing the tubes, she stowed the entire apparatus in her pack, wrapped a clean silk around hers and the woman's punctures, and stood. Too fast. Weakness arose from her stomach, rushing to her head. Swaying, she fought the blackness swelling in her mind. Her symbol wavered, the blue glow flickering.

Strong hands gripped her elbow and supported the small of her back. "Have you grown ill, my lady?" Long Sand asked, his lips close to her ear.

Though his steadfast grip helped her gain equilibrium, Crystalyn pulled away the moment she could. His musky scent stirred something inside. She had no time for it. "I can walk now, but the woman will have to be carried, gently. Do you know her?"

Long Sand stooped and slipped his arms under the woman. Straightening, he cradled her head on his shoulder. "The woman hails from the Red Rock clan, a warrior leader we know as Railee, though she has followed a new master, the revered one," he replied.

Crystalyn sent her symbol ahead but only far enough to light the way. "Continue with the lead, Atoi. Hastel, keep an eye on the rear, trade off with Long Sand when he gets tired. Everyone stay alert. This woman, Railee, would've expired from the loss of blood within a few minutes. We are close. One last thing. Leave Darwin to me, I don't want anyone else hurt."

"Aye, mistress," Hastel replied.

"I expected no less," Long Sand said.

Flitting ahead, Atoi set an easy pace. Pausing often, the little girl allowed her to catch up and gain a breath or two before dashing to the edge of the light. A half bell crept by, longer than she'd expected at catching the quarry.

Long Sand's pleasant voice broke the silence of the gloomy hall. "The Red Rock woman awakes."

Crystalyn paused, allowing the nomad to overtake her with

his burden. The nomad set the warrior woman on her feet.

The dim light made it hard for her to gauge the woman's balance. "Can you walk?" Crystalyn asked her.

Reaching up, the woman yanked the *shroudin* down around her neck, wincing when it took dried blood and possibly hair with it. As she looked around, her flowing head of flaxen hair moved wildly back and forth and then settled on Long Sand. "Whom do you share water with, Sand Reader? Where is the revered one?"

"Call me Crystalyn, my companions are Atoi and Hastel," Crystalyn interrupted, pointing to each in turn. "We can extend pleasantries when we're out of danger. Can you walk?" she asked again.

Railee rested a hand to the pommel of her sword. "My strength is limited, but my will is not. Please, continue, if I fall behind, leave me."

"No one gets left behind," Crystalyn said, meaning every word. "Atoi, keeping the same pace will do for now."

The little girl dashed off, and Crystalyn kept the radiance symbol an even distance from the little group and her.

"What magic lights the way?" Railee asked as they walked. "Even the revered one has no such power."

"My Lady Crystalyn has proven resourceful with her…using of symbols," Long Sand replied.

"Why is she different than others?" the warrior woman asked.

Long Sand hesitated. "I do not know," he finally said, his voice barely carrying along the hall.

Crystalyn left them to their conversation. An intersection had appeared out of the gloom ahead. Atoi paused at its center.

Crystalyn moved close. "Which way do their footprints lead?"

At the end of the hallway to the right of them, Atoi pointed toward light streaming from an open set of shiny gold doors. An explosion, followed by several others, belched cloudy balls of dust into the hallway. Stalking close to the wall, Crystalyn slipped beside the doorframe, leaning beyond it for a quick glance inside opening up a view that put a frown on her face.

The quarry was not alone.

# DIVINE LIGHT

Not bothering to aim, there were too many to miss, Darwin launched another salvo of his Dark flame balls at the horde of beetles. Scarabs, as Malkor had called them from the old lore, or death beetles, delved under one's skin and ate one alive. Whatever they were, they filled the floor with their countless numbers, crawling from the now gaping eyeholes of the people depicted upon the main hieroglyphic pillar centered in the enormous room. One, or perhaps both of them, had stepped on a pressure stone in their rush to get to the end wall mosaic. The magnificent porcelain-colored tiles depicted the Valley of Forgotten Kings in its prime, before sand had buried the bulk of it. Somehow, they had released the nasty creatures, though he had not heard the telltale click.

In whatever manner they had set free the skin creepers, it had no bearing now. He had little energy left, certainly not a sufficient amount to destroy all the bugs. His exploding balls of flame had cleared a wide rounded area with each hit, but the skittering mounds refilled the space in less than a heartbeat.

Darwin reveled in the sweet power of the Flow flowing into him, but he could not keep drawing so much at once. The point of no going back came about quickly. It was the bane of any intelligent User, Dark or Light, and feared by all, with good reason. Draw too much too quickly and the Flow would be unstoppable; one would become a pillar of raw power and be consumed. Nearly there, he severed the link to the Flow retaining what he could though it would weaken him the longer he held it. A body made a poor container for the Flow.

On an impulse, he installed a half wall of the flame, letting the skin creepers mindlessly march into it, though it was a heavier drain than the Dark flame globes. There was no need for a higher barrier. Even if the skin creepers stacked upon each other, he would have sufficient time to raise it. "Perhaps, you would like me to fetch your last meal from a tavern in Gray Dust as you look for the key to the pattern that will open the final door," he said to his servant with a casualness he did not feel.

Malkor's eyes brightened to a deep red glow. The whites, irises, and corneas were hidden behind the radiance. "I am truly sorry, Master. My mind has slowed a bit for comprehension and assimilation. Even so, I have read far back in our history, farther than I have yet delved. No mention of this grand montage has surfaced. It is likely the old scrolls never had the key inked on them, perhaps due to the intricacy of the work. Our one small hope is that a lore master viewed the proper sequence for pressing the eleven raised blocks in the past. Sadly, I have sifted through most of their minds and now do not have much optimism for an outcome in our favor. The one thing for certain is pressing the raised stone pieces in an improper order will set off the final trap the Ancients mention in the codices. If it was, in fact, the Ancients who wrote the codices, as most previous lore masters believe."

"Keep sifting through it, right to the beginning of the knowledge, if you must. I shall hold the skin creepers off for as long as it takes," Darwin said though he knew it for a lie. Flashing a smile of reassurance, he added weight to the falsehood. He meant to ease the pressure on his servant, thereby providing a route to a thorough search, though the drain from his half wall of flame had grown strong. It tugged upon him, as if an immense wild creature chained to his vitality struggled for freedom.

The red of Malkor's eyes burst into a crimson radiance, consuming sight of all but the glow in both sockets. "I shall strive for speed," he said, the tone of his voice echoing, as if he spoke from the end of an immense hall. In a way, his servant did—the hall of ancient knowledge.

Darwin returned his focus to the Dark flame wall.

A woman and a girl strode into the room.

*The bloody betrayer and the Dark Child!* Fear of Crystalyn's power and rage at her interference roared through him, battling for dominance. For an instant, his concentration wavered.

A mass of scarabs skittered past his weakened flames, some burning. Still they came, scurrying forward in a V-formation, a large scarab the size of a small sand crab at the tip. His momentary lapse would cost them dearly. There was no time to remove the wall and come up with something capable of handling both threats.

A red globe of fire swept the V-shape away. "It is clear in my mind now!" Malkor exclaimed. Spinning on a heel, he faced the grand mosaic sprawled across the room's great wall. "Rising from the east, the valley's youngest light shines first upon the tomb of the high king!" he declared. Then he pressed the raised portion flush with the top rear of the temple-like tomb they stood in, the tone of his voice loud with excitement. "The light shines next upon the tombs of the queen, and the king's beloved maidens," he intoned. Using both hands, Malkor pressed the raised stones on two smaller cathedral-like structures at the same time. Again, he chose the two easternmost raised mosaic pieces.

Darwin held a shaky breath weakened by the drain of the flame wall. If his manservant guessed wrong, they would know soon enough.

Pressing a raised stone piece on the rear haunches of the great warden guarding the front of the complex, Malkor continued along the wall, pressing stones on the resting places of the lesser kings and their smaller retinue, walking a path of the sun until he stood below a depiction of the great orb in the west.

Darwin started toward his servant, but Malkor waved him back. Pressing a round raised stone in the center of a magnificent representation of the sun, Malkor returned to the mosaic of the tomb of the high king. He pointed to the first stone he had pressed, now raised. "Young light shines first on the high king." He pressed the stone tile flush again. An audible click sounded from within the wall.

The tomb of the high king split down the center and across the top, dispersing a fine dust as a massive stone door swung inward. The gap between the top and side widened with a surprising rapidity for all the apparent weight of the thick limestone. Inside, a golden light shone.

Darwin rushed into the room oblivious to the gilded objects, jewelry, and precious stones strewn about the small room in piles. He sought and found the source of the divine light. All else fled from his thoughts.

# MELTED STONE

Crystalyn froze a step beyond the golden doors. Countless black beetles marched into a straight line of black fire, burning soundlessly to cinder. Behind the flames, the man whose betrayal sank deeper than the blackest depths of the Wasted Sea, the one whom she'd once thought to build a life with, stood in front of a beautiful tiled mosaic. He glanced across the room and met her eyes. A scowl marred his handsome features.

Crystalyn missed a breath and then two.

Atoi tugged on her arm. "Skin creepers come," she said, pointing.

The beetles on the back rows had broken from the mass, skittering across the floor toward them. Having her ice symbol hovering in the air in front of her made her reaction almost automatic; she sent it sailing into the sea of churning bugs. Expanding and elongating many times the original size, it flipped horizontally, landing in the densest concentration of beetles, freezing the floor with a thick coating of ice throughout its oval shape and half again its size surrounding it.

Rows of beetles reacted to her action. Skittering in waves toward her, they veered around the ring of ice.

"They don't like the cold," Hastel said from behind her. "Do it again, quickly."

Combining the two symbols took but a moment, yet the

rippling black wave had closed over half the distance. Crystalyn released it into the forefront of the charge, stretching it from side to side as far as it would go. Only a small path remained uncovered on both ends where the beetles piled higher trying to get through without touching her ice.

Long Sand sprinted past her holding a crackling torch. The flame flattened, nearly licking his hand from the speed of his rush. "You have the left side, warrior! Do not let a single creeper touch you!" Sliding to a stop, he waved the torch back and forth, stringing fire along the front rows from the wall to the ice channel her symbol had become. Beetles scurried up the wall, moving higher to outflank the heat.

"We all die if you stop now, User," Railee shouted.

Though it sounded weak, Railee's shout raised Crystalyn's anxiety and her ire. She wasn't a User. Users drew upon the Flow, something she could never do. Pushing her anger to the side, she prepared another symbol and then combined a second one.

Behind her ice channel and on the right untouched side of her frozen ring, the black bugs gathered. On her left, the beetles climbed to the roof, slipping around the flames and Hastel.

"I cannot stop them all!" the one-eyed man bellowed. A group the size of a tray of ale scurried down the wall toward him.

Then Atoi was there. As soon as they touched the floor, she danced atop them, her booted feet blurring with the speed of her feet tapping back and forth beside him.

Crystalyn stretched a symbol from her ice channel up the wall to the roof and partway across the left side. Repeating the move with the second one on the right, the symbol elongated as far as the pattern would, leaving an opening the size of a barn door. Staying back from her ice, the beetles climbed the walls to the stone ceiling on both sides, heading for the center. Quickly, she created her ice symbol, filling the gap as the first of the creatures arrived.

Though she'd grounded herself to the planet, such heavy symbol use had taken a lot from her; her head throbbed in time with her heart. Behind the ice, countless beetles swarmed from floor to ceiling, a crawling tunnel of black bumps. Already her first ice symbol was fading.

Beyond the bugs, Darwin slipped through a doorway as it opened, the black flames dwindling down to nothing. Golden light lanced outward from within. Wherever the light fell upon the beetles, the creatures vanished in a puff of steam; wide swaths disappeared in an instant.

Atoi's graceful twirls slowed to a standstill. "The skin creepers leave us," she said, pointing.

Scurrying with surprising speed and precision, ordered rows of beetles climbed a column and vanished through the gaping eye sockets of carven beings wearing exotic clothes and headdresses. In a matter of seconds, the room cleared.

"Would you look at that?" Hastel asked no one in particular. "Wherever that light came from, we should go. I'm not at all certain we were winning."

Crystalyn rubbed her temples. "Come, those we came for have opened a doorway," she said, splashing through the small puddle her melting ice made.

Hastel passed by her, his crossbow cradled in his arm. "If you get a shot at his manservant, take it. Leave Darwin to me," she said firmly. At least, she hoped her voice was firm. Her head ached so badly she couldn't tell. She leaned beside the door, giving it a moment to lessen.

"No! No one touches him. He is for me alone," Railee said.

Aching head or not, Crystalyn wasn't about to argue. Forming her black net symbol without the spikes in the knots, she combined it with one that felt "sticky" under the heading defenses from the black-lettered *Tiered Tome of Symbols* and sent it hurling at Railee.

Plunked from the floor and hurled against the wall, the warrior woman grunted in surprise and pain. "Ungh…what have you done, betrayer? I cannot move naught but my feet. What have you done?" she repeated, her voice a snarl.

Crystalyn barely heard. Her head reeled. Weakness bloomed from her stomach. The sensation passed with a few pulses of her heart, allowing her to stay upright. "I don't have the energy to keep you alive. Stay there and keep quiet," she croaked, her voice hoarse as she stepped through the wide doorway.

Railee's shouts followed her into the room. "You cannot leave me like this, blast you! Cut me down! Long Sand, come back here! Somebody! Little girl, use your dagger, please!"

Hastel squatted behind a row of tall gilded urns. Grounding herself, Crystalyn again drew upon her symbols, weakening herself further in order to provide protection from magical attacks. Once her absorption symbol covered her, she swept it over Hastel, motioning for him to stand beside her. She sniffed. Her nose bled.

Together, they strode boldly between lustrous mounds of jewelry and past a wheeled, two-men abreast, horse-drawn contraption made from the precious metal gold. They halted before a golden sarcophagus painted elaborately like the columns of a race of peoples unknown to her in the previous room. Beyond the coffin, a gilded throne reflected golden light from a dazzling double-tipped half-spear hung high on the wall above it. Darwin straddled the arms of the throne, reaching for the Spear as Malkor watched oblivious to everything else but his master.

The red robe's profile looked odd, the back of his head longer than it should be. Perhaps an illusion created from the shimmering light of the spear overhead. "Don't touch it," Crystalyn said calmly.

Facing the wall, Darwin froze, his arm outstretched upward. "You dare confront me?" he sneered without turning around.

Sniffing, Crystalyn prepared her acid wheel symbol in her mind, hoping she had the will to use it. "Don't make me destroy you. We need to talk, you and I. You have much to explain."

Darwin rose to the tip of his toes. "I explain nothing to no one," he said softly. "Kill them, Malkor." His outstretched hand closed upon the Spear.

Flaming red spikes flew from Malkor's right hand, striking her absorption symbol. Dissolving on impact, the missiles had no effect.

Hastel's answering bolt did, however. Flying straight and true from out of her barrier, it thumped into the red robe's chest, sending him crashing into a mound of golden breastplates.

"Blast you!" Darwin's shout preceded a shimmering ray of golden light emerging from the Spear and slamming into her symbol.

The light blew Hastel and her amidst her barrier backward into the wheeled vehicle and pushed it through mounds of gold coin and urns before it crashed into the far wall, reverberating into them. Swept from her feet, Crystalyn slammed to the floor, her hold on the symbol breaking from the impact of the coins.

*"Do'brieni? Do'brieni! You have sustained injury!"*

Crystalyn sent assurance of her survival into the link before toning down the connection.

She needed to think. Something dug into her back. How long she lay there, she had no idea.

A moan drifted through her sense of hearing and comprehension. A little girl moan. Atoi. The child lay nearby, her eyes closed. Atoi's small feet pointed the wrong direction, blood seeped from compound fractures on both blackened thighs, and her dress had burned away, creating a high hemline on both legs.

Judging from the fractures, she'd taken the brunt of the gold urns, a direct hit from the light going by the burns, or both.

Gathering her waning strength, Crystalyn crawled to the girl, her head and stomach remonstrating every movement with waves of wretched weakness that left her gasping for breath. She despaired. The little girl's wounds were grim. Likely, the sacroiliac joints on her lower spine had twisted. Certainly the ligaments that encased each joint had torn, though she couldn't know with any degree of certainty without an internal look, which was beyond her.

Though her legs ached, she couldn't even check herself for damage. Atoi would die. Why the little girl hadn't died instantly was something she failed to comprehend.

Incredibly, Atoi's eyes opened. She sat up. The vivid emeralds that were her eyes stared at Crystalyn, unblinking.

Amazed, Crystalyn could only stammer. "I donnnn't think you, you should move—"

Calmly, Atoi put her knuckles to the floor and lifted her tiny body, twisting her legs around until they faced the proper direction. No blood seeped from burns that already faded. Lowering herself back to the floor, Atoi modestly pulled her dress as far as it would go over her upper, fast-healing thighs.

Long Sand strode into view. Several gashes on his arms and face trickled blood. Stopping beside Atoi, he looked down. "The legends have proven true," he breathed. "The Dark Child keeps her eternal."

The warrior woman, Railee, hobbled to a stop on Atoi's other side. Someone had wrapped a *shroudin* around her left leg above the knee. "Onan's light truly shines bright upon her," she said, her voice soft.

"Here now, let's not make such a fuss. This has happened a time or two," Hastel said, stepping past Crystalyn. Offering his hand, he helped the little girl to her feet and then turned, his one eye gazing where Crystalyn lay. "Can you move, or be moved?" he asked. Of the four, his wounds appeared the most superficial, with only coin-sized bruises on his forearms and thick biceps.

Performing a quick cursory internal and external assessment, Crystalyn found no major damage other than she'd drained her energy reserves. No healing would be forthcoming from her for a day or two. Even then, she'd still have to exercise extreme caution. "Nothing broken, but I need a few moments before I dare stand. What of Darwin, have I lost him?"

Long Sand pointed toward the end of the room. A jagged-edged circular doorway gaped open to a late evening sky fading toward darkness. Gobs of melted stone dripped downward, glowing redly like the lava they'd crossed.

Crystalyn struggled to comprehend. "He had us helpless. Why would he leave us alive?"

"He has the great artifact he came here for, the Shimmer Spear," Long Sand said. "Now perhaps, he desires to use it, to save its power for whatever malice he has in mind for it. Or, the desire to gauge his manservant's wound motivated him. Who can say for certain?"

Crystalyn frowned. "If that's so, where did he go with them?"

"To the gateway," Atoi said, matter-of-factly. The tone of her voice contained no trace of pain, and she sounded normal. Well, as ordinary as Atoi, anyway.

"What gateway?"

"The gray one the spear holder keeps in his tent."

As the little girl's, the Dark Child's, words sank in, Crystalyn smiled. Darwin Darkwind had made a serious mistake. He'd left them alive. He'd left *her* alive with a way to follow. She would find him and end it.

# HEART OF THE DARKNESS

Crystalyn's first thought of Gray Dust was grungy, yet it had a certain appeal to it. Though the incessant ashen dust encrusted everything, the buildings had an appealing construction of gray or brown limestone trimmed with dark wood that loomed from the incessant gusting wind with grace and intricate carven beauty. The many people going about daily errands ranging from haggling with merchants, slipping furtively through the shadows of buildings and parked wagons, or strolling deep in conversation seemed used to the dust. No one had a cloth wrapped over the bridge of a nose.

After leaving the small cul-de-sac alley the somber gray gateway had dropped them in, she'd followed Hastel and Atoi out in the streets, not bothering to ask if they knew where they were going. They obviously did.

Motioning to the others, Crystalyn pulled the *shroudin* from her nose, letting it fall about her neck with reluctance. Her nostrils flared as she inhaled; the gray dust scent packed them so fast she coughed.

Long Sand's face remained impassive, though there was a stark glare in his eyes for everything and anyone. Haggard men, despondent women, and even ragged emaciated children used to begging, moved away as they came close.

Railee's brow crinkled as she gazed around, her darting blue eyes also rife with revulsion and distrust.

Even Broth's great sienna head stayed low to the ground.

Atoi and Hastel had removed their facial wraps after leaving the gate. "When were you going to let the rest of us know when to remove these rags? Crystalyn asked.

Atoi's bland look was as expressionless as her smooth young face. "Only nomads or bandits wear *shroudin* in town. You should have known this once we left the Shimmering Sands Desert behind."

Crystalyn shared a glare between both her oldest companion and her protector. Atoi had the distinction of being the youngest in the group, making her the oldest-youngest travel mate, but that did not give her the right to take liberties on what she should know. "I'm well aware of the reason why one wears a head cloth in that stinging sand-filled withering desert the nomads call home. I have never been to Gray Dust, so how would I know the customs here? The big question is, why haven't either of you mentioned you've journeyed to this wonderfully filthy city of Gray Dust before?"

Atoi blinked slowly, her expression as unreadable as ever.

Hastel looked like he'd had to swallow some of the dust floating around, which wouldn't surprise anyone considering how much drifted about stirred from the passing of many feet. "My apologies, Mistress, one tends to forget you are new to this world. On horseback, you would disgrace anyone, and you always seem as if you know where you're going."

Crystalyn ignored the praise. Nevertheless, it was nice hearing it from a warrior who had long been comfortable riding, and leading, or both. "So you admit to knowing your way around?" she asked, raising an eyebrow. "Where's the best inn in this dust haven? I require a bath, then a real meal after that. Make it better quality than Staunch the Flow Inn."

"That would undoubtedly be the Quench Quarters," Hastel replied hastily.

Perhaps too quickly. Crystalyn looked at him sharply. "We're not here to drink ale all night," she warned.

Hastel blinked. His one visible eyelid opened and closed slowly. "Aye, mistress, I had no intentions of imbibing the night through," he said, his voice mild.

"You will keep it to a minimum, is that clear? I can't have the militia detaining us here. Darwin is getting farther away," Crystalyn said.

His one eye brightening, Hastel glared, though he looked away when Crystalyn matched it with one of her own. "As you say, Mistress," he mumbled over his shoulder.

Crystalyn kept a smile of satisfaction from showing. "Good. I want everyone to stay alert. Who knows how many contacts Darwin has here? He may already know we've arrived," she said.

Railee's serious features grew more solemn at the mention of Darwin's name. "The Quench Quarters should serve our needs, Mistress Crystalyn. Expect me there after inquiring of my contacts for word of the betrayer. Do I have your leave?"

"Go inquire. If he's not here, I want to know by morning, early—where we can catch up to him," Crystalyn replied.

Railee gave a slight nod and then departed.

Taking the Red Rock warrior woman's place, Long Sand strode beside her. Crystalyn took the opportunity to ask him something she'd been wondering. "Who's leading your people, Sand Reader, if you're here with us?"

"The Searing Sun sect follows me still; my plea for release met denial inside the tent of the elders at the great sun's rise before we departed the Valley of Forgotten Kings. Irun, our strongest, leads the sect's swiftest to this place. My people come to band with you; their arrival is in two days hence."

Crystalyn was startled. "Huh? Why would they want to join me? I chase a dangerous man."

"The great lord's magic is strong, but your power is believed higher. After I recited the events inside the monolithic tomb while you slept the sleep of healing, the elders have acknowledged the debt of service I declared in the desert. The sect travels the path of the Creek Clan."

Crystalyn consciously reminded herself to close her open mouth. She'd pushed the matter of the Searing Sun clan's debt to her from her mind when they left the Valley of Forgotten Kings, figuring the matter closed. "I'm not certain we'll be around when your people arrive. Darwin will decide that. I can't let him get away, not this time."

"Then I leave word of our destination. The sect shall follow."

"And what of the bloody merchant Guail, have you executed him?"

Long Sand hesitated, his blue eyes penetrating. "I await your word. His actions are perplexing though. He claims no recollection of the event, and his movements are stiff. Perhaps you injured him worse than believed."

"What of his retinue of followers and slaves? Have they been freed to go where they will?" she asked.

Long Sand flashed a brief smile, his white teeth bright upon his white-skinned, handsome face. "They were informed of their freedom. Nearly all have chosen to follow the way of the Creek clan."

Crystalyn bit back a groan. The merchant had many wagons. All those lives to cause her worry for their well-being. She'd traded the large Valen refugee force for one-half again as large and all the nomads of a sect. How would she find food and lodging for them all as she hunted for a man? What about when the search ended, after destroying Darwin? What then?

However, she hadn't traded the refugees, not in any real sense of the word. The entire people of the Vale awaited her at the outskirts of Brown Recluse, not far from where they were. What would she do with everyone? Yet another detail for her to store under her list of things to take care of.

"With your leave, Sect Mother, I shall ask with discretion around the city for interactions or sightings of the great lord. Perhaps wind of him and his servant shall come with haste, particularly if I perform a reading," Long Sand said.

"Granted. I want him found. But tell me, why do you call him great lord? You no longer have to bestow such a high honorific on him," Crystalyn asked. Then something he said struck her. "Did you just say sect mother?"

Long Sand smiled, though he continued to glare at all who passed them as he replied, which made him look even more menacing. "The great lord commanded no one call him by that title. Now he shall carry it to the grave and beyond with the sect."

Executing a quick bow without missing a stride, his hard look relented briefly as he gazed at her. "As leader, you are sect mother with…certain duties. I shall report to you at the tavern." Inclining his head a final time, he strode away, the crowds scattering before him.

Crystalyn gave a small shake of her head. The nomads were an odd people, Long Sand in particular. What duties had he meant? She had her own agenda and questions. "What is a sand reading?" she called after him, but he'd moved beyond hearing.

Hastel dropped back beside her. "Allow me to answer, mistress. Though I'm no expert when it comes to such a taciturn people, I have viewed the readings with my own eyes a time or two."

"Eyes?"

"Yes, back then, I still gazed upon great Astura with both naïve orbs."

Crystalyn smiled warmly. "I wish I'd been there to see it.

When was back then?"

Hastel coughed. "Hmmm, that is a tale for another time, should it arise. Where were we? Oh yes, a reading from one of the nomad sand readers—there are only a few, it involves a life of constant training and much ability with the Flow. They use it sparingly…" Hastel said, trailing off.

Swiveling his curly, brown-haired head back and forth, he looked for Atoi. He found her as they rounded a corner. The small girl strolled ahead, moving onto a wide busy street where wagons pulled by horses and oxen jostled with covered carriages. Threading through the chaos, townspeople on foot moved to and from whatever errand betook them.

"Sand reader?" Crystalyn prompted.

Hastel jumped, though she hadn't spoken loud. "My apologies, mistress, a sand reader can glean a lot from something given, discarded, or a plucked personal item, even something as tiny as a grain of sand that has ridden in a beard or hair line for only a few bells. A reader gathers knowledge of the person the longer the association is with the previous owner. Such as where that person came from, what their affinity with the Flow is, how long they've used, if they're addicted or not, that sort of thing. The rare ones, like our Long Sand, can sift through countless grains of sand blown in by the wind. Eventually, the three or four rare readers, like Long Sand, will find the person sought by interrogating and reading those whose path the tracked granule has crossed."

"How can they do that? By using the Flow? He seems to have a lot of knowledge of it," Crystalyn observed.

Hastel stepped upon a slatted wooden front porch in front of a building. "I assume so; they've deemed me unworthy of this knowledge, not that I've bothered to ask. They are a secretive and touchy lot. You'll have to inquire it of him when he gets here. This fine establishment is where drink and dinner await," he said, waving his arm expansively. "In that order."

The Quench Quarters looked grander than Staunch the Flow Inn and Tavern back in Brown Recluse or Hastel's Muddy Wagon Inn at Four Bridges. Though the large sign hanging from the front alcove depicted a voluptuous woman drinking ale from an overhead cask, the décor inside shone with an obvious expensive taste. Crystalyn perused the sturdy, beautifully carved mahogany wood as they strode inside. The dark round tables and high-backed chairs invited groups of eight or less to drink and dine together.

A tall buxom woman late in her middle seasons wearing the low-cut outfit of a tavern maiden stepped in front of Crystalyn, stopping her and Broth from following her three other companions. White locks streaked the woman's blonde hair, but her face was smooth, free of most lines. "Please forgive such an abrupt interruption, sweet lady, but I have no recollection of meeting a warden outside the Virun border. I had been led to believe they do everlasting patrol only there."

"Not all of them. Who are you?"

The woman lowered her blonde head streaked with white locks quickly. "I must ask your pardon a second time. Sabella, owner and operator of the Quench Quarters Inn and Tavern, and Happy Fulfillments, is at your service," she said, dipping with an elegant, though quick curtsy.

*"Remain alert, Do'brieni. This woman is more than she seems. A strong power emanates from her, though I detect no outright signs of malice."*

Crystalyn gazed at the woman with renewed interest. Violet flecks raced subtly across her gray corneas. The tavern keeper had used for seasons for such a saturation. "It is fortunate to have met you then. I am Crystalyn, and I require several rooms for the night. This is Broth, my closest companion and advisor," she said, waving her arm at the warden with a flourish. If the woman wanted to treat her as a lady, she'd act the part.

Extending his foreleg, Broth bowed low.

Sabella laughed with delight. "I love his beautiful amber eyes, are the two of you linked? What does he have to say?"

"He has a great hunger."

*"My appetite is large, though I do not recall mentioning it."*

Sabella's tinkle of laughter was brief. "Then I shall not keep him waiting. Select any free table and I shall have you served."

Crystalyn gave a small inclination of her head. "Thank you. I do have one specific requirement."

Sabella's eyes brightened, she lifted her chin. "I am certain you are aware special demands have further costs."

"Yes. One of the rooms has to have a vaulted ceiling and come fitted for Valen."

"Is that all? I carry five Vale-sized rooms as do all the larger taverns," Sabella said, her chin lowering.

Crystalyn noted the woman's disappointment; a merchant had to sell extras to make a living. "One of those will do for now. See my child companion for payment; add a silver rectangle to your total for the night for your troubles."

Sabella flashed a quick smile. "The Dark Child has a lifetime tab, I shall work through her. Please, make your wishes known, and I shall see it done." She turned to Broth. "I am greatly pleased to make your acquaintance, sire." Nodding a final time to Crystalyn, she sauntered off.

*"There is much more to that one than she allows anyone to see,"* Crystalyn sent. She motioned for the warden to continue with the others, following as he set out.

*"Agreed. One who claims to have never met one of my kind has an extensive knowledge about us."*

*"She only claimed to have never met one of your race outside the border. Perhaps she met some of you at the dark border of Virun."*

*"Ah, my Do'brieni is right. The human woman is intriguing."*

*"Don't get too enamored, that one has a bite that may equal yours."*

*"Yes, my Do'brieni."*

Lore Rayna had halted behind a high-backed chair though she made no move to sit down. Several water-filled mugs resided near every other chair on the table. "I have agreed to assist Long Sand at the stables," she said as soon as they neared.

Crystalyn frowned as she selected a chair by the wall. "Now you tell me. You could've accompanied Railee. You don't care for her much, do you?"

Lore Rayna shrugged, the living dress rippling as it adjusted to cover her shoulders and then pulled back, leaving them bare. Her new emerald hair color went well the dress. "She gave herself to a Dark User, one with a proven record of malicious intent. But that has little relevancy with the present situation. The stables have access from the back of this inn if you require me soon." Lore Rayna strode away, moving farther within.

"Wait!" Crystalyn called after her. "What food should I order for you?"

Without slowing or turning around, the big woman vanished through an archway at the rear.

"Great," Crystalyn muttered.

"I'll order for her," Hastel offered. "She gets meat with her vegetables like the rest of us."

Crystalyn had no inclination to disagree. Whatever her big friend wouldn't eat, she would. Her stomach growled and a wave of irritation pulsed through her at odd intervals, a certain sign she needed to eat before taking it out on everything around her. Where was the blasted tavern maiden?"

A handsome man in a gray robe left Sabella and her too-low cleavage at the end of a long well-oiled bar and wandered toward them. In no mood for flirtations, she hoped he would stride by, but he stopped at the opposite side of the table from her. His brown eyes looked friendly and wary at the same time.

Crystalyn pushed a lock of her hair away from her eyes. "What do you want?" she asked, not at all nicely. Whatever he thought to gain, she had no time for it.

"A trade, if you will. A large pitcher of the finest ale available in this wonderful establishment in exchange for simple information."

Hastel thumped his mug on the table, sloshing water over the side. "I cannot vouch for him, don't know him personally, I say send him on his way."

Atoi's otherworldly voice echoed around the table. "He has not been long on this world."

Startled, Crystalyn glanced at the little girl; judging from the way his tongue slid out the side of his large muzzle, even Broth seemed surprised by the unexpectedness of it, losing his noble demeanor.

To his credit, the man proceeded with his plea, though his eyes had drawn wide. "Will you allow me to provide some dinner then? I'm a traveler only just arrived, as your young companion has made known. I require knowledge of travel gateways."

Crystalyn couldn't believe what she'd heard. Here was someone who spoke of a gateway casually, openly. She glanced at Atoi. The little girl gave a small shrug, though big for her.

*"What opinion do you have for his request, Do'brieni? Should we let him stay and talk of these gateways? Perhaps we can find one to put us closer to ridding the world of Darwin."*

*"All information on the gates, large or small, carries a higher worth than a king's treasury."*

*"Agreed."*

"I say let him move on. Nothing he's said has changed my mind," Hastel said when she looked to him.

Hastel's reply was about what she expected from him. She turned to the man. "You'd better sit down, and get that food on its way. We're famished. Two of our companions are attending the horses; order for them too, if you will. After we eat, we'll talk about how gateways are difficult to come by and what you want with one."

The man signaled to a tavern maiden carrying a tray of filled mugs two tables away. Behind her, a man wearing the black plate armor of the Dark Citadel tried to get her attention with a light touch on her bare shoulder. The woman stiffened, but her eyes remained upon the stranger at Crystalyn's table.

Satisfied he had caught the tavern maiden's attention, the brown-eyed man took a chair. Crystalyn caught a glimpse of something odd about the clothing he wore under the robe. Glowing lines traced intricate patterns wherever she could see.

Crystalyn waved a hand toward her companions, pointing to each in turn. "This is Hastel, our self-imposed guardian. The girl is Atoi; beside her is our warden companion. His name pronunciation is too long for human lips. Call him Broth. You should know who you are about to dine with. I am Crystalyn…Crystalyn Creek. Do you still want to remain at our table?"

"Why wouldn't I?" he asked, glancing over his shoulder for the serving maiden. "I'm Trenton Bonner."

His quick reply surprised Crystalyn. Most Asturans would want to stay as far away from the symbolic User as possible.

Her steps coming in abrupt jerks, the maiden was nearly to their table, drenched from the empty drink tray she carried.

The newcomer frowned at the maiden. "Hey, you're spilling it!"

Broth growled.

Atoi's otherworld voice echoed around the table. "It comes, Vessel of Ages."

Hastel fumbled for an axe. "Blast it! What comes?"

Crystalyn brought out her green symbol with its many spinning cones inside, similar to the radiation funnels that afflicted Low Realm on occasion. She sent it streaking across the table toward the woman, but it caught Trenton first. The concussive gust blew him backward into the woman, pressing them both to the floor as it spun past, dissipating in the center of the tavern.

Trenton reached for the serving woman, the same woman whose robotic movements had spilled their drinks. Something about her was off. "Don't touch her! There is something going on here. I suspect a flicker is involved," Crystalyn said.

Trenton frowned, pulling his hand back.

The maiden suddenly moved, snatching his hand into hers.

His back arching with pain, Trenton stiffened.

Crystalyn formed her healing symbol. Stretching it over the rigid man, she attached her awareness to it and sank into Trenton. Immediately, she found what ailed him. A malicious cognitive presence assailed his brain, blowing inside him like black acidic smoke, consuming all it touched, like the darkness behind the flicker that had attacked Jade.

Perhaps it was the same entity; if so, it had grown in power with faster aggression. Little remained of his mind. Without a second thought, she sent her symbol flying into the heart of the darkness.

# OUTLANDER

On her knees beside the small down-filled bed, Atoi leaned over the well-proportioned man, staring into his handsome face with interest. The girl's pale brow furrowed. "He's stirring," she said. The tone of her voice was petulant. "You said he was going to stand before Onan, but he awakes."

Crystalyn moved to the other side of the bed, across from her little guide and companion. "I *said* it was likely he would meet the Great Father, Atoi. He appears to have made the decision to remain with the living for a while longer, though I cannot say if his neural processes survived fully."

Her pale face smoothing to her customary one of dispassion, Atoi withdrew, moving behind Crystalyn to gaze out a window.

Lore Rayna took the little girl's place. "Can he speak?" she asked.

Crystalyn gazed into Trenton's almond eyes wondering what manner of mind lay behind them. Perhaps she should've touched a neural wall while her awareness was attached to her symbol to get a sense of the man, but she'd barely had enough of her pattern to push the mind eater out as she'd come to think of it. "Can you?" she asked him.

Trenton opened his mouth, but only a guttural grunt came out.

Yet he had opened his mouth. A good sign his lack of

vocalizing and movement was temporary. With luck, the mind eater's touch had only numbed his motor facilities. "There you have it, Lore Rayna. He cannot answer your inquiries, at least for now. It is likely he cannot even move, though the paralysis should pass."

Lore Rayna sat back, raising her knees. Even sitting on the floor, she was nearly level with Crystalyn standing. "As far as we are aware, only your sister, Jade, and I survived a similar psychic attack. Now, *he* makes three. Are you certain the tavern maiden was not infected with a mind worm?"

"Positive. My gut instinct says something different pursues us; this makes the second similar evil I grappled with after cleaning it from Jade in the Vale. The attack in Brown Recluse had the strongest power. I nearly succumbed to that one."

Lore Rayna stood, towering over everyone. Her leafy green dress adjusted of its own accord to cover her upper thighs. "As my mistress believes, so shall I," she said. Lowering her head under the top of the doorway, she left.

Crystalyn eyed Trenton again. "When you can speak, we will talk. I would like to know how you have in your possession an artifact *I'm* familiar with." Reaching into her dress pocket, she pulled out the red crystal orb she'd taken from him and showed it to him before putting it back where she'd found it. "I have put it back in your pocket."

Then she put on her emperor face. *Wear the right emotional mask and people will respond.* "Know this, Trenton. I *will* have the truth from you, or I'll take it from you using less pleasant methods. I have the capability and the determination. Complete honesty is necessary. There are many lives I hold dearly at stake, one of them my own."

The man opened his mouth slightly, but nothing came out.

A *thump* resounded from the direction of the door, followed by two others.

"Should I let her in this time, mistress?" Hastel asked from his customary stance of leaning on the wall by a door.

"I suppose you must."

A small creak of floorboards preceded a woman she'd met.

Sabella sauntered into the room, the sway of her hips exaggerated. "He's awake," she said. Flashing Trenton a coy smile, she spoke to Crystalyn. "You should rest now, my lady. You're nearly as pale as your little companion is. My girls and I will attend to his needs."

Crystalyn's hands went to her hips of their own accord. "He *needs* the healing of rest. Keep your...ministrations and those of your girls to assisting him with it, for now. Notify me the moment he's able to speak."

Sabella smiled. "He's with expert care. I'll send one of the girls to inform you the moment he utters a syllable, if he does."

Crystalyn folded her arms at her waist, staring at the shorter woman. Finally, she gave a brief nod. "See that you do. Come, Broth, attend me to our rooms. Hastel, take the first watch outside this one." The soft creaks of four padded feet and the thump of her two booted feet accompanied her into the hall.

*****

Crystalyn gazed into the mirror, considering the blue dress—one of her trimmest fit— and it looked good on her.

*"Your choice of apparel is of no significance, Do'brieni. You make every piece regal."*

Crystalyn giggled. "Why, Broth, coming from a noble like you, that is high compliment, indeed."

"Keep that one," Atoi said, appearing beside her in the

mirror. Her wide green eyes seemed overly large on her too-pale face. "He will like the way it hangs on your high hips and bare shoulders."

Crystalyn frowned at her little companion. Dispassionate, Atoi's emerald gaze gave nothing away. There was no indication if the little girl made sport of her. "I have little caring what he likes, though putting him off guard won't hurt. Coming from my world of Terra, he somehow has acquired an artifact I'm familiar with; I'd like to know how he came by it. Should I discover his profession as thievery, I will destroy him."

Atoi's composure slipped, her eyes widening.

Crystalyn left her gaping there as she made her way into the hall, Broth padding beside her. Three doors down on the left, they stopped at the room she'd had Trenton carried into last night. Lore Rayna arose from a cushioned bench placed in the sitting alcove situated atop the wide stairway leading down to the tavern. The big woman looked tired, her streaming emerald hair unkempt and needing a brush. The big woman had asked for second watch, and Crystalyn hadn't argued. Trusting Long Sand or Railee wasn't prudent yet; they were too new to her group.

Though slower than her usual vibrant self, Lore Rayna's single stride brought her to Crystalyn's left side.

Lore Rayna removed the sturdy iron key from her bodice, offering it to Crystalyn. "Except for Hastel's failed attempt to take an added shift even though his eye drooped lower than his scar, the night passed without incident."

Flashing her biggest companion a quick smile, Crystalyn took the key and put it in the latch, raising her arm in preparation for a thumped warning of her entrance.

"The outlander has departed," Atoi said, lower on her right.

Crystalyn gaped at the little girl. Slowly, she lowered her arm. "Whatever do you mean, little one. I left him six hours—bells—

ago. How would he leave? There's been a constant guard on him the night through."

Atoi regarded her in silence. Then, turning toward the stairs, she scampered from view.

Lore Rayna tapped a sandaled foot. "Do you wish me to go after her?" she asked. "The Dark Child displays little respect for her elders."

Crystalyn turned the key. "Nay, if she wanted, she could mention she's older than both of us put together and be right." A gentle push swung the door inward. A quick glance around the room affirmed Atoi's brash statement; the room was empty.

*"Look to the window, Do'brieni."*

Cut close to the frame, a squared edge was all that remained of the glass. A bath rag draped along the bottom had protected the Terran's hands and fingers.

Crystalyn grappled with an anger that boiled, an ire threatening to spill over her self-control. "Perhaps you'd better go find the bloody little imp," she said as evenly as she could, her voice only cracking at the end.

Executing a small curtsy, Lore Rayna left without a word.

Crystalyn marched to the window and looked upon a narrow alley. Three stories down, shards of glass gleamed in front of the Quench Quarter's rear entrance door. Quelling her fury with a slow breath, Crystalyn looked out upon the hazy town of Gray Dust and fumed.

She wondered if she'd made a vast mistake by giving the red orb back to a thief, a thief from her home world. The very orb she hadn't found after killing her Indenture Service Provider though she'd searched for some time after. Seasons ago, she'd sensed a power within the beautiful crimson ball of crystal. The crystal had not been lying in its customary bed of velvet in the mausoleum, nor had several other items she'd had her eye on though there was still plenty for the taking.

Again, she wondered if she'd done the right thing by giving it back. Even with the black crystal candle augmenting her symbols, she may not be a match for Darwin and the immense power of the Shimmer Spear. One bolt from it had nearly taken all of them.

The soft tramps of booted feet outside the room preceded the sound of the door creaking closed behind her. Then Long Sand spoke, his quiet voice revealing little of the fatigue he must feel from a day and night of searching a fair-sized city. "Our quarry has entered the Stair of Despair," he said without preamble. "They may already be dead." His quiet statement hung in the room.

Crystalyn whirled, staring from human to nonhuman host to the broad and beautiful Valen face. Even the usually unflappable Hastel looked taken aback. Only Long Sand and Railee remained unperturbed. Crystalyn had a sudden irrational urge to float one of her symbols back and forth in front of them to see if that would elicit a reaction, but she quickly discarded it. *Don't act like a petulant child,* she admonished herself.

She allowed herself a glare at Long Sand. His visage remained impassive. "Are you positive your reading read what your contact heard correctly?"

*"Can we fight our way through this Stair of Despair, Do'brieni?"*

*"There is an ancient power there. The White Fur clan and all my people have not risked an entry into its dark abyss."*

Railee spoke in Long Sand's place. "I give witness to the words. The sand reader's source took note of the mention of such a dangerous place. No one, legend or otherwise, has made claim of surviving a climb up the Stair. Those that have tried were not seen or heard from again."

Centered under the vaulted ceiling, Lore Rayna paced the lengthy room at her full eight-hand height. Three of her steps took her to the end wall. Spinning, she continued back, her dress shifting high up and down her upper thighs. "We cannot follow the path he has chosen. Even in the sanctuary of the Vale, my people know better than to stray too close to the Stair of Despair."

Turning her back to her companions, Crystalyn contemplated the city outside the window; the same one Trenton had escaped through with the orb. In the distance, the columns of a roofless coliseum stood with magnificent grandeur atop a small hill. "What are my options then? Letting such evil escape isn't one of them."

As if reluctant to speak them, Hastel's words came quietly. "There's an old belief, nothing more than an obscure passage in a codex, I forget which, that names a cave leading from the Dark Citadel to the Stair. Unfounded or true, I know not."

Crystalyn faced the room's interior. "That must be it! It's where he's going." Then she froze, crestfallen. "He has two days' lead on us, and the citadel is so well manned. He'll have all the soldiers he needs to fight us when he arrives. If only we could get there first, take out the guards, and ambush him when he arrives."

Atoi spoke from the doorway. "The topaz gateway would take us ahead of him possibly."

The room erupted into a chaos of sound.

"Such a move would not be wise," Long Sand declared.

"They'll strafe us as we step through," Hastel protested.

"The hooded man's soldiers nearly destroyed mine and your mother's forces, *Sarra'esiah*, please reconsider such an action. But if we are to go, you must wait for my people. They are two days from here," Lore Rayna begged.

Crystalyn silenced them with a raised hand, her vision fixed on Atoi. "Where is this topaz gateway?"

Atoi crossed the room and took her by the hand. Turning her around, she pointed to the coliseum. "There," she said. "Where the outlander went."

The protests began anew.

Crystalyn ignored them. Perhaps now, she had a way to get ahead of, and waylay, the two men she most desperately wanted to catch while searching for the intriguing outlander—a designation most people on Astura would still consider for her.

# POWER GAINED

Darwin gazed long at the Stair of Despair. The great stairway rose from behind and climbed above the massive black wall barring entrance to the southwestern plateau. For all of his twenty-four seasons of life, he'd heard of the dangers inherent to the place, a dark place rumored to hold the power to consume souls.

From the overwhelming sense of dread leeching his resolve the longer he stared at the stairway, he suspected the rumors had some truth. He waved his companion forward.

The bloodstain on Malkor's red robe looked as fresh as it had two days ago when he had pried the crossbow bolt from the back of his servant's ribcage. Pulling it from Malkor's lung and out the front had been easier since the cruel steel bolt had ripped a wide hole through two of the bones. The healing had drained him, but his well of knowledge lived. "I do not see a way through. How much is known of the stairs and the Black Wall?"

Malkor kept the hood of his stained robe lowered, refusing to look at either subject of Darwin's question. "Are you certain this is…wise, Master? Access to the red pit might be less of a danger if we go by way of the Dark Citadel. We can always return to Gray Dust. Surely the symbol wench will not have followed us there."

"We have had this discussion, do not call her that. The chance of someone identifying us once we enter the Dark Gate is too great, so is the likelihood *the betrayer* now has the gray gateway I took from Guail. I have little doubt she is in Gray Dust. Now, let us move forward with what we came here to do. You have the lore infusion; I ask one final time. What is known of the obstacles barring my way?"

The red hood rose slowly to the wall. As he peered from under it, Malkor's jaw trembled and then grew slack. After a time, he looked away, lowering his head quickly. "There is no passage through the wall, hidden or otherwise."

"What? Why would the Black Wall have no door?"

Malkor's hood snapped up, a stunned look upon his narrow face. "There is no…wall. It is a seal."

"Why would a wall be a seal?"

Malkor gripped him by the arms, his brown eyes wild. "The seal is there to keep something inside from getting out, something *dark*. To get inside we may have to break it. Please, Master, there has to be another way."

Using the butt of the Shimmer Spear, Darwin prodded his companion away from him, roughly. "You forget your place, servant. You would do well to remember you are here to accomplish what I command, *only* as I command. We shall get past the seal with the knowledge of its making. As a lore master, sift through the wisdom streaming into your mind soundly; concentrate on anything pertaining to the construction of the wall."

"As you command, *My Lord,*" Malkor hissed. "Sorting through eras of material, searching for oblique references, may take some time. Judging from my brief scan to locate the seal, not much knowledge has been passed down from the Ancients."

"Nevertheless, you shall put all you have into the effort."

Malkor gave a brief nod. Then he stiffened. The red flecks racing across his corneas expanded and grew pronounced. Soon they covered his orbs completely, turning them a glowing blood red as he accessed the library of countless tomes streaming into his mind, infused into memory.

Darwin had seen the process before, though not from Malkor. A Servant of Eons in the southern land of Shimmer had provided a demonstration. The woman had given up stable sanity to retain the lore, became a living Flow-powered knowledge base. That person had given him the idea for discovering the Shimmer Spear's location.

He returned to his contemplation of the Black Wall. They had found no other cover near the wall. Someone had cleared a wide swath in front of the wall making it a barren place, devoid of even so much as a weed. Standing out in the open in front of the Black Wall was foolish beyond measure. Dark things guarded it. He could attest to a dozen winged shapes as he sat waiting for Malkor to sift through the lore.

Someone had also exerted immense energy not long ago, perhaps a season. Filled with timber, topsoil, and rock, the path to the citadel that used to wind around a series of waterfalls, called the Plunging Chasms, stood tall and forbidding now as terraced cliff faces.

Malkor's recent infusion—his sacrifice—had been the deciding factor that brought them both to such an ominous place as fast as the gates could bring them and before his companion's insanity set in fully. Darwin had already seen the first sign of it with his frequent pauses during conversation. A tinge of regret for requiring his lifelong manservant to undergo the infusion crept upon him, but he quelled it ruthlessly. Malkor's place in life was to comply with his decrees. Having a lore master to command would substantially decrease the time it took to dominate the whole of Astura.

Darwin napped and ate, waiting without impatience as the morning wore into early evening before Malkor stirred. Abruptly stumbling forward, Malkor fell. Darwin caught him in his arms.

Supporting his older servant friend, he walked him around the little clearing tucked inside the heavy foliage bordering Fetid Fern Swamp.

A dozen passes around the small clearing allowed Malkor's leg muscles to loosen while storing the memory of walking inherent to them. Darwin released him afterward, letting the man continue twice more on his own. When his red-robed servant made it without mishap, he stopped him by extending the double-tipped spear in front of his chest. Malkor had to stop or risk a gash across his chest. "What have you learned?"

"The risk is high, but you have the power to make the attempt…with assistance."

"Whose help do I need?"

"Mine."

Darwin was annoyed yet jubilant at the same time. "Why did you not just say that? What is required?"

A flash of something unidentifiable flitted across Malkor's narrow face, vanishing in an instant. Perhaps fear. "The cost is high and we shall only have the power to attempt it once. Should we fail, we die."

"Then we die. Get on with it. Tell me what it is I am to do." Again, something flitted across his manservant's face, but now Darwin knew it for what it was, glee. Why would Malkor be happy with his choice to gamble both their lives? He dismissed the thought. What his manservant believed did not matter. By the time his friend discovered his fate, it would be far too late. "Did I not command you to get on with it? No cost is too high."

Malkor smiled, as oily and obsequious as the merchant Guail. "As you wish, Master," he said, extending a hand. "First, you must give me the Spear."

Darwin drew back, gaping at the hand. "What could you possibly want with it?"

Malkor's smile faded, and his swarthy features smoothed. He kept his arm extended. "You must trust me if it is truly your desire to slip quietly beyond the Stair of Despair."

A great reluctance to part with the Spear gusted through him. Glaring at his manservant, Darwin dropped the center grip in Malkor's hand. "Whatever you have to do, make it fast, the Spear belongs with its master."

Malkor pulled the Spear close and then jabbed it forward, the tip pointed down. "As you wish, Master, the Spear shall return to the master."

A sharp pain to his groin caused Darwin to bend over where his confused sight fell upon the Spear embedded in him, its golden glow growing red. The red haze of his pain fell away, enveloped by a fog of blackness, darkness he knew as final. He grew weak, his mind lethargic. Strength bled from him.

Then Malkor's comforting healing settled inside him, adding strength without the pain. The darkness grew lighter.

But it was wrong. The red tint of his friend's healing light had changed, turned black. The blackness was somehow lighter and felt different from the final darkness of the storm. Flickering with the promise of pain's end and power gained, it waited for him to accept it, to draw it within, and drink deep from its dark supremacy. Tasting the surprising influence of the Flow inside the dark heart of omnipotence, Darwin drank.

*****

Clutching the Spear in his maimed hand, Darwin strode to the Black Wall, maintaining a tight grip on the dark aura that surrounded him and his manservant. The key to their survival lay with his ability to exude the Dark power of a great master, a soul saturated with Flow corruption.

As they neared the base, four maimwrights dropped in front of them, two at a time, the thump of their landing echoing dully from the hard granite construct of the Black Wall. The way forward blocked, Darwin halted. When the four monstrosities stood side by side, their multifaceted eyes glistening silvery and motionless under the midday sun, he raised both arms. "Lift us to the stairway of darkness, the path of bleak and utter despair," he commanded.

The tallest, most brutish-looking wright with the largest pinchers taking the place of a right hand cocked its head to one side. The gesture would have been human-like if not for the beak of a mouth and bee-like orbs where the eyes should reside.

Screeching something unintelligible, the maimwright, along with the creature next to it, stomped to his side bringing the strong smell of rotting carrion. Gripping him under the pit of his arms by their pincher members, the wrights lifted him from the flattened rocky ground, and then four powerful wings flapped, raising him and their own heavy bodies upward.

As he rose, Darwin had time to reflect on his current situation. He tried to ignore the uncomfortable awareness that one closure of their pinchers—accidental or not—would result in him falling armless to his death. Such thoughts lowered his mental grip on the aura, and the smaller beast swiveled a thick human neck to scan it with both sets of its silver foiled eyes.

Deigning not to dwell on the beastie, he concentrated on the aura, drawing more of the Flow into his infused body from the Spear through the undetectable blood pathway Malkor had created. It was an ingenious way to infuse one to an artifact, requiring a direct route to a main artery to function at the fullest, though at a high cost as his servant had promised. Emanating the arrogance of power absolute while ignoring the ghost pain, the emptiness of one side of his groin, was difficult, but he would prevail.

As they neared the top, he thought about his next move beyond the Black Wall; one mistake there and both he and his manservant would burn in darkness. Worse, they could become a mindless shell, made that way by the Dark guardian of the stair. He had heard such tales from scholars his entire life, stories he expected held much truth.

With the Spear, he should be able to bypass the guardian, if Malkor's information held true. Everything hinged on the great artifact's ability to store the Flow for him to draw upon and maintain the façade of a great master, one with true immense power.

Infused to him now, he felt the Flow resonating in the Spear with an undeniable acuteness. It throbbed through his body like an icy dark entity seeking release upon any that irritated it, all instantly at his command. No longer did he have to ground himself before drawing upon the Flow, nor did he need to use and discard an Interrupter to augment his power. He could take it from the artifact until emptied. Precisely what he required, for his feet no longer touched the ground, the one great limitation of the Flow.

The beasts carried him over a wall one could stretch out upon with room to spare. The descent into an ancient courtyard, kept dark by the looming cliff above, took half as long. Dropping him roughly in the center, the maimwrights trod into the shadows.

He waited for his servant, trying, and failing, to ignore the palpable sense of great power moving around him with uncanny speed, an alien intelligence that harbored an almost uncontainable rage at his invasion into its domain. Yet for all its power, it had an uneasy caution. Darwin carried something it was wary of, and the power he and Malkor projected stemmed from it. *It knew.*

Wary now, Darwin gripped Malkor by a shoulder and then covered his mouth with his free hand as soon as his two carriers withdrew. His manservant nodded, signaling his understanding.

Satisfied he would maintain silence for the duration of the climb, Darwin wasted little time setting out for the deeper shadows of the stair. Unseen, the dark presence paced them, a dark stain of malice against a shadowy background.

Narrow and steep—nearly a ladder—the ancient stairway climbed a vertical thirty stories; it took well over a bell to reach the first landing. From the start, he found it prudent to maintain a grip on the stair above though it made for a slow awkward climb with the spear scraping against the granite now and then. A fall would be fatal for both of them.

Darwin released his hold on the top stair and crawled upon the first ledge, his breath burning in his lungs.

Flickering with darkness deeper than shadows, the large black spot of malice slipped up the cliffside beside the stairs. Pausing on the ledge, it waited and watched. The rage the dark thing exuded bombarded his senses along with the intimations of what its baser instincts were—it wanted to control, to rend, and to tear. But his false auras kept it at bay, made it uneasy. It could not have mastery over them.

For ages, it had skirted the dark power under the rock mountain, a natural evil not born of this world. Now, such powers invaded its realm, breaking the eons-unspoken truce born from the respect of equal power. It now considered testing the strength it had so long avoided.

Alarmed by the revelation, Darwin drew from the Spear intending to shore up his façade, make them appear even stronger, but the reserves had depleted within it, drained by the necessity of maintaining two auras as he struggled with the climb. A glance upward raised his alarm to something bordering fear. A full day of ascension lay ahead.

The malice grew noticeably greater. The large flickering spot of blackness shifted closer.

Malkor gripped his shoulder. "Do not let your fear rise," he whispered.

The darkness paused, the flickers of darkness slowing.

"It is uncertain. We attack now, if we are to survive," Darwin said quietly though he had little hope the two of them would prevail—even if they had twenty of the most powerful Dark Users at their disposal. The creature's power was beyond any he had experienced. With every word, the flickering inside the shadow slowed, increasing as soon as he stopped talking.

Malkor's grip grew painfully tight on his shoulder as he whispered in his ear. The bony index finger of his free hand jabbed toward a dark opening in the cliff wall behind the flickering blackness. "No, Master, we cannot win, but we may surprise it enough to make it to that cave."

Seeing little choice, Darwin drew deeply upon the Flow, filling the spear and his reserves with the radiant glow of blackness surrounding the light of the catalyst. Malkor followed his example, drawing likewise. Instinctively, he knew their combined might would fall short, but if they were to die—or worse, become some sort of monster—he wanted the thing to feel their sting. "Stay close," he whispered.

Striding forward with a boldness he wished he truly had inside his traitorous gut and weak knees, Darwin held the Spear out before him, brightening the way with thoughts of luminosity. Surrounding the blackness of the Flow filling the Spear to the tips on each end, a brilliant white radiance lit the way forward.

The blackness recoiled.

Darwin strode ahead. The blackness moved away, skittering to the side, dropping back as he passed. Keeping the Shimmer Spear pointed at it, he twisted around, walking backward, the cave not far away. He froze. Malkor hadn't moved. Flickering faster, like a sputtering candle, the creature slipped up on his servant. "Malkor," Darwin croaked, his mouth suddenly dry.

The darkness enveloped his friend; Malkor's form flickered inside, seeming to rise inches from the ground. Then, incredibly, Malkor flew from within, running toward him as fast as his ruined leg allowed. "Make for the cave, Master! Run!" Malkor shouted, running past him.

Darwin ran.

# HIGHER POWER

Using the Flow to lift the heavy circular stone cap from the ancient well, Darwin exposed the shaft glowing redly underneath, an inch at a time. A burst of hot air arose, spreading outward, heating his beard; it broke his concentration. The carven lid of stone ceased its scraping crawl along the raised lip. Releasing the Flow, he wiped his brow with his good right hand.

Three and a half days descending partially collapsed tunnels and crude, crumbled staircases after escaping the dark thing at the Stair had led to this seemingly insurmountable barrier—even with the added benefit of the Spear. He could not allow it to end here. He would not. If he had to, he would command Malkor to cease maintaining the firewall that blocked the underground denizens from gobbling them up for their evening meal, as a last resort. The bloody ingrots had stalked them for bells.

Drawing on the Flow, he redoubled his efforts. Grinding chunks of stone from the lip, the heavy lid swung slowly open, widening the gap by several inches. Perspiration beaded on his brow again, but he had no hand free to clear the sting from his eyes when they dripped. His mangled hand clutched the Spear, and his good hand held the dark glow of the Flow as he lifted and pushed. Leaning forward, he tilted his head downward and let the rivulets fall. The Shimmer Spear grew hot in his hand.

Scraping a protest, the lip cracked and popped, releasing a

final plume of white dust. Drained, he released the flow. The lid ground to a halt, wide enough for him to squeeze through, much to his relief.

He checked on his manservant. "Contain the blasted toadies until I stand at the shaft's bottom. Set your flame to burning the first few rows then follow with haste. The granite walls of the shaft are too smooth for them to climb down, yet drawn by the promise of a meal, some of the baser ones may try anyway and cause you to fall as they would."

"I hear your commands."

"A brass ring resides atop the lid. I am going to tie the rope to it and drop it down the shaft. We shall use it until it gives out."

"Are you certain this is wise? How are we to make the return ascent? I'm not certain our combined strength will lift even one of us far."

Darwin wondered why the man was loyal to him, following him so blindly with complete trust. If the man could not figure it out on his own, then he would keep him in the dark. A place he preferred for his manservant anyway. "I am certain of many things. One of which is that we shall not come this way again, *if* we survive."

Keeping his brown eyes on the wall of flame, Malkor untied his red robes with only two fingers.

Darwin stopped him as he reached for the ropes tied around his slender waist. "Keep your flame burning, do not let them through. I shall untie the rope." Tugging the knots loose from the rope with his one good hand and using his mangled hand to hold it in place was awkward, putting him too close to his manservant, but he managed. Soon he had most of the rope coiled in a circle on the ground; the end he kept a hold of he wrapped through the ring, securing it with a square knot.

Sitting on the lip of the well, he wrapped the rope under him.

Thankfully, his left hand still had the strength of a good grip, unlike the useless arm attached to his shattered elbow. Gripping the rope with his good right hand, he swung out into the well's center, straddling the cord on the arches of both feet. "Once I have reached the bottom, I shall cast a small Flow of light to the top. Follow as quickly as you can."

Without waiting for a reply, he started down, dropping his weight inches at a time. The air warmed around him, and he was soon perspiring heavily from that and his exertions. Perhaps he should have left his black robe with Malkor, but he did not savor the thought of roaming around underground caverns in his underclothes. The caves could turn frigid from one chamber to the next.

He went relentlessly down, trying his best to ignore his moist, itching skin, though he was glad for the light of the red glow. It was one less detail to handle to reach his goal.

Darwin could see the bottom when the rope ran out more than halfway down from where he hung. He used the Flow to create an updraft strong enough to almost support his weight and descend at a controlled rate. The concentration to perform the task was enormous, but his feet finally met level ground a half bell later. He barely had the strength left to send a small burst of light through the tiny opening of the well's lid so far above.

He sat down, drank some water from his flask, and waited until he had the strength to stand and rise. Above, Malkor descended at a quick rate. His manservant fell much faster than he had, excessively fast. At the last moment, Darwin had the presence of mind to string a black web of the Flow across the well, removing the stickiness from the center.

As it was, Malkor's backside nearly touched the floor when the webbing stretched from the weight of his body. Then the dark web flung his manservant upward as it tightened. Malkor flapped his arms and legs attempting to right himself from his horizontal position. Darwin let him bounce once before dissolving the web on his second stretch. Malkor thumped to the ground, landing on his bottom.

At any other time, Darwin might have laughed. "Are you injured?"

"No, Master, only my pride. I had not the strength nor concentration to control my fall; I am again in your debt."

"Nonsense, I would expect you do the same had our circumstances been reversed."

Climbing to his feet, Malkor gave a quick bow. "Truly, Master."

A sense of a vast open chamber ahead drew Darwin past his servant, through a narrow door, and out into a carven hallway hewn from black granite a long time ago.

From there, they traversed a series of crumbly narrow ledges; the heat rising with each step forward required two additional stops to splash water into parched throats. Cracked white marble columns carved with the forms of nude or scantily clad beautiful women stood out starkly against the black stone, lining an ancient roadway going the direction that tugged deep inside of him.

For bells, they followed the columned road, shuffling along in silence as they wound around and climbed over the rubble of statues fallen. The roadway ended at a great cavern he had somehow known he would find the moment they slipped into the tunnels beneath the Dark Citadel after escaping the Stair.

A pit of molten rock swelled at the edges of a great plateau of dark granite. A blast of shockingly cold air dried his sweat, chilling him as soon as he stepped onto the rock.

His destination was easy to see. As lovely as it was alien to the cavern, immense, glossy pillars of black granite ringed a polished silver dais. Standing high and resolute in the silence of the cavern, the dais shone with intricate engravings of a crowned skeleton raising a short spear at a mass of prostrating people. In place of eyes, flame engulfed the skeleton's eye sockets.

Other images, as sharp as the first, filled him with awe the closer he came. Immense funnel cones tore about inside a vast sphere in the center of the magnificent chamber, sucking earth, water, and clouds into a spinning twisting fury.

Alone, the flaming-eyed skeleton stood at cliff's edge on a high and enormous dais with a half-spear raised like the one in his hand, the tip pointed to the great sphere. A pulsating pillar of power radiated upward from the spear. Prominent at the base of the dais, the Flow wound below. Darwin sensed the black tint of darkness roiling within its frothy curls.

Silver steps cut into one side of the dais rose to the top. He climbed them, his stomach churning with the first fluttering of anxiety as the magnitude of what he was about to do cascaded throughout him. Malkor followed in silence behind, something he could not fault. What was there to talk about anyway? He intended to prostrate himself before the Dark Master, the Great Spirit to some, to some the Undying Darkness. It was not something even the most powerful could take lightly.

An irregular-shaped rock lay centered on the dais. Stark in its simplicity, the piece of granite sat rounded on one side and flat on the other, as if a great sword had hewn it in half. The flat side gleamed darkly with stains darker than the gray stone.

Darwin performed a slow circuit of the dais, uncertain what to do. Then a thought struck him; perhaps he had to make himself known. "Dark Master, I have come to speak with you!" he shouted. His voice seemed shallow, swallowed by the immensity of the cavern. A thick stillness settled over it. Nothing moved; silence reigned.

A half bell slid past. Darwin's excitement faded. He sat on

the rock, dejected. *Did I come all this way only to fail?* His fingers brushed a smoothed indent on the rock, and suddenly, he knew what he must do. Twisting to lay on his back, he placed his neck in the boulder's impression, extending his head over the edge, looking upward.

An immense presence descended upon the dais blotting all light on one side. A voice, ancient and raspy, boomed throughout the cavern, vibrating the rock with a power long contained. "At last, someone comes with a mote of intelligence," the voice said, gaining strength with each word. "You supplicate before the incarnation of the true shadow on this world. What do you seek?"

Malkor wailed. "Master! Why have we come here? We are nothing, nothing!"

The cries of his manservant came from his right and behind. Darwin ignored them. "I humbly offer my speck of intelligence as the Great Shadow's world travel vessel."

The Great Shadow paused for a time. Then, a silhouette of a double-headed axe appeared, held by hand too dark to see as it rose.

Darwin tried, but failed, to see the dark shape of the Dark King's crown that the scroll *After the Third World War, Before the Dark Empire* had hinted at. He couldn't raise his head high enough without losing his balance.

High above, the great axe paused. "You would offer your head to the greatest power your world has ever known? You would offer your head to ME?"

The last word boomed and thundered throughout the cavern fading slowly, stark and final.

Darwin gripped his resolve. The time for a change of heart had long past. "I come offering my head to eternal darkness."

Again, there came a pause. "You have a temporary vassal?"

"The vassal awaits within this chamber."

"Master?" Malkor asked.

His manservant's query came as a plaintive whimper, drifting forlorn and alone past his hearing. Again, he ignored it.

The great axe rose higher. "You would offer your thoughts, your life, and your soul freely without reservation? You would give yourself completely to the higher power, the majestic darkness?"

"I would."

The great axe descended.

# DIRE NEED

Trenton stood dumbfounded. A wide hallway cut from dark stone spread out before him. Dark-armored soldiers stood nearby or spoke with robed or leather-clad men and women. His mind stumbled with grasping his surroundings. The topaz gate was supposed to send him home, back to Terra. Where was he?

Two helmed soldiers grabbed him by the shoulders, dragging him a few yards from the gateway.

A bee-like helm turned toward him, on his right. "Are you daft? Loitering in front of a travel gateway, particularly one of the greater ones, could get you killed," a feminine voice said, sounding metallic coming out from the headpiece.

A masculine metal chuckle came from the helm on his right. "Or worse, you could merge with a woman and spend the rest of your life not knowing whether to sit or stand in relief rooms," the voice said.

"Your humor is as degraded as your mind, Deit Sa," the woman said.

Deit Sa laughed. "It is why you are helpless to stop thinking of me, Rinn.

"Hardly," Rinn declared.

Trenton squirmed, but their holds were strong. "Let me go. What is this place?" he asked.

"I will answer that," a new voice said.

A man strode toward Trenton, a horned helm upon his head. Like the bee-like helm, the helm covered his face.

The two soldiers, whose grip kept him in place, stiffened, the laughter dying quickly. "I greet you, Lord General Tsan," the soldiers said, one after the other.

Lord General Tsan ignored the salutations, his horned helm leaning toward Trenton. "Or rather, I shall ask the questions. State your business, what do you wish with the Dark Citadel? How did you get through the gate?" he asked.

"I had a marker, a medallion depicting a hooded man. The guard on the other side took it as he let me through."

Lord Tsan laughed. "I do enjoy her little ruse. That medallion marks you as captive. You have delivered yourself to us by your own admission."

Trenton could scarcely believe what he heard. "There is a mistake! I paid well, a steep price to travel to my world!"

His three captors laughed.

"I bet you did," Lord Tsan said pleasantly. "She enjoys younger men." Then his voice hardened. "Search him well; he admits he is an outlander."

The woman released him. Removing her gauntlets, she handed them to Lord Tsan. Quickly, with no regard to any part of him, the woman riffled through his robe. She pulled it open when she got to his suit. "What is this, Lord General?" she asked stepping to the side for Lord Tsan to view.

"What Dark using is this? Use extreme care, Rinn. Check him well. Though he wears the gray robes, underneath is armor infused like I have not seen. This one is a User of some power or he has high connections. Search there, something bulges," Lord Tsan commanded, pointing at Trenton's front pocket.

With her long and slender fingers, the woman deftly fished the crimson orb from his right leg pocket. Trenton groaned, though he tried not to. Crystalyn had only returned it to him the day before.

The woman soldier dropped the orb in General Tsan's left gauntleted hand he had outstretched, emitting a soft *plink*.

Cupping his fingers around it, General Tsan moved the orb close to his helm, leaning over it. "So this artifact is precious to you, I can see why, it…has something about it. The Dark Lady will want to know of this. Bring him," General Tsan commanded.

"Wait—" Trenton started to say.

"Silence!" General Tsan shouted. The sharp horns of his helm came close as the big man leaned down. "Speak without permission again, and I shall take an eye. Do you understand this?" he asked softly.

"Yes," Trenton said.

General Tsan turned and strode away without another word.

Roughly, the two soldiers, Deit Sa and Rinn, marched him to the center of the wide hallway, leaving the gateway, the only escape in sight, behind.

They followed General Tsan's broad back to an intersection with three branches where massive pillars shouldered the gray rock ceiling three stories above though every path appeared carved from a mountain of rock.

The lord general selected the left branch. Striding toward a watering hole or fountain that groups of armored and robed people clustered around, the general turned right before Trenton could get a good look. Ahead, another stretch of hallway, this one with pillars lining both sides of a soft red rug they soon trod upon, going off in the distance.

Trenton mulled over his situation, working on a course of action. General Tsan had taken the crimson crystal orb from him, but the man hadn't found the ion laser cutter grafted to his finger. Flesh-colored with nail and prints, fashioned to look like his digit, it extended his finger slightly longer than the rest, though they hadn't noticed. Nor had they taken his climate suit from him.

Though his situation was dire, it could still get worse. He tried not to think about it as he looked for a way out. Though their grip slackened somewhat, the two soldiers did not fully release him. Escape seemed hopeless.

The hallway pillars changed, becoming ornate and amethyst in color. Carved men and women in armor or robes engaged in some activity, mostly battle from the look of it. Two rows of the magnificent pillars led toward a wide half-circle set of beautiful cobalt granite stairs. A set of golden doors, as high as the hallway, reflected sunlight from a square hole bored through the ceiling. Two guards holding long spears with the tips pointing toward the sun vent blocked the doors with their persons. Two others stood on each side with crossbows readied.

Lord General Tsan climbed the steps and halted before the guards. "Move aside," he commanded.

The guard on the left frowned, his open-faced helm sliding forward on his brow when he did. He pushed it back into place with his free hand. "The lady of the citadel has met with you prior to this, Lord General Tsan," he said. "Everyone gets only one greeting from the esteemed Lady of Darkness, you know this."

"I have…acquired an item she will wish to view with her cold green eyes, as wondrous as they are," Lord General Tsan said.

The general's voice changed, becoming softer, less brash when he spoke of the lady. Trenton wondered if could exploit Tsan's apparent attachment in some way—perhaps parlay his release in exchange for silence. Likely, he was the only one who could hear the tonal differences in the big man's voice. His training with PallTech back on Terra had ensured he noticed.

"I shall send a runner to notify the protector, that is the best I can do," the soldier on the left said.

The soldier standing at the right-hand door stirred. "The lady knows all. It is her wish Lord General Tsan shall pass," the woman said, her blue eyes dull. Her pallor was ashen, as if she had strayed too long from the sun.

Her blonde hair was cropped short in a provocative style, and Trenton tried to catch her eye with his own, but she stared only forward.

"What about the general's men and the gray robe?" the male soldier asked.

Staring at something or nothing along the hall, the woman failed to respond.

"They are part of this and have to go through, you bloody imbecile!" General Tsan snarled.

The soldier's brown eyes glared with stark hatred for a heartbeat. "Have a care, General. Not all in the Citadel are intimidated by you. The Dark Lady has my loyalty," the soldier said. He stepped to the side, refusing to look at them.

Lord General Tsan shouldered the golden door open without another word.

Deit Sa released Trenton's shoulder and took the lead.

Rinn pushed Trenton stumbling forward through the door, staying right behind him.

Inside, robed and armored men and women stood in a line along one wall in a great room. The huge vaulted ceiling housed statues on either side reminiscent of those below who barely reached their pedestalled feet.

Trenton did not glance at the people who waited; he had eyes only for the person sitting on the high-backed gilded throne. As they strode closer, he was surprised, but happy, to note the lady on the throne was barely a woman, perhaps twenty, twenty-one, seasons. Dressed in a nearly sheer, low-cut black dress, the girl-woman spoke to a large warrior, bigger than the general, who interrupted what they were saying with a few quick words. His despair over his predicament lessened. The girl-woman's beautiful locks of auburn hair cascaded to her shoulders as she slowly turned his way.

His chances at convincing her of his dire need to return home had risen. Perhaps, with a little flattering, he could get her to agree to discuss how the gates worked and fill him in on what he needed for a return trip to Terra.

One glance of her cold green eyes destroyed the notion.

# TAKE IT AWAY

The One Mind slowed the images rotating around the general, focusing on the dark one, the timeline leading to the point of termination. Shuffling the image faster and faster, a shadow of the man appeared. Moving choppy at first, the image flowed into the fluidity of shadowed life. Background images followed, luminous and colored when compared against the shade of the man. The shade moved beyond a group of men wearing citadel livery squeezed together by a slim black band wrapped around them, glowing darkly.

Though Jade had seen her ability used in such a way several times before, the One Mind's expert manipulation of it in a short amount of time horrified and fascinated her. The Over Mind, the alien hive intelligence, was growing too powerful, too fast. And, gathering all the Dark Citadel's leaders in one place—this room of thrones—was a bold move. Though the Over Mind had most of its subverted stationed on both sides with bows and swords at the ready, the line shuffling to the dais was hostile for the most part.

The scene continued. A shadowy weapon raised, the shade slipped toward a man in a dark robe…*Darwin Darkwind!* Clutching a shimmering black spear, Darwin gave a flick of his free hand. Lifted from the stone floor as if made of smoke, the dark figure of the general flew across a courtyard, vanishing from the scene.

The images spun, revolving into the cyclone of the aura

surrounding the man in dark plate armor.

A slender hand, her hand, came into view, palm facing forward. "Hold!" she heard herself say. "Protector, record this. General Bowman is now commander of the Dark Gate. How many regiments are stationed there?"

Her dad glanced at a ledger he held. "Six full regiments and one-third of a seventh," he replied.

By the whim of the One Mind, Jade heard every word. "Leave him with one-half of a regiment. The rest go with you to prepare for the battle at Surbo," the One Mind said.

Smiling at the mention of his new position, General Bowman's smile faded fast. "Is that wise, My Lady? We would not have enough men to open the Dark Gate and send out sorties while defending it."

"You will not be opening it," her dad said, the tone of his voice cool. "You are dismissed, general. The next leader class may come forward!" he called to the line of people sprawling out from the great throne room.

A woman in a red robe with the hood thrown back climbed the three wide stairs to the throne, and then she executed a bow as deep as a man would. Her luxurious hair created two silky black piles on the floor as she waited for acknowledgment.

The One Mind kept the woman doubled over for several long moments as Jade's vision gave a cursory glance about the great room. The row of people waiting to meet the Dark lady of the citadel stretched beyond the massive angry statues of Dark Users and dark-armored soldiers that lined the cavernous walls. "You may rise, Correlda," the One Mind finally said.

Correlda failed to keep the surprise from her smooth face. She smiled, satisfaction alighting her dark eyes. "It is fortunate my lady has knowledge of me. I shall be of great service to you."

"There is awareness of your loyalties from some that follow

you. You may approach," Jade heard herself say in her most pleasant tone.

Correlda stepped near, her mouth working, and failing, to maintain a solemn composure. "I must say, I am ecstatic that a woman, even one of your youth, controls the citadel. Selecting me for my experience shows wisdom beyond your seasons. How may I serve you?"

Jade's arm reached toward the woman; it was painful to view without her brain giving the command or having the smallest feedback flow into her mind that her muscles obeyed. "You shall start by kissing my ring," the One Mind said.

Correlda's smile was beautiful as she bent. "You will find I am a great one to have in your retinue, My Dark Lady," she purred, pursing her mouth for a light touch.

The One Mind shifted Jade's hand at the last moment, and Correlda's dark-shaded lips landed upon her knuckles, missing the ring altogether. The woman froze. A torrent of fruitful manipulations and murders, both hired and performed by Correlda, blew past Jade's protective bubble, latent memories of past deeds and experiences. The woman had led a deceitful life; plotting to kill Lord Charn, Crystalyn, and Jade seemed mild by comparison. At one time the woman had been friend to Jade's mom, Sureen, part of an elite team known as The Watch, until joining with the Dark Citadel. Jade found it hard to feel bad for her even though she was now one of the controlled.

Her slow movement unnatural and awkward to look at, Correlda straightened, her facial features slack.

"Gather your followers at the Oracle one bell from now," the One Mind, the Dark lady of the citadel said. The One Mind had promoted the name in the early stages of claiming the fortress.

Correlda staggered away, her movements stiff.

A male voice spoke from within the line. "The crone is

getting old or in heat again."

A chorus of male and female laughter ensued, dying quickly when Correlda staggered past without looking at them.

Her dad took a step forward. "The next in line may come forth," he said, his voice carrying to those at the forefront, quelling all conversations.

With the soft *chink* of chain mail, a soldier climbed the dais, looking too young to fight, let alone lead. Though his face was a little broad, Jade thought him handsome, and close to her seasons.

Before the sandy-haired soldier could bow, the One Mind spoke. "Stay where you are," Jade's voice commanded.

The soldier stopped moving.

The One Mind slowed the cyclone raging around the man. The three images slowed, and again the thing inhabiting her selected the darker image, shuffling through it as one would a deck of graphical cards. The shade of the soldier swung his long sword at something indiscernible, as the background bled into clarity. A gray fog permeated the air so dark swaths of it had turned black, giving all things a faded hue.

Slobbering and grotesque, the thing the soldier fought beside a foul algae shoreline was something horrible, nearly too frightening to look at. At some point, it may have begun its existence as an isopod. Now, it strode forth on four legs. Squirming tentacles dripped something foul on its belly. A shell on the creature's putrid back had the color and texture of putrescent flesh, the same stuff as the scale spikes at the tentacle ends.

At first, the shade of the soldier did well by countering each jabbing tentacle, but his movements dants quickly grew slower, less frequent. Soon, a spiky tentacle, then two, impaled the shade; a third sent the sword tumbling from his hand. The One Mind let the image go; it twisted, the colors elongating and elastic as it picked up speed, blurring back into its rotation.

Jade was stunned. She knew the area from the holographic of it and her dad's stories of when he grew up there. The soldier fought on her world, on Terra, in the polluted air of Low Realm.

Jade's vision swung to where her dad came into view. "This one remains with The Gap project. Keep him in leadership," she heard herself say.

Her dad bowed his head slightly. Then he motioned to one of the soldiers stationed at the rear, a middle-seasoned fit woman she didn't know by name. "Take him to The Gap's guard regiment, give him a full regiment, and outline the duties with the understanding he is to not speak of it except at strategy meetings with other commanders."

The woman nodded to her father, bowed to the One Mind, and then regarded the young soldier with stern blue eyes. "Follow me," she said.

The One Mind watched the sandy-haired soldier leave. Jade feared for him. The Gap of Thundering Darkness, the place of the project, confined a beast that frightened her as much as the One Mind did.

*****

Garn grew weary of the pomp sliding glibly past the lips of some of the Dark lords. Their transparent attempts to curry favor from the Dark lady of the citadel, his daughter, Jade, were tiresome. The line had ceased to stretch beyond the golden throne room doors. He'd had to stand and listen to every word for the longer part of a day.

He hated having to stand beside his daughter doing the bidding of the thing controlling her with no way to do a blasted thing about it. The helplessness of the situation made him want to lash out at every obsequious lord or lady that climbed the steps of the three thrones.

Some of them even attempted to climb together, which came against his explicit order. In those cases, he'd had to separate the offending parties, forcing one to step back to the head of the line. In one case, he'd had to draw his sword before the toady scurried away. Garn had then sent him to the rear as punishment.

Perhaps the alien monster controlling Jade was growing impatient or weary. More often than not, his daughter raised a palm, halting the person before they came within range of its evil touch. The thing was devious. Somehow, it had discovered how to select the leaders of the citadel from the others, reserving its foul ability for them. With the deviousness came a high intelligence. It had known allowing him to live with his mental capacities intact would keep Jade in check.

Not only that, Garn had a feeling it knew overtaking the Dark Citadel would be easier with him in command. Most of the citadel's authorities were familiar with him as the Alchemist's most trusted protector. Their ruse that the hooded one had appointed her as the lady of the citadel until his return had happened better than expected.

At the back of the immense room, a commotion started. Several people moved to one side. Then the entire line shifted left, a quickly growing wave of bodies rolling his way.

Lord General Tsan, a particularly cruel man, though a well-rounded fighter and Dark User, strode the throne hall. For reasons known only to it, the thing inside his daughter had left the man intact. Behind the general, two soldiers under his command escorted an unknown man wearing the neutral color of a gray robe.

His daughter turned to him. "Tsan has something to show, peruse it. Decide if you can make use of it."

With a quick flick of his hand, Garn signaled Captain

Lanniss. Lanniss, a good soldier, halted the next person waiting. He had specifically asked his daughter to leave him alone. Too many leaders had the blank-eyed stare of the mindless.

Garn watched the group approach, focusing on the man second to rear early in his adulthood. Smaller than the general in stature, he only got flashes of the man behind, just enough to spark his interest. The man wore something besides normal clothing under his robe.

General Tsan strode to the top stair and executed a small bow. "My Lady, I have found a great artifact for you to use as you see fit." Holding up his gauntleted fist, he opened it. A crystal orb gleamed with a dark red hue.

Garn stepped closer. Something black flickered inside.

Jade shrank back into the seat of the throne. "Take it away, I do not desire it. I do not want it," she said quickly.

Lord General Tsan closed his fist on the orb, dropping his hand to his side. "What would my lady wish for me to do with it?" he asked, the tone of his voice soft.

Jade, his daughter, the host, looked away. "I do not care, take it away."

General Tsan regarded her for a long moment. When she did not return his gaze, he spoke softly once more. "And what shall I do with the prisoner, My Lady?" he asked.

Garn interrupted. "Lock him and the artifact at the military confinement in the Dark Gate courtyard," he commanded.

Lord General Tsan's horned helm swung slowly toward him, as if reluctant to take his eyes from his daughter. "As you wish, Protector. Shall I interrogate him?"

Garn regarded the great artifact's owner. Brown eyes stared back warily, an expected reaction when mentioning any form of the word interrogate. One never knew if only questioning would be involved, or torture, perhaps both. "Nay, Lord Tsan. I intend to handle this myself."

"Trenton, my name is Trenton," the gray robe, Trenton, said.

Garn ignored the man's outburst. "You are dismissed, take him to confinement," he said, nodding at Tsan.

General Tsan looked at Jade once more. When she failed to look at him, he stomped down the steps, his steel-heeled boots *tinging* on every step. "Bring your charge," he snarled at his two soldiers.

Each soldier gripped the gray-robed man by a shoulder, spinning him around.

"One other thing, Trenton," Garn said.

The soldiers stopped. Trenton looked over his shoulder, his curly brown hair masking one eye. "Yes?" he asked.

"I suggest you give the general your full cooperation if you wish to live beyond today," Garn said.

Trenton gave a curt nod. Then the two soldiers pulled him roughly away.

Garn watched them go, hoping he hadn't lied.

# DARK SOUL

Squeezing the darkness tight around the last group of ingrots that had dared attack him like a giant extension of his own fist, Darwin compressed the subterranean dwellers. Green, glowing pulp oozed from the darkness, squeezed as high up as a dwarf standing on a man's shoulders. Releasing his hold, the radiant gel plopped into the tunnel's standing water.

Darwin's smile was grim. The flow of power had shifted; he had not even needed Malkor's substantial help. A wealth of strength, dark and commanding, burned within him; an agonizing sweetness both painful and succulent flowed into his stream of Dark User resource from the roiling blackness that had once been his soul.

He could now draw the Flow from two places, through his body as before and from within the blackness surrounding it. The Spear acted as a catalyst and power source, storing and shuffling the power to whichever tip he chose to fling it with. Ultimate supremacy raged through him, searing away compassion, eroding remorse. At last, he had the means to destroy those who had maimed him and the one whose power *had* surpassed his own.

Yet, such power came at a price he had not prepared for. The darkness sought dominance. It had expected no less than complete mastery of him from the moment the axe sliced into the sentient part of the soul, the awareness one has of one's own ambience, the part attached to one's body from the neck up. Instead, it had found a prison, containment inside his soul.

Enraged like any beast caged, the darkness within his soul clawed and tore at the boundary the Shimmer Spear and the Flow set for it, a separation he had not been certain would hold, even with the old lore's assurance Malkor had dredged from his eons of experience to call upon. He had to make haste; reclaiming the Dark Citadel would take time, even with the added power.

The constant fending away the beast wore at him, draining his patience. "Your ineptness is surprising, Malkor. You and all your lore gave assurance the glow frogs would give us no trouble."

"My surprise is as great as yours, Master; ingrots are known to fear man with a proper demonstration. They are aware of the futility from attacking a User of no little power. Always in the past, groups of the creatures would test the mettle of a single traveler or small company of travelers by sacrificing one of their own. Once dominance is established, they slink back to their holes."

"A continual wave of attacks hardly counts as 'slinking,'" Darwin sneered.

"I simply meant to imply that—"

"From this point on, reply only with something useful. How far do we have to reach the citadel?" Darwin interrupted. Malkor's whines had grown irritating.

Made brighter by the dim light of their surroundings, Malkor's eyes glowed red as he accessed his lore base. Darwin noted the ease with which he slipped into the mode of searching with each use.

"Next is a short ramp upward leading to the lower holds, which may have guards," Malkor stated. His eyes kept their crimson brightness.

Darwin frowned. "Why are the subterranean dwellers this close to humans?" he asked aloud. "Why such high numbers and showing so much aggression? Do not answer, my servant, my friend. I speak of things handled once the Dark Citadel's forces are under my command. A proper cleansing shall come then."

Malkor sloshed past without replying. His eerie red eyes dimmed only slightly from the bright white of his flawless glimmer shard.

Marching through the tepid water, Darwin quelled his rising irritation as he caught up to the red robe. His manservant would soon know his place or accept punishment for such a slight. For those below him, showing respect was something he would insist on implementing once the dark throne and the Obsidian Table were his. Of course, having those two stations meant all *would* be beneath him. His time had come.

As his servant expected, a pair of soldiers stood on each side of a wooden door banded with thick and wide strips of black iron. Darwin's dagger-sized black splinters protruded from their eyes and cheeks before they could raise an alarm. Had they worn helms, he would have had to come up with something more draining on his stores. Something else to make note of when established as great lord and faction leader. Helms were standard issue for a soldier; they would always wear them on duty or face severe recriminations.

Darwin signaled for Malkor to stay close behind, and then he pulled the door open, stepping through without pause. Two additional guards stood at duty on the inside. Not one of them moved or even looked his direction. He continued past them, going farther along the hallway and then stopped in his tracks. *"What are you doing, worm?"* the Great Shadow asked. Raspy from disuse, the dry voice in his mind continued. *"Only a fool would leave an enemy alive behind him."* Darwin turned around abruptly. "Drop," he said simply to his manservant.

Malkor froze. Then he fell to his knees.

Surprised at the speed of the Flow available to him, Darwin executed the same fate to the two men as he had their counterparts on the other side of the doors. Both men dropped without voicing a sound.

Satisfied they would continue undetected, he nevertheless wondered at the soldiers' lack of action. At the very least, the guard duty called for the script proof of patrol requirements for anyone accessing the Endless Caverns. The soldiers should have detained them and demanded to see it. Had protocols changed so much under the hooded man's rule? Had they become lax?

If so, the Alchemist was going to pay dearly for it. At first, he had considered convincing the Dark One to serve him but discarded the notion quickly. The man was too dangerous, such cunning had no match, and it was best to dispose of him immediately along with those in his command hierarchy. *"The fool learns,"* the Great Shadow said, laughing maliciously. Darwin ignored the voice in his mind.

Though his confidence grew with each unguarded doorway he passed through, he slowed his pace. Overconfidence had maimed him for life; vengeance would soothe the hatred for those who had made it happen.

He detoured along a side hallway that opened into the natural cavernous rooms the Ancients had left with little enhancements, only boring hallways to and from it.

The Caverns of Creation had changed. Well, the main cavern, the first and largest, had. Its seven pools of water had changed to a glossy black color from seasons of Flow experimentation, which was normal. The square tower rising five stories, halfway to the enormous stalactites stretching down, was not. Many had broken off, or blown apart from the caverns grip by an errant bolt from a young or arrogant Dark User.

Darwin shunted the images of past time spent in the caverns

to the back of his thoughts. The dark creation towering three stories beside the wooden structure captured his attention, filling his vision. The Alchemist's Dark Users had developed a way to make the raggedy doll-like creations bigger and stronger. Several of them must have collaborated on the project.

Having no care for the mechanics of such using—though at a certain time in his life, he would have thought of little else—he desired only the power, the enhancement to strength.

Reaching out to the Flow, drawing it through a pool of dark water, he filled the colossal creation with the sludge of life, making it his own. Behind it, another awaited in the same state. He brought the Flow into it also. Wide, yellow-orange eyes lit upon both faces, standing out sharply on the burlap-textured skin of the creations. Neither one had a nose or mouth to catch the eye. It was just as well; he wanted a weapon not a companion.

Darwin left the room going back the way he had come; the Great Master could call the juggernaut creation with a thought, if he should need it. A short hike along the hallway of his original starting point brought him to a long stairway rising upward.

As Darwin climbed the first set of stairs leading toward the Dark Gate, he prepared every step of his assault on the citadel in his mind. Revenge was close.

As he did so, the blackness within him raged.

# GRIM GRANDEUR

As they galloped along the Black Road, Camoe had sufficient time to reflect on the irony of his life. A few short months ago, he had avoided the dangers of the Black Road while aiding with the escape of the young woman from the Dark Citadel. Now he rode on a dark horse out in the open on the Black Road, heading back to the same blasted place he had worked so hard at leaving.

Worse, he could not help but think that if he had not brought Maialene with him to the Dark Citadel those seasons ago to pinpoint the exact location of the Dark Oracle, his daughter would still live. Kara Laurel would not have hated the sight of him for it and joined with the enemy. The same enemy he now escorted to the Dark Gate. Why did fate keep him returning to the place of heartache and bitterness, his greatest error in judgment? Why had he ignored the foretelling then?

Easily recognizable on his red stallion, the hooded man caused an about face from every patrol leader who thought to detain them during the last three days as they moved toward the Dark Gate. For two nights, they'd kept a cold, fireless camp. Interestingly, they encountered no one, military or otherwise, coming from the citadel.

Camoe urged his mount beside the Alchemist and motioned for him to slow; something he had wondered about more than once had resurfaced. "Why have we not encountered your army's return from the Vale? A token force would hold it, the Valens have fled."

The black cowl swung toward him, all but the Alchemist's beardless chin lost in shadow. "Some knowledge is dangerous to glean, druid," he replied.

Camoe nearly drew his sword. "I shall only warn you one last time. Do not toy with questions. Answer all that I ask or die in this barren, blackened, and defiled place. Another headless corpse shall gather scant notice, not even a hooded one."

The dark cowl swung to the front and behind, the hood settling to face back in Camoe's direction. "As you wish, but do not speak aloud I did not warn you. You are correct; a regiment ensures the taking of the Vale stays with the citadel, the rest march to join those assailing Surbo. The capitol city of the White Lands shall likely reside under Dark User control, under *my* power within a week," the Alchemist said, the tone of his voice soft.

Camoe, too, spoke soft. He did not want added danger upon the shoulders of his life mate's warriors. "Why have you assailed Surbo in the first place? There are much easier, less defensible places to hold in the central and eastern lands. Your losses against the city are great."

For a long while, the dark cowl faced him in silence, the sound of the horses' hooves clopping against black cobblestone the only sound. Finally, the Alchemist stirred, checking the road ahead as he spoke. "I expect not one of you on this foolhardy expedition shall survive. Revealing to you that taking Surbo is imperative, or so it looks, shall not cause harm to the desired outcome of the plan at this point."

"Why? What is so important there it is worth throwing so many lives away, killing so many innocents?" Camoe asked.

The beardless chin lifted slightly. The thin lips of the Alchemist shifted upward, forming a grim smile. "Surely you have an idea, druid. It is not what is there but what lies beneath."

Camoe drew in a sharp breath as the enormity of the Alchemist's words hammered him, causing his heart to race. "The Flow, the great river of power, is strong there," he breathed.

The Alchemist's smile widened. "Precisely," he purred. Spurring his horse with the heels of his boots, the hooded man pulled away.

Leaning only slightly forward, Camoe urged the dark horse into a gallop. The big stallion needed little incentive; the great horse was unused to following, and he had had to rein it back more than once, dropping behind the Alchemist to maintain the ruse his little band of warriors had joined with the Dark One. Camoe watched the expert way the man rode and knew anxiety over his devious brilliance. With the power of the entire Circle of Light at his disposal, the Dark One may become unstoppable. For now, all Camoe could do about it was ride on.

Rounding a bend, the grim grandeur of the Dark Gate came into view. A hundred meters wide, the gate curved outward a half kilometer to its center, finishing the arc from there at the opposite canyon wall. Built with the same dark gray granite as the citadel, the gate defied imagination with its sheer size. Two gigantic, black iron doors stood closed halfway along each side of the center arc, hanging on massive poles bored through the wall.

A second wall, made to blend in with the cliff face of the plateau, towered above and behind the main one. Four great iron doors were spaced evenly on it with room to slide to the side, which released flying creatures according to stories Camoe had heard in a past age. He hoped never to see what would come screeching out of them firsthand. Each exit was nearly as wide and high as a falun tree.

The Alchemist galloped at full speed toward the gate until it loomed with the presence of a hill sliced vertically by some gigantic axe, and then stopped abruptly.

Pulling hard on the reins, Camoe slid past the man by a horse's length. "What is it?" he asked.

"There, in the dark shadows of the far left arc, what do you see?" the Alchemist asked in return.

At first, Camoe knew confusion at the question, and then a blackness darker than the shadows gaped where the wall met the canyon. A doorway, opening to the inside, stood ajar. "Where are the gate guards?" Camoe asked.

"Precisely, the gate is only opened for returning patrols without mounts, always heavily manned," the hooded man said softly. "Before getting this close, a horn should have sounded, the first warning to halt and declare ourselves."

"What is the second warning?" Kerna asked.

"A hail of arrows," the Alchemist replied.

"That is pleasant," Peers said. "I assume if one makes it to the third warning, it is the worst?"

"An assault by magical means," the Alchemist said. "None of this has happened, but something has. Keep a sharp watch; it is likely we go to battle." The Alchemist leaned on the pommel of his saddle, his dark cowl facing Camoe. His smooth blocky chin and grim mouth were the only view of his features. "Perhaps, your decision to ride the Black Road in lieu of the topaz gateway shall have merit after all," he added. Urging his horse on, he made for the gaping hole in the wall.

Not happy with the look of the situation, Camoe urged his black stud into a fast trot until he caught the hooded man, slowing to match the wine-red stallion's pace. "Perhaps you organize different than your predecessor, but recalling from my limited experience, the Black Road had as much activity coming out from the Dark Citadel as going into it."

The Alchemist slowed. "Your memory serves well. There has

not been commercial or military travel both ways as there should have; it is disturbing. I am not surprised you noted this," he said softly. Coming up to the doorway with caution, he dismounted, letting the horse continue to the wall's base without him.

Camoe did the same, keeping the horse between him and the ominous blackness beyond the doorway. "You shall continue to lead, but know this. The first sign of treachery, and you receive a dagger in the side. Your death will be slow and excruciating," he said. Sidling close to the man, he followed the Dark One's example of keeping his back to the canyon wall out of sight of the door.

The Alchemist deigned not to respond to his threat. He waited until Peers and Kerna slipped from their horses, and moved quietly behind them. Then, he strode boldly into the darkness.

Camoe had a brief moment of despair. He hated how fate and the foretelling of Flow threads, his curse, had forced him back into the lair of his lifelong enemy. This very fortress had taken his loving daughter from him one time and then allowed him to escape with another dear to him the next. As he strode beyond the Dark Gate, he doubted if he would survive a third excursion. He had no care. Jade needed him.

# HER RESOLVE

Crystalyn admired the great gates. The sheer size of them, towering from the Old Town Coliseum's floor to where the ceiling started its magnificent arch, made her feel small. Their very function added a backward sense to everything one knew about technological disciplines. The alien technology that kept them sustained for so long was nearly incomprehensible, far beyond anything known, even on her Terra. Her hand came to rest on the bag belted to her hip she'd brought for the expressed purpose of carrying the black crystal candle. Did artifacts like it owe their existence to the same technology? Whatever the answer, the bag matched her light kell leather shirt and pants Lore Rayna had brought her earlier, a gift from Long Sand, though she hadn't noticed at the time.

Sabella stepped in front of her. Her low-cut dress revealed much of her large bosom as she inhaled and exhaled deeply, as if she'd run for some distance. The tavern keeper put her brown hands on her slender hips. "Without the hooded man's marker, the guards will not let you pass through. Each of your people is required to have one, there is not that many markers in existence that you need. Why are we here?"

Crystalyn glanced over her shoulder. The six ordered rows of Valens, Shimmering Sands nomads, and Red Rock warriors stretched beyond the stoic, stern-faced statues of the coliseum's courtyard. Each grouping had a good contingent of Users and archers, but the bulk was warriors. Though she had chafed at the delay, Crystalyn had to admit waiting for the Valens made an impressive display of force joined with the others. She hoped they were enough. According to Lore Rayna, they were going to need as many as she could get to follow her. Her focus shifted back to the immediate task. "You know a lot about the hooded man. Why is that?"

Sabella blinked. Dropping her hands to her side, her gray eyes glinted with a hint of steel. Her hard gaze flicked to the troops lined up behind Crystalyn and then back again. "Anyone in these parts with even an inkling of sense knows the hooded one controls this side of the topaz gate. The Dark One has made no pretenses with it. You would do well to learn this quickly. Do you not see the futility of such a foolish notion as taking the ascension gate by force? As your warriors overpower the twelve guards, the contactors hidden within the room and spread about the bystanders shall raise the alarm. The city watch will respond long before your people have made it through. Now, I have done as you asked and brought you here. I must return to the tavern. Without me watching, the girls sit and drink or sleep. Two of them have favorites they wish to net and give away free samples. Such actions degrade the business."

"Is that wise to let her go, mistress?" Hastel asked.

Crystalyn gave a look to her one-eyed companion she hoped would silence any further questions. Putting her hands on her hips, she formed a symbol in her mind, a long-lined pattern with 180-degree curves on each end. One she hadn't yet tried. She'd only just read it in tier three of the *Tiered Tome of Symbols* two nights ago as she waited for the Valens' arrival. The pattern brought to mind hemp. "I'm afraid you're not going anywhere but with me, dear. We cannot run the risk of having you contact the gate's present…caretaker."

Sabella looked around, her eyes narrowing. Lifting her left hand, she motioned toward the six rows of people lined behind soldiers stationed at the podiums a modest distance away from the topaz gate. "What is this? You accept my help and then think to detain me? You dare, here in this place of innocent patrons?" Her right palm arose level with the floor.

Two armed and plate-armored soldiers stood, perusing the lines and the people milling around near the walls, behind each of the carved wood podiums. Four others stood in pairs on each side of the great gate.

Crystalyn smiled her sweetest. "Then using the Flow is not a good idea, is it tavern keeper? Yes, I know you can, I've seen the flecks in our eyes. Even if you managed to fight past me, you wouldn't get far. In case you hadn't noticed, my people are fiercely loyal."

Sabella moved carefully backward, her eyes darting back and forth from front to back. "In case you have not heard, my lady, *my* people need me at the tavern. You cannot stop me." She held her left palm level with the floor, starting to draw upon the Flow.

Bringing out her symbol and releasing it, Crystalyn restrained her rising anger, anger at herself. Had she reasoned it out, she might have known Sabella would fight. Those whose arrogance makes them believe they have substantial power—merited or not—nearly always chose battle over negotiation.

Unraveling, like a kite tail that grew longer as the masthead shrank, the symbol flew at the woman. Radiating with a deep green, it wrapped around Sabella's shoulders, winding around her as a black cone detached from the tavern mistress' left hand.

A blunt force slammed into Crystalyn. Knocked from her feet, the cobblestone flooring jarred her right side as a heavy weight of soft brown fur pressed down upon her right.

Broth's paws scraped cobblestone as he twisted upright, clawing for purchase. Regaining his natural four-footed stance, he lowered his head, his hourglass eyes glowing with a light red, a certain sign of distress. *"Do'brieni! Have I injured you?"*

*"No, dear one, again you have kept me out of harm's way."*

Ignoring the burning abrasion making its painful presence known on her lower cheek, Crystalyn pushed off the floor and climbed to her feet, glancing at the shocked faces of those lined up behind. One of the desert nomads was down. Crystalyn nodded for Long Sand to attend him.

"Shall we terminate her?" Hastel asked. He'd pulled the crossbow, still attached to his back sling, around to the front of his waist.

With eyes large, round, and shiny, Atoi stood to one side of Sabella, her jeweled dagger pressed against the tavern keeper's bare thigh below the high hemline of her short black dress. "Allow me to scratch her, one tiny nick shall do," the little girl said, the tone of her voice a soft caress.

Crystalyn's rope symbol had dissolved when Broth had jumped on her. Bringing it out once more, she sent it wrapping around the woman again, pulling her arms tight to her sides.

Lore Rayna came near. Stooping, the big woman dabbed at Crystalyn's cheek with a soft cloth, kell from the feel of it. Pushing Lore Rayna's arms gently away, Crystalyn strode beyond the big woman's ministrations, her eyes locked with the tavern keeper. A trace of worry furrowed the woman's fine brow, vanishing as Crystalyn moved near. "Such a foolish move from one facing so many. Have you grown desperate? What are you protecting?"

Again, a look of concern, or fear perhaps, flashed through Sabella's eyes as she spoke. "I cannot go with you. Only death awaits me beyond the topaz gate."

"Your death awaits you here and now, in front of all these

people," Crystalyn said, waving her hand expansively about the wide room.

A hushed stillness had fallen upon it. The armed and unarmed soldiers, the poorly and richly dressed patrons, her oath-bound people behind her, all stood silent. Even her familiar companions, Broth, Lore Rayna, Hastel, and Atoi, listened to her every word as if caught in uncontrollable reverence.

She had refused to consider this before—no one could ever worship her. She was unstable, her mind broken beyond repair, and unworthy of adoration. "Hastel's crossbow bolt sinking into your breast will mercifully end the slow agonizing death of Atoi's dagger. Answer me, or I will not give him the order to shoot when I let Atoi slice into you. Her dagger hungers for flesh," she said.

Atoi pressed the flat of her dagger into the woman's thigh, smiling up at her.

Sabella's tanned skin paled slightly, though her features remained smooth. "You would not do such a thing because of the people, not with witnesses."

"Try me. What care do I have of these people, most who likely know you? They watched you attack and injure one of my people. Killing you is justified and you know it."

Sabella's eyes widened. Then, her gaze a mixture of haughtiness tinged with uncertainty, she scanned the entire room. No one looked away. She lowered her head, her eyes downcast. "Ask what you will," she whispered hoarsely.

Crystalyn moved closer. Slipping her hand under the woman's unyielding chin, she lifted firmly. Expecting higher resistance, Sabella's head snapped upward more roughly than she intended. "Good girl. You'll provide complete and truthful answers when I ask for them."

"I have one," Atoi said.

Broth's warm familiar thoughts flowed through Crystalyn's

own. *"I believe the Ancient young one has an inquiry about the outlander."*

*"As do I,"* she sent into the link. Though Atoi had mentioned the outlander had crossed through the gateway, she'd claimed no knowledge of anything more, which Crystalyn hadn't really believed. "Ask away," she said aloud, keeping the tone of her voice neutral. What question the little girl spouted would reveal much.

Atoi spoke without hesitation. "Have you lain with the hooded one as you have the outlander?"

Crystalyn kept her face smooth with difficulty. Not a question she'd expected.

Sabella's chin rose, her eyes ablaze. "Such a question would befit someone older. How old *are* you really?"

"You ask a question to my question. Decease and respond," Atoi said sweetly, though her green eyes narrowed.

"Answer mine and I shall determine if your improper inquiry shall receive an answer!" Sabella sneered.

"Enough!" Crystalyn boomed. Beyond the woman, two of the soldiers at the gateway drew swords.

Crystalyn turned to Lore Rayna. "Bind her," she snarled, her anger mounting for reasons she'd long ago given up on ever knowing.

Gripping Sabella's shoulder, Lore Rayna spun the woman forward, making her face the gate. "Remove your bindings, *Sarra'esiah*; I cannot put her hands behind her. If she has a desire to access the Flow, I will know. Such a move shall cost her dearly."

"I almost hope she does," Crystalyn said, dissolving her symbol. "Stay with her, Rayne, and keep close, I don't want her out of my sight." She turned her back on the woman, dismissing her. "Long Sand, is the injured one able to be brought forward?"

Centered in a row of warriors ten wide, the nomad strode past her. "He claims no need of healing," he said, nodding to a man at his left who wore a kell bandage soaked red with blood. He wore it proudly wrapped around his upper arm like a badge of honor.

Perhaps it was. Crystalyn knew little about them. "Where are you going?" she asked.

"We go to clear the way through the ascension gateway," he replied as if it was obvious.

Perhaps it was. On Astura, who knew? Crystalyn sighed. "Don't kill more than you have to," she called after him, but the tall Shimmering Sands warrior strode on.

Crystalyn looked to the mirror image of the tallest pair of obelisks she'd found on Astura so far. On the other side, two sister obelisks provided the entry to a place she'd once known love—the very place where she now intended to destroy that adoration from the man whose betrayal had nearly destroyed half the known world. Could she do it?

She was about to find out.

Gathering her resolve, she signaled the order to march.

# SOMEWHERE INSIDE

Following its orders, Garn led most of his men to the east wing along with those that followed it. He had to think of whatever manner of creature inhabited his daughter as an *it*; calling the thing Jade would rend him mad. Not being able to view it bothered him more than he would admit. How was he going to kill something he couldn't see without harming his daughter?

Leaving a token force at the topaz gate, they'd marched the length of the citadel collecting soldiers and Dark Users as they went. His questions about where they were going had gone unanswered so far.

He tried again. "You've gathered the bulk of the men left in the citadel, several hundred. Not many for the size of this fortress, the Alchemist left a couple regiments to patrol the Vale. Tens of thousands assail Surbo. Has someone besieged the citadel?"

As they climbed the eastern stair tower, it was silent. When Garn started to believe no answer forthcoming, it spoke. "A regiment of those attacking Surbo was sent to forestall endeavors crafted seasons ago. The rest have been called back, though they shall not arrive until after. For the One Mind's citadel is under attack, in a way. No longer is the Great Shadow content to dwell in the caverns below; it has claimed a host and makes a gambit. The One Mind's offspring let the host pass two days ago."

Garn was heartened to hear the attack on Surbo had ended; a

lot of wartime innocents would've suffered. He was curious about the endeavors, but other thoughts occurred to him. "Why let the host move past then? Why not exterminate the threat there?" he asked.

With his daughter's round eyes, it looked at him then. They were no longer innocent. A calculating intelligence lurked there. Garn's heart lurched in his chest.

Thankfully, it looked away as it answered. "The Great Shadow will fail; the Over Mind shall grow stronger."

Garn had no idea what it meant, but he guessed who it spoke of. The Over Mind, the One Mind, used the two names for itself interchangeably. "You sound certain of the failure. How can you know? Nothing is certain with battle." At the top of the tower, they turned west, following the wall. The courtyard behind the Dark Gate lay at his left ten stories below.

They continued in silence. At the halfway point where the wall's arch was the greatest, it spoke again, picking up the conversation as if there was no lapse. "Agree. Only the future is assured, the Great Shadow will fall," it said.

A thought struck Garn and he stopped. It kept going, moving fluidly. Hurrying, he caught up as they came upon the grand stairway. "Wait! Are you saying you know what is coming?" he asked.

It continued speaking conversationally. "Your offspring has a great mind, a unique ability. Such a one the One Mind has not encountered on countless worlds, nor has the Over Mind knowledge of it from those thoughts and memories consumed on other planets. On this one, your progeny is known as an anomaly, an inconsistency with something long foreordained by a long ago ancestor with a variant of this power. With your brood's significant talent, the One Mind knows the need for twelve Dark Users there," it said, pointing to one of the two house-sized gears used to open the gate. "They are to remain hidden. However, their focus has to lie with the One Mind and the protector throughout the battle."

"Why do the Users need to focus on us? Who are we fighting?" Garn asked quickly, glancing around. "I need to plan our defense." He squashed the urge to sprint to the wall and look over.

Clasping his daughter's hands behind her back, it strode along the top of the grand staircase, halting partway past center. "The protector and the One Mind shall stand at this point, your sword at the forefront. Inform the twelve to install a barrier for repelling Flow-based assaults; they are to maintain a constant vigil. Position the soldiers on each side of the stairs. Prepare the archers and power Users to move to the edge overlooking the courtyard with a signal. The protector shall know when they should move forward and attack."

Garn was stunned. Such a strategy was one he would have staged for the courtyard. Yet whom were they fighting? And when?

As if it read his mind, it continued speaking. "The Great Shadow is not far, you have less than half a bell, Protector. The commanders come forth for their orders. Make use of the foreknowledge the One Mind provides wisely," it said.

Garn watched the generals lumber toward him, part of the Dark Regiment controlled by something so strong it had consumed worlds and the beings on them. Now the thing had the power to view the future. How would he ever destroy such a powerful creature if it knew what he would do beforehand?

Garn stole a glance at his youngest daughter. He had to find a way. Though the thing had donned a black lacy gown cut too low and painted on black eye shadow with matching lip coating, it was his daughter's body. Part of her had to be somewhere inside; she *had* to be. He could believe nothing else. Only when he ceased to draw breath, would he give up on his child. Perhaps, not even then, if the Great Father allowed intervention from beyond.

# RELATIONSHIP

A bolt of sizzling white light rent the wide hallway in front of Crystalyn the moment she materialized on the other side of the topaz gateway. The bolt struck two men as they fought with sword and scimitar, blasting them away from each other, hurling them a distance to the granite flooring where they lay unmoving.

Garbed in the black kell leather of the Red Rock clan, several bodies lay scattered in the great hall of the Dark Citadel; two others had the Shimmering Sands attire with the open front robes covering the brown kell underneath. She hoped Long Sand wasn't one of the two. As she moved from the gateway's threshold, Broth loped beside her. Hastel and Atoi sprinted for one of the colossal roof support pillars many long yards from the gateway.

Her worry for Long Sand diminished when the nomad leader slipped from behind a wide pillar to the right of the topaz gate and dashed to her. Gripping her arm, he pulled her to the hard stone floor behind a body and then lifted another on top it, grunting with the effort. Dropping prone next to her, he quickly quieted his rapid breaths. Battling the living and stacking the dead had to be exerting.

Broth dropped to his long stomach next to her. *"We are at a great disadvantage, Do'brieni. The enemy has the entire citadel at its disposal while we are limited to four coming through safely at the same time."*

A bolt of crimson lightning brought the gagging smell of

burning flesh wafting past. Concussive booms heralded the screams of the dying. Fear permeated her link with Broth. No, not fright, but worry, anxiety that they gated into a deathtrap. Though hers or the warden's, she couldn't tell.

Crystalyn shifted close to Long Sand, her lips brushing his ear. "Where are they? Why didn't they burn us down as soon as we came through?" she whispered. His scent filled her nostrils, blessedly replacing other far less pleasant odors. Even with danger so near, his masculinity made her head reel.

"As expected, there was a fierce battle with the soldiers guarding the gate on the citadel side as the forward clan arrived, yet it was over sooner than anticipated. The clan won almost effortlessly." Shifting, he gestured toward a dark intersection left of the great hall. "Our only losses have derived from a small band of Dark Users making a stand there; the clan's archers are nearly in place to remove this threat."

A bolt of radiant blue flashed high in the great hall. Spreading out and downward, the lightning flashed, like an upside-down tree flickering within a mirage. The smell of burning flesh grew unbearable. Crystalyn's stomach lurched.

*"Something is askew in this foul place, Do'brieni. The smell of rotting flesh is strong."*

Broth was right. The scent came nearer to that of decay. Crystalyn took a closer look at the body she lay behind. A sickly white, the gate corpse's pallor was devoid of pigment, more so than the skin tone of the cadaver of the clan member stacked underneath the former gate guard. Granted, the clan had darker skin tones having lived a life in the sun, but the sentry's pallor was gray, as one dead for hours not minutes. The smell emanated from the top body.

Crystalyn crawled back from the corpse pile. "Long Sand! How long has that one been dead?" she blurted, pointing.

The nomad leader looked where she pointed and then glanced at the intersection.

Crystalyn followed his gaze. Several dark-robed Users lay about. Nomad warriors moved cautiously toward the opening. The short skirmish was over.

Rising to his feet, Long Sand came over. "A half bell, perhaps less. Why have you asked?" He offered her his hand.

The sand reader easily pulled her to her feet. Crystalyn bent and patted the dust from her knees, nodding toward the makeshift barrier. "Please do something for me. Pull the deceased guard off to one side."

His face blank, as if he thought she'd lost her mind, Long Sand complied, wrinkling his nose.

"I take it you smell it?" Crystalyn asked.

"The scent of death is very potent," Lore Rayna said, coming over from the gateway. The big woman escorted Sabella, gripping her by one arm. Railee held the other.

"Your wisdom shames me," Long Sand said, bowing slightly. The sand reader's quiet voice was reverent. "Something as blatant as this I should not have missed. There is something happening inside this dark place we have no knowledge about. Please, accept this long knife as added protection," he said, offering the sheathed weapon in his outstretched hand.

Crystalyn took the weapon without protest and strapped it to her side. "You had a distraction, such as securing the area, remember? Don't let it concern you. How many do we have on this side now?" Crystalyn asked, shunting the matter of smelly corpses to the back of her mind.

Railee answered. "With our arrival, we have thirty-two. Four additional have come through by now."

"Already?" Crystalyn asked.

Railee glanced at the woman whose arm she held. "This one

commanded the sentries on the Gray Dust side to stand aside, which they did without question. Our captains file our soldiers through with timed pauses."

Crystalyn regarded the tavern mistress.

Sabella stared back, her chin tilted slightly upward.

"Thank you," Crystalyn said simply.

A flicker of annoyance crossed Sabella's gray eyes. "There was little point to them dying; the militia would have arrived long ago if they were coming."

Crystalyn's ire with the woman rose, but she quashed it. "Agreed. Needless deaths expend resources," she said, keeping the tone of her voice even. "We make for the courtyard behind the Dark Gate, and from there, underground. Are there any hazards I should know about?"

"No."

Keeping her eyes on Sabella, Crystalyn spoke to the others. "When we have five hundred strong with half of them Users and archers, we go on. I will lead us. Should we encounter unexpected resistance, kill her."

Sabella blinked. "The Dark Gate will have soldiers, above and below," she said quickly.

Crystalyn kept her face smooth. "Yes, that is a standard for the citadel, the same as it was when I was here last. Is there anything else?"

"With the hooded one's rule, the guard and confinement barracks are upheld," Sabella said, the tone of her voice getting small at the end.

Now it was Crystalyn's turn to blink. Such information imparted a lot about the Alchemist. The current great lord was far less secure than the previous one. "You've given me a little, bordello mistress. I'll do better. Help me destroy the one we came after, and you'll be freed to return to your…tavern."

Sabella's brow scrunched, as if in pain. "I shall not aid you with harming him, I cannot."

With blurring speed, Railee's dagger pressed against the tavern woman's throat.

*By the Great Father, that one can move fast when she wants,* Crystalyn thought.

Broth growled his unhappiness with the situation.

"Why do you help when he has betrayed you? He has, has he not?" Railee asked, her voice a deadly hiss. "Darkwind betrays all who come within contact of him," she added, muttering.

"Darkwind, Darwin Darkwind? I have no care for him," Sabella said.

Crystalyn expected her frown matched the tavern woman's furrowed brow. "Then who do you protect?"

Sabella's frown deepened, marring her lovely face. "Is it not obvious? We stand in his domain. You should all leave, before it is too late."

Railee lowered her arm to her side though she kept the blade from the sheath.

Crystalyn at last understood. "Your hooded one is safe as long as he allows us to handle the filth we came for."

Sabella's blonde hair flung back and forth as her gray-eyed glare shifted to include all, the white locks hanging prominently. She fell silent.

"One-arm Darwin chose the Stair of Despair. He may already be lost," Lore Rayna said, her glowing eyes fixed on Crystalyn.

Crystalyn shook her head. "He would've had a way to make it past planned beforehand. A coward like him would never make the attempt if he wasn't certain of success."

"You overestimate Darkwind," Sabella said. "No one can survive the Stair. Those who are so foolish to try have vanished from society. Even so, I will help you search for him. Command your people to release me, if you wish my help."

Crystalyn hesitated, letting her delay at giving the order sink in. "There is one question I want answered," she finally said. "What is your relationship with the Alchemist? Speak truthfully, or I'll have you locked up, and we go on our way."

Sabella hung her head, the white lock shining bright against the backdrop of the Dark Citadel. "He is my father," she said nearly too soft to hear.

From behind, Atoi's dark laughter rang out.

Crystalyn almost wished she hadn't asked the woman. She knew what it was to be a daughter, what she would do to protect her dad.

# DARK FLOW

With the Shimmer Spear wedged firmly under his mangled arm, Darwin Darkwind, the Great Shadow, strolled through the courtyard behind the Dark Gate, killing soldiers and civilians with abandon. He reveled in the feeling of power snuffing out the puny lives of men and women with the simple flick of his hand from the power within. All ran before him. Even veteran warriors backed away with care.

The bows and crossbows had ceased when he had blown apart most of the weapons masters from wherever they had fired, hidden or not. They had believed they were safe from view, and he could imagine the look of horror when the Great Shadow had located the energy traces their projectiles created when piercing air. The Great Shadow, the dark stain within him, laughed with glee at the thought of it.

Once located, the master, no *he*—he was the Master of the Great Shadow now—had burned the bolts and arrows to cinders by following the released energy back to the source. Darwin did not have to do anything. After commanding the raging blackness in him to take out the first steel missile, it had handled the rest automatically. The raspy voice in his mind laughed malevolently. *"A command to destroy is my desire, worm,"* the voice said. Maniacal laughter boomed inside his skull.

Darwin closed his mind to the sound, his own glee drowning

it out. Everything he so desperately sought, the hardship and pain endured, the atrocities committed, had culminated at this point with nearly limitless power at his disposal. For the power gained, it had all been worth it.

Lifting a dark-armored soldier with a captain's insignia marked on the right shoulder, Darwin sent him crashing into the back side of the Dark Gate with a wave of his hand. He barely noticed the drain of Flow as it flowed through the Spear.

The blackness within surged with every use, seeking control. Again, Darwin fought it back, pushing it into the Shimmer Spear where it belonged. The task took longer this time, even though he had expected another such attempt. The crowned shadow with the great axe laughed, a dry ancient laugh.

"Master?" Malkor asked hesitantly, his raspy voice hoarse. "After we have destroyed this rabble, may we stop for water at the guardhouse? You should drink your fill, perhaps some wine?"

A band of soldiers and red robes charged out of an interrogation room. He wrapped them in a tube of darkness, glaring at his servant. "You need nourishment. I no longer have such base requirements; I feed on the nectar of power. Why do you not do as I do? The great knowledge I have provided you should sustain you for eternity," he said. Reveling in the way his voice boomed when he spoke, he pulled the tube tight. The screams of agony ended with gurgling that quieted with a satisfying abruptness.

The darkness within him exulted.

A man wearing a gray robe stumbled from the room the red robes had come from. Blood ran from a cut lip. Both his eye sockets had the dark purple and red tint of heavy bruising. "I do not know who you are, but I thank you for my release," he said.

Drawn to the front pocket underneath his robe, the Great Shadow responded to a power emanating from the man. Reveling within the grasp of the Dark Flow enhancing his strength, Darwin gripped the man's robe and yanked. Twisting violently around, the man spun to the flooring minus the robe Darwin now held in his hand. Sliding partway across the room on his back, he lay still. An odd pattern glowed softly red on the armor suit he had worn under his robe.

Darwin ignored the man and the suit. Reaching inside the pocket with his free hand, his power hand, he closed upon a thing of great power. Drawing it out, he let the robe fall away.

Pulsating in his palm, a red crystal orb gleamed darkly. He smiled. With it and the catalyst for the Flow stowed in the Spear, the Great Shadow's power would increase tenfold, *his* power. The Great Shadow surged strong within, immensely pleased.

Malkor's nasal whining voice cut his satisfaction short. "As you say, Master, you likely do not need such a mundane thing as water. I do, however. Without it, I shall die. And, if you want followers, we should leave some alive," his manservant said.

"Silence!" Darwin boomed. He would punish his servant after all in the fortress if it served him. Growing annoyed with losing his fulfillment, he looked for those living to regain it. He found none, only his cowering manservant clinging upon his lustrous black robes.

Though his head bowed slightly, Malkor looked up at him, his arms held at his chest in a ridiculous defensive posture as if he meant to block blows from a brawl. Did such a puny human roach think it could stop the Great Shadow?

How much did he truly need his servant? Once he had the citadel contained, he would go forth and conquer the land, beginning with the lore masters. The wind door would no longer be a deterrent to one such as him. Darwin drew more of the Dark Flow into the Spear though it was near capacity and thrummed with power. Malkor cowered lower before him, which pleased him.

"Please, Master, do not look at me so," his servant said. A

malevolent smile fixed upon his ragged lips. Malkor straightened and pointed. "There, Master, is someone for the great one to play with."

Darwin spun. A large group had gathered at the north courtyard as dozens more streamed through the great hall's double doors in orderly rows. He barely noticed. The betrayer stood at the forefront.

He smiled. The confrontation he knew had to come since leaving the Valley of Forgotten Kings had arrived. It had come to the courtyard behind the Dark Gate. Finally, he had the strength to destroy her and suckle upon her latent power.

The power within, the Great Shadow, surged with anticipation.

Beside the betrayer stood one he had used and left to die, yet the sand woman lived. No longer had he such base instincts. He would slaughter her and the plant woman with the eyes of white radiance towering behind.

A motion beside the gate caught at the Great Shadow. A figure cloaked under a dark cowl strode with a familiar boldness through the guard door—someone he recognized, another betrayer. The Alchemist had brought only a mere three warriors for support. Such a puny fool, a minor distraction, though he carried some supremacy. The Great Shadow would terminate him first and eliminate his power.

Screaming, the sand woman suddenly charged, racing toward him as if such a puny mortal with her little sword had the power to hurt one such as *him*. Wrapping the insolent woman in Dark flows of air, he hurled her across the courtyard, slamming her into the Dark Gate near its peak with a wet-sounding, satisfying *splotch*. Slowly, then with speed, the woman fell.

The betrayer screamed with gratifying anger. Perhaps, he would destroy all those around the symbolic User in like manner.

From the top of the great gate stairs, a voice rang loud and clear. "Use your strongest, Crystalyn! His is stronger than you know!"

The Great Shadow sent a dark spear hurtling at the disrupting voice as the betrayer shouted something. Annoyingly, the tall warrior easily deflected it, though the man's movements gave a view behind him.

The anomaly waited.

Darwin smiled.

The power gathered beyond the Dark Gate had grown from fortuitous to fortunate. No longer would it have to send creatures after the girl and subvert her to its will from afar. The Great Shadow would envelope her now, firsthand. Then, its power would expand exponentially. The anomaly's innate ability with reading auras, to know the possible futures rotating around every single soul, was here for the taking.

It would *take*.

With all the power the Great Shadow had collected over the eras, the Shimmer Spear, and the red orb, it would not only see the future, it would control it. Resistance from anyone or anything would be ineffectual. The power within would dominate them all.

Darwin, the Great Shadow, was greatly pleased.

The betrayer and her substantial strength could wait. The target had changed.

The Great Shadow hurled much of what it had at the one blocking the way to the anomaly where ultimate power awaited.

## *SARRA'ESIAH*


Crystalyn thrust open one side of the great double doors of the Dark Citadel interior. Railee kicked the other. The black-iron-banded wooden doors hit the gray limestone wall with a thunderous *bang*. Lore Rayna's tree-branch arms slid past. Slamming both doors to the wall, the versatile limbs kept the heavy wood and iron from bouncing back into them and then withdrew. With Railee slightly behind and Lore Rayna following, Crystalyn brought out her golden cyclone symbol and advanced into the courtyard.

Robed and armored bodies lay strewn about the long, wide area behind the massive gate and dark stone wall constructed to hold it. Crystalyn tried not to look at them too close. Someone had been particularly violent with some of them, the heads twisted at unnatural angles.

The courtyard had changed. Carved columns of beautiful women dressed in sheer robes were interspersed with large statues of powerful men wearing naught but loin coverings. Made from stark white marble and placed with an eye toward complementing the austere dark granite of the flooring and walls, the marble lined the perimeter, the largest and most intricate carvings around the fountain. Left alone in the center, the deep gray dais stood out.

A memory flowed through her mind as she viewed the Dark Dais where challenge for lordship occurred with a duel to the death. Stained with dried blood, blackened by combat both magical and physical, the raised circular area in the courtyard's center dredged feelings of disgust and revulsion from the depths of her mind.

A motion beyond the dais caught her attention where the one person she'd seen battle upon it strode. Darwin bloody Darkwind.

Sword in hand, Railee dashed toward the black robe. "You shall go no farther, Dark King! I see you for what you are!"

"Railee, stop!" Crystalyn screamed.

Something unseen, unrelenting, and unforgiving wrenched the nomad woman from her feet midstride, lifting her high into the air. Blood streamed from her clenched lips, and her sword *clanged* to the stone floor. Soaring at a high speed across the courtyard, she slammed into the Dark Gate. Hanging in stasis for a double heartbeat, she dropped many stories to the floor.

"Blast you, you bloody murderer!" Crystalyn screamed. Boiling with rage, she failed to hold onto her cyclone symbol and it dissolved.

"No!" Lore Rayna screamed.

At the top of the grand stairway leading to the top of the gate wall, a voice rang out. One she knew and loved. "Use your strongest, Crystalyn! His is stronger than you know!" Her dad's voice was easily recognizable but not the person he was now. Trim and fit, he looked capable of taking on anyone, even Hastel or Long Sand. Someone stood behind him. *Jade!* "Are you two all right?" she shouted.

Dark spears of power flew at her dad, which he deflected. Then, a buzzing hail of blackness blotted out half her family.

Crystalyn's anxiety exploded, bringing on panic. She formed a symbol, the old and familiar knockback, her first aggressive one. Releasing it, the gray star pattern with the white outline streaked to the target, striking Darwin in the chest.

Lifting the black robe from the stone floor, the symbol thrust him into Malkor. Shoved through a wide doorway where steps led downward, they vanished from sight.

"Everyone take cover! I doubt I hurt him much!" Crystalyn shouted. Not heeding her own warning, she looked toward the top of the stairs, fear knotting her stomach.

Incredibly, her dad stood unscathed, a great sword in his hand. Behind him, Jade gazed over his shoulder at her. The glint of something translucent flickering with a light blackness surrounded them both. Crystalyn understood. A barrier covered them.

*"Do'brieni! The enemy marches!"*

Four unordered rows of soldiers marched past her father and sister, climbing down the stairway. Oddly, they moved with an inelegance unbefitting those trained in martial affairs. Archers and Dark Users slipped along both sides of the gate wall, lining the top of its arc.

Crystalyn's warriors filed through the great double doors six at a time, Hastel's archers and the Users fanning out as soon as they could. The Shimmering Sands clan had already spread out around the eastern side of the dais. The Valens, lined to come through, would take slightly longer, as only two could go through together.

Grinding her teeth with frustration, Crystalyn watched the progress of her warriors; it was taking too long. The open area of the courtyard made her uneasy.

*"Broth, go check on Darwin's condition, report back to me. Stay hidden and don't engage him under any circumstances."*

*"I shall go with stealth, my Do'brieni."*

*"Good. Then hurry back. I need you at my side."*

Beside the Dark Gate, four figures moved. One, she'd overheard consorting with Darwin months ago. Even from across the courtyard, the gold bands were unmistakable. *Blast! Another enemy to take on. There's no end to them on this bloody world,* Crystalyn thought. The four ran to a fallen person wearing a gray robe. The hooded man stooped over the crumpled form.

A violent wind gusted into Crystalyn, sweeping her legs out from under her, slamming her into the dais. Gripping the rough stone at the lip of the dais, she held on with all her might. Finally, it slowed enough to pull herself upright.

"Blast her! Someone put an arrow in her!" Lore Rayna screamed, shouting from where she lay upon the granite floor.

Sabella dashed toward the group gathered around the fallen man at top speed.

Hastel sat up, raising his crossbow.

*"Darkwind returns, Do'brieni. He has started the climb."*

Crystalyn had no time to worry about the hooded man or Sabella now. The rest of the Shimmering Sand warriors were marching into the courtyard, rows of soft flesh beckoning for arrows and strafing assaults of the Flow, six abreast. "Forget about her, Hastel! Set up the archers around the perimeter, cover those still coming in if the enemy decides to fire upon us from the wall!"

"Aye, mistress," Hastel said. Crystalyn barely took note of Atoi moving beside her as the one-eyed man climbed to his feet and sprinted away.

"Long Sand, get your people out of the open. Move them to the stables over there," she said, pointing. "Have them set up barricades in front. Bring out wagons and stall doors, pull down statues and columns, anything you can find to protect against those archers and Users. Keep in mind, wood is flammable. Ask someone to check if Railee somehow survived."

"Your command is my honor, Clan Leader," Long Sand said, crouching and moving away.

"RaCorren!" she shouted next, bringing the big Valen running to her. "Position the Valens in the hallways and doors of those barracks next to the stables. There is access to deeper within the citadel—guard for rear attacks. Have the Users install barriers in front of the archers and nomads where needed. Prepare aggressions for retaliation against the Dark Users rimming the wall."

"I shall, *Sarra'esiah*," the Valen leader said. Giving a quick bow, he, too, left at a run.

"Lore Rayna, come with me. You too, Atoi, since you won't go anywhere else when we battle, it seems. I'm going after Darkwind."

*"You have hurt the red robe, Do'brieni. He has remained behind to heal. The black robe comes. I come,"* Broth sent. A moment later, he loped though the southern door.

Crystalyn hurried toward her *Do'brieni*. With luck, she would have time to gather her little group on each side of the doorway and ambush Darwin when he stepped through.

She made it halfway to her link mate when the walls and doorframe exploded outward.

# CRIMSON BEAM

The Great Shadow rolled off the servant using the fist grasping the orb to push the body to a stand. The two artifacts appeared intact, though the deformed arm's grip was weak. The Great Shadow had the strength to renew it and give back the power and mobility it once had. But it would take a constant dribble of Dark Flow. It was not worth such a high expenditure, not yet. Perhaps after all of Astura had submitted to its power.

The Great Shadow gazed up the stairs. The symbol of power cast by the tall outlander woman had hurled it and the living host, Darwin, many stories deep. The host should have failed, yet all but the old wound of the arm appeared intact.

A glance downward revealed the reason. The servant lay unconscious on one side, his left arm severely damaged. The shoulder's blade protruded through the red robe. On an impulse, the Great Shadow split its essence, installing half of its dark spirit inside the red robe, expending a few bits of its Dark Flow to heal. Sitting up, the servant opened eyes of radiant red rimmed with the darkness of its essence. "Follow when you have healed enough to do so. Do not use more than necessary to provide healing to make you mobile. Stay in the shadows. Add power, or healing, only when I request it of you. You now stand in as my reserve," the Great Shadow rasped.

The servant rose and bowed.

The Great Shadow climbed, immensely pleased. Having a failsafe had on occasion insured survival through the millennia.

At the top, the Great Shadow paused on the landing. A warden bolted away from the open doorway. A small group of humans ran toward it. The symbolic User, *the betrayer,* dashed in front of them.

The Great Shadow cast the translucent image of its true essence, overlapping the human host. Expanding, the Great Shadow rose to a tremendous height. In one hand, the Great Shadow gripped the infused Dark Flow spirit approximation of the weapon that had made it king so long ago, when it, too, had been a man. As an afterthought, it sent out the silent call for the colossal creations, getting them moving, bringing them nearer.

The citadel's ceiling was now too close and the doorframe too small. One swing of the great axe demolished the obstacle. The door header and the walls on both sides crumbled. Bending only slightly, the Great Shadow stepped into the courtyard. "You insects dare attack the Great Shadow? Fools!" the Great Shadow boomed.

Exulting in the power it now wielded, the Great Shadow drew the Dark Flow deeply into the Shimmer Spear, ignoring the heat of it, raised the human's right hand that held the orb, readied the great axe, and attacked. The Great Shadow, the Dark King, bore down upon the puny humans scurrying around below.

*****

Crystalyn dived to the floor and rolled to one side, narrowly avoiding a chunk of stone the same size of her head as it sailed past close enough to billow her hair. The dark gray stone clattered in pieces upon the limestone flooring. Dust curled into the air, rising nearly as high as the first two of four massive black steel doors mounted onto the cliff face of the plateau overlooking the courtyard.

Bending, Darwin stepped through the ruins of the doorway, allowing the top half, a translucent shadowy form of a crowned man with flaming eyes of red, to come through.

Crystalyn gaped. The figure of the man attached to Darwin's feet was translucent, though high in detail, wearing war boots and plate armor. It towered above the black robe by more than two stories. The apparition held a double half-moon axe. Darwin had Trenton's orb in his right hand; his left clutched the Shimmer Spear.

The flaming eyes of the crowned apparition fell upon her.

The monstrosity attacked, swinging the axe as if chopping wood. Crystalyn rolled, one hand holding onto the bag containing the black candle. The axe smashed into the floor beside her, buckling it upward. Thrown to one side, her arms flailed as she twisted around and landed on her hands and knees painfully. She rolled to her back. The great axe rose and fell, dropping toward her at an incredible rate.

*"Use your symbols, Do'brieni!"*

Forming her magic absorption spell in her mind, Crystalyn brought it out and laid it horizontally above her as the axe struck. The force was enormous. The white crosses on her symbol gave off blinding white sparkles as it dissolved from the impact. Again, Crystalyn rolled to one side, springing to her feet this time.

Arrows and white bursts of light peppered the crowned figure and Darwin, some aimed at the monstrosity and others going for the man. None had any effect. Red and black bursts and long arrows joined the fray.

Blindly, the great axe flailed crumbling statues and carving gashes out of the courtyard's south wall. A water cistern burst, flooding the floor. As he splashed around, tree branches penetrated

Darwin's barrier, snaking around his wrists and legs. "No! Lore Rayna, let go! He's too strong!" Crystalyn cried.

Crystalyn was too late.

A black cloud shot from Darwin's hand. Arcing around at the inside edge of his barrier, the cloud separated into four parts. Darting forth from the cloud with chilling accuracy, black quills struck the four branch limbs, sinking deeply into them. Lore Rayna's scream rent the air. The branches retreated, carrying the quivering quills. Blood welled at the bases.

The great axe turned toward Crystalyn.

*"Run, Do'brieni!"*

Crystalyn ran. The only path without debris led toward Sabella and the group of four. There was no time to climb a stair.

*"Run faster, Do'brieni! I shall slow it for you."*

*"No, Broth!"* Crystalyn sent, glancing over her shoulder often. One swat of the broad side of the axe hurled her link mate from sight as if a pest bothered it. A single abrupt *"Urp"* echoed in her mind. *NO!*

Darwin charged, gaining ground by leaning forward, putting the crowned figure at her level. The axe swung backward, preparing a swing. Then it hesitated. Darwin slowed. Atoi stood in the way, her dagger held forth.

"Atoi, no!" Crystalyn shouted.

Surprisingly, Atoi listened, dashing to the side and slipping behind the head of a fallen statue.

The little girl's diversion allowed her to get to the group. Standing side by side, the five people left her an opening between a woman with a bow and Sabella, closing the gap behind as she ran through. Crystalyn slid to a halt, spinning around.

Darwin had changed targets and tactics. Red flame burst from the orb, shooting forth in long lines and setting fire to archers. Protected by personal barriers, Dark Users scattered away from the burning pillars that raced wildly around. Lunging, the great axe cut through some of the Users, blowing through barriers as if they did not exist. Then the great figure turned, focusing on the little group of five.

"I need an opening to get within range of a potion," the Alchemist said in a rush. "If Darkwind is still human, it will have great effect."

The druid Camoe replied. "Aye, I will capture the bad one's attention. Perhaps I can slip my sword through the barrier surrounding him."

Crystalyn pulled herself upon the dais, keeping her eyes on the monstrosity lumbering toward her. It paused to swing at a row of soldiers marching down the steps, razing a huge swath of death through their ranks. A red beam from the crimson orb burned through additional archers and Users. "Get behind the dais, all of you," she said. "I'll provide the diversion."

Crystalyn selected a symbol out of the multi-aggression chapter she recalled from the black-lettered *Tiered Tome of Symbols*. Next, she chose an airy one from the pushbacks chapter of the white-lettered one. Her third and final selection was a lovely white snowflake one from the decent defenses section from the same book." Unraveling all three in her mind, she combined them, creating a compact one, black on one side and white on the other. Octagonal in shape, the pattern inside, the symbol drawn with thin stick lines formed a myriad of pinwheels tipped with spikes at the points.

Keeping the white side pointed toward her at all times, she released the symbol spinning at the man shape inside the translucent shell of a crowned man. Rotating faster than the turbines on a hovercraft, her symbol of splintery death streaked toward the man she once loved.

Then it dissolved before it got near him, struck by a red

beam from the orb. Crystalyn tried another, all she had time for, only to watch it destroyed as Darwin reached the edge of the dais. Then she brought out her golden absorption symbol, wrapping it around her.

The great axe fell, chopping at her barrier while she stood centered in the dais, looking up at the wicked curve of its descending half-moon head. Again and again, it rose and fell, pounding on her symbol as if a chunk of green wood persisted against a split.

Crystalyn reached into her kell leather bag, her hand enclosing the black crystal candle, feeling the strength return to her decaying symbol. It wouldn't last long. Already the candle thrummed, growing warm in her hand from the draw of power flowing through it. Cracks appeared at her head. Weakening, she dropped to her knees.

Abruptly, the pounding ceased. Darwin smiled, raising the orb. "Perhaps this is stronger, betrayer," he said, his voice a dry raspy boom.

A crimson beam shot forth from the orb focused beside the cracks at her head. The crystal candle burned hot in her hand in an instant, melting her flesh. She couldn't let go.

Crystalyn screamed.

# DARK SHAPE

Camoe trundled around the side of the dais on his hands and knees, keeping low. He did not have to look back to know Peers and Kerna followed. They would not have listened to a command to stay back had he dared take the risk Darwin Darkwind, and the Dark King apparition, would not overhear.

Rounding the dais, Darwin's foot came into view. Camoe froze. If all had gone according to the hasty plan, the Alchemist and the User woman would have arrived at the same position on the other side.

Atop the dais, Jade's sister screamed, long and loud.

Camoe stole a glance at her. Darkwind had activated a focused beam from the crimson artifact, attempting to penetrate her barrier. The woman's beautiful features scrunched with pain. Why that would hurt her, he had no idea, but it had, putting her in dire peril. They all were. Darkwind, coupled with the blasted Dark King apparition, was powerful, a greater foe than anything he had ever fought. His entire brash plan hinged on the bloody hooded man performing his part, something that should have happened by now. Had he make a grave mistake by trusting him?

As Crystalyn's scream faded, the sound of glass breaking signaled the attack, which sounded the reason for the delay. Camoe gave a quick prayer of thanks to Onan for the Alchemist's foresight. Then he dashed the few yards remaining to him at a crouch.

Darkwind waved his hand back and forth trying to dispel the Alchemist's thick black smoke rising inside the front half of his barrier. As Camoe reached him, Darwin abruptly stopped waving his arms and then flicked his right hand with an abrupt motion. The smoke dissipated from within his shield.

Committed now, Camoe jabbed at the side of the man's black robe as if he held a spear instead of a sword. Partway in, plate armor scraped against his blade, or so he thought.

An arrow flew past his ear, bouncing harmlessly away at the same point his sword was. He pushed the long sword harder, jarring his arm. Though the sword had passed through the magical barrier, it encountered another one—a shield within a shield. Stunned, Camoe froze, trying to comprehend. How could someone maintain two shields? The drain on the Flow would be horrible, expending huge amounts every second for each type. How had he done it?

He was still wondering when a dark shape loomed over him. Then, something enormous smashed into him.

****

Dashing headlong downward, Garn took the grand stairway steps two at a time, Crystalyn's scream adding strength to his legs. At the bottom, he sprinted to the dais at full speed. His previous captor, the Alchemist, squatted beside the place of challenge. Using the hooded man's back as a springboard, he launched himself at the shadow of a man assaulting his daughter, ducking under the apparition's great axe swing, the edge coated with fresh blood.

Raising his great sword in midair, he brought it chopping down with all his might on the source of his daughter's pain, the hand holding the orb. A myriad of sparks flashed in front of his vision. Landing on the dais, he rolled, using his momentum to follow through with a handspring to his feet, holding his sword at the ready to block the next swing of the axe.

There was none. The axe remained suspended above as the man shadow inside the translucent apparition clutched at a severed wrist. The Spear grasped in the shadow's other arm shimmered brightly. An arrow, then two, suddenly protruded from the stump.

The shadow of the man screamed low and hoarse. *Good, it can feel pain*, Garn thought. A ball of purple flame landed between the arrows, exploding. Gobs of flesh and blood drained out of the shield to the elbow. The shadow man's screams ended with coughs. A potion sent smoke up the tube of its arm, drawn upward as fast as a chimney.

Slowly, from a great height, as if a gigantic pendulum, the great axe swung downward at the potion thrower.

Garn had seen enough. Things were heating up too fast. Grabbing his daughter by the wrist, the one with her hand grasping a black artifact, Garn pulled her to the edge of the dais. Though she yelped with pain, Crystalyn clamped the severed hand between her ankles.

At the edge, Garn let go of her and hopped off the dais. Turning, he sheathed the great sword and got both hands under her shoulders, pulling her to the floor and the relative safety of the dais edge. As he straightened, a dark shape clamped upon his shoulders, carrying him away.

*****

Jade sensed the One Mind was not pleased. The protector, her dad, had abandoned his post. As the One Mind paced back and forth along the wall, it was difficult to determine where he'd gone from the stilted view of the barrier maintained by the twelve Users. She'd last seen her dad race down the grand stairway.

A grizzled-faced red robe came into view. "You there," she heard herself say in the formal way Asturans had of speaking, "Why has the lot of you not attacked? Who is in command?"

"I have that honor," a new voice said.

The view changed. Swinging around, she looked along the wide walkway of the great wall.

A woman wearing the silky black robes of a master User strode toward them, bowing when she came close. "Great Lady, there is reason for withholding," the woman said, raising her firm chin slightly. "Whenever we strafe the target, it has no effect. In return, the apparition attacks with that monstrous axe. The weapon cuts through our personal barriers as if none exists. Two-thirds of our Users and archers have joined the Dark Regiment."

"Why have you not concentrated on the invading force then?" the One Mind demanded to know.

The woman's beautiful, though austere, features clouded. "The order came to hurl everything we had at the Dark King. As I mentioned, two-thirds of our long-range capability are decimated, two of those my siblings. Unless you have reserves you have not spoken about, the risk for the enemy strafing us with return fire is too high," the woman said, lowering her eyes. "I have now reported when no one else would. Destroy me if it is your will."

"Reserves are not your concern; following orders is topmost," the One Mind said using Jade's mildest tone of voice while slowing the cyclone spinning around the woman. Inside every image, darkness swirled, which saddened Jade. The woman's death was imminent. The One Mind released the rotation. Jade watched as her hand reached out and touched the woman on the cheek. She listened in as the former free-willed commander's thoughts and memories became part of the Over Mind's Dark Regiment, not the one the Dark User believed.

*"Return to the regiment, commence an assault on the soldiers and Users in the courtyard,"* the One Mind commanded as the woman's last memory of her two sisters cut in half from the red beam of Darwin's power drifted past. Jade hated the alien efficiency of the process. It was all over in a few seconds. The woman's actions would now no longer be her own, nor would she ever again think for herself.

Jade's view shifted once more, rising upward to the four great black iron doors carved into the side of the plateau above the courtyard. The right topmost doorway gaped with darkness, rolled open on unseen rails by an unviewed mechanism of some sort.

A call went out from the One Mind then, a command for the beast to come forth. Two, great-clawed forelegs appeared at the edge, the dark shape of a long snout above them. Bending low, a head filled with sharp teeth scraped the top frame.

Not for the first time, locked in the silence of the little bubble in the corner of her mind, Jade wished fervently for the ability to scream.

The One Mind had released the reserve.

# CREATIONS

With her free hand, Crystalyn hooked the red orb from the severed hand. Her left hand ached badly, but there was nothing to do about it now. Her fingers had cramped around the black candle with a death grip, refusing to let go, her flesh seared to it.

A dark shape shadowed the light above.

Trenton, the outlander, bent over her, his hand outstretched. "Give me the orb, I can help," he said, his voice hoarse. His brown eyes glinted earnestly.

Crystalyn put her hand in the one extended, her fist still closed around the red crystal orb. "Help me up," she said.

Trenton complied, raising her to her feet with ease, though he remained hunched down, taking no chances.

Crystalyn glanced around. Holding his mangled arm up to slow blood loss, Darwin flailed around with the axe, swinging wildly at Sabella, the hooded man, the woman with the bow, and a warrior holding two long swords. Camoe was nowhere in sight. Several Dark Citadel soldiers swung wildly, almost lazily at his back. The apparition above Darwin, the Dark King, twisted and cut them all down with one swing of the great axe. They fell without a sound.

"Where's my dad?" she asked the outlander.

Ignoring the question, Trenton reached his hand toward her, but he did not straighten. "Give me the orb, I can help," he repeated.

Crystalyn was annoyed. "Here, take it," she said, dropping it in his hand. "Just don't let Darwin have it again." Her left hand throbbed.

Trenton stood. "Why would I?" he asked. "That creature took it from me. It's going to pay for what it did," he declared, holding the orb chest-high gripped in his right fist. An orange-red fireball blazing bright and tailed like a comet shot forth from his fist, striking Darwin in the face.

Dissipating, the attack had no effect, except for making the monstrosity look at them. Darwin strode around the dais toward them.

Too weak to run, Crystalyn prepared her absorption symbol.

A dark shape loomed behind Darwin. Gaining size as it flew closer, the shape extended a pair of reptilians claws attached to powerful legs, two parts of its elongated body and fierce scaly snout. As an eagle would with prey, the black dragon reached down and clamped it claws on Darwin's shoulders.

Flapping its massive wings, the dragon rose, though not high. Sparks flew as the great claws lost their hold, scraping against Darwin's barrier. Letting go of its load, the dragon flew on, dropping the apparition onto its back beside the dais.

The absorption symbol faded away as she formed her diamond-shaped symbol. Inside, the pattern's glowing lines formed intricate crystals that she sent soaring into the area unprotected by any barrier. The bottom of Darwin's kicking feet.

The symbol dissolved on impact, dispersing a sharp crystal shard from each of its four points. As long as a blade, the first two shredded Darwin's legs; the final two sank into his groin and stomach.

Darwin screamed.

The apparition surrounding him shrank, dwindling into the

man until only Darwin, the former love of her life, remained.

The barriers winked out.

"Malkor! Heal me!" Darwin shouted. Though his lifeblood pooled quickly, Darwin's voice was loud still.

Malkor was already running across the courtyard, dragging his shattered leg a half step behind. Hopping over small debris, he slid to a halt, going to his knees beside his fallen master. He put a hand on Darwin's deformed one, the only limb left to the black robe. "This time, I cannot," the red robe said softly.

"I…called…colossal…No time…no—" Darwin said. Spitting up dark red blood, he stiffened and went still.

Malkor drew back.

"I'm sorry, Malkor, but it's over—" Crystalyn said.

"Do you hear that?" Sabella interrupted.

The tall woman with the bow cocked an ear. "Yes, loud thumps," she said.

The man with the swords sheathed at his back reached for her hand, clasping it gently. "Something big is coming," he said.

Crystalyn had no time to wonder about it. She had to get to Broth. Camoe would help locate her link mate, but she'd lost track of where the druid had gone.

Above the same doorway Darwin had burst through, the remaining upper wall collapsed, clattering to the floor. Huge blocks fell near where she'd last seen her *Do'brieni*.

"*Broth!*"

A massive body stepped through the wall. Pausing, enormous yellow-orange eyes regarded her from beneath burlap-textured skin. Moving to one side, the towering creature made room for a second to enter. Then, in unison, both lumbered toward her, kicking large chunks of shattered stone spinning away with each footfall.

Crystalyn could only stare.

Hastel appeared beside her, the patch over his eye slightly askew. "I don't think those creations are coming to ask if they can help us, mistress," he said mildly. Adjusting the patch as if conversing over a mug of ale, he continued. "You'd better do something to slow them, or run before those on the wall decide to target practice."

As if his words brought it about, an arrow shattered against the dais, narrowly missing him. Another whizzed past Crystalyn.

"Move!" the Alchemist shouted. "Put the Dark Dais between us and the wall!"

Crystalyn ran, following Sabella who stayed close to the hooded man. Sprinting around the dais, a hail of red splinter missiles struck near, narrowly missing.

"That was close!" Trenton shouted from somewhere behind.

Crystalyn slid next to Sabella at the eastern radius of the dais, squatting behind the circular stone. Hastel slipped beside her, keeping his head down.

With their tree-sized legs, the colossal raggedy men had gained on them. The first symbol that came to mind was a circular one, entwined double lines surrounding a vague shape in the center. Both struck in rapid succession at the feet of the colossal creations, placed there by design. Darwin had been vulnerable where foot touched floor.

The symbol's radiance brightened with a golden light briefly—the shape in the centers now visible as a circle with a tree inside. As the radiance dimmed, the stone underneath the towering creations buckled and heaved. Tossed in differing directions, the raggedy men landed hard upon their backs on the left and right of each other.

The black candle warmed, causing her hand to throb with a deep piecing pain.

A violet ball of flame soared to the creation squirming for

footing on the left. A second ball struck the creation on the right. With each, the flames burned quickly and then died out.

"Blast it! They were created with something flame or Flow resistant!" Sabella cried.

Hunched beside Hastel, a red beam shot from the crimson orb in Trenton's hand striking the rightmost raggedy man in the side of the chest. A wisp of smoke plumed into the air leaving behind a hole that oozed a black tarry substance. The creation continued flailing its arms and legs, attempting to stand.

Hastel glanced over the dais, ducking behind quickly as more arrows and explosions clattered and banged on top of it. Waves of heat raised the surrounding temperature noticeably. "It's no good. We have to make a run for the barracks. We're too exposed out here; either those things will stomp us into the floor or the bloody Dark Users will destroy us." He looked at Sabella and the Alchemist. "No offense, you two."

"None taken," the hooded man said. "You have the right of it." Then, turning to Sabella, his voice grew softer. "Which is it going to be? What will you use, your physical or magical barrier? I hope your guess is a good one and the damage taken minimal."

Crystalyn interrupted a reply. "Sabella can cast a physical; I'll hold back the User attacks."

"I can only shield one person. Either me or someone else," Sabella protested.

"Don't ask me to assist," Trenton said. "I don't know how to make a barrier, or even if I can. Besides, the orb weakens me too fast. At least, the crimson beam does."

It was then she noticed the woman with the bow and the man with two swords had left. Peering over the dais, she found them sprinting toward rows of Dark soldiers moving in unordered groups down the stairs. The woman fired arrows as she ran, covering the man as his whirling swords cut down the men and women alike, whether they wore plate armor or not.

Crystalyn wished she could send an aggression symbol their way to help, but doing so would cost her the barrier she hadn't yet put in place. They would all die. Oddly, most of the Dark Citadel soldiers clamored toward the dais ignoring the two assailants. She wished them the speed and the endurance of the Great Father.

Setting the absorption symbol with its myriad of white crosses hovering in front of her, Crystalyn stretched it over the five of them who remained. "Decide who you protect, Sabella, we haven't much time. They're getting up!"

The dark creations had managed to roll over. One after the other, they stood upright using blocks of stone and pieces of statues as handholds.

Translucent with a faint hint of violet, a flicker of radiance surrounded Sabella.

"Make your barrier as wide as you can," Crystalyn said.

Resuming their silent march, the creations made for the dais. Though arrows, dark cones, and flashes of white detonations struck them, the creatures strode onward, undeterred.

"Keep Sabella and me between you and the Dark Gate as best you can!" Crystalyn shouted. "Go now!"

They moved in an awkward line, Sabella, then Crystalyn, the hooded man, Hastel, and Trenton. Crystalyn was anxious for the Terran; not only did he have to time his movements for four others, but it put him closer to the colossal creations who moved faster than she liked. "They're coming too fast, run!" she screamed.

Sabella dashed ahead, leaving them exposed. Something whizzed past Crystalyn before she caught up to the woman and checked on the others. The hooded man had dropped back but pushed through into the protection of her symbol. Blood streamed onto his biceps from damage to his right shoulder. Hastel and Trenton had stayed within the symbol's boundary. Crystalyn focused on the way forward. "Go to the east of that fallen statue," she said, raising her voice so the blonde-haired woman would hear.

Sabella complied. For a short time, they had the protection of the statue. The barracks came into view.

Behind, the dark creations' thumps vibrated the floor, growing louder.

Nearing the barracks, archers appeared at the windows. Light Users, Valens, and soldiers hunkered down behind a crumbling fountain. Warriors took shelter behind wagons and debris piles, staying well back from the two piles of rubble that burned.

Sliding to a halt behind a mound of stone and statue blocks jumbled beside the main fountain, Crystalyn spotted Valens and nomads as they ran past, her eyes automatically following them. The dark creations had nearly overtaken her.

The warriors hacked at one of the towering raggedy men, to no avail. Massive hands swatted them and their tiny swords away; even the larger Vale people were flipped broken and crushed from sight.

The way to her was suddenly clear of defenders.

His right shoulder drenched with blood, the hooded man ran up behind the first creation and tossed a flask that landed near mid-thigh. With a succinct *clink,* the glass broke apart on the creature leaving a dripping yellow liquid that detonated with a loud *pop.* A large chunk of thigh vanished, replaced by a hole oozing the oily black substance. Leaning to one side, the creation continued on, dragging the leg.

As its gigantic foot rose to crush the life from her, Crystalyn ran underneath, bringing a symbol to bear in front of her. The overall shape octagonal, the pattern inside formed a myriad of pinwheels with thin stick lines, tipped with round spikes at the points. She had but a moment to release it as the creation's near wall-sized hand swept down toward her.

Spinning, the symbol connected with the ruined thigh, flinging dozens of spikes in a tight line, cutting through the leg. The creation fell, thankfully, away from her. The leg teetered and then fell over toward her. Crystalyn shuffled backward, stumbled over a chunk of stone, and fell.

Oozing the thick black liquid, the severed thigh caught at her ankles, pinning her painfully to the stone and drenching her with the oily substance. Lifting onto its elbows, the dark creation commenced pulling itself around, crawling for her.

Slowed by a mound of rubble it chose to plow over, the first colossal creation clattered over it, moving ever closer. Each of its canoe-sized feet rose high with every step. Crystalyn could only stare. She couldn't tell which monstrosity would get to her first.

# THE LAST CREATION

As RaCorren lifted the giant leg, Crystalyn pulled her legs out from under it. The big Valen let it go. The heavy limb *thudded* wetly on the ground. Before she could utter a word of thanks, Long Sand grabbed her hand and pulled her under a column lying on its side, the crown resting on the fountain wall. A double hand's width from the column's far edge, a wall of rubble blocked the way onward, though there appeared to be space for her to crawl past the timbered column and climb the mound if she had to, albeit barely.

The second dark creation stomped toward her at the only speed it seemed capable of, a slow, steady march. She was grateful for that. Reaching her makeshift barrier, the towering raggedy man halted. Raising a foot high, it stomped on the column leaning on the fountain above her, crunching half the base to chalk on the courtyard flooring. Slowly the foot ascended again.

Ignoring RaCorren, the first colossal dark creation moved past the Valen, walking on its hands, pulling the body and its maimed useless legs behind it.

The Valen man slipped a broad sword from his back sheath, chopping the weapon's width into the colossal arm above the elbow. The creation shuddered but kept moving. "Everyone with a blade weapon aid me! Defend *Sarra'esiah*!" he roared.

Heaving forward, the colossal crawler moved ahead another

hand's reach, gaining half the distance to Crystalyn.

The gigantic foot of the towering creation descended, slamming into the column. The base crumbled, shifting close to her head. Jagged cracks appeared along the column and covered her in a white dust that stuck to the black tarry substance from the dark creation. The great foot ascended.

Scrunched beside her, Long Sand shifted slightly, glancing through the gap between the column and rubble. "The stone cannot take another hit. We have no choice except to fight our way past. Can you run?" he asked tersely.

"I think so," she replied. Until she slid out from under the column, she had no way of knowing for certain.

Hastel arrived at the crawling creation first. Working on the opposite side of the Valen, his muscular arms swung with synchronal precision. As one axe bit deep, the other rose and then fell as the twin side of the half-moon chopper ascended again. His broad shoulders glistened with the sweat of his exertions, and splotches of the tarry substance coated his brown kell vest and bared arms before long.

Joined by a nomad and his scimitar, RaCorren and the warrior took turns hacking at the gigantic creation in the same place.

Long Sand slipped out from under the pillar, taking her by the hand.

The one-legged creation lunged forward as Hastel and the other two cut through its arms. Sliding forward with an inhuman effort, the colossal head slid beside Crystalyn. Losing momentum, its burlap-textured skin rubbed her shoulder.

The colossal foot slammed into the column. A sharp *crack* rent the air.

Long Sand tugged at her hand.

The heavy white marble fell in two halves, the upper torso of a lovely woman taking her place. The sand reader had barely pulled her to safety.

The dark creation had not been as fortunate. Lying unmoving, the huge head was buried under the thick column. An image of yellow-orange eyes fading from the loss of the spark of life flashed through her mind.

From where she lay beside it, Crystalyn formed her absorption symbol, combining it with the air elemental one under the heading wrathful aggression, which she'd read in the black-lettered *Tiered Tome of Symbols*. Flowing with liquid-like consistency, the black-and-white pattern hovering above her converted to a radiant gold. Snaking outward to a triangular point, it swirled into a raging cyclone containing thin fragments of gold.

Blowing into the descending foot, the golden tempest flew upward, spiraling partway up the leg before fizzling out and dissolving. The black crystal heated in her hand, and her throbbing hand ached all the way to the bone. Crystalyn moaned from the pain and weakness. The golden symbol had drained her of much energy

Atoi appeared from out of the shadows of the barracks, dashing under the withdrawing leg.

Shredded and oozing streams of black goo, the dark creation supplanted its damaged leg beside its intact limb and stooped to a pile of rubble. Arrows sank into its back, fist-sized balls of white detonated all over it, and thick green vines entwined around its legs, crawling toward the waist.

Long Sand lifted her upright. "If you are well, Clan Savior, I shall join the battle of destroying the final abomination."

"Go for the eyes, the spark of life there needs extinguished," Crystalyn said, wincing. Her left hand ached. "Trenton may have the best shot at it with the orb."

Atoi slid to a stop beside her. "The Dark Citadel soldiers are attacking." The little girl ran to the foot of the broken column, peering around it. "They are many," she said.

Spread in a line spanning the width of the courtyard, the dark-armored soldiers marched. The black dragon stalked behind, a beast towering as high as the dark creation.

"Gather to me, Sect Leaders!" Long Sand shouted as he joined Atoi at the downed column.

RaCorren strode up to her. "I shall rally my people and bring them to the Dark Child. It is a good place to make a final stand. Will your one-eyed companion survive?" he asked, giving a nod back the way he had come.

The humongous creation had managed to lift a heavy marble depiction of a planet resembling Astura, cradling it in his arms. Hastel chopped with wild abandon at the shredded leg. "He can take care of himself," she said. "As you collect your fighting force, have your archers and Users attack each of the enemy's flanks. If you can get them to create pressure, it will remove some from us, while I regain strength."

RaCorren executed a brief bow. "As you say, *Sarra'esiah*," he said. Turning, he ran into the darker area at the front of the row of barracks, giving the creation a wide berth.

The creation limped toward Crystalyn carrying its heavy round payload.

A glint of something shiny caught Crystalyn's eye, the steel of a bared weapon. Before she could sound the alarm, skirmishes broke out at the barracks. The enemy had crept in behind, cutting her people off from any hope of escape. Her people were doomed.

Following her, they'd left their homes and loved ones, trusting her to keep them safe. She'd repaid them by leading them all to a dark place where they would die. Every death would be on her bloody incapable hands.

The mere thought of it made her angry. She'd go out with a

boom, giving it all she had. They would not perish for nothing.

Her mind clear with what she must do, Crystalyn visualized the absorption symbol with its many crosses of white and stretched it over her. Picking up a fallen warrior's shield, she slid it over her right arm and strode on. It wouldn't do to have the symbol's source taken out with an errant arrow.

Preparing, she strengthened her barrier, looking over her shoulder. The last creation limped toward her, the sphere hugged to its immense chest. Ignoring the swords hacking below, the vines seeking to tether or pull it down, and the arrows quilled on its burlap-textured skin, the yellow-orange eyes fixed on her as it came.

When it raised the ball of marble slightly, she judged it close enough and broke into a run.

She'd barely made it beyond Atoi's lookout spot beside a mound of rubble before missiles and cones streaked toward her. The enemy's power struck her barrier at half-point. A throbbing migraine caused her to wince, dulling the pain in her hand. She'd reached her limit of symbol use. Creating more would drain her life. But did it matter? She'd give those who came with her the best chance at survival.

Her companions, her followers, her people, shouted at her with urgent voices, but she tuned them out, keeping an eye on the last creation. The thing had gained. Reaching deep inside, she picked up her pace.

An image of Jade grasping her hand flashed through her mind causing her to long for her sister with a fervency that surprised her. *"Together we are stronger,"* she clearly heard Jade say somewhere close. Startled, Crystalyn glanced around. Or, had she imagined it? A bolt of red lightning crashed into her absorption symbol, bolstering her head throbs and drawing through her aching hand with an intensity that staggered as she moved forward.

Behind, the creation stomped past the barrier of rubble, past her friends, moving fast for it.

Not far ahead, Dark-armored soldiers advanced many rows deep, their movements unordered in places. Choosing an ordered group in a direct line with the dragon, Crystalyn dashed forward, running at top speed.

Without slowing, the dark creation heaved the marble sphere.

Waiting until the last moment, Crystalyn dashed sharply left, running in front of the first row. Pikes held at the ready banged against her shield edge, jarring her shoulder.

A wide swath opened up at her heels as the sphere bounced into the front row.

Skidding to a halt, she reversed direction, dissolving her symbol and installing a new one, the absorption for a physical barrier. Then she charged after the ball. The marble sphere rolled through soldiers, crushing or throwing their mangled bodies to the sides, opening a path to the dragon. The dragon dodged nimbly to one side.

The massive marble ball ground onward, its momentum carrying it smashing into the gate wall where it bounced once and rolled to a stop. A great crack raced upward, knocking several Users from atop who stood too close to the edge.

The enemy force closed in around Crystalyn, raining blows on her barrier. Jagged cracks appeared with a quickness that worried her, only to have them stop the next moment.

Gasping for breath, she'd reached the dragon.

Preparing her golden cyclone symbol, knowing it to be the last of the power she had in her, she half-turned, gauging the distance to the thing behind. With luck, she could include it and the dragon within the area of her symbol's effect.

The dark creation thumped through the soldiers, kicking and smashing them as it followed the path of the marble boulder.

An enormous force slammed into her wrenching her from the floor. Blunt force crashed into her side, stopping momentum. Blackness bloomed.

# HORRIBLE CHOICE

Garn gazed at the fighting force below with increasing frustration. The thing controlling his daughter and his commanders had wanted to give the order to attack the invaders not long after the black dragon had dropped him. He'd argued against involvement as they battled the gigantic creations the Alchemist had created. The being that inhabited his daughter had taken his advice, at least part of it. The thing had moved the citadel soldiers to the courtyard while Crystalyn had fought the creations. One of the creatures still stood, bent over a pile of rubble. Garn worried since he hadn't seen his daughter in some time.

Now his soldiers, no *its*, advanced in rows along the courtyard, those groups without officers moving with precision.

Garn's heartbeat accelerated as his oldest daughter sprinted out from behind one of the pillars the invaders had pulled down for cover. Crystalyn ran toward the Dark army. What was she doing?

Close behind her, the creation threw a massive green and blue stone ball before its advance. His daughter had run from danger into worse peril. Garn wanted to ask *it* for the dragon's aid, but there was no time.

Slipping nimbly to the right, Crystalyn somehow avoided the front row of Dark soldiers. Then she vanished behind a wall of metal shields. His concern deepened until he noticed her running behind the great ball as it rolled through the regiment rows.

The black dragon sprang to the side. The marble ball rolled past, banging into the gateway, and seven Users fell to their deaths. Garn barely noticed. His daughter had turned to face the creation following, forgetting the danger so near. Knowing she wouldn't hear from this distance, he vaguely heard someone shout look out with his voice, as he ran toward her.

The dragon whipped around, its great reptile tail catching his daughter in the side. As if nothing more than a doll made of rags, Crystalyn thudded into the gate wall a partial story high and then slid to the floor, unmoving.

Racing once more down the grand stairway, the fear in the pit of Garn's stomach for his eldest daughter accelerated his heart and constricted his throat. His practical mind nagged no one could survive such a blow.

A group of five from the Dark Regiment, the controlled ones, captains all, spread out to bar his way at the bottom. Barely slowing, Garn's great sword disposed of two. He shouldered between the two as they fell and raced on.

With its left fist, the creation pounded on the dragon's head. The beast had clamped its great jaws upon the right arm.

Giving them ample room, Garn hugged the wall. Making it to the crumpled form of his daughter, he dropped to one knee, checking her pulse. At first, he found none and feared the worst; his heart hammered in his chest. Calming his fears, he slowed the thumps of his internal organ until they faded beyond detection.

Then, though weak, he felt the pulse he hoped to find at her neck.

Standing, he turned, a shout for healers dying at his lips. *It* stood near, wearing his youngest daughter's body. Flanked by three dull-eyed, slouching generals, the translucence of the smoky barrier glinted around it still. A glance upward revealed the twelve mages grouped in front of the grand stairway.

"Again, you abandoned your post," the creature inside his youngest said. "The Over Mind wishes you flogged for each episode at our private quarters once the enemy is eradicated."

Elated, Garn barely heard. "Some of the Users maintaining your barrier will have the healing ability. Command them to aid me, quickly. There is not much time left for her."

Jade's emerald eyes regarded his oldest. "This offspring of yours has no use to the One Mind, quite the opposite. Request is denied."

Garn leapt, drawing from his sheath as he did. The tip of his great sword rested in the small of his daughter's neck before he could change his mind about what he was doing. As one, the three generals drew long swords and then lumbered toward him. "Call them off or I plunge this through her throat," he snarled.

Though it did not give a flick of the hand, nor say a word, all three generals froze. "You would slay your remaining progeny? The Over Mind believes you now use deception. The One Mind will not provide aid to your fallen offspring," it said.

Gripped within the sounds of the carnage happening at the front lines, the fierce battle between dragon and creation, the sizzling bolts of Dark and Light exchanged from both sides, it came to him he had a horrible choice to make. Destroy one of his children for the unlikely success of saving another. How could he take the chance of losing both daughters, one by his own hand? How could he not?

# TRUE CLAN

As Seonid, the last of the master healers left the bedchamber, Deonna stuffed another pillow behind the small of Crystalyn's back. Declining the offered brush the woman held in a tray with a wave of her hand, Crystalyn grabbed the hand mirror and raked her deformed hand through her hair, pulling it in place with decent results. No healing yet had been able to straighten the curls from her fingers, fingers that may forever remain locked around an unseen object the shape of the black crystal candle. At least, according to the string of Dark User master healers that had come and gone throughout the day, the digits on her left hand would remain deformed. Perhaps when she'd healed a day or two, she would attempt her brand of deep healing from the inside out. She couldn't wait long or any of the melted ligaments improperly repaired would heal too short and she'd have to live with the mend. The only healer's capabilities she trusted fully were her own.

Once satisfied with her hair, Crystalyn put down the mirror and glanced at head mistress Deonna. "Let them in, I'm ready," she said, even though she wore the silky, semi-sheer nightdress the healers had put on her. She hadn't the strength to change.

*"Are you certain of this, Do'brieni?"* Broth asked, lying in his customary place on the floor beside her bed. *"Another twelve bells of rest shall help you mend."*

*"I know, you would benefit too, my Do'brieni, the healers told me your*

*wounds were as dire as my own. But I can't wait to hear everything that happened."*

Another thick strand of usually immaculate hair poked through a bun too loose from neglect as Deonna lowered her dull blue eyes. "Yes, my lady," she said. Turning away, the head mistress shuffled toward the antechamber, her movements stiff and jerky as if her arm and leg joints pained her.

*Perhaps arthritis had finally caught up to the crotchety old woman,* Crystalyn thought. Oddly, Deonna had not shown any of her former sauciness; in fact, she'd been quite docile during the frustrating ordeal of getting her ready for this morning's meeting. Such clumsiness from the woman had come as an unexpected and unpleasant surprise.

Crystalyn put the matter from her mind. Since she'd woken from the deep sleep required after a near-death healing, she'd spoken to no one but the head mistress, the healers, and Broth. Today, her family and companions waited to speak with her. Why was she so nervous?

Her dad and her sister strode inside the bedchamber first, Jade going to the maiden vanity with its round gilded mirror and plush stool for a place to sit.

Charging across the room, her dad wrapped his strong arms around her shoulders, giving her a fierce hug. "Careful," Crystalyn said with a fond laugh. "I'm still breakable."

"I know, Seonid hissed a warning to keep the visit short and go easy on you, but I've missed you," her dad said, speaking into her hair. Giving her a final squeeze, he backed away.

"I've really missed you too, Dad. And, look at you. You seem seasons younger, how?"

He shrugged, a roguish grin flashing upon his smooth face. "Flow potions and unparalleled exercise," he said with a flourish. Then, his tanned face clouded with concern. "But that is for another visit. The real question is, how are you feeling? I nearly lost you."

Crystalyn covered her left hand with her right, hiding the deformity, the blatant imperfection upon her youth. "I will mend, mostly. It's nothing I can't handle. What happened? I only recall making it through the rows of citadel soldiers, little else after."

Her dad exchanged a glance with Jade who sat docilely on the stool as if nothing out of the ordinary had occurred. "The black dragon, Jade's dragon, struck you with its tail," her dad finally said.

Crystalyn gaped as he paused, presumably to let it sink in. *How am I still alive?* she wondered.

"When I got to you, you were in bad shape," her dad continued, his voice getting hoarser at the end. He swallowed. "Jade then called for the five healers from her retinue of twelve Users who maintained her barrier. The rest set up a shield around us while the dragon and Jade's rear line soldiers battled the creation, finally destroying it. A truce was called with your soldiers when the dragon fled to recover from the wounds it received."

Crystalyn locked eyes with Jade. Her younger sibling wore too much black eye shadow, and she had smeared lipstick across her full lips, *black* lipstick, and donned a lacy low-cut dress. Her black high-heeled boots, though matching her outfit, didn't fit Jade's usual look, at all. None of it did. What happened to her innocent sister?

"How does a young woman acquire an army?" she asked.

"Perhaps, one should ask you the same," Jade replied without a smile.

"Stop acting above your seasons," Crystalyn scolded. "I asked first, and what's with all the black you're wearing? Aren't you glad to see me? Don't I get a hug?"

"The Dark Citadel has named her lady of the citadel after the Alchemist's extended absence," her dad interjected, speaking quickly.

Crystalyn frowned. "What do you know about running a fortress?" she asked Jade.

Lined with black, Jade's emerald eyes were impassive, round and unblinking, reminding Crystalyn of the frustrating antics of Atoi.

"She doesn't have to know," her dad cut in. "There are lords and Users here giving council, not to mention me."

"Is that why you attacked me? Sent the black dragon after me?" Crystalyn persisted, still looking at Jade. "How does one get a dragon, anyway?"

Her dad replied again. "She…we thought you were invading. Well, that *is* what you did. Nevertheless, we had no idea it was you. The dragon bonded with Jade after we came here, it's quite protective. Particularly after that apparition appeared and attacked everyone."

Crystalyn raised an eyebrow. "You bonded with a dragon? You impress me, sister. Come, give me a hug while you fill me in on the state of my army, running of yours, and the welfare of my companions," she said, holding out her arms.

Jade stood.

"No!" her dad said, too loud. His deep blue eyes had fixed on Jade.

Jade looked at him sharply.

So did Crystalyn.

"I mean it, Jade, you are not to touch her," he said, scowling at his youngest. Visibly smoothing his features, he turned to Crystalyn. "I have spoken with your friends. They also have received warning of this. There is something important I have to ask you as I asked them. Jade is fighting an illness, some sort of disease we know little about, which might be contagious. I cannot take the risk it is. Please don't make contact with her until my scholars have researched it. Will you promise me this?"

Crystalyn frowned. "What type of disease? What are the symptoms? Though I haven't tackled ailments of that scope yet, I might be able to cure her when I have my strength. I can heal, Dad. I'm stronger than anyone I've met, so far."

With a quick smile, her dad folded his muscular arms at his chest and leaned a shoulder against one of the polished gray granite columns. Crystalyn still found it hard to get used to the change in him. "I heard. I'm quite proud of you. We'll discuss that when you've healed."

Though she said nothing, Jade still eyed him.

"Is it dangerous to her? What are the symptoms?" Crystalyn repeated.

"Not now, I mean it. When you're stronger and only if you don't need to touch her. Jade's safe for the time being," her dad replied. "Your friends wait in the antechamber. I'll let them inform you of the state of your soldiers," he added.

"My people," Crystalyn corrected. "Which companions are out there?" she asked, suddenly afraid. How many had she lost?

Her dad's smile was soft. "You will soon know, and I'll let them speak of it. There were many who fought bravely." Standing to his full towering height, he strode to her and squeezed her shoulder gently. "I shall return after you've had a night's rest. Don't allow their well wishes to keep you awake overly long." Giving her a last fond look, he strode to the doorway, turning to wait for his youngest daughter.

Jade gave her a brief stare and then strode from the room in silence.

"Dad! Mom's here. She's been on Astura the whole time," Crystalyn blurted.

Her dad froze at the threshold. "I know that now," he said, nearly too soft to hear. Then he slipped through, vanishing from sight.

Crystalyn frowned. Though she'd finally reunited with most of her little family, they had something to hide. They'd only told her the bare minimum of how they'd come to be at the Dark Citadel and only those parts concerning her. How had easygoing Jade come to run a place of such war mongering and in-fortress violence? Didn't her dad want to hear about his wife who had been missing for so many seasons?

*"Though I heard and understood your true clan's words, I have no sense of their inner selves."* Broth sent, breaking into her tumultuous thoughts.

Crystalyn stared at the empty doorway. Sadness replaced anxiety. It was almost as if she didn't know her family either.

# QUIET REVELATION

Atoi slipped inside the bedchamber first with Hastel right behind. "You live," the little girl observed as she halted at the foot of the luxurious queen bed. Inlaid with gilded white porcelain tiles drawn in fine black paint, the bed was a masterwork depicting animal life on Astura. "Have you mislaid your instinct for it?" the little girl asked her green eyes round with curiosity.

Hastel spoke quickly. "What she means is, we thought we'd lost you when you charged into the enemy like a young dragon lion on the rampage." He sat stiffly on the cushioned benched footboard. A wide kell leather bandage compressed his chest and stomach.

"Aye, what caused you to do such a thing?" Lore Rayna asked, as she, Sabella, and Long Sand filed into the room, spreading out around the bed.

Crystalyn gazed fondly at them all, even Sabella. Then she grew sad; there was one missing and bound to be more. "I am sorry for the loss of Railee, Long Sand. She was a great warrior."

"Aye, that she was. She earned a place inside the Tomb of the Warrior, an honor bestowed only upon the greatest of our peoples. Two of the Red Rock clan are transporting the frozen remains. With your consent, I would like the great honor of attending the ceremony in your place," the sand reader said.

Though surprised by the abrupt request, Crystalyn nodded.

"You have it. Who better to perform it? Go now, ask the clans to gather those fallen inside this dark place of stone. Let them also have a final resting place in your lands. Take whatever you require from here."

Long Sand bowed deeply, his forehead nearly touching the bed. "I thank you, *Kalaesanamun*," he said, straightening. "Most were already honored with a pyre. Their ashes shall be returned to the sand in private ceremonies."

"What did you call me?" Crystalyn asked.

"The clans have now bestowed upon you the highest honorific, given only once throughout our long history, for your bravery and power. *Kalaesanamun*. No one has ever succeeded in assaulting the Dark Citadel. Roughly translated from the ancient histories, it has a meaning of Warrior Queen of Sun and Sand."

Crystalyn flashed a brief smile. "I'm no queen, far from it. Nay, I'm only a simple broken-minded woman who wishes to care for loved ones."

Long Sand shrugged. "Give them their beliefs. Until we meet again, *Kalaesanamun*," he said. Turning, he strode from the room.

Gazing at her remaining companions, Crystalyn took a deep breath, steeling herself. "Who else? How many did we lose?"

"RaCorren lives, though we lost a few of the Vale. The druid Camoe has gone to stand before the Great Mother," Lore Rayna said. "It is a great loss for humankind and Valen alike. He shall return to the soil as soon as your father assures us citadel soldiers have withdrawn from the Vale."

Crystalyn nodded though she wondered why Jade hadn't mentioned someone so dear to her passing. Was her sister grieving? "I shall see to the withdrawal myself as soon as I can get my dad back in here," she said. "Has he been preserved?"

"There is time for your full recovery. Our Users keep him within ice as is the Red Rock woman." Lore Rayna said.

Crystalyn moved on to her next question. "How did you survive the quills? Did you heal yourself?" she asked.

Lore Rayna flashed a quick smile, lovely on her broad face. "I tried, but they were saturated with the poison of Dark Flow. Fortunately, two of our Users with healing affinities came to my aid. Between the three of us, we slowed it enough for seven master healers to be found and cleanse it." The thought of her ordeal causing her stress, the green-leafed dress shifted back and forth with agitation, revealing too much.

Crystalyn could empathize; she'd thought a lot about the battle upon awakening. "Darwin had become nearly unstoppable. Without my dad and all of you, the outcome may have been different. Which reminds me," she said, looking around the spacious room. "I'm sure there's a way back to Terra available in the citadel. Where's Trenton? He helped us; I want to do what little I can for him, for all of you."

"I have a portion of the answer you seek," a soft masculine voice said from the doorway.

*"Have a care, Do'brieni. I have no sense of this one as well. There is high suspicion in the White Fur clan that he may have engaged some of my race for reasons unknown."*

A shadow detached from the darkness of the foyer outside the room coalescing into a hooded man wearing a half cowl that left his stomach bare. The gold bands clamped around his muscular biceps shone with new polished brilliance. "The gray robe was last seen fleeing the courtyard with the red robe Malkor during the battle with the creations."

Sabella's gray eyes glinted as she frowned. "Did you not believe it relevant to inform us of this sooner, Father? Between them, Malkor and the outlander have considerable power I—we— could use them."

Crystalyn cut into the conversation. "Use them for what?

They are not tools to use as you see fit, Sabella. Nor are any of us." The woman opened her mouth to protest. Crystalyn silenced it with her imperious empress look. *Wear the right emotional mask and people will respond.* She turned to the Alchemist. "Your daughter is right to ask, however. Why have you not mentioned this sooner?"

The hooded man's golden hourglass eyes were shadowed, revealing nothing. "Knowledge of the two was only gleaned two bells ago. Since then, an investigation regarding the murders of your warriors left guarding the topaz gate has revealed they likely fled through it. Their whereabouts from there are unknown."

Silence followed the quiet revelation.

After a time, Sabella stirred. "How many have you sent after them? When will they report back?"

The Alchemist said nothing.

The thought of Malkor slinking around out there made her stomach turn. What would make Trenton join with such a man? Had he really helped murder her people?

Crystalyn put the matter away for the time being. Something else came to mind, something vital to this world. "What is your plan now, Alchemist? Do you expect to rule the lands with your potions and cunning after removing the stain of the Flow from the lands? Was that it all along?  It makes little difference to me; I don't use the great river of power."

Folding his arms at his chest, the hooded man froze. Then, leaning forward slightly, his golden feline-like eyes peered from the shadows of his hood unblinking. "How would you know about that?" he asked. Without waiting for a reply, he continued. "Your connections are more extensive than I believed. There's no harm in telling you now. The Flow is doomed. Soon, there shall only be the power of one's ingenuity, steel and armor, and your symbols. With my flasks as support, no one would stand a chance of defeating you."

Sabella's smile was wide. "My father has done you a great service, Crystalyn. You should thank him by rewarding him from the citadel's coffers."

Crystalyn did not smile back. She couldn't trust either one.

Instead, she locked her eyes upon two golden hourglass ones so like her link mate's. Though she didn't like it, sometimes when it came to the matter of trust, one had little choice. The worms had a weakness, she knew, one that had caused the hooded man concern in the past. If only she could recall what it was, perhaps she could restore Astura if it came to that. Her adopted world wouldn't be the same without the great river of magic flowing through it. Something she would have to deal with at some point. Not now, perhaps when she healed.

Broth rose upon his four great paws and laid his head in her lap. His now large blue hourglass eyes, symbolic of his contentment, looked up at her as she scratched gently behind his sharp ears. She returned the gaze with a fond one of her own. At least she had her family together again, both old and new. Once her mom was contacted and asked to make haste to the household, to Creek Citadel as she would demand it known, they would all come together again. Crystalyn smiled from the thought of it.

The End

Read on for an excerpt from book three of the thrilling epic fantasy series, *The Flow of Power.*

# SHADOWY FORM

Sureen blinked. Evening's golden light replaced the darkness of hood and blindfold. Foliage faded into view, matching the scents and sounds she had smelled and heard for some time from horseback. Teal ferns grew near fallen logs clumped with lime green moss. Thick roots of the great falun trees dived under a long ago cultivated wagon trail. The trunks rose beyond sight on both sides, *creaking* now and then from a light breeze. Not far ahead, an arced wooden bridge raised high at the center spanned the Even Flow River, one of four crossings accessing the town of Four Bridges.

Stuffing the kell leather hood and soft cloth in his bags, the graying, grizzle-faced Captain Bronaham rode to the front of the line, six horses away.

Sitting her horse on Sureen's left side, Kara Laurel gripped her appaloosa stallion's reins in her left hand. The right held the white crystal staff and her roan mare's reins. "You shall remain with your hands bound behind your back for a while longer, my dear. I would hate to have you lost in such a backwoods town."

"Why are we here, Kara? What is it you wish of me?"

Kara Laurel smiled with the same sweet radiant smile Sureen recalled from their youth, the one that lit her green eyes with an inner glow of vibrancy. "There is someone you need to meet, someone you shall befriend and bond with."

"Are you quite certain of that?" Sureen asked. "I choose friends with much care."

Kara Laurel's laugh was a tinkle of tiny silver bells, as rich as her mood. "How well I know," she said. "Come, we have little time left before darkness falls."

Urging her roan mare forward, Kara Laurel followed the black Shire warhorses, strolling at an easy clop in single file. Soon they were thumping over the high arc of the bridge and then plodding onto the well-packed trail on the outskirts of town.

They passed a wagon lined with straw leaving town. With the passage barely adequate for two carts abreast as the trail narrowed for the bridge, a farmer gazed at her openly, his brown eyes bold with curiosity from under his wide-brimmed kell hat.

Sureen stared back, hoping he would ask the meaning of her binding and perhaps gain interest from the many other horses and wagons trailing him to cause a scene of many inquiries. Instead, the man's eyes shifted from her as soon as he noted her arms bound behind her, which denoted her as a User held under guard. Quickly, he looked to the road ahead, his body rigid as he moved from sight.

Disappointed, Sureen tried the same boldness with several of those exiting the providence, her eyes imploring them to speak. Every eye slid past her; most noticed the reins Kara Laurel gripped led to more than her horse.

Giving up, Sureen focused on her surroundings. The town of Four Bridges spread between the eastern side of Lake Ever Cold and the base of Glacier Mountain, the rambling wood and stone structures small underneath its looming presence.

The place had a festive air about it. Townspeople and visitors flocked about going about some sort of new spring event. Colored ribbons and banners hung from nearly every storefront. Young men and women chased after each other dressed in garb gaudier than even the most flamboyant merchants wore.

Reining sharply to the left, Captain Bronaham swung into a side alley filled with refuse. Guiding his warhorse around the larger piles, he halted beside a nondescript wooden door.

Dismounting, he stepped gingerly over to where Kara Laurel had brought their horses to a halt and helped the woman dismount. Then Sureen found his strong arms around her waist as she slid to the muck, wincing when it splashed wetly.

Kara Laurel handed the reins of the horses to him. "Meet inside, after the animals are stabled. The booth is at the back. Set your men up with drink, but remind them of the need for discreetness."

Captain Bronaham inclined his head. "Aye," he said. Climbing into the saddle, he rode off leading the two horses. His twelve leather-clad men followed in silence. The dark armor of the citadel had long ago been replaced.

Kara Laurel laid her delicate hand upon Sureen's lower back, clasping her bound hands within it. "Come, dear, we are to go through the servant entrance to the Muddy Wagon Inn and Tavern. We must make haste. My master has waited with little patience."

Sureen did not bother with an answer.

Thumbing the latch, Kara Laurel pushed her firmly inside. Pressing on the small indent of her back, her intimate friend from early adulthood channeled her through a kitchen active with the meaty smells of broth and fresh vegetables. Cooks wearing splattered aprons worked in a frenzied elaborate dance, slicing at counters, stirring cast-iron pots, and flipping sizzling meats over a large flat-topped stove. No one glanced overly long at them.

Leaving the kitchen, they entered a smoky tavern filled with the drone of many raucous voices. The booth at the back proved to be the first one they came to, dimly lit and occupied by three shadowy forms.

Kara Laurel's touch indicated she should sit at circular bench seating. Sureen did so, shuffling inward and making room for her captor. One of the shapes across the round table leaned forward and adjusted the wick on the oil lamp centered on the table. The light flickered brighter.

A voice Sureen had heard many times spoke softly as a face she knew well leaned into the light. "What have you told her?" Durandas asked.

Kara Laurel chuckled. "Not much, only that there is someone coming to our little gathering she will want to meet."

"Which is much more than you have revealed to us, First Light of the Circle of Light," Malkor sneered. As the light flickered across his narrow face, his eyes seemed lit with an inner, smoky red fire.

The third person, a handsome man Sureen hadn't yet met, drew the hood of his gray robe over curly brown hair. "I told you not to trust him. You are a fool, Lore Master," the man said.

Durandas' dark eyes smoldered. When had his eyes darkened? "Your trust is not required, outlander. Only your power, if we cannot convince the Azure User to join with us."

Sureen gaped like one afflicted without the ability for coherent thought. What in the name of all bloody subterfuge was going on? What vile plan had these people taken her prisoner to implement; more importantly, why did they need her? There was enough power at the table to lay waste to the entire tavern, even without knowing what the outlander was capable of.

Outside the light's reach, a shadowy form slipped into the booth.

Other books by R.V. Johnson: *Beyond The Sapphire Gate*, Book 1 of the thrilling *The Flow of Power* epic fantasy series, and *Beyond Terra,* An engrossing novella set in the same two worlds. FREE DOWNLOAD. Sign up for the author's new release group and receive a free copy of the stunning novella. Get it here: http://www.authorrvjohnson.com

R.V. Johnson grew up in Utah wandering through beautiful tranquil forests, exploring the unique alien-like setting of the red rock desert and climbing the rugged trails of the high Uinta Mountains where mountain goats roam. Indoors, he read from his large library or wrote in his journal. One can now find him writing and reading outside.

He strives to be the gem the dragon hoards.

http://www.authorrvjohnson.com